I0838443

Blood Tribe

Iris Kain

Also by Iris Kain

Shadow Hunter

Eternal Spring

Offshoot

Sour (Book #1 of the Murphy Blackwell Chronicles)

Sweet (Book #2 of the Murphy Blackwell Chronicles)

Salty (Book #3 of the Murphy Blackwell Chronicles)

Blood Trials: Book #2 of the Blood Tribe Trilogy

Blood Treason: Book #3 of the Blood Tribe Trilogy

Acknowledgements for Blood Tribe:
Romeo and Juliette, (1.1. 138-141) Univ. of Chicago Press 1906.
The Art of War, Sun Tsu. Translated from Chinese by Lionel Giles, M. A.. Original publication 1910.
Essays: First Series (1841). Ralph Waldo Emerson.

ISBN 978-1-957244-06-8

For Jamie.

# Blood Tribe

I offer you peace. I offer you love. I offer you friendship. I see your beauty. I hear your need. I feel your feelings. My wisdom flows from the Highest Source. I salute that Source in you. Let us work together for unity and love.

- Mahatma Gandhi

Chapter 1

October 1943

Vivian's only clue that her mother was home when she got back from the American Legion Hall was the presence of their run-down Ford sedan in the driveway. She strode through the door, hung her jacket on the coat rack, and went straight into the roomy living room to her favorite item in the house—the radio. It stood as high as Vivian's waist, and even though on cloudy days the reception was at best so-so, it was her and her mother's pride and joy. She turned the power knob. Duke Ellington's "Mood Indigo" poured from the speaker.

She headed to the oak rolltop desk and sat down in the high-backed chair. She tried to dispel the unforgettable sensation of Jude's touch, but the more she tried to distract herself, the more pressing the memory became.

Duke Ellington ended, and Tommy Dorsey picked up with "Marie" on his famous trombone.

Maybe if I try to write Phillip a letter, she decided. She rolled back the desk's cover and reached into the right-hand drawer where her mother kept the stationery. She grabbed a fountain pen, dipped the nib into the ink, and determined she would put down whatever came to mind.

"My Dearest Phillip," she wrote, and was stumped. Before tonight, the thought of Phillip hunkered down in a foxhole reading one of her perfume-scented letters always made her smile. Tonight, as she sat back and tried to think through the past few days to find a topic to write about, all that came to mind was Jude's silk voice, his touch, the graceful way he danced, and the way the soulful voice of the crooning singer mirrored her heart's mood.

Her hand started for the page two or three times as she considered telling him about going to the dance with Ruth, but she stopped herself.

And what would you write? "The American Legion Hall held a dance, but I only stayed for a few minutes. Ruth dragged me out after a handsome stranger started flirting with me." Don't be stupid.

The phone rang. Vivian leaped from her chair and nearly spilled black ink all over her skirt. It was late; her mother would most likely be asleep. She reached for the phone before it had a chance to ring again.

"Hello?"

"Vivian?" Wesley's voice barely carried over the background noise. He had called from the hall. "Is that you?"

"Yes, Wesley," she responded. "What's up?"

"Well, I'm not sure," Wesley said. "I just got back, and I can't find Ruth. Did she say anything to you about when she was planning to go home?"

"Um, no," Vivian tried to recall any part of her conversation with Ruth she might have forgotten. Anything might have been said. But nothing came to mind. She was so flustered when Ruth practically pushed her into Wesley's car and made her go home.

"I don't see her," he said. "I was wondering if she'd said anything to you."

"Sorry, Wes, but I don't know anything that you don't."

"Well, if she calls you, let me know. I'm going to go see if maybe I missed her," Wesley said. His voice didn't sound hopeful.

"Keep me posted, alright?" Vivian asked.

"I'll let you know as soon as I find her," Wesley said. They hung up.

Her concern rose. It wasn't like Ruth to wander off by herself. Overprotective parents, loving friends, and a doting boyfriend—now fiancé—had made it uncommon for Ruth to be alone, and her friend seemed to like it that way. That Wesley had to look for her was puzzling and a little disturbing.

Well, it was a busy night, she reasoned and tried to put it out of her head.

She sat down with pen and paper again and forced herself to pen a page full of nonsense and small talk for Phillip as she waited for Wesley's call. It never came. Agitated, she put up her writing utensils, closed the desk, and went to bed.

That night, she tried to steer her dreams toward rational thoughts of Phillip, marriage, and their future together, but it didn't work. She was haunted by nightmares of a beautiful, dark man who seduced her, no matter how hard she tried to ward him off.

C3 80

Her mother's voice woke her in the morning.

"Vivian, honey, you have a phone call."

She sat up sluggishly and peered through half-open eyes at her bed-side clock. It was only a few minutes after six in the morning. Anyone who knew her well enough to call her should know that she would not be crawling out of bed for another hour. It had to be Wesley, calling about Ruth. She hurriedly slouched into her robe, felt around for her slippers with blurry eyes, and stumbled to the living room.

Her mother waited in the doorway to ensure Vivian was awake. As usual, Rose Black had pulled herself together early, a store-bought cotton dress pulled snugly over her trim figure, a cup of coffee in her hand, lipstick blotted on the bone rose cup. When Vivian managed to make it to the living room, Rose smiled and handed her the telephone.

"Hello?" She fought to keep the grogginess from her voice but failed.

"Vivian? It's Wesley," he stuttered. He sounded as though he were trying to talk around a bone stuck in his throat. "Listen, I need to talk to you as soon as possible. It's urgent. I'd have come over to tell you, but they needed me here...."

"Wesley, you're not making sense," she interjected. "We're talking now. Why come over? What's wrong?"

"I don't want to tell you over the phone—"

"Wesley, what happened? Is this about Ruth? Don't make me worry. Tell me what happened."

There was a sigh and a choked sob. Wesley was *crying*!

Oh, God. How bad is it?

Vivian waited with a furrowed brow for Wesley to find his voice. All thoughts of sleep vanished. She tapped a nervous foot on the floor. Her mother brought her a steaming cup of coffee in a china cup, and Vivian nodded a thank you rather than speak. She did not want to interrupt Wesley. Rose disappeared, probably to the kitchen, to finish reading the morning paper.

"It's about Ruth, Vivian. Remember how I couldn't find her at the dance?"

"Yes, of course I remember."

"Well, I never did find her. I asked some people if they'd seen her, but they hadn't." He drew in a shuddering breath and continued. "A bunch of us started looking for her, calling around, that sort of thing. I knew something was wrong...." He broke off and sobbed hysterically.

Vivian was desperate to hear what had happened, but part of her knew. Somehow, she knew.

"Wesley, what happened?" she barked. There was another pause, and Vivian tapped her foot harder. The wait was torture.

"I'm going to come over," he sniffled. "I don't want to say this over—"

"Wesley William Scott, you tell me right this second! Where the hell is Ruth? What happened?"

He still didn't want to say. This time, Vivian swore she could have reached through the phone, grabbed him by his shirtfront, and shook him until he spoke. She endured another static-filled, shaky breath.

"I took the woods behind the hall," he said. "I don't know why I looked there, but I did. She shouldn't have been there. Now I wish... Why couldn't someone else have...?"

"Have *what*, Wesley?"

His voice struggled, delivering the news in fits and starts. "I found her, Viv. I found her. Dead. I. Found. Her. Dead. *Dead*. She's gone, Viv."

"*No*," Vivian murmured. "How?"

"How?" Wesley sounded angry. "I don't know. All they tell me is that she lost her blood somehow."

"Lost it? How does a person *lose* their blood?"

"From the looks of it, she lost a lot on the ground."

"Wesley!" Vivian cried.

"I'm sorry," he apologized. "I'm so... so.... Listen, is it alright if I come over? I'd like to talk to you. I need to talk to someone."

"Of course," she said. She could use someone to talk to as well. She wasn't sobbing yet, but her throat felt blocked, and tears poured down her cheeks.

"I'll be there soon," he said

"Alright."

She hung up the phone in a stupor and felt for the chair next to the telephone table. She shuffled over and sat heavily.

Ruth... gone? How? *How does someone lose their blood and die?* She had never heard of such a thing. It sounded like some crazy jungle disease or something out of a novel, not something that happened in New Bridgeport, Michigan. She sat several minutes until her shaky legs worked again and walked to her bedroom, her coffee forgotten.

Hot tears poured down her cheeks as she laid curled into a ball on her bed. Ruth, her closest friend, was gone. While her mind grasped the concept, her heart refused to budge. She remembered Ruth's flustered face as she forced her to leave the hall the night before. She saw her rosy cheeks, her dark, curly hair, the determined set of her mouth. What had possessed her to go into the woods at that hour? Ruth wasn't a nature-lover, no matter what time of day it was. The thought of Ruth strolling through the woods crawling with heaven knew what kinds of bugs and four-legged creatures… No. Not Ruth.

Poor Wesley. What is he going to do? Ruth was his whole life. How will he go on without her?

As she sobbed into her pillow, she wondered how she would get along as well.

持 持

By the time Wesley arrived, Vivian had showered and put on a fresh pot of coffee. She nearly forgot to comb her hair, and when she looked at her reflection in the mirror, her eyes were red-ringed and swollen, as if she hadn't had any sleep at all. Her mother asked what was wrong, and after finding out a few details, graciously stepped back to let her daughter deal with the situation the way she usually did—on her own.

Wesley looked even worse than she did. His button-down shirt and slacks were as wrinkled as if he had slept in them. Then she recognized the shirt and slacks as the same ones he had been wearing when he dropped her off last night. His eyes had circles so dark it looked as if someone had slugged him. His sandy hair was uncharacteristically un-kempt, and his face was a sickening gray-white under his tan.

She let him into the house and showed him the way to the large, white kitchen, where she handed him a cup of black coffee. Wesley looked at the fabric-covered white chairs nervously, afraid to sit down.

"It's alright," Vivian assured him, sitting across from the chair she directed him to take. "They're washable."

He sat down and sipped his coffee, his face distracted. His eyes steered clear of hers as if he feared she blamed him for Ruth's death. She sat, her arms on the table, her eyes unblinking and dry, and listened.

"I don't know where to begin," he murmured. "When I couldn't find her. I asked around, tried to find folks who might've known where she was. No one knew anything. So, I called you, then I checked again, but that was no good. She just wasn't there. That's when I started to panic.

"I got the guys together, and we started to call people, friends she might have left with for one reason or another. Nobody knew anything, and by now, it was getting late—around midnight or so, I figure. The guys and I all wandered everywhere we could think of around looking for her. Thought maybe she'd walked home, and we just missed her. But I drove the route to her house and didn't see her, and her folks said she wasn't there. And then *they're* worried. That's when someone called the police—her father, I imagine.

"The guys suggested we start to search the whole area near the hall for her, on foot, you know? I thought it was a great idea. I knew that Ruth wouldn't…. Well, you know Ruth. She never does the unpredictable.

"The other fellas, they took different roads. Thought maybe she just took a long way home or something. I took the woods behind the hall with Artie and Frank and one or two others."

He paused to sip coffee, and Vivian followed suit. Her mouth had grown dry as she listened. He put the chintz cup back in its saucer, and it struck Vivian how strong and capable his hands looked holding the tiny piece of china. He did not look as though he felt capable at that moment, though. He looked beaten down.

"I don't know why I took the woods," he continued. "It was the last place I suspected she'd be. I think maybe somehow, I knew… It only took a couple of minutes for me to find her. Even in the pitch-dark part of the woods, she was so pale…."

Vivian didn't press for details. She didn't want them. He had already hinted at how gruesome the scene was, and she didn't want to picture it; it would make it too easy to imagine how her friend may have suffered. Yet, he looked so burdened by pain and confusion that Vivian did not ask him to stop. He needed to unburden himself by sharing the details. He hadn't stopped staring at the tile floor since he took his first sip of coffee, and his voice was level and detached.

"The coroner explained that her body was drained of nearly all its blood. Imagine that. Like a Goddamn vampire got a hold of it. Oh, sorry. You know I don't like to swear in front of a lady, but jeez. It looked to me like there was plenty of blood there. It was all over the place."

He broke off to regain his composure, his eyes brimming with tears. Vivian waited for him to go on.

"I'm really sorry to be the one who has to tell you this. I didn't know where else to go. You were Ruth's best friend. I suppose a part of me thought you'd want to know."

"I did, in a way," she admitted. *However, I could have done without all the details.* "I don't understand it any better than you do, but it helps to know I can be here for you."

"You don't know why Ruth was in the woods, do you?"

Vivian shook her head and agreed it was both puzzling and maddening.

They finished their coffee in silence. Vivian struggled for something to say. They were both lost in thoughts of Ruth. Wesley patted her hand several times in reassurance, and she did the same, as if by strengthening each other, they could help themselves.

The phone rang. Vivian crossed the kitchen, entered the living room, and answered it. She guessed it would be another grieving friend—possibly Daisy Milner from English class. She had been a close friend to Vivian and Ruth. But no one was there.

She hung up.

She returned to the kitchen, where she found Wesley on his feet. The two of them made plans to visit Ruth's family in an hour or two after Vivian had freshened up. The phone rang again.

Vivian held up a finger, and Wesley nodded. She entered the living room again and answered the phone.

Once more, no one was there.

"That's odd," she commented. She looked up, and Wesley was watching her. She flushed, embarrassed that he caught her talking to herself, but he didn't mind.

"I'll be around in a little while to drive you to the family's house if you'd like," he offered.

"Thank you. That'd be nice," she said, and the phone rang a third time. An annoyed expression crossed her face, but she lifted the receiver.

"Hello?"

"Vivian?" It was the voice of her neighbor, Frances Drake, New Bridgeport's leading rumormonger. Vivian had a vague memory of seeing Frances at the dance the night before, on the arm of her very long-standing, very henpecked boyfriend, Paul. Frances had waved briefly before catching Rita Schmidt by the shoulder, giving her an intense conspiratorial look and running her mouth at what appeared to be faster than the speed of thought. Which, knowing Frances, might not be far from the truth.

"Yes, Frances?"

"Have you heard about Ruth? Of *course* you have. What was I *thinking*? It's *awful*. And to think, it might have been any one of us."

"Any one of us?"

Wesley motioned at his watch and mouthed the words, "Two hours." Vivian nodded and waved as he let himself out.

"You know Ruthie would never go into the woods alone at night. She's not *that* ridiculous. And from what I heard, her body was in an awful state."

Vivian ignored the comment that her friend was ridiculous and said only, "Yes, Wesley told me."

"Wesley? Oh, yes. Poor Wesley. So, he's been with you, *hmm*? Well, at least he has a *friend* to talk to." Her voice held a knowing tone that made Vivian bristle, and her mouth opened to rebut her, but Frances continued. "Well, my *father's* friend works at the coroner's office, and he won't stop talking about it. Honestly, Vivian, it's *terrible* the way they're making such a *dreadful* commotion over this."

I'm sure you're terribly *upset*, Vivian thought. Frances continued seemingly without taking a breath. "I know it's not often someone passes in that fashion around here—you know, murdered—but they woke me up at five this morning, and the phone hasn't stopped ringing since."

Vivian didn't doubt that Frances had been on the telephone all morning, but she would wager that Frances was doing the ringing. She backed out of the conversation as tactfully as possible. Talking about Ruth with Wesley, who had loved her every bit as much as Vivian did, was one thing. Talking to Frances was like trying to tiptoe through her mother's flowerbeds blindfolded. She never knew when she was going to step somewhere she shouldn't.

She headed down the hall to her room, opened her closet door, scanned the rack for her navy dress, and wished she owned something black for the funeral.

The phone rang again. She hesitated and let it ring twice before deciding to answer it. It did not seem fair to put her mother out since it was most likely for her, anyway.

This is the last call. I'll wait outside if I must, so I don't have to hear the phone, she thought as she lifted the receiver.

The line was dead.

Chapter 2

Vivian's next few days passed in a fog. Ruth's funeral came and went, and the town circulated with rumors. Half of the town—which included those inclined to believe the grandiose or far-fetched—speculated that it was something like spontaneous combustion or clouds that rained frogs: improbable, but not unheard of. The other half viewed it as a horrible murder, regarded neighbors with suspicion, and started locking their doors at night.

Just as the phone lines and back fences cooled, the unexpected happened. Another body turned up.

If the rumors were true, the second was more gruesome than the first. The casualty was a young man this time. Vivian heard from Frances that the throat in the newly found body had been savagely torn out. Equally shocking, this body was also drained of blood. Vivian learned the coroner's office called in a pathologist from the state university to examine the blood and the victim. The pathologist was incapable of shedding any light on the reason for the missing blood.

The newspaper had frustratingly little to say about the baffling circumstances.

Confusion surrounds the case of two recent deaths in Vernon County. Ruth Weaver, 19, daughter of Max and Dorothy Weaver of Far Harbor, was discovered early morning October 17th after she disappeared from the can drive at the New Bridgeport American Legion Hall. Sixteen days later, the body of Robert (Bobby) Schaffer, 15, son of George Schaffer, owner and operator of Lakeland Books, was found only a few miles from the woods where Miss Weaver was located. No suspects have been linked in either death, and murder has not officially been declared the cause.

Pathologist Gray Wyllie was unable to provide the *Palladium* with a definite cause of death. Said Wyllie: "Although I personally cannot verify the cause of death, I will do my best to help this community put this tragedy behind them."

She had almost put him out of her mind. Almost. Just when she thought that horrible, wonderful night had faded from her every thought, she saw him again.

It was a calm Sunday afternoon. She was working in the garden, a corner about half an acre square bordering the road. Her face was flushed and sweaty under a wide-brimmed straw hat. She had covered her arms with a pink, long-sleeved shirt, now covered in dirt and chlorophyll stains at the elbow. Her hair had fallen out of kilter. The pins that struggled to hold it in place had failed dismally in her thick, dark blonde hair.

She had filled a wheelbarrow with pumpkins when she became aware of a car idling on the street corner beside her.

Jude struck a breathtaking pose behind the wheel of her dream car, a black 1940 LaSalle Sedan.

"Hello. How are you?" he said. It was enough.

Vivian blushed to the roots of her hair. She brushed one of the larger dirt chunks from her apron front and smoothed her skirt. Then she caught herself. She was determined not to be shy this time. She'd had it with feeling intimidated around him because he was so handsome.

"Fine, Jude. Thank you. How are you?" *Much better. Let him know you remember him.*

"Doing well," he crooned, clearly implying, *Doing well, now that I've found you.*

"That's a pretty garden," he said. Vivian blushed again. He had the uncanny ability to say innocent things sensually. She decided to match his banter.

"It's a lot of work, but it's worth it," she breathed and made a slight adjustment to her brassiere. His eyes went to her chest, which was the effect she had hoped for.

"I imagine it is. My mother had a wonderful garden when I was younger. She loved it. She raised all kinds of herbs and vegetables, and I'd help her weed."

She nodded.

"I enjoy it. I mean, look at these pumpkins."

He smiled that crooked smile again. Vivian hoped a sunburn disguised her blushing cheeks. She returned his smile.

"Vivian, may I take you to dinner tonight?" he asked.

She blinked. As much as she had hoped for this moment, now that it had happened, she wasn't sure what to say. He was handsome and charming, but he struck her as a man used to experienced girls. She didn't want to put herself into an uncomfortable situation. She wasn't "that kind of girl," and, despite how she flirted with him, she didn't want to become one.

Still…

She smiled, and he had his answer, but he waited, his car idling in the middle of the intersection with no regard to nationwide gas rations or an oncoming driver.

Her eyes wandered to the heavy, low-hanging clouds in the sky. The day had grown late. Not much time to clean up for a date. What would she wear?

"I… um. I mean, I don't…"

"We'll go to the Charthouse," he offered.

She blinked. *The Charthouse? That's so expensive! He looks too young to be able to afford that. I wonder how old he is?*

"Sure," she said. It sounded to her as if someone had answered for her.

"Eight o'clock?"

"Eight is fine."

"See you then." He put the car in gear and was gone.

It wasn't until after she poured her basket of weeds onto the compost pile that Vivian thought about Phillip.

What on earth am I going to tell Mother? It wouldn't be polite to go on a date with Jude and not introduce him. Her mother had taught her better manners than that. Sneaking out to the car wasn't an option— what kind of girl sneaks out to a car? Backing out before he arrived at her house was of the question since she did not know his telephone number.

Jude didn't know about Phillip, so that was not a problem. Not really. No young man gets too sociable with the parents on the first date, so her indiscretion wasn't likely to come out unless Mother said something.

Ugh! What am I going to do?

Vivian dreaded the idea of presenting Jude to her mother—and not only because of Phillip. Jude had a seductive, wicked quality that parents dread in a suitor for their daughter. Her mother would find a way to work Phillip into the conversation. Jude would think less of her for accepting his date. He would leave. Or worse, he would want to take her out anyway, thinking she was a trollop. She had to come up with a way to lead her mother into believing her date with Jude wasn't a genuine date.

Impossible.

Maybe sneaking out to the car wasn't such a bad idea. If she conveniently placed herself on the porch as Jude pulled up, strolled out to the car, and disappeared before her mother saw who she left with…. It might work.

☙ ☚

Vivian put the pumpkins in the garage and reached for the doorknob just as the door drew inside. Her mother held the interior handle of the knob, dressed to the nines in her favorite blue dress and matching pumps. Her perfectly curled hair accented her youthful face, and her lipstick was a brilliant shade of red.

"Mother?" Vivian breathed. Her mother looked like she was going out on a date.

"Vivian! Oh, I was just coming to get you," her mother gushed. Her voice, however, reflected surprise, and what sounded like a bit of disappointment. Car keys dangled from her hand, and under her arm was her black clutch purse.

"Mother, are you going out?"

"Yes. There's a bond rally in town, and I thought…" her voice tapered off in uncomfortable hesitation. Her mother wasn't a good liar, and it made Vivian uncomfortable to see her struggle to search for one.

"Yes, of course."

There was no "of course" about it, but Vivian wasn't about to squabble. Now she had a way to avoid introducing her mother to Jude.

"I was hoping maybe you might want to come with me, but you looked as though you were having so much fun in the garden," her mother added. "You've been doing such a wonderful job in keeping it up all summer long. I've been neglecting it too much. Anyway, I thought you'd need to rest tonight. You've been out there all afternoon!"

Vivian smiled.

"Yes, well. Thank you," she replied. *Don't ask how long she'll be out. Act natural.* "I may go to Rita Schmidt's house later." *Rita? Do you think she'll believe you're willingly spending time with Rita?*

But her mother didn't as much as blink. She seemed to be functioning but not thinking—very out of character. *Whoever he is, he has Mother in a tizzy,* Vivian thought with bemusement.

"Well, off I go!" her mother chirped. "Have a good night, honey. There's some leftover food in the icebox if you want a bite of supper before you go over to the Schmidt girl's house. I may be running a little late tonight." She didn't bother to explain why, nor did Vivian ask.

Vivian's father, Matthew Black, had been dead for years. She didn't remember much about him. She knew his face from pictures around the house of a smiling, blond, ruggedly handsome man, and she had vague memories of a soothing baritone voice, but that was all. She didn't remember if her mother had told her how or when he had died. It had happened before Vivian remembered, which was unusual since she had the impression that she should remember, that it wasn't that long ago. Some nights, she heard her mother crying, and she knew her father's death must be the cause. She was afraid to ask, afraid that Mother would think Vivian was intentionally trying to be cruel by dragging up painful memories. Most of all, she was scared that her mother would doubt her sanity. How on earth had she forgotten her father?

And now, her widowed mother was dating again. It was about time.

"Have fun, Mom," she said. Her mother looked at her with blank surprise, like a child caught in a forbidden act, and she smiled.

"Thank you."

Vivian heard the old Ford crank up. She closed the door and turned on the radio. WRBD was playing "Glenn Miller's Friday Night Swing Hour," perfect getting-ready-for-a-date music.

She took a quick shower and powdered her body lavishly with lilac-scented talc. She borrowed a bright red dress from her mother's closet, one she had just mended. It wasn't too short, and it plunged just right in the front. She swept her hair up into a hairstyle that resembled one she had seen at the movie theater last week, reminiscent of Katherine Hepburn. She also borrowed her mother's bright red lipstick and the high-heeled shoes that matched the dress. As she admired herself in the standing mirror in her mother's room, she thought: *If mother saw me now, she'd kill me.*

She was having second thoughts about her choice of clothing when the bell rang. *Too late to turn back now.*

Jude beamed at her and took in her appearance with a swift and appreciative glance.

"Good evening, Vivian," he purred.

"Hello, Jude," she replied. He wore another handsome dark suit. She wondered if anything but elegant, tailored suits hung in his closet.

"I apologize, I wish my mother was home, but she's gone to a bond rally." *Thank God.*

"No need to worry. I'll meet her another time," he assured her. She was happy to hear he was already planning another time.

"Are you ready?"

"Let me grab my purse," she said.

It never occurred to her that her brown purse did not match her outfit. It didn't matter. From the way he looked at her, a matching purse was not on his mind.

Chapter 3

Dinner lingered over candlelight, and pleasant conversation flowed as smoothly as the Chianti. The headwaiter knew Jude, and brought them a second bottle as soon as they'd finished the first. Vivian tried to decline—she was already giggling too much—but Jude insisted. Then again, she reflected, perhaps it wasn't the wine. This was her happiest night in months.

He did most of the talking, but Vivian found him a captivating subject, although he remained closed about any topic more recent than his teenage years. He told her stories about his youth in Europe, and that he was an awkward child. Vivian found this hard to believe, but he confirmed his statement by displaying his scars. The largest one, a jagged scratch on his right hand across the palm, he claimed came from ice-skating when he was eight.

As the dinner wound down, he took her hand firmly in his. His fingers traced ticklish circles in the palm of her right hand, and his black eyes focused on hers.

"Vivian, let's go for a walk on the beach after dinner."

"Alright," she agreed without hesitation. As he took his eyes from hers and motioned to the waiter for the check, she questioned the wisdom of her decision. The beach at night with a man who was a stranger could be dangerous. Her heart pounded as she considered what might happen while she was alone with Jude on the beach. She both looked forward to and dreaded the possibilities.

What is happening to me?

They finished the wine. Jude paid the bill, leaving a generous tip, and they drove down the dark country roads to Wallenberg beach. The night was as beautiful as it had been the night Ruth disappeared. It occurred to her that she hadn't thought of Ruth all evening, though her friend had rarely left her thoughts before this magical night.

She watched Jude as he drove. Either he did not notice, or he pretended he not to. She took in his polished profile the same way her mother viewed the pastries in the bakery window—the ones she never let herself buy. She was sure this had to be love. Love for a man she hardly knew. How she wanted him! She wanted to touch his face, to feel the texture of his skin under her fingers. She wanted to press her lips to his, to see what it felt like to kiss him, to taste him. She wanted to run her fingers all over his body, to take it all in so whenever she looked at him, she remembered how every inch felt.

They arrived at the beach. He got out, circled the car, light and assured, and opened her door. He took her hand and led her down the trail through the woods that led them to the shoreline.

If someone had told Vivian that it was possible to see every star on her side of the universe that night, she would have believed them. They were awe-inspiring, innumerable. A brilliant crescent moon hung over Lake Michigan, creating waves that glittered like falling stars and caressed the shore as Jude took her hand.

"I love the beach," she murmured.

"Who doesn't?" he asked with a smile.

"It makes me feel so small. Like I'm just a speck in an infinite universe. It helps me realize how insignificant my problems are. The lake looks huge, and it's not even a drip when compared to the oceans. Oceans must look enormous."

"Not so much different from this," he said. "I've seen the Atlantic and the Pacific. The Mediterranean Sea."

"What are they like? How are they different?"

He sighed pensively, and his brows knit for a moment.

"The oceans are foamier. Choppier. There are no fish on the shores. Too many scavengers around to eat them."

Well, this conversation certainly has gone in a strange direction. Foam and dead fish.

"Jude, where were you born?" she asked. It was personal, but she felt an urgent need to devour everything about him, a thirst for knowledge she never had with Phillip. With anyone.

"Spain," he replied casually. Unlike during the conversation they carried over dinner, his eyes neglected to meet hers. Vivian studied him unflinchingly.

Why does it sound as if he's lying? Why would he lie?

"You're kidding!" she exclaimed. It sounded forced.

"No. I lived there for a large part of my life." Still, the dishonest tone to his voice. Why now? What was different? Was he more nervous?

"Do you speak the language?" she said.

"Claro que si," he replied.

"Well, I'll be," she murmured. The obvious fluency with which he delivered the short reply might have been practiced, but it sounded real.

"When did you see the Pacific?" she pressed.

"Off the California coast a few years ago," he said.

A few years ago? Jude, how old are you? How have you been able to do all these things in such a short lifespan? You can't be more than twenty... thirty at the most. Why am I so hesitant to believe you? But most importantly, why don't I care if it's the truth or not?

"What you're telling me is that you've been everywhere," she quipped. It came out with more force than she intended.

He looked at her so intensely it took her aback. His black eyes were ebony storm clouds. She tried to back away, but his grip on her hand increased.

"Vivian, you have no idea," he sighed. She got the impression there was a lot more weight in those five words than was evident.

It wasn't said in anger, so why did she feel like a reprimanded child?

They walked in silence, holding hands. She had the urge to throw back her head and let out a scream of combined happiness and frustration. She felt elated that she was with Jude, but also frustrated as hell. Was it the lies she suspected he was telling her? Or that she still wanted him despite them?

She felt herself shiver and wasn't sure if it was from the night air or nervousness. Jude looked at her with concern.

"Cold?" he asked.

"A little," she fibbed.

He put his arm around her and drew her close. She sighed contentedly, or tried to. A breeze blew by, and she listened to the drum of the waves on the shore.

She lost track of how far they walked in silence. Step by step, they passed widely spaced homes on the sparsely populated section of shoreline.

Seclusion, she thought. She was alone with Jude. Incredibly alone.

She examined his handsome profile, and imagined her hand touching his cheek, caressing his cheekbone with the tip of her thumb... but it wasn't her imagination. She was doing it, and Jude did not mind.

The breeze picked up. Vivian inhaled the strength it carried with it. For a moment, she thought she could fly. She felt her mind spinning like the leaves fluttering in the trees lining the shore. Jude kissed her. Not a soft kiss, not the type of kiss she had grown used to with Phillip. Jude kissed with the strength and assurance of a man who knew how to please a woman.

They kissed like long-lost lovers rediscovering each other. Jude showed her his excitement with every nuance, every touch, every time he looked her in the eyes as he kissed her. Her breath came in ragged gasps. She wanted him so passionately, so desperately, she would have done anything.

She closed her eyes as he touched the back of her neck with his long fingers. She felt herself falling to the sand, no… floating. As if she drifted to the ground. Jude covered her with his strong, lithe body. He kissed her neck roughly, and she responded. She felt her dress come down around her shoulders and the unfamiliar sensation of his hardness on her thigh. She felt electric and powerful to be the cause of it, and it did not frighten her.

He stopped, and Vivian nearly panicked. *Why'd he stop? Did I do something wrong?*

His face was torn, confused.

"Vivian, I—I…"

"Jude, what is it?"

He turned away, and his inattention alarmed her. She touched his shoulder, and his hand on hers reassured her.

Jude seemed to have difficulty finding the words he wanted to say. With every second that ticked by, she became increasingly aware of the cool air on her exposed flesh. Doubtful that he wanted to continue, suddenly embarrassed at her nakedness, she pulled the dress back to her shoulders.

Jude noted this out of the corner of his eyes, and it swept away any misgivings. He pushed her down gruffly, pulled the dress back down, then further, past her breast. He took her nipple in his mouth. She was shocked but not horror-stricken as the pain and pleasure mixed in breathtaking surges. Jude struggled with the clasps on the back of her dress until it came loose and gave way to his insistent tugs. She reclined nude in the moonlight as he hastily removed his clothes.

He placed his undershirt under her bottom and again covered her with his body. His agile fingers found their way to her unexplored parts. She moved her hips in time to his experienced touch until her body approached a crescendo. Her back arched, displacing the shirt. She did not care. He stopped just short of her peak and entered her.

It hurt. Just an ache, a sharp pain, and then a slight soreness. Jude took his time, and soon she pushed him in harder and deeper.

When she finished, she dug her fingers into his back so deeply she thought she might have drawn blood. She felt him throb inside her with his perfectly timed climax.

If minutes or hours passed afterward, it made no difference to her. Time and worry had lost all meaning. She lay nestled in the crook of Jude's arm as he absently stroked her hair. The slim moon shone down. She had never had such a perfect night.

Chapter 4

Vivian always felt like a commanding executive when she sat behind the solid oak desk in the office at Rogers and McMillan, an advertising firm with dozens of cubbyhole-sized offices tucked into the floors below. She spent her days at a typewriter, copying documents from her boss's nearly illegible handwriting. Occasionally she was only an errand-runner. The company was so sprawling she considered herself lucky that Mr. Stewart, her boss, remembered her name, though she had worked for him for over a year. Her mother knew an executive who'd played golf with her father, and she had coffee with his wife at the country club. Consequently, Vivian landed a job out of high school. Her typing skills were excellent, she had a keen grasp of the English language, and she also had a mother who raved about her drive, determination, and intelligence.

May, secretary to Vice President Spanozzo, dropped in to see her the day after her date with Jude. May spent more time wandering the halls, gossiping, and "taking private dictation" than anyone Vivian knew. She was also very Italian and very Catholic, which meant she spent a lot of time in confession as well. Vivian could not remember a single instance of catching May performing any work. She spent hours painting her nails, which were long and extremely orange. Not red. Orange. Vivian had no clue where she found a polish that color.

May had dressed in a garish purple outfit which set off her olive skin. It was low on top and high at the bottom, with an attention-getting quantity of ruffle and frill around each. She complemented—or at least accessorized—the outfit with a prodigious set of fake pearl earrings and a necklace to match. Vivian suddenly felt dowdy in her tailored ivory dress.

"Hey hon," May said in greeting. She called everyone hon. Vivian took no offense. "How was your date?"

"My date?" Vivian asked. Everyone she was familiar with knew that Phillip was overseas. How did May know about her date?

"I was at the Charthouse last night. I saw you looking cozy with a certain attractive someone across the table." May perched her curvy rump on the opposite side of her desk and smiled knowingly, wrinkling her nose. "Who is he?"

Vivian lowered her eyes, and a smile escaped her lips. She had been dying to tell someone. May was the perfect candidate. With her rather colorful history at the office, who was May to criticize Vivian's indiscretion?

"His name is Jude," she said.

"Where did you meet him?" May cried. "Is it over with Phillip?"

Vivian sighed.

"At the Legion Hall, and I don't know."

"Aaahh," May sympathized.

"I really like him, May," she confessed.

"Well, far be it for me to criticize. I mean, with your man so far away and all. And even when he was here… Well, I hate to be so critical of your Phillip, but 'Faint heart ne'er won fair maiden,' ya know."

"What do you mean?" Vivian asked, knowing what she meant but wanting to hear it from someone else's lips.

"Well, Phil never struck me as a lady-killer. Nice, yes. Passionate, no. This… what was his name? Jude? Hon, from the way he looked at you, he wanted you for dessert. I know that look."

Vivian blushed.

"So did you?" May prodded with arched eyebrows.

"May!" Vivian gasped. Then, on reconsideration and a perceptive look from May, she found herself confessing with a nod.

"*Hot* damn. It's about time somebody loosened you up. No pun intended. I wouldn't mind trying him on, myself. I mean, if you weren't seeing him already."

Vivian looked at her knowingly. May wouldn't wait her turn, and both of them knew it.

"Have you decided what you're going to do during your vacation?" May inquired, changing the subject.

"My what?"

"Your vacation. It's posted for this coming week. I was wondering what you had planned."

"You're kidding," Vivian moaned. "I didn't want it this week. I thought I had penciled it in for November! I was going to take off during Thanksgiving. I wanted to help my mother since it's at our house this year."

"Well, Stewart had Evelyn coming in next week to take your spot, and half the floor has asked for Thanksgiving. Besides, I think it's kinda late to change it now."

Vivian pursed her lips in frustration. She had hoped for the holiday off, but on the other hand, the idea of having the coming week off had merit.

"Well, I guess that's that, then," Vivian said. She put the final typescript on Mr. Stewart's memo and pulled it from the typewriter.

"That's it, Hon. Make the best of it. Spend some time with your new man," May said with a knowing wink. She stood up and straightened the wrinkles out of her dress.

"Then you can come back here and tell me all about it. Maybe I'll learn somethin'." Her emerald eyes rolled up, and she fluffed her hair. "Or maybe not."

Vivian grinned.

May waved, shaking her hips and wagging her orange-tipped fingers over her shoulder as she toddled out of the office. "Better get back to work," she said in parting. Vivian wasn't sure if May meant the comment for Vivian or herself.

α β

The rest of the day was useless. She couldn't concentrate, even to type the simplest memos. In her mind, she saw Jude's face, felt the passion of it as if it were a fresh wound still bleeding. She stared at the documents in front of her until the words swam together.

The phone rang.

"Benjamin Stew—"

"Hello, Vivian," a silken voice said. It was Jude.

"How did you—"

"You told me where you worked. Remember?"

She didn't.

"I've been thinking about you," he confessed, and her confusion dispelled when she heard the somber tone in his voice. She nearly said the same but decided instead to be coy.

"Oh?" she asked, trying to disguise her pleasure.

"What do you think?" His tone said that any other thought was ridiculous. "Didn't you have a nice time last night?"

No, I take my clothes off with every guy I cheat on my boyfriend with,

Vivian thought. She had to admit, however, that May was right. His straightforwardness was refreshing after Phillip. Jude acted like he knew how she felt, and she was pleased with his intuitiveness. She pictured him drifting off to sleep the same way she did last night, holding a pillow to his chest, smelling her on his hands. She could almost imagine he knew that he had starred in all of her dreams last night.

Almost.

"You know I did," she admitted.

"Care to have another nice time?"

She did not know if he meant another date or another chance to have sex on the beach, but the answer was the same to both.

"Yes, I would love to."

"Is seven o'clock too soon?"

"Seven is fine."

"I'll be there."

C֑ ֑֑

She signed out at five o'clock on the dot and embarked on the mile hike home. Her mother had always been stern about how often Vivian drove the car, and had become stricter since the start of gas rationing last year. It was foolish for Vivian to drive, she said, when her job was a mile away. When Vivian had asked about what she should do in rainy weather, her mother had bought her a large, black umbrella and raincoat. Rose Black was no-nonsense, but Vivian respected and loved her for it.

The late afternoon sun shone brightly, and only a few white clouds lolled in the sky. She inhaled deep, full breaths of crisp, fall air and thought for a moment of skipping home like a child. After a few moments of rehashing the content of her recent phone call with Jude, she found herself pondering what she always thought about when given long periods alone.

Her nightmares.

It seemed that her mind had replayed the same gruesome dreams for as far back as she remembered. In them, she lay paralyzed while a dark, menacing man—typical nightmare material—came to her bedside. She never remembered much more than that. Some mornings she woke up with vague impressions of blood or flying. Other mornings she remembered blood and a feeling of intrusion. They varied in small ways, but there was always blood.

She had tried asking her mother about them. Her mother explained that it was most likely triggered by the horror of her father's sudden death. While that seemed plausible, it also raised more questions. Was it possible that she didn't remember her father because of some weird subconscious repression? It scared her that she couldn't remember someone who must have played an important role in her upbringing.

What frightened her most of all was the idea that maybe her father was the *cause* of the nightmares.

She hated to consider it, but there were connections. In her dreams, it was always a man who invaded her bedroom. She recalled feeling conflicting emotions of both love and fervent hate for the man. Why would she hate her father? There was also a sense of helplessness that made Vivian think of a childlike acceptance of a dominant parent.

At times she wondered if the memory of the dreams changed when she tried to remember details. Could it be that it wasn't that she *could not* move so much as she *did not want* to move? But why wouldn't she stay and fight? It just didn't make sense.

And why couldn't she remember anything about her childhood?

After months of delving into books on human psychology, two theories rose above the others. The first was that she was having a hard time accepting her burgeoning adulthood. The blood symbolized her menstruation and, concurrently, her maturity. The man stood for her future spouse. The second was her awareness of death, brought on by the unexpected death of her father. Although she was proud of her theories, they did not give her the sense of satisfaction she expected to feel after having worked through a longstanding fear.

She paused at the rise of the small hill where the train tracks passed through the center of New Bridgeport. She noticed how the beams ran like veins in the arm of the tracks. They looked so unbreakable. Imbedded. Permanent.

Not permanent, Vivian. Nothing is permanent. Everything, every person, every town, every city is as fleeting as rain in the immensity of history, with only a few exceptions. ...

There. Right there. She had had a fleeting insight, but it vanished before she grasped it. It was infinite, phenomenal, like when she stood on the shore of the lake at night and tried to see where the lake ended and the sky began.

The thought of the lakeshore reminded her of her date. She wondered if tonight would be as wonderful as the night before. She quickened her steps and hurried home.

Chapter 5

*D*amn. *Damn, damn, damn. Where did the time go?* Vivian rushed around the house looking for earrings, for shoes to match her navy dress with the slightly plunging neckline, and for her black purse. It felt as though gremlins had come into her house and rearranged everything. She caught a glimpse of flushed cheeks and her exasperated expression as she rushed by the mirror in her mother's room. If she didn't stop scurrying everywhere, her hair would come tumbling down like it always did. She tried to tell herself that she needed to calm down or she would never finish in time.

The earrings were on her nightstand, where she had left them the last time she took them off. The shoes were in her closet, hidden under a skirt that had fallen off its hanger. The purse remained a mystery.

I'll borrow Mom's. She won't mind.

Strangely, or conveniently, enough, her mother was absent again that evening. Vivian supposed that her mother's date the night before had gone well, also. She was pleased that she wasn't around to ask questions or get in the way, but felt guilty for feeling that way.

She snatched her mother's tiny black purse from its place on the closet shelf, added a tube of lipstick, her change purse, and a little money into the small mouth. As she thrust her money to the bottom of the purse, she found a scrap of paper. At first, she thought it was crumpled money, but it was too small.

This was the purse mother used when she went out last night. Vivian withdrew the tiny scrap. She knew she shouldn't read a message about her mother's private business, but part of her was dying of curiosity about her mother's new beau.

It was difficult to read. First, it had been crumpled into the bottom of a clutch purse. Second, the handwriting was a challenge. It looked like some of the characters were formed strangely, like whoever wrote it wasn't used to writing with the English alphabet. Third, the faintly smeared ink had gotten a little wet. Her mother must have spilled something on it.

> You have plans for tomorrow. We will get back to you.
> —*Cartaphilus*

What sort of name is Cartaphilus? Vivian puzzled over the piece of paper, but the scrap's origin and meaning remained a mystery. Her need to prepare for her date overcame her curiosity, and she tossed the scrap into the nearest wastebasket.

She went down a mental checklist to make sure she was ready. Her shoes were at the door. Her mother's purse was in hand. Her earrings were on. Perfume... she grabbed the bottle from the vanity and gave herself a squirt, careful to avoid staining the dress. Now all there was to do was wait. She checked the time. Twenty to seven. A little early, but not bad. And here she thought she was running late.

She paced the floor for about fifteen minutes because she didn't want to sit and wrinkle her dress. She thought about her mother, wondered again where she was, and then dismissed the line of thinking since it was pointless.

Where would Jude take her tonight for their date?

At five to seven, she turned on the radio intending to use it as a distraction, but nothing was on. There were only three local stations, but sometimes they caught a station out of Chicago on when reception was excellent. Today wasn't that day. The three usual stations were playing commercials. She turned off the radio.

Seven o'clock.

She pulled the curtain back and peered out into the twilight, but saw no headlights on the lonely street. A restless sigh escaped her lips, and she let the curtain fall back into place. She didn't want him to think she had nothing better to do than stand in front of the window and wait.

What to do? She was too edgy and absentminded to try to write a letter to one of her friends. She had already tried the radio. It was too close to the hour anyhow; all the stations would be broadcasting the news. She had no urge to listen to countless stories about the war, which would only depress her and cause her to worry about Phillip.

Even if she was about to go on a date with another man, she still cared.

She considered the phonograph, then sat on the floor of the living room, her resolve to leave her dress unwrinkled forgotten as she thumbed through the records with an uninterested gaze. She gave up.

Seven fifteen. He was late.

How old was Jude? Maybe twenty-five? And he drove a LaSalle Sedan Convertible, wore tailored suits, and left generous tips.

Maybe he inherited money, like you.

What else had he told her? He had seen the Mediterranean, the Atlantic, and the Pacific. He spoke Spanish. He knew how to ice skate. He had been to California. That was all, despite how much he had talked the night before.

But was it? Hadn't his expressions and manners spoken volumes? Why had so much of his conversation last night struck her as false? Why did she feel that his character wasn't genuine whenever she was around him? She felt as though she were the protagonist of a play, and that their dialogue had been written long before. Or, more accurately, that she was acting out a part in a play she had seen several times before. Most importantly, she felt that she had no control over the plot, that her future was decided, and that her fate would not be pleasant.

It didn't make sense. Nothing made sense. Her passion for a man who only confused and frustrated her made the least sense of all.

There was a gentle rap on the door, and she stood up nervously, hesitantly.

Don't answer it.

But why shouldn't she? This was what she wanted, wasn't it? To be loved by a man as handsome, intelligent, and caring as Jude?

Caring? How do I know he's caring? What has he done that would lead me to believe that?

She opened the door. She didn't remember crossing the living room, but the door was in her hand, and there was Jude, smiling his dashing smile and handing her a single red rose.

She invited him in while she got a vase for her flower. Jude followed her. He openly took in his surroundings but did not comment. Vivian found a vase in the cupboard and nearly dropped it on her way to the sink. Her hands shook, and her mind traveled a hundred miles an hour—it argued with her, told her to back out of this date, that she did not need to see him again. Water flowed into the trembling vase and overflowed into the sink before she remembered to shut off the faucet.

"I wish my mother were here, but she's gone out again," she stammered. "I'm assuming she has a new beau, too."

"How nice," Jude said. He lifted the rose from the counter and placed it into the slender glass vase. He took it from Vivian's shaking hand and rested it on the counter.

"Vivian, are you alright?"

"Yes. No. I—I'm not sure."

He led her to the table and chairs, pulled out a chair, and directed Vivian to sit. His face was awash with concern, and Vivian felt a bit guilty for her doubts about him. He covered her hands with one of his and felt her cheeks and forehead with the other. Vivian flushed, but not from any illness. His touch, if anything, made her rosier than she had been.

"I think I saw some brandy in the living room. I'll get you a glass," Jude offered.

"Yes. Thank you, that would be good," Vivian murmured. Jude left the room with long, confident strides. She heard the tinkle of glass as he poured brandy from the decanter her mother kept out for company. He brought the drink back nearly as quickly as he had left.

"Thank you," she murmured, accepting the glass. She lifted the glass to her lips and took a tiny sip. She had never tried brandy before and was surprised at its potency. It tasted wonderful. She tried to place the flavor but could not pinpoint what gave it its metallic tang.

"Oh, you're bleeding!" she exclaimed, taking Jude's hand in hers. Across his palm, a tiny scratch dripped blood in a slow but steady flow.

"Yes, the rose and I got into a bit of a tiff," he explained with a modest grin.

"Hmm," Vivian murmured. She sipped more brandy.

◌ ◌

"Thank you again. It seems the brandy was just what I needed," Vivian said on the way to the car. Her head had cleared, and her qualms about Jude had died down.

"I've found that when I'm feeling stressed, a drink often puts me in the right state of mind," he replied glibly. He opened her door and helped her in before circling the car and taking his seat.

"I wish you'd let me put iodine on your cut," she said.

"I'll be fine. I'm a quick healer," he reassured her. She smiled at him tenderly.

"So, where are you taking me tonight?" she asked.

"My house," he said. Vivian sat up to her full height, her eyes bulging. Jude chuckled. Vivian wasn't amused.

"Don't worry. I'm not planning to take advantage of you. Not unless you want me to. My company is celebrating its centennial year in America, and I'm having the party at my home."

"What? Did you say 'your company'? Do you mean you own it, or do you work there? What is it that you do?" Vivian stammered. Her confusion was evident in her voice and easy-to-read face, and Jude smiled at her bewilderment.

"I'm the president of a large company."

"President?" she asked, resenting her failure to keep the doubt in her voice. "I mean, you look so young."

Jude first appeared amused. Then a grave expression shadowed his features.

"It was forced upon me. Inherited, you might say."

Vivian was impressed.

"It must be nice to have so much power so young."

Jude shook his head.

"No, Vivian. It's a curse."

挈 按

Jude drove for nearly thirty minutes. She marveled at the beauty of the late fall foliage that still clung to the oaks and maples lining the roads. The sky was clear and blinked with stars, which gradually vanished as they drove under a canopy of thick elm limbs. They reached a countryside unfamiliar to Vivian, largely wooded, with houses spread out between sizable parcels of land.

She hadn't realized how long she had been stargazing, and she was reluctant to break the silence. She cleared her throat.

"Are you sure your guests know how to get to your house?" she asked.

Jude nodded.

"Yes. Most of them have been to my house for one reason or another."

"At night?"

Jude suppressed laughter, and Vivian was glad the darkness hid her blush. Had she missed something obvious? She didn't see what was so funny.

"Yes, at night," he said, the laughter now absent from his voice.

"Well, the only reason I ask is that places look a lot different in the dark," she added defensively.

"No, no. You're right. And had most of my guests not already been present at other nighttime functions, I would have ensured they knew their way. You're absolutely right."

His firm defense of her comment waylaid her discomfiture. She smiled in the dark, and her clenched fist relaxed.

He pulled onto an unlit gravel road. Despite its breadth, it was nearly hidden in the darkness. If he hadn't pulled onto it, Vivian would have missed it.

"Your home is very secluded," Vivian remarked. Jude indicated his agreement.

"What can I say? I enjoy my privacy," he said, and Vivian believed him. Jude struck her as the type who rarely made friends, and kept the ones he had for life. She felt privileged to be accepted in his circle of acquaintances, and to be meeting his work associates so soon after their first date.

The road continued for about a half-mile when Vivian realized it wasn't a road at all but a driveway that ended in a broad, circular sweep in front of an enormous, well-lit mansion. About fifteen cars were parked on the grass on either side of the house, but Jude wasn't the slightest bit put out over the abuse of what looked like a well-maintained lawn.

Jude's "house" was a mammoth white Georgian composition of wood, iron, and marble. Vivian gaped at the tall ionic columns that held up a massive second-story overhang, the arcaded flues on matching chimneys, the breathtaking second-story Palladian window. A third story rested in the center of the roof with its own porch, its roof held in place by miniature ionic columns. Freshly painted black shutters framed every window.

Jude walked around the car to open her door. She put her hand on his arm, and he led her up the expansive white marble steps to a broad door with stained glass diamonds and sidelights. She already heard the tinkle of crystal and murmur of conversation drifting out with the faint sound of a violin, piano, flute, and was that a cello?

"Why do you hide such a beautiful home so far from where people can see and appreciate it?" Vivian asked.

"I didn't build it for other people," Jude replied. "I built it for me."

He opened the door, and they headed inside. Vivian expected a bombardment of hails and handshakes, but the response from his guests could not have been more subdued. The conversation came to a stand-still as eyes from all corners of the house centered themselves on their host and his guest. Vivian allowed a servant with a strangely dazed expression to remove her jacket.

"Ladies… Gentlemen… This is Vivian."

He pushed her forward with a firm hand as he presented her. His opposite hand stretched out, and Vivian would have sworn it was the hand he had scratched earlier that night, but the injury wasn't there. His voice put a heavy emphasis on her name.

How sweet. He doesn't want them to forget my name.

But the faces of his guests were anything but sweet. Eyes from every corner of the room stared at her as though she had risen from the grave. She raised a hand in greeting and smiled a weak smile. No one spoke.

Something is wrong. Something is terribly wrong.

Chapter 6

October, 1997

She awoke with a sharp inhale of stale air, her mind in such a thick fog she wasn't sure for several seconds if she had awakened at all. Her first instinct was to panic, but she didn't know why. Blackness surrounded her, and as her senses slowly came alive, she sensed a barrier in front of her, and she knew that any movement within an arm's reach would be obstructed.

She reached out and discovered she was in a firm box with a pillowy surface. Her fingers traced the silky fabric and found seams and buttons, but no handle.

Her panic grew, and so did her claustrophobia. Desperate for freedom, she pushed on the barrier. It didn't move. She pushed again, harder, but it was like trying to move a brick wall. She tried to curl her knees up to add more power, but the box was too narrow to allow her legs to move. Screaming in panic, she braced herself and shoved with all her might. The barrier didn't move upward, but it gave a little from the right. Was it hinged?

She focused her attention near her right, now putting all of her force behind it, and the top half of the box pivoted upward and outward on hinges.

She was in a casket.

She forced herself to stifle a gasp, sensing silence was critical. Some part of her intuited others were sleeping inside the caskets surrounding her.

Her brow furrowed. *Sleeping? Why would I think that? People don't sleep in caskets. I don't sleep in a casket.*

So why was she here? She wasn't dead.

Her memory danced a shadowy ballet. Cognitive thought wasn't easy.

My name. What's my name? Where am I? She kneaded her brow feebly with a fist at the end of her bony forearm. *Why do I feel so weak?*

No ideas arrived except one: *Get out. Quickly.*

The silk lining hindered her getaway. Her atrophied muscles didn't want to cooperate, and she repeatedly slipped, her long, thick fingernails abrading the silk. After a few frustrating tries, her muscles cooperated, aching as she climbed out of the casket and set her feet onto the chilly ground.

Clueless and frantic, she clung to the casket for balance as she tried to remember who and where she was from her surroundings.

The room was dark, with a hard, dirt floor. The proportions and construction were impossible to make out in the gloom. A stone staircase rose to her left, and around her stood about eight other caskets and coffins, not counting her own. Most of them appeared weathered, time-worn, and had been there for decades judging from the musty smell. If her casket was as old as the others, it didn't look it.

Strange thought, she decided. *My casket.* That was when she noticed the lid was missing from the center coffin.

He's in there.

Her breath came in shallow gasps. Her heart jumped impossibly high in her throat. She backed up as silently as her leaden feet and shaky legs allowed. Her eyes darted in every direction as she prepared for an attack. From what, she didn't know. Some distant part of her knew the reason she was in this cold, dank, dead place hid in that awful box, and she was loath to look.

But she had to. She had to know.

She struggled not to make any noise, not to so much as breathe. She begged her frustrated muscles to cooperate and creep up. Stealthily, she tiptoed closer. There was a man...

Jude.

a dead man...

That bastard captured me. Imprisoned me.

...lying asleep in an ancient coffin.

No! It can't be!

Dried blood obscured his chin and chest and trailed down the front of a double-breasted black suit. Wrapped around him like a python was a beautiful, raven-haired woman. A dreamy, smug look covered her bloody face. Half-dried blood was spattered on her white silk gown.

Her heart broke as memories of her and Jude tumbled crazily through her mental fog. A black dress yanked down over her shoulder as she fell backward. Naked skin. Pain. Powerful emotions too strong to decipher. She trembled and hyperventilated as she backed away from the putrid sight. The images tumbling through her mind were far too incredible: blood, death, an ocean—a feeling of flying.

Stay calm. Stay calm.

Her heel hit a large, sharp pebble and sent it clattering across the dusty floor. The echo rebounded off the walls of the crypt. Vivian gasped quietly, covered her mouth, braced herself, and waited for Jude to sit up, leap toward her, and put her back in the coffin.

Vivian. My name is Vivian. And that bastard...

She ran.

☃ ☗

Vivian reached the outside of the crypt without knowing how. Once there, she paused and folded her arms across her chest as she collected herself. Slowly, her thoughts gathered from the far corners of her mind like pieces of metal drawn to a weak magnet.

Nothing she had seen in the crypt explained anything—who she was, who Jude was. She caught fleeting mental pictures of naked bodies, of talons and sharp teeth. She didn't know how many of the crazy thoughts spilling through her mind were real and how many were nightmares, and they were too unpleasant to dwell on.

Under the light of a gibbous moon, she saw a landscape of head-stones, each about two paces from the next. Vivian had no urge to read any of the names. Intuitively she knew they offered no answers, and intuition was all she had to go on.

She gradually became aware of the cold rain, and that she was shivering. Her feet were bare, dirty, and slippery with the moss from the crypt steps. Like the woman wrapped in Jude's arms, she was dressed in a long, white, silk nightgown, which offered no protection from the weather. And she had lain still for far too long. She needed to keep moving. It didn't matter where, just away. Far away, and quickly.

She began to walk.

☃ ☗

Inside the crypt, Jude's eyes fluttered open. He used his ears to attune himself to his surroundings more shrewdly than a bat uses radar. He collected details from the universal knowledge that only the oldest life forms know.

So, she decided to try to leave me. He heard her footsteps as they pattered away uncertainly on the ground above. He was surprised she had made it so far. Usually, her trips involved a feeble struggle to cross whatever room held her.

It was only a matter of time. They all try to escape, or think about trying. He suspected this was Vivian's third try in as many years. It was of no importance. He would arise soon and find her. She would not be gone long, if she survived at all. He always made certain of that. She was too weak. Undernourished. Susceptible to anything. Death would be the easy way out.

She won't die. You know she won't die.

And so what if she didn't? He would have fun hunting her. He always did. It had been fifty years since his last good game of cat and mouse.

And why is that? You've never let her sleep so long before. And what if she gets away? Don't you think you ought to get up now and make sure she stays where she belongs? Make sure she doesn't cause any trouble?

He squelched the depressing thought. The smile on his face widened when he thought of the various ways of punishing her. She *was* his favorite pet, and punishments could be sweet. Jude thought about her young breasts and long, dark blonde hair, how her lithe body yielded to his every thought. He felt the first stirrings of arousal and decided to wake the pet beside him.

ζ η

Vivian's cold feet gradually became a dark shade of red, and walking was a lot harder than she remembered. She felt like a drunken toddler.

She had been held captive in a private cemetery on a large plantation. Fortunately, the grounds on the estate were well maintained, and the grass, although cold and wet, was soft and free of pebbles and sticks. Her white gown was now so soaked it was transparent. She might as well have been nude.

Her stomach growled loudly and clawed inside her body. She licked her dry lips, and her tongue pricked on sharp eyeeteeth. *Hmm. I wonder.... No, don't think. Keep walking, think later.* The world spun in gentle circles, and she paused to stabilize herself. Stars danced in front of her eyes when she looked up from where her feet trod on the spongy grass. The world danced, and she swayed. She felt a blackout coming on.

No! I've gotten too far now. Never made it this far before .. I have to keep moving, I have to... she coaxed herself.

It was as though two Vivians dueled in her head. The part of her that knew what had happened before she gained consciousness refused to talk to the conscious side. Occasional transmissions would break through like a radio with another station buzzing in periodically. It was infuriating. No, it was beyond infuriating. She felt as though she was running on nothing but impulse. Her mind grew duller as she became hungrier.

Radio. She thought of her cozy living room, where she and her mother sometimes listened to the radio shows. Where was her mother now?

Don't think about that! an angry voice interrupted. *Keep one foot in front of the other and stay straight. Just keep moving. March.*

Was she going crazy? Or maybe delirious with hunger? *Yes, that must be it.* She had to find food, and soon.

She raised her tired head and surveyed her surroundings. There was still no sign of a house, although the trees ahead appeared to be a grove. If she was lucky, maybe something was in season. She had no idea what season it was, but the thought filled her with a small measure of hope.

As she reached the trees, she saw they were part of a peach orchard. Hanging from the branches were the remainders of a harvested crop. None of the fruits looked appetizing, but she couldn't afford to be choosy. She trudged under the closest branch she could find, grasped a low-hanging, overripe peach, plucked it from the tree, and bit.

Juice dribbled down her chin. The sliver of clarity she had grasped with the help of the cold weather vanished. Her surroundings faded, and she saw herself in a candlelit room with Jude. He was smiling and offering her something...

This is wrong. It doesn't taste right. It's plain, it's not...

Not what?

A similar memory skirted her grasp. She chewed. It was like chewing paste. Piercing the skin felt bizarre, too, and she fought the urge to suck the juice from the fruit's meat.

Skin, and blood...

She closed her eyes, and shook her head against the bombarding images and the sudden urge to lie down and let them wash over her.

Can't think about that now. Later.

She ate the peach, despite its bizarre taste, and followed it with another. She had become far too thin, too frail. She needed to get strong. As she ate, the drizzle stopped, chased by strong and chilly breezes. Vivian decided food could wait; it wasn't helping anyhow. She needed clothing.

Her teeth chattered, and she still felt dreadfully hungry, but she continued her course. First light was approaching. The sun hid behind gray clouds ready to burst any moment with more rain. The only sign the sun existed in this strange waking world was the encroaching light filtering through the clouds. Vivian squinted at the dawn.

It seemed days before a farmhouse came into view. The clouds had formed a halo around the sun, revealing a beautiful, golden dawn. She plodded on listlessly and hoped that she was traveling in a straight line. Her head beat like a bass drum, and her eyelids were lead.

If I can get to the house, I'll be alright, she told herself. Her feet were purple and bruised from walking for so long without shoes. She had forgotten to feel self-conscious about her state of near nakedness in her desperation for shelter from the God-awful sun, which was giving her an excruciating headache. Her pale skin was already feeling the early stages of sunburn, though it was barely dawn.

Shivering, her teeth chattering, she lumbered up to the farmhouse. It was two stories, freshly painted white, wooden siding with black shutters. White beams supported the porch, and between each beam hung a Boston fern. White, wicker patio furniture rested on the porch. It looked warm and inviting, and Vivian had no doubt its occupants must be nice.

Almost there. Almost.

She climbed the four steps to the porch with a great deal of support from the wooden handrail. There was a clean, yellow towel on the chair closest to her. She blinked and swallowed, sucked in her breath nervously, and subconsciously tongued her pointed eyeteeth again. What would she say to whoever answered the door? How would she begin?

Vivian grabbed the towel, dried off, and wrapped the towel around herself. On the cushion, hidden under where the towel had been, were a pair of denim jeans, a black T-shirt, and a warm, red flannel jacket alongside a pair of black wool socks. There was also a set of underwear.

Vivian resisted the urge to put them on. The towel and clothing were there for someone else, and she had already assumed too much just borrowing the towel. But it wouldn't be wise to knock on the door looking fresh from the grave.

Voices came from inside the farmhouse. Feeling like an intruder, she crept slowly over to the picture window and peeked inside.

What she saw both awed and confused her. The window looked in on the living room. The soft, beige walls, sofa, and coffee table were typical, as were the plants in the windowsill. What mystified her was the glowing box with buttons on the front resting on an oak shelving unit across from the sofa. It emitted moving pictures, like a cinema, only in color. The voices she had heard were coming from the movie-box.

Vivian had heard about television but had never seen one before, and a color picture was still in the experimental stages—she thought. She stared, captivated. A blonde woman spoke of actors from early cinema. John Barrymore flashed onto the screen, black and white, as she remembered him from the movies, dressed in a flamboyant pirate's costume. The following picture was of a pretty blonde woman with red lips. Vivian could not hear what she was saying, but underneath her were the words, "Drew Barrymore, Granddaughter."

Vivian gasped and turned away from the window.

Granddaughter?

How long have I been sleeping? Could it have been decades? She studied the back of her hands and her thin legs. They didn't look older, just much thinner. What was going on? Vivian wouldn't have guessed she had the strength to cry, but tears burned behind her eyes.

She couldn't ask these people to help her. She wouldn't know what to say. They'd never believe her. She didn't believe it herself.

Quietly, rapidly, and with as much modesty as possible, she donned the clothes left on the chair. They were a little too large, but she couldn't afford to care. She needed to protect herself from the weather. Judging by that morning, the nights were going to be cold. Who knew where she would be by nightfall?

As she sat in the chair to better put on the socks, she uncovered a pair of black leather boots hidden under the seat, which fit her almost perfectly.

Once dressed, Vivian rose from the wicker chair and hurried for the steps. As she stepped on the first one, the door squeaked open behind her. A plump, middle-aged woman in a kitchen apron, denim pants, and flowered blouse peered at her curiously from behind a heavy screen door. Her large, brown eyes smiled at her.

"Are you coming in, honey? Or you leaving already?"

Chapter 7

Vivian's response to the woman's sudden appearance was to break stride mid-dash and almost fall down the porch steps. Her sticklike arms flailed frantically before clamping down on one of the porch pillars. Her mouth sagged open in astonishment, and her face burned.

I stole her clothes. Why is she acting so nice?

"Come on," the woman said. She moved gracefully from behind the screen door, put her arm around Vivian, and led her into the house. She effortlessly steered Vivian into the kitchen. Like the living room, the kitchen was warm and inviting, separated from the living area by a tile-inlaid island lined with barstools. The walls were painted brick red with walnut cupboards. Apples decorated everything from the plates hanging on the wall to the macramé bowls suspended from the ceiling. The décor made Vivian think of cinnamon and apple pies. Her stomach growled again.

"My name is Beth," she told Vivian, easing her onto a barstool. "And you're Vivian." Vivian leaned onto the brick-colored countertop as Beth strolled around the island into the kitchen. "I knew you were coming. You were in my dreams last night, and they're rarely wrong. Not that I have them often. But often enough." Beth moved like a dancer tossing various items from her cupboards into a pot.

The drugged feeling returned. Life was like a vast puzzle she had worked on before, but none of the pieces fit for some reason.

"First things first," Beth said. "You need to feel better, don't you? Don't ask me how I know what it is you need, but I know. I ain't asking questions. I know you're not wicked, honey. You're misunderstood. You need help, and I ain't the one who can fix you, but Lenny and I will get you on track."

Beth warmed a dark liquid in a double boiler on a stove built into the kitchen countertop. *Amazing,* Vivian thought, *a flat stove.* She wondered despondently if the world would ever be familiar to her again.

"Oh, don't you worry about that," Beth assured her. "You'll catch up. You'll see." And with that, she opened a pantry filled with spices and liquids which only a marketplace could match. Smells wafted across the kitchen and tickled Vivian's nostrils—odd aromas, like dirt, old sandalwood, and eucalyptus leaves. She realized Beth had answered her without her ever having uttered a word.

"Lenny's m'husband," Beth continued as if nothing unusual had happened. She shuffled through the pantry, moved aside candles, and tinkled jars and bottles as she went. "He should be home any minute now. We didn't want to use the phone here at the house." She found the jars she was looking for and blended the ingredients into the mixture on the stove.

"Normally, I prefer to use fire, but we're in a hurry today, and I'm sure the Lord will understand. Now for the main ingredient."

Vivian was curious what that main ingredient was. How did Beth know what she needed? Beth grasped a small bowl from the refrigerator. She removed the top pot from the lower one, placed it on a cool burner, and slowly stirred the liquid contents into the bowl. Vivian strained as much as her feeble neck would let her, but Beth's body blocked most of it from view.

"I killed one of my hens this morning after I woke up, before you got here. Hopefully, it'll be enough."

Voodoo? Witchcraft? Vivian wondered. She recalled a man, Jack McCrory, who lived across the sharp turn in the country road that formed the barrier between her mother's property and his. Her mother had invited the greying widower over for dinner on more than one occasion. One night, after a few snifters of brandy, he spun long, wild tales about voodoo, but she had never believed him. He claimed to have seen instances of it in his travels as a salesman, and had used the stories to frighten misbehaving children wandering close to his yard.

"No, child, not voodoo. But somethin' similar. And it's a good thing, too, or you'd be in sorry shape." It was the second time Beth had displayed telepathy, and Vivian shook her head in disbelief. Beth gave her a wry smile. She removed an enormous white ceramic cup from the pantry and slowly, carefully, poured in the warm, dark contents of the pot. Vivian strained to see the contents so hard that she almost didn't notice Beth's closed eyes, her lips moving silently as she poured. As soon as she filled the cup, she righted the pot. She hadn't opened her eyes, but not a drop was lost. *Amazing.*

She brought the cup to Vivian. "Here, honey. I imagine this will taste a little better than them peaches."

Vivian took a long draft from the mug. It was delicious: spicy and metallic in perfect harmony, like nothing she had ever tasted. As she continued to sip, she felt warmth spread from her core to her extremities. The more she drank, the better she felt. It was as though a housekeeper came into her thoughts and cleared away the cobwebs. The pain vanished, her feet grew warm, her color returned, and her eyes focused. She managed a feeble smile.

"I have a little more left if you need it," Beth offered. Vivian nodded eagerly. As Beth poured the rest of the strange, almost cider-like drink, Vivian asked, "What is it? It's delicious."

"Chicken blood, garlic, and poppy, mostly, but there are other herbs mixed in."

Vivian nearly dropped the cup. She quickly caught herself and forced herself to swallow the stuff in her mouth.

"Did you say chicken blood?"

Beth nodded fervently. "It's what you need, honey. The blood is what'll keep you on your feet." Now it was time for Beth's brow to furrow as she studied the sad, bewildered look on Vivian's face.

"You have no idea, do you?"

Vivian recalled the bizarre thoughts that had tumbled through her head as she bit into the peach. Blood and skin. The finished picture still hadn't surfaced, but the effort didn't stress her now.

"What's happened to me?" she murmured. Her voice was drowned out as a large, dark-skinned man bustled into the front door. Beth turned and smiled lovingly at her husband.

"Is she ready?" he asked. He tossed the car keys nervously from one massive hand to the other. He was dressed like a hardworking farmer on his day off: dark jeans and a warm sweater pulled over a t-shirt. He restlessly ran a hand over a peninsula of hair on the front of his slightly balding head.

"Almost, darlin'," Beth replied. She scurried over to the pantry, removed two daintily wrapped objects, and brought them over to Vivian.

"This," she said, handing her a tiny red velvet bag, "will help you remember. Your recent memories will come to the surface without a struggle, but the others, well... this'll help. A little. Be strong of mind if you decide to take it, or you'll put yourself in danger. Remember this: If you decide to use it, be ready to fight for your life, even beyond the grave. Death is not the end.

"This one," she handed Vivian a similar bag, only black, "will help you end it if you decide to finish the fight. Unless you want it all to be over, don't untie it. Don't smell it. Don't *look* inside it. It's that potent."

Vivian swallowed hard and took the two bags. Although she had only had mental clarity for a few minutes, she sensed the truth in Beth's words. A million questions came to mind, but Beth turned her back and strode to a coat rack near the door. She pulled off a small, black leather handbag, which she gave to Vivian. Vivian put the tiny packages inside the purse.

She thought of the bizarre turn her life had taken, and she didn't know where to start. Clearly, a substantial amount of time had passed since she had first met Jude. He had done appalling things to her. She also knew that her struggles were only beginning.

"My life will never be the same, will it?" she whispered.

Beth shook her head solemnly.

"Baby, I wish I could keep you here forever, even if it meant killing off all my chickens," she replied, and smiled feebly. "But if you stay here, we're *both* dead."

Chapter 8

Trying to appear more confident than she felt, Vivian followed Lenny to the large, blue Chevy pickup in the driveway. She climbed into the passenger seat, and when Lenny buckled his safety belt, she followed suit.

"Put this on," he said gruffly and handed her an enormous parka.

"Thank you, but I'm not cold," Vivian said. Lenny looked at her as though she had sprouted a third eyeball.

"It's not to keep you warm. It's to put over yourself to block the sun. Cover your skin if you want to keep it. Otherwise, you'll discover the hard way that you're awfully photosensitive."

"Oh," Vivian muttered. Though she knew there was no way for her to know—she wasn't even sure what photosensitive *meant*—she still felt foolish. She obediently covered herself with the parka from head to mid-thigh.

"Where are we going?" she asked once she settled underneath. Her voice sounded ridiculous and muffled.

"To a safe house. Well, to what Beth and I believe is a safe house. Anymore, there's no way to know for sure. They'll tell you there what you can do about your situation."

Her situation. She still had no idea what her situation was. She thought about the red bag and its mysterious contents that Beth claimed would bring back her memory. Be strong of mind, Beth had said. This was the strongest of mind she supposed she would be for a long time; the chicken blood had helped her the way her mother's chicken soup had when she felt sick. Hard to say what would happen once the brew Beth had concocted for her wore off. Was she ready to fight for her life?

Damn right I am. Better take it now.

"Will we be on the road long?" She asked. She felt foolish for trying to carry on a conversation from under the parka, like a child playing hide-and-seek yelling, "You can't find me!"

"About four hours. You'll probably want to get some sleep, if you can."

Vivian reached toward the floorboard, and tried to get her purse and stay under the parka at the same time. She found it and pulled it onto the seat. It was easy enough to fish out the red bag, as there were only two items inside.

She opened the bag and pulled out a large pill. It looked like hard gelatin covered in hair. *Disgusting.*

"Do you have anything to drink?" she asked. She was beginning to feel like a massive thorn in Lenny's side.

"There's some tomato juice in the thermos to your left, there. Beth thought you'd want it. That pill will probably knock you out for the rest of the trip."

She groped for the thermos, found it, and unscrewed the lid. *Well, here's hoping.* She placed the pill in her mouth and briskly followed the nauseating pill with some flavorless tomato juice. She replaced the lid and sat back.

She closed her eyes and tried to sleep. The truck bobbing and dipping on the country roads was a little bothersome at first, but as the tiring effects of the pill overcame her, she closed her eyes, and prepared to remember.

☙ ❧

This was bad.

Jude arose shortly before sunset and tried to get a fix on Vivian, but it was like trying to get a grip on a handful of water—she kept slipping out of his grasp.

She's fed—at least a little bit. I don't have the same hold on her. Her mind isn't as scattered as it should be, but still...

Still, it was too scattered for him to grasp. And she was on the move. He could not tell where. The direction seemed erratic, undetectable. As if she knew someone was following her, and was dodging without seeing which way she was going.

She's in a vehicle! Damn that witchy bitch. I'm going to kill her. I'll kill her whole family for the trouble they've caused.

Vivian's mind was too muddled to get a grip on her location. If she was close, it would not have been a problem. She must have traveled at least a couple of hundred miles by now.

Damn it. I'll have to tell them. Fuck. There's no avoiding it now.
Releasing his search for Vivian, Jude focused on the minds he knew best.

❧　❦

It was as if she was there, living and breathing it again. She slid down the tricky slope of memory as though it were a horrific carnival slide. Fifty years of cruelty and horror came flooding back. She remembered Jude's exquisite, deadly kiss. She remembered meeting Jude's friends, how they'd appraised her as though she were a work of art in a museum not to be touched, but to respect. She recalled Jude's rages. All the insults and abuse came back with perfect clarity.

She recalled her futile efforts to fight him off, and how he swatted her like a cat playing with a fly. Again and again, she tried to resist him, but it was useless. That he controlled her was indisputable. She was weak, and her ability to think became weaker the more he kept her malnourished.

Finally, she saw the bloodletting. She lived the nightmare night after night. He visited her bedside and fed her his cold blood. For a few moments, she would be able to move on her own, but in those moments, his mind still dominated hers.

Jude had kept her a prisoner, unconscious, and he visited her only to feed her or to use her physically. She was his servile concubine, powerless to fight him off physically or mentally.

She awoke only on occasion, and always ravenous. Jude would feed her, usually from his chest or arm. When he finished with her, she would lie down again and sleep until she was hungry or Jude wanted her again. When he wanted her, there was no act too depraved to soothe his twisted passion. Her cheeks flushed as she recalled countless episodes of perverted cruelty.

Eventually, he wanted her less and less. She stirred less often, and when she did, she was incoherent from hunger. She knew she was losing her touch with reality, or what had become her reality, and she hated herself for it. More than that, she loathed Jude for what he had done.

She was Jude's property, his toy. And when he finished with her, she had no doubt he would kill her and throw her away, but there was no telling when that would be. Ages had passed since he'd taken her prisoner, and despite his bouts of disinterest, he refused to let her go. Nevertheless, she was his, and not to be had by anyone else. Ever.

Chapter 9

Vivian awoke around two o'clock and felt surprisingly refreshed. She remained under the parka, silent, hot, and introspective. She didn't know what she was going to do, but at least now she had an idea where she had been.

So that's my past, she ruminated. *How did I let this happen to me? Me? I never allowed anyone to control me like that.*

Music emanated from speakers in the doors. Both the style and the artist were unfamiliar. She decided to chat with him to keep the trip from becoming tedious.

"What are we listening to?" she inquired with a muffled voice.

"What, this?" he asked, amused. "Girl, you *have* been gone for a while. This is Marvin Gaye."

"What's a Marvin Gaye?" Vivian asked, feeling foolish.

"'What's a Marvin Gaye?'" Lenny laughed. "He's a soul singer. One of the best."

Vivian hesitated.

"Umm, not to sound stupid, but what's 'soul'? Aside from a kind of music."

She could almost *hear* Lenny shaking his head. His tone of voice had softened, though.

"Soul is music that talks to your heart, says what you think, and makes you wanna be with the one you love."

Vivian thought about that for a moment.

"I thought *all* good music was supposed to do that."

Lenny chuckled.

"Yeah, but soul does it with *style*. Hey, I know I told you to stay under the parka, but there's a good view coming up if you want to take a peek. I don't think it'll hurt."

Vivian cautiously slid the parka past her eyes. The sunlight struck them, and she was temporarily blinded. Still, she watched nonetheless as they climbed an enormous arching bridge, a beautiful, mammoth structure of steel and concrete. Below the bridge flowed a wide river.

"Normally, we don't come in over the Talmadge Bridge, but I had to take a detour into South Carolina while you were sleeping. I think someone was following us, but whoever it was, I lost 'em. The view's coming up on your left."

The Chevy chugged to the top, and as they descended, Vivian glimpsed the peaks of an old city to their left. Trees lined many of the streets like sentinels. The buildings looked as though they hadn't changed since the founding of the colonies. The sun gleamed off the top of a gold-domed building, and church steeples stretched beseechingly toward heaven. Along the riverfront stood weathered four- and five-story brick buildings with tiny balconies framed with wrought-iron railings. A cobble and ballastone road wound along the riverfront, flanked by brick sidewalks. Two white riverboats with bright red guardrails and paddlewheels were docked near the sidewalk, waiting patiently for the next lazy jaunt down the river.

"Where *are* we?" Vivian gasped. A long way from Michigan, she was sure.

"Welcome to Savannah, Georgia," Lenny bellowed in an exaggerated Southern drawl.

She nodded mutely. The well of tears she thought was bottomless had evaporated, at least for the moment. Reliving her nightmare during her drug-induced sleep had both angered and motivated her. Jude had taken her life and everything she had ever known away. Now it was time to get it back.

Once off the bridge, she and Lenny wove through a town of historic buildings and live oak trees laced in Spanish moss. Lenny skillfully maneuvered his way through traffic squares, and Vivian peered at the well-cared-for monuments that stood in the center of each. She gaped at the monumental, marvelously preserved homes with brick steps and iron handrails. Bright flowers, topiary trees, and bushy plants decorated many broad windowsills and verandas. She caught glimpses of manicured gardens hidden behind the fences and gates. And there were churches around every corner.

"A lot of the downtown houses have names," Lenny told her, "Some of these places have stood since before the States were a country. Savannah's one of the oldest towns in the U.S., and they mean to keep it looking just as it did over two hundred years ago."

He turned the wheel onto a street at a right angle to the river—or at least, so Vivian thought. She had lost track of her sense of direction.

"Don't worry, you'll learn your way around soon enough," Lenny said. Vivian smiled. Lenny had at least some of the psychic talent his wife did. "Michael and his family will take good care of you."

The houses down this street were in no way comparable to the beautiful homes of downtown. About fifteen feet from an alley entrance, they pulled into what she supposed was a driveway—a small, empty patch of sandy dirt able to hold about three cars. The house was two stories, red brick, and unremarkable. It was more modern, yet far from new. This was a house Savannah forgot. All the windows were boarded up. White paint peeled on the dilapidated remnants of a porch with rotting steps. Sparse, long grass grew bravely in the patches where there was any grass at all. In place of a welcome mat was a square, emerald green carpet remnant.

Lenny didn't hesitate to get out of the car. "Cover up again, as much as you can," he said. "You're going to have a bad enough burn as it is." Vivian conveniently neglected to hear him. After all, how bad could sunburn get?

He looked at the house quizzically and consulted a piece of paper in his hands as though to make sure he had the right place. One of the shabby, white doors on the porch opened as he studied.

"Lenny!" shouted the young man bounding down the steps. He crossed the distance in about two paces and greeted Lenny with a bear hug. Lenny was a tall man; this young man had him beat by a stretch. Vivian meekly slid out of the car, gripping the purse Beth had given her, and never taking her eyes from this newcomer. Built like a Norse god and *impossibly* tall—probably close to seven feet—he had bright blue eyes and a blond head full of curls that looked as though they'd be more at home on a toddler. The inconsistency in this thought made Vivian smile. He probably hadn't been a toddler in about, oh, four and a half feet or so. She guessed he was roughly her age, maybe about twenty-one.

"So, this is Vivian," he said, still friendly but now staring at her with a critical gaze. He smiled and revealed a row of bright, white teeth. "I can see why Jude didn't want to let you get away." Vivian blushed and turned her eyes toward the dusty ground.

"Vivian, this is Lukas," Lenny said.

"Oh, shit, what am I thinking?" Lukas gasped as if suddenly remembering something important. "I'd better get you inside." He walked around the car and grasped Vivian by the elbow. "Can you make it? Are you feeling alright?" The display of chivalry spoken after the vulgarity was amusing.

"I'll be OK," she breathed shyly. A hint of a genuine smile made it to her lips. It felt foreign to her, as though her muscles had forgotten how and needed to remember.

"I'd better get going," Lenny said. Lukas shut the passenger-side door to the Chevy and stared at her curiously as she headed around to the front of the truck to where Lenny sat with the door still open. She handed Lenny the parka and looked at him evenly.

"Thank you. Thank you, and thank Beth for helping me. I know you put yourself at risk for me, and I don't know why you did it. I want you to know, I *am* sincerely grateful to you and your wife. I won't forget this."

Lenny accepted the parka and smiled.

"You're welcome," he replied earnestly. And with that, he shut his door, started his Chevy, turned on Marvin Gaye, and drove off in a cloud of gray Savannah dust.

Ϩ　Ϫ

Hashepsut Ketut heard a familiar, sinister voice calling her just as dusk settled on her makeshift dirt grave meters below the earth in Togo. In Scotland, Wynda Moireach heard, and a glower settled over her delicate features. In Australia, Peter Dale listened to the voice and arranged with his second-in-command to ensure that things ran smoothly in the event of his extended absence. Zivon Duscha took flight from Saint Petersburg with a modicum of resentment as soon as he understood. Their destination: Atlanta, Georgia.

Known to them now as Jude Shepherd, the voice summoned twenty ancient, malefic creatures. They were all given the same cryptic but incontestable message. Meet by nightfall, Atlanta time, in the usual chamber.

They were not curious or driven by the will to serve. They were merely obedient. It was a price they paid for the power they enjoyed, for the privilege of holding a portion of the planet under their control.

Although their lives dated back centuries, Jude Shepherd was by far the oldest and most evil. He claimed to be the father of the vampire race, and none of them could dispute him. None of them had lived long enough to see the genesis of their kind. Jude had killed off their predecessors in a calculated attempt to hold the greatest strength that comes with age. He had eliminated his earliest progenies, whose names lived on only in records. He was at least two thousand years old. Charles Dunning was said to be fifteen hundred, and there was speculation that Maysun Khatri was older. No one knew. No one dared to ask. Acceptance was part of the game, a nod of the head, and executing orders part of what kept them on top of the Tribe. The rules were simple: Obey Jude, and they were free to behave according to their whims. They had countries to run, to handle as they saw fit.

The price was that Jude controlled the world. It was one they were willing to pay.

Chapter 10

Lukas led Vivian up a flight of stairs into an apartment on the second story. Almost no natural light penetrated the boarded windows. The only light was from the dim yellowish glow of dust-covered bulbs. A thick layer of dust covered *everything*. The rooms consisted of a kitchen, a large living area, a tiny bath, and two bedrooms.

"Sorry about the shape of the place," Lukas apologized. "It's temporary."

The place was a mess. It looked like a Taj Mahal for hobos. Two mismatched couches had been set in the corners on the left of the living room. A third folding couch against the far wall was the only piece of furniture that matched anything—it was the same bright, emerald green as the carpet on the stairs. To the right was a small, boxy, black stereo. Vivian guessed by its neglected appearance that it wasn't up to modern standards. Fruit crates with candles on top posed as tables. Emptied cigarette boxes and used matches littered the floor next to scraps of crumpled paper, beer bottles, and several filthy articles of clothing. Above the stereo hung three large posters depicting a sultry-looking young man with a painted face. Drab, dark wood paneling covered every wall.

"Who *lives* here?" Vivian asked, trying not to look disgusted with the condition of what she assumed was her new, albeit temporary, home.

"So far, just you, me, my dad, and our friend, Gina."

"How long have you been here?"

Lukas shrugged. "Off and on for about two weeks. Be glad it's October. This place has no air-conditioning. Here, take a seat." He pushed a pile of dirty clothes off a couch cushion. Vivian sat down daintily. Lukas brushed off another seat on the couch beside it and reclined in it comfortably.

"You don't like it here, do you?" He asked pointedly. Vivian tried to think of a delicate way to put what first came to mind, and decided against it. He struck her as open to candor.

"Not really." She laughed.

"Don't ask me why we come here. Michael and Gina love to party here. I think it's because they don't have to worry about cleaning up afterward."

"Who's Michael?"

"My father."

"You call your father Michael?" She tried to imagine calling her mother Rose, but couldn't.

Lukas laughed. "Trust me. It'll make sense soon enough."

Vivian shook her head. "*None* of this makes sense. I was dropped off in a new town, literally years from what I'm familiar with to live with *homeless* people?"

This time Lukas's laugh bordered hysteria. When he calmed down, he said, "You make it sound so *bad*. And I wouldn't say homeless. We have *lots* of homes. We pick and choose which ones we want to stay in from day to day."

"Do they all look like this one?" Vivian asked, her voice full of dread.

Lukas shook his head, bit his lip, and turned the corners of his mouth down to keep from laughing again. "Not hardly. Michael chose to stay in this one tonight so you can get a glimpse of what's going on. He's out now, rounding up the troops."

"He's not like me, then," Vivian said. "He doesn't have what I have." She instinctively knew Lukas wasn't like her, which was odd, since she couldn't pinpoint what was different. But Michael was out "rounding up the troops" in daylight. Lenny had told her she should stay out of sunlight. *What was the word he used? Photosensitive?*

Lukas shook his head. "No, he is. He's just well-fed."

"OK, so let me ask you a question."

Lukas raised his eyebrows and waited for the question. Vivian gathered her courage, and let it all out at once.

"What the hell is going on?"

At this, Lukas took a deep breath as well. Obviously, he had known this was coming and had prepared himself with an answer that wasn't easy to reveal. His eyes rolled back in his head as he searched for the right words to begin.

"OK, lemme ask *you* something. What do you know?"

Vivian sighed in exasperation. She clenched her hands into fists and released them, taken aback at the length of her fingernails, which bit into her palms.

"I know I woke up this morning in a crypt, in a coffin, casket...

whatever. I ran away, scared as hell. I know that a man I thought I loved lied to me and kept me as a prisoner for years, but I still look the same—I mean, I haven't aged. I know I drank his blood to stay alive. I know some witch woman gave me a mixture of chicken blood and herbs at her house and a disgusting pill to help me remember what I'd forgotten during the years I was a prisoner. It was her husband who brought me here. I know that I'm not supposed to wander off in the sun for too long. And now I'm here in a dirty apartment in Savannah, Georgia, talking to some guy I hardly know about things that don't make any damn sense, hoping he'll clear it all up for me."

All of this gushed from her lungs in what felt like two breaths. She studied Lukas, who held her stare, and whose eyes registered no shock at any of her statements. He had leaned forward as she rambled, and now he eased back into his seat. Again, he searched for the right words.

"Vivian, do you believe in the supernatural? The existence of things outside of normal… reality?" Vivian supposed that he needed to know she wasn't on the verge of cracking, that she could handle earth-shattering news.

"After this morning, I'd believe just about anything."

He smiled, but it faded as he gazed into Vivian's eyes. He leaned over again and took her hands in his. They almost disappeared in his massive grasp.

"I hate to be the one to have to tell you this. You may not believe me, but *try*. Vivian... you're a vampire."

Vampire. The words echoed inside her head like the bang of a judge's gavel at the verdict of life in prison with no parole. She had been aware of this eerie possibility on some level since she took the trip inside her nightmarish memories, but to hear it from someone else's lips confirmed it. She was a vampire, a monster from myth and storybook, from ancient legend. It couldn't be true, but there it was. The impossible had been made emphatically possible.

"How do you know?"

Her lips quavered; her hands shook inside Lukas's hands. Her heart had misplaced itself inside either her throat or her stomach, maybe both.

"Vivian, my father's a vampire, just like you. Right now, he's only three years older than I am, to look at him. Still, he's my father. He lives by drinking the blood of other people, and sometimes animals."

"He kills people? Do I have to kill people to stay alive?" She knew if that were the case, she would rather die than go on living.

"No. That's the part so many people don't understand. You don't have to take another person's life to survive. Are you familiar with the vampire bat?"

"Vaguely," Vivian admitted. She had heard stories, maybe read a book a long time ago. Right now, every memory was a long time ago.

"Well, that's kind of how you can live. I mean, yeah, you drink more blood than a bat. But that whole death issue, it's avoidable. Very avoidable."

"Unless you're like Jude," Vivian added.

Lukas nodded sympathetically.

"Unless you're like Jude. Jude gets his kicks out of killing people, slaughtering them like cattle. Most vampires do. It's unfortunate, but it happens more often than not." He sighed. "Now here's the hard part–"

"There's a *hard part*?" Vivian asked incredulously. *Surely, it can't get any worse.*

"Jude, your... captor, is a lead figure in the *Shévet ha Dam*," he pronounced the Hebrew words *Shev'bet ha Dawn*. "That's basically Hebrew for 'Blood Tribe.'"

Why does that sound familiar? Vivian wondered.

"The *Shévet ha Dam* is a huge underground network—a society of bloodsuckers that help keep vamps anonymous, make it possible for them to continue moving, changing identities. That way, no one wonders why they never get any older. Jude's sort of the president, you know? He's been around a while. A long while. No one knows how long, but he's the oldest vampire anyone knows about. He's not the kind of guy you want to go against, so we stay away from them. They're bloodthirsty demons, and they treat human beings like cattle. We don't do that. We don't use the *Shévet ha Dam* to survive."

Vivian removed her hands from his and sat back on the couch with a deep breath. *If I'm dead, why am I breathing?* Her mind reeled.

"Who's 'we'?"

"There's a small group of us, getting larger all the time, who don't appreciate the way Jude and the *Shévet ha Dam* run things. We're kind of like the Rebel Alliance in *Star Wars*."

Vivian gave him a blank look. Lukas waved when he realized his mistake.

"Bad example. Anyway, to make this as brief as possible, we're with *you*. We'll hide you. We'll help you. We're the folks nobody talks about, but everyone knows we are there. Jude is for sure going to come looking for you, and if you don't want to go back, you don't have to."

Lukas sounded like he was trying to be brave. She looked at his bright, baby blue eyes and smiled.

"You know I'd rather die than go back," she murmured. Her voice, though soft, was as sure and steady as a tank.

Lukas nodded.

"We know. We'll keep you safe. Somehow."

Chapter 11

The door at the bottom of the staircase slammed. A booming voice sang in the style of a 1940's crooner over the stomping footsteps of people taking the stairs. Vivian's ears perked up, and she smiled despite herself.

Lukas raised his eyebrows at her and stood up.

"Dad's home," he said. He strode into the kitchen, ducking his head as he walked through the doorway, and opened the door at the head of the stairs. Two people trooped inside, their arms laden with cases of beer and plastic grocery bags.

The crooner continued his tune as he heaved a case of beer into the refrigerator. A young-looking woman trailed him. They both appeared in their early twenties, but Vivian knew not to assume anything by appearances. She knew the second she saw them and smelled them that they were like her. Vampires. The living had the trace odor of pumping blood under the surface of their skin. These two did not.

The crooner dug into one of the bags, his back turned to Vivian and Lukas.

"Dad, Vivian's here," Lukas said. Michael turned around. He was tall—not nearly as tall as his son, roughly five foot ten—with a pale complexion, brown eyes, and short hair so dark brown it neared black. He extended a strong-looking arm as Lukas and Gina raced downstairs as if they were in a competition. When Vivian extended hers to shake, Michael turned her hand gracefully and brought the back to his lips.

"Hello," he said, his eyes burrowing into hers. He turned away abruptly as Lukas and the woman thumped up the stairs again. They dumped the groceries they carried onto the kitchen counter.

"You got here just in time for your welcome home bash," Michael told her as the they bustled around putting their groceries away. "Let's see what we got here. Beer..."

"Check," said the woman. Gina, Vivian guessed, remembering the name Lukas had mentioned.

"Snack food..." Michael continued.

"Check," said Lukas, who'd dug bags of chips out of a shopping bag.

"Milk, orange juice..."

"Check, check," said Gina. Her large, sultry brown eyes, tiny waist, and long blond hair made Vivian think of a pinup model. She wore a blue shirt with a butterfly sandwiched between ample breasts.

"Trojans..."

"Trojans?" asked Lukas. Michael shot him a look of tried patience.

"We don't want our guests to get sick and die, do we?" he asked pointedly. "Ever heard of AIDS?"

"Good point," Lukas agreed.

"What are Trojans?" Vivian asked, regretting what she knew was a question that would make her appear foolish. The look Michael gave Lukas implied it should be understood.

Michael turned and smiled at her wryly.

"I *knew* I was going to like you," he quipped, which got a round of hearty laughter from the others. Vivian blushed. He tossed her a purple box with "Trojan" written across the top in bold letters. *Condoms*. Vivian read the box, smiling with amusement.

"You came from Lenny and Beth's, right?" Gina asked, breaking into her train of thought. "How long were you held there?"

"I-I don't know," Vivian stammered. "What year is it?"

"That long, huh?" the pretty blonde said, giving her a sweet, sympathetic smile as she busied herself with putting the groceries in various cupboards.

"Let me see... today is Thursday, October ninth...nineteen ninety-seven," Michael answered.

"Wow," Vivian breathed. "That would make it... fifty-four years."

They all stopped what they were doing and looked at her in shock.

"*Damn!*" said the blonde.

"Yeah," Michael added, "You look really fuckin' hot for a seventy-year-old." Once again, his humor was met with laughter, and Vivian appreciated his lighthearted remark. She knew then that if this clan had a leader, Michael was it.

They paused and looked at one another without commenting. Vivian felt defensive.

"Why? When were you changed?" She looked at Gina and Michael in turn.

"Well," Michael began, leaning across the island in the center of the kitchen and fixing his eyes on Vivian, "I was changed in 1984, when I was twenty-six, and Lukas there was about two years old. Gina..." Michael turned around and directed his question toward Gina's back. "Gina, how long have you been in?"

"Seven years," she answered. She had a beautiful voice. Vivian wondered if she could sing.

"Yeah, seven. That makes you by far the oldest one in our group. I think you might be the oldest in Savannah."

The oldest and least experienced, Vivian thought wryly.

"Who brought you in?" Gina asked. Finished putting away her share of the groceries, she sat down in a leatherette kitchen chair beside the glass-topped table.

"My..." She struggled to find the right word. Captor? Lover? She had only been on two dates with him before he imprisoned her—there wasn't a word for that. "Um, my boyfriend, Jude. Jude Shepherd."

Once again, she was met by a shocked look from Gina. Michael remained unaffected.

"Joseph Cartaphilus himself," Gina said. Vivian didn't follow, but Lukas spoke before she did.

"You must be strong," he surmised.

"I-I don't know."

"That's what we're going to find out," Michael said. "But not tonight. Tonight, we have a good time and introduce Vivian to the town."

"Yeah, like, *all* of Savannah," Lukas crowed. "The whole friggin' *town* is going to be here tonight." He broke off into a little dance to a tune only he heard.

On a Thursday? Vivian thought. Plainly, the day of the week had no bearing on their willingness to host a party.

"Tonight, you're our guest," Michael. He came around to the island, pulled out a chair, and motioned for Vivian to take a seat. She accepted. He walked around the front, sat, and took her hands in his. He focused on her with a mixture of admiration and authority that would have looked ridiculous on anyone less handsome.

"Tonight, you stay with me. I'll introduce you around, show you the ropes, give you an idea of what's going on. I understand you're probably nervous. That's okay. We'll take care of you. But promise me one thing, and this is critical. If you start to feel scared for any reason, if you get a bad feeling that something is about to happen, even if you don't know what, *tell me.* You probably have a lot more power than you realize, and you need to learn to trust your instincts. Your life may literally depend on it." With his brief sermon delivered, he stood.

"Do you want to freshen up before our guests arrive?"

The next thing Vivian knew, Gina handed her a change of clothing and herded her into the tiny bathroom.

"Don't worry, the water's not blessed," Michael joked

After a gloriously long, hot shower, Vivian emerged feeling like a new woman. She dried herself on the scratchy towel Gina had given her and put on her borrowed clothes.

After she brushed her hair, which had grown beyond the center of her back, she considered herself in the mirror. Her eyes were still wide, the color the same blue-green they'd been in life. A light smattering of freckles still covered her nose, and her skin was smooth and soft, thanks to Gina's lotion. *Not bad for a dead woman, I guess,* she decided.

Twilight was falling as Vivian stepped out of the steamy bathroom. The only lights were from the handful of overhead bulbs, and candles lit the shadowy corners all over the house. Someone had also made a feeble attempt at picking up a little of the mess.

"Oh, yeah, the mirror thing's a lie," Lukas said, reclining on the corner of one of the couches with his legs stretched out across all three cushions. He had changed into a sports shirt and wide-legged jeans and topped it off with a visor.

"Mirror thing?"

"Yeah. I didn't know if you caught that. Y'all can see yourselves fine unless you don't want to be seen. There's a lot of myths about vampires. Some of them are truer than others, or partly based in fact, but the facts got mixed up over the years."

Vivian took a seat on the couch opposite him.

"Such as?"

"Well, the garlic thing. I've heard it makes your eyes kinda water, but it sure as hell won't kill you or drive you away. Michael loves the taste. He says it's one of the few foods that almost taste like he remembers. Like horseradish. Umm... stakes through the heart, well, yeah. That'd kill anyone, though, wouldn't you think? I don't think vampires explode or anything, though. Not like in the movies. I've heard they turn to ash, but I've never seen one die. There's more to it, but Michael explains it better than I do. The whole good/evil shit is more his specialty."

"What about sunlight? Does it kill us?"

"That's avoidable," Michael said. He gently pushed his gigantic son's feet off the couch and took a seat next to him and across from Vivian.

"We become photosensitive because of a lack of live blood in the body. If you remain in the sun too long and haven't been eating well, you'll get sick, burned, or both, and possibly die. Vampires need to stay well-fed and build a tolerance to it. Young and weakened vampires can die of malnutrition and exposure to sunlight. They may die ugly deaths, but as Lukas so eloquently put it, we don't explode like in the movies. Sunblock helps to an extent, but it's easier to make sure you stay fed. The *Shévet ha Dam* has its own little invention—photoprotection—that works wonders for young and undernourished vampires. And the stake through the heart thing only works on young vampires like us. I'm not sure if it'd kill you."

"What about regular food?" Vivian asked.

"What about it?"

"Do we eat? Regular food?"

"You can," Michael shrugged, "but it doesn't taste the same. Sometimes we eat to blend in. Smoking, drinking, and drugs... we're still physical beings, and we suffer minor effects from them. Our bodies are still carbon-based. We still breathe—the myth that we can go without oxygen is exaggerated. We can go much longer, but we can't live without it. We're potentially immortal beings with great healing powers. We also get stronger as we get older."

"In other words, you can put an eight-ball up your nose, and you *might* stay up all day," Lukas said. Vivian had no clue what an eight-ball was, but she did realize hearing the phrase "stay up all day" was going to take getting used to.

A thunderous knock at the door turned everyone's head.

"Gina, get the door, please," Michael asked. Gina did.

"S'probably Josh," Lukas said.

Michael nodded. "It is. Can you take Vivian here downstairs and get her ID'd?"

"Sure." He motioned a frisbee-sized hand in her direction. "Come on, Viv."

Vivian followed Lukas down the stairs, crossing paths with Josh and Gina as they carried unfamiliar electronic equipment in the opposite direction. Vivian heard Michael tell them to set up in the corner by the windows.

Lukas led her to a door next to the one that led to the upstairs apartment. He let himself in with a key.

"We don't live here," he told her as they walked across the threshold, "'Course, we don't live upstairs, either, really. The people who live here are squatters too, only for different reasons. We told them as long as they leave us alone to party, we wouldn't bust them out to the cops."

As soon as the door was open, Vivian smelled a nauseating chemical vapor in the air. A handful of people sat on the dirty floor, passing around a glass pipe. Unlike the mismatched family upstairs, these inhabitants looked the part of homeless scum: dirty and unkempt. Filthy clothes hung from their thin frames, and their eyes showed a disturbing vacancy.

"Goddamn crackheads," Lukas mumbled in disgust. None of them looked up. He took her through the apartment to a room in the back.

"We have to keep this locked up," Lukas informed her quietly. "We can't let the crackheads know what's in here. They'll steal the shit and try to sell it for drugs. We don't keep it upstairs, 'cause... well, we need the space to party."

He took her to the door and started to work on the locks. There were two doors, one inside the other—four locks on the first door, four on the second.

"We don't keep this stuff here often, but we need to keep it safe when we do," Lukas said as he finished with the final lock. He stepped inside and flipped a light switch. When Vivian entered, he shut the door, locked it behind her, and then walked around switching on numerous pieces of equipment.

"What is all this stuff?" she asked.

"Computers, monitors, scanners, modems, printers... ID stuff. You're going to be a new person, as far as the city of Savannah and the US Government are concerned. Sit over here." Lukas patted the top of a stool with a brilliant green backdrop behind it. A tripod-mounted camera pointed at the backdrop.

Vivian sat, and Lukas turned on a bright light. He lit a cigarette and adjusted the shot. He tapped keys in quick succession and clicked a couple of icons with the mouse. Vivian watched in amazement. Computers were only a commercial concept when Jude had taken her. To see someone adept at using one, especially in a raggedy, ill-kempt home, was an idea from a futuristic story.

"Whaddya think?" he asked. He turned the monitor so she could see the picture.

"I think I look dead," Vivian said with a weak laugh. "I mean, pale. I mean..."

"You don't like the picture. Got it. Let me try again. And whatever you do, don't smile."

This time the picture was flattering, and Vivian nodded.

"Good," Lukas said. "I hate that part. Now I gotta think up a name..."

"I can't choose my own?" Vivian asked. Lukas shook his head as he sat down in a shabby, orange office chair and took a deep drag on his cigarette. His fingers flew around the keyboard. The screen reflected all kinds of digital information foreign to Vivian's eyes. She took a seat on the stool next to him to watch.

"Not a good idea." Another deep drag on the cigarette.

"Why not?"

"You and Jude ever talk about getting married? Having kids? Relatives? Maybe names you liked? He's gonna remember that shit, and when the time comes, those are the first names he'll look for. You might not remember them right now. Trust me: Jude Shepherd won't forget. Besides, we need a modern name. You don't look like a Daisy or a Betty." He pulled up a screen and fixed the cursor on the line marked "Name." He paused, took a long, appraising look at Vivian, and crushed his cigarette out in an overflowing ashtray.

"Hmm... Kelly? Nah. Rebecca? No, you don't look like a Rebecca or a Becky. Melissa? No, I've known one too many Melissas." Lukas sighed in exasperation. All at once, his eyes lit up with an epiphany.

"I've got it! Melody! That's *perfect*."

"Why Melody?" Vivian asked. She mouthed the foreign name with a wrinkled nose.

"Haven't you heard that song... it's an oldie; you might know it. *A Pretty Girl is Like a Melody?*" Lukas said with a smile. Suddenly the name wasn't so bad.

"Let's see... driver's license... passport..." he clicked various boxes on the screen.

"Did you want a job?" he asked.

"I don't know. I hadn't thought about it."

"Ah, hell. We'll give you a Social today as well, just in case." He continued tapping various buttons for what felt like a long time, then pointed the arrow to a button that said *print*. Vivian jumped as multiple mechanisms around the room came alive.

"You like that? I've got them all set up to print at once," Lukas smiled smugly.

He removed the first identification card—a driver's license—and handed it to Vivian for her approval. She was, according to the card, from Naples, Florida. Name, Melody Burgett. Birth date, August tenth, 1976. She had just turned twenty-one. The card appeared impossible to forge but was nothing compared to her passport, which confirmed that she was born in Florida.

"How did you do this?" she asked.

"Stolen government equipment. How else?" Lukas snorted. He walked around to a third printer and removed a social security card. Vivian added it to her other identification items gratefully, and placed them in her pocket as they headed from the room.

"Now remember to get someone to change those for you every five to ten years or so. Preferably more often, and at least every time you relocate. Don't worry. As far as we're concerned, you're still Vivian. To everyone you meet tonight, though, you're Melody."

He bolted the last lock, put his hand in the small of her back, and guided her through the reeking smoke.

"What's your real last name, anyway?" he inquired.

"Black. What's yours?"

Lukas smiled as though she had told a joke. "Graves."

Vivian got the joke. They headed up the stairs to the growing din that was Vivian's welcome party.

Chapter 12

When Vivian and Lukas reached the top of the stairs, nearly twenty people were milling around the apartment. She found Michael hunkered under a makeshift table—two crates with a wide piece of plywood on top—helping Josh get some equipment in working order. There were two turntables and a plethora of records in milk crates behind two huge speakers.

They still use records, Vivian thought, delighted.

"I need music to work to," Michael said, his head poking up from behind the table. "Lukas?"

"Yeah, Mike," Lukas replied.

Michael gave him a fatherly reproving look. "Put on some damn music, would ya? Something lively," he requested.

"Sure thing," Lukas agreed, and he dug through a small stack of what Vivian assumed to be music. They looked like tiny silver records in plastic covers. He selected one, turned on the tattered stereo, and inserted the disc. What she heard was nothing like what was playing on the radios back in the forties. She found herself liking it, at least a little.

"Drum and bass," Lukas told her.

She noticed a short, blond male vampire beckoning her from the tiny niche between the bathroom and one of the bedrooms, and she wound a path through the crowded living room. When she reached him, he startled her by grabbing her elbow and steering her hastily into the unoccupied bedroom. Her first instinct was to punch him and let out an earsplitting scream, but once she saw the innocuous look on his face, her fears died down.

"Don't scare her, Josh!" Gina ordered her friend from the other room with a grin.

"I won't," Josh replied, his eyes hidden from behind a visor and long, shaggy bangs. "But Michael said she needs some schooling, and I have a minute." He closed the door behind them and faced Vivian.

"Michael asked me if I'd have a little heart-to-heart with you before the party gets rolling tonight," Josh said. "He thought he might get a little caught up at first, and we can't have you feeling lost."

"OK," Vivian agreed. That sounded acceptable.

"First off, you *have* to feed tonight. Soon. No ifs, ands, or buts. You need your strength back quick, fast, and in a hurry, and there's no two ways about it."

Vivian wondered if it was possible to put more clichés one after another, but she didn't interrupt. Josh motioned her to join him on a mattress and box springs resting directly on the floor. She did, gingerly taking a spot on the dirty cushion and feeling more than a little uneasy about losing track of Michael in the growing party.

"Michael said you've got to follow him around tonight, once everything gets going. Just do what he does, and you'll be fine."

"How? I mean, won't they notice? I don't think I've ever done this with an unwilling person."

Josh shook his head, amused. He leaned in uncomfortably close and asked her, "Are you familiar with snake charming?"

"What do you mean?"

"It's an example Michael uses, so sorry if I jumble it up. Snakes supposedly hypnotize their victims before they strike. Vampires are like that. We can make people not know they've been struck. On top of that, if you drink from someone who's *already* fucked up, they won't know what hit'em. I like those best, 'cause then the next day, they blame the drinking or drugs for feeling shitty. Just don't fucking drink from another vampire. There's nothing grosser than drinking a suckhead."

"What's it like? Feeding off a human?" she asked. The idea intrigued and repulsed her at the same time. She supposed the best way to get over her apprehension was to ask. Josh was right about needing to feed that night. Her alertness was already starting to fade. *The chicken blood must be wearing off.*

Josh looked at her quizzically, and Vivian suspected it was due to her ignorance. His reply caught her off guard.

"Ever had sex?"

She almost retorted that it was none of his business but decided against it. She had a feeling he was a man of few profound thoughts, and if this was his best analogy, it would have to suffice.

"Yes. With Jude."

"Hmm. That's it? Oh, sorry. No offense."

Her eyes narrowed, but she said, "None taken."

"Well, you know how you feel when you're making out, and you've gotten so hot, so into it, any doubts or any fears are gone, and instinct takes over? You just gotta have it? That's the best way to describe it. And by the way, if you haven't figured it out, Lukas is off-limits."

Vivian gave him a No Shit look.

"I want to make sure I get all the details out," Josh said defensively. "Lots of women have tried and learned to regret it. I don't know that Lukas would mind much, but Michael is protective and especially strong for his age, too. Trust me on this one. Oh, and one more thing."

"Yes?" Vivian said, growing impatient. Josh was far too full of himself, and it was getting annoying.

"Scratch that. Two things. Be careful what you think. A few of these fuckers can read your mind, or at least your intentions. If you're not careful, you'll piss someone off. If you can, hide your thoughts or distract yourself. Don't worry. I'll cut this off soon."

Oops, Vivian thought.

"Yeah. Oops," he said. Vivian wasn't sure if he was irritated or hurt. Maybe both.

"Last thing: try not to look so damn surprised. That one's on me, not Michael. I mean, I know he thinks it's adorable that everything is new and exciting to you, but you don't want everyone to wonder where in the hell you've been for the last half a century. *Capice?*"

The expression in Josh's eyes had turned from warm and friendly to cold and steely. Vivian felt a little repentant for her thoughts.

Damn. I didn't mean to hurt his feelings, but it isn't like I can stop thinking. I can't change that I've been enslaved for the last fifty years while the world evolved around me.

She hated that she was ignorant of so much. Nothing was the same— not the cars, technology, clothing, and not the people. And what of the vampires? They weren't human; they might not even have souls for all she knew! And they were just like her.

Dear God, what's happened to me? Am I dead, or am I alive? Maybe I've already been condemned to hell, and I'm living it.

Josh's eyes softened. He rested a supportive hand on her shoulder. "Hey, don't worry. It'll be OK. You'll feel a lot better once you've had something to drink."

Music as loud as an onrushing train suddenly burst through the doorway. To Vivian, it sounded like someone had wound a clock too tight and found a way for it to play a drum. Vivian tensed at the thought of rubbing elbows with so many bloodthirsty strangers. Gina waited outside the door with her arms crossed. When she saw that Vivian was OK, she graced her friend with a forgiving look and laced her arm through Vivian's.

"Go have some fun," he said. "Just remember what I told you."

Sure, no problem. Either I find some sap that lets me bite his neck, or I wither away and die.

She looked around the room anxiously. *Where's Michael?*

Chapter 13

Jude stirred as dusk settled over the plantation, incensed and ready for blood. His dreams had been of Vivian, and they seemed more like nightmares than dreams. In them, he faced the wrath of the Tribe for her escape, and this time, they were able to overpower him. At the end of the dream, he surveyed an angry crowd from his position on a cross. The feel of nails in his wrists and feet was far too vivid. So was his fury at his impending death, a mimicry of the one who'd cursed him.

Ungrateful bitch. Whatever made her think she was woman enough to leave me? Has she no sense?

He took his time rising from the coffin, shook the grave dust off with a clawed hand. His current lady had already risen to feed. He sought her thoughts in his mind, felt her hunting in the nearby village. He was eager to hunt and would join her soon. Now there were more pressing matters.

He had to try again to find Vivian.

He rested on one of the cold stone steps and cleared his mind. *Vivian... Vivian... where are you?* He closed his eyes and concentrated. *Focus. Ah, yes. There you are.*

❧ ❧

Vivian felt a prick in the back of her head. She was so sure something was there that she reached around with her hand to feel what it was. She kneaded her fingers in her hair but didn't find anything. She nearly dismissed it when it happened again, this time with a feeling of unease, like a snake uncoiling in her stomach.

Jude.

It was Jude. Nothing else could make her feel simultaneously bewildered, disgusted, and frightened. His grip on her was like fingers caressing her brain. Her thoughts grew muddled, and she felt nauseated.

Michael! Where's Michael?

The room was loud, dark, and full of cigarette smoke and strangers.

Where in the hell is—? Then she remembered what Josh had told her: Be careful what you think. *What if Jude is trying to find me? What if he can read my thoughts?*

At that second, she knew he could. He was trying to find out where she was, prodding her thoughts as cautiously as a thief in an unfamiliar house. She knew, and, just as certainly, she knew she was reading them right back.

❧ ☙

Jude saw the room, not clearly, but well enough to know it was crowded, hazy with smoke, and loud. Perhaps a club. *Why would she go to a club? She's always hated crowds.*

He shook his head in irritation. If she was adapting to her environment so soon, things were not going well. Ever since taking her captive, he had ensured that she drank enough to stay alive but remained pliable, her thoughts his to contort and control. Her prior escape attempts hadn't succeeded because her lack of blood ensured she remained meek and immobile. This time she hadn't only walked away, but she was adapting, her thoughts growing independent of his. He felt it, sensed it in her mind.

This is not good.

She did not feel far away. Her heart raced, and he felt her frantic search for... whom? There was someone there she was counting on, someone who was important to her. A man. If he found the man, it would be all too easy to find her. The *Shévet ha Dam* had many means of tracking at its disposal.

Give me a name, Vivian. Just give me a fucking name.

❧ ☙

Don't think. Don't look. Don't make it easy on that bastard. She buried her face in her hands and sat down on an arm of a couch. People were looking at her curiously. She closed them out, too. *Blackness. Clear your mind of anything he can use. Think of home. Michigan. Anything other than here.*

She felt a hand on her shoulder and heard an unfamiliar voice ask her if she was alright. She nodded, not trusting herself to talk, not wanting to walk, only wanting that cursed feeling that Jude was inside her head to go away. God, he was *strong!* Her legs shook down to her ankles, her hands trembled. She felt desecrated, knowing he had entered her with such ease. She flashed back to their night on the lake, how she had wanted him—*wanted him*—to enter her. After that night, he had taken her whenever he wanted.

Will he ever stop violating me?

She felt as though he was pushing her out of her body and mind. His psyche was searching, sending feelers through her recent memories. She struggled to halt his advance, and it worked at first. Then he pressed forward slower, but with more strength. She bit her lip; the taste of blood as it flowed back into her mouth almost sent her over the edge. She was hungry, weak, and had to take action soon, or she would lose her mind.

In desperation, Vivian tried a course of action she wasn't sure would work: she pushed back. She didn't think she knew how by God, but she did. Vivian pushed back. *Hard.*

Cₛ ₛᴐ

Jude smiled. *So, she wants a fight, does she? Not a problem.* He locked his mind on hers and prepared to settle in.

Cₛ ₛᴐ

"Melody? *Melody!*"

She heard a familiar voice but avoided focusing on it. She refused to let Jude see what she was thinking. Her eyes stayed clamped shut, and she tried to focus on the music. *That awful, pounding music, that's all. Concentrate.*

"Where's my lighter? Somebody give me a lighter, quick. *Who's got a goddamn lighter?"*

She heard people shuffling around her, heard the music drumming in her head. Someone grabbed her hand from in front of her face and then...

A white-hot pain shot through her palm, and Jude vanished.

Cₛ ₛᴐ

Jude sat up. The link was broken. Incredible as it was, she had managed to slip away. But how? Traces of the connection still lingered, buzzing around his head like flies. It wasn't enough. All he had was the knowledge that she was with a large group of people in a loud place, which could be anywhere. He deduced that it wasn't far, maybe as close as Savannah. Wasn't there a little band of renegades down there?

He shook his head, incredulous. *She was a moving corpse, for Christ's sake! I saw to that. Right now, she shouldn't even be able to handle abstract thought!*

He had kept her drained to the point of death for half a century. That she had walked away was unfathomable.

I must have been too generous when she fed from me the last time. And then, with a bit of help from the witch woman... He had unwittingly provided her with the means to walk away and the strength to focus enough to evict him from her thoughts.

Who knows what else she might discover she can do? If she feeds tonight, it will only increase her resistance, strengthen her resolve.

His mouth twisted into a malicious grin. *Vivian, my dear, you have no idea what you're up against.* This would be a most entertaining, albeit brief, hunt. Naturally, she would lose. He calculated that she had two days at the most once he recruited the help of the *Shévet ha Dam*. He wasn't looking forward to the confrontation, but their support was necessary. Besides, why should he tire himself?

He sighed in frustration. *You're going to make this difficult on yourself, aren't you?*

ଔ   ଓ

Vivian slowly opened her eyes, not trusting that it was over, not believing that Jude had given up. Michael watched her with concern reflected his brown eyes. He swept her hair away from where it curtained over her forehead and brushed away a tear with his thumb. She hadn't been aware she was crying. She didn't know vampires could cry.

"Don't talk," he whispered. "Don't think. If he's going to try to reestablish a link, it will only make it easier. Come with me." He offered her a hand up. Her legs still shook violently. Feeling as though she was walking on rubber bands, she followed him down the steps and outside.

They took a seat on the edge of the rickety porch. Michael produced a pack of Marlboro Lights and a lighter from his front jeans pocket and lit one expertly.

"Wanna cigarette?" he offered. Vivian shook her head.

"Don't smoke?"

"No. I've always hated the way it smells. I was never one of those people who bought into that 'smoking is cool' attitude."

"Me neither," he said with a grin as he took a long drag. He flicked the ashes from his cigarette, took out a second cigarette, and lit it with the first. He dangled the second in front of her face.

"Take a drag," he directed her. The corners of his eyes crinkled up in handsome crow's feet as he pointed the butt of the second cigarette in her direction.

"What are you, crazy?" she laughed. Nevertheless, she found herself accepting the cigarette.

"One puff. For me," he said without taking his deep brown eyes from hers. She put the cigarette to her lips and pulled in a lungful of smoke. She coughed on the horrible taste, but it wasn't as disgusting as she had expected. Her undead lungs shook off the smoke with ease.

"Feel better?" he asked. She shook her head.

"I feel like I have bad breath," she laughed. "That's... nasty." She prided herself on using some of the slang she'd picked up.

"Do it again." His eyes never stopped staring into hers. She had the crazy notion that he wanted to kiss her, and the thought kept her smiling. She did as he asked, trying not to giggle as she inhaled.

"Feel better?" he asked. She shook her head again.

"Now I have *really* bad breath."

"Yes, but are you distracted?"

She understood, now, that he had been trying to get her to think about something other than Jude. And he was right. It worked.

"I have no idea what I was trying to forget," she said with a teasing grin, and took another drag.

೮೩ ೮೦

The apartment was teeming when they reentered. Michael led her around and introduced her to an assortment of vampire and human guests. Randi, a vampire whose scantily clad body was much perkier than her disposition. As it turns out, Randi's boyfriend was Josh, whose boyish face peeked out from under a towheaded shock of hair. His baggy clothes hung from his skeletal frame, seemingly by will alone. In the living room, she met Avery, a tall, dark, lithe vampire blessed with good looks, but who hadn't been gifted with brains. Every time she spoke to him, he responded with an unfortunate laugh that conjured up images of cartoonish feeble-mindedness. His body, however, was flawless and so graceful he looked boneless as he arched his arms from side to side. Gina joined him for a few moments before luring a human from the couches to dance with her.

Michael flitted around as swiftly as the white rabbit from Alice in Wonderland, first talking to one person, then another, towing Vivian with every step. She soon lost track of names in the flood of conversations. Michael and his crew reminisced of parties past. People came and went, their conversations competing with the music volume. Someone on a phone dodged outside with a hand pressed to one ear. At one point, Vivian took a seat on the couch and smoked a cigarette to stop fidgeting. Josh had reclined, ostensibly comatose, on the other couch. An hour and a half had passed, and Vivian was beginning to wonder when she would learn the lesson Michael wanted to teach her.

Randi sauntered into the living room from the kitchen.

"Josh, we need some acid in here," she barked. Skeletal Josh rose, blew his bangs from his eyes, and shuffled into the kitchen.

"I like how he listens to me," Randi laughed. "Josh. Acid. And he goes." Randi curled up onto the emptied couch and grasped her feet. She looked tired. Vivian had never seen anyone take drugs before, so she got up to watch.

At the kitchen counter, Josh unwrapped a small piece of paper with tiny grid-like lines on it from a flat square of tinfoil. He cut two tiny flecks off and set them on the countertop. The pieces were hard to distinguish from the flecked pattern on the counter. Gina and a nervous, homely-looking female tapped the flakes of paper and set them on their tongues.

"Don't swallow. Just let it sit there," Gina instructed her friend. "It takes about fifteen minutes to kick in."

And you won't feel a thing, will you, Gina? Vivian thought.

Josh began selling more acid. Most of those buying were human, but a few vampires joined the throng. Vivian remembered Josh's words. *If you get someone who's already fucked up, they won't know what hit 'em.* Evidently, "fucking them up" was the preferred method here.

"It's less painful for them that way," Michael said, interrupting her reverie. Vivian jumped and turned around to find Michael at her elbow. So he could read minds as well.

"You left me," he scolded. "You weren't supposed to do that."

"I was curious," she said defensively. "And you were busy."

"You know what curiosity did for the cat."

Vivian's brow furrowed. She shook her head subtly as she looked on at the spectacle. Josh's customers had all the charm and grace of sharks in a feeding frenzy. She didn't see the appeal. Why would someone take anything that would make them act like anything other than themselves? It was one reason she hated Jude so much for what he had done. She could not understand what motivated people to feel out of control and self-destructive, much less why Michael and his cohorts encouraged those they claimed to value, for food if nothing else, to engage in such degenerate behavior.

"Do you *all* encourage your 'friends' to do this? To take drugs so flagrantly?"

"Flagrantly. Good word," he said. "But in answer to your question, no. Most of them drink, not dose up. Those who use drugs were abusing themselves long before we came along, and we don't bring any new people to the scene. They come on their own. It's one of our unwritten rules. Besides, we look over them better than they do one another. None of these drugs cause significant long-term damage if done in small doses, and if we feel that anyone is starting to get too fixated, we try to cut them off. Failing that, we exclude them from the group."

"It's an awfully big group," Vivian observed.

Michael smiled. "So are we."

Chapter 14

The party raged on, a spectacle of debauchery that left Vivian speechless. People bought and consumed drugs so unashamedly she almost believed they were legal. Women removed their tops to entice the men and danced over their laps provocatively. Two men walked around with nothing on except a sock covering their genitals and their shoes on their feet—sans socks. At one point, a couple decided they wanted to take a bath in the apartment's only bathroom, and they didn't care who had to use the toilet in the meantime. Anyone was welcome to use the toilet if they didn't mind being watched. Josh wrote "fuck" on the wall in lighter fluid and set it on fire. The most unsettling part to Vivian was that no one felt unsettled in the slightest. She didn't know whether to be amazed or appalled.

Now she understood why they partied where they did.

Michael continued to lead Vivian around, looking for humans to introduce themselves to so they could pursue what Michael called "sustenance." He gave her the "lowdown"; the five steps he used to acquire a victim: "Introduce, identify, impress, ignite, imbibe." Details were to follow.

After nearly two and a half hours of fruitless wandering, he became frustrated with the mass of humans stumbling through the apartment in various states of mind. He handed Vivian a jacket, put on a long, black trench coat, and led her outside by the hand.

They walked into a brisk, moonless, starless night. Vivian was awed at how swiftly her vision adapted to the darkness. As they descended the porch steps, Josh silently joined them from around the corner of the house and smiled. Vivian shivered. His teeth were dark with blood, and she could smell it. Her hungry stomach clawed at her.

Cars and partiers filled the tiny lot and adjoining alley. Even the neighboring streets were packed. The three of them took a left and headed down the alley. Vivian heard loud, slurred voices rising from a group gathered around the lowered tailgate of a pickup. Michael smiled and motioned his head toward the truck. He had found their prey. The three of them crept up as silent as cats.

"There's no *way* Led Zeppelin is as good a band as Pink Floyd," she heard a stunning blonde with spiral curls argue. "The best band *ever* is Pink Floyd, and the best album is *The Wall*."

"*The Wall* is overplayed," a young man argued.

"And why do you think that is?" the blonde asked, as if the man had proven her point.

The back of what was an otherwise beautiful truck was littered with beer bottles and an empty fifth of Jack Daniels.

"Nice truck," Michael interrupted. "Whose is it?"

"Mine," the young man said proudly. "Only paid thirteen thou for it. Got a brother-in-law at the dealership. Got me a deal."

Michael extended his hand.

"Dillon Moriarty. These are my friends Melody and Josh."

"Moriarty, huh?" the man said, impressed. He took Michael's hand firmly and pumped it a couple of times. "Well, I finally meet the man behind the myth. I'm Mark, and these are my new friends Jenny and Katie." Jenny was the blonde he had been debating. Katie was a frumpy-looking brunette with round glasses and a body to match. She reminded Vivian of an adorable owl. Vivian recognized her as the female who'd taken acid in the kitchen with Gina.

Well, he's got introduce, identify, and impress down in one step. I'd better catch up.

"What kind of truck is this?" she inquired. "It's gorgeous."

"Dodge Ram Two-fifty," he said. His chest swelled slightly, delighted at her interest. "I rebuilt the engine. Four-barrel carb, dual overhead cam—"

"Nice," Michael interjected diplomatically, subtly covering up Vivian's lack of response. She nodded, pretending to be duly impressed. Out of the corner of her eye, she caught sight of Josh talking animatedly with Katie, or rather *at* Katie, who clearly didn't mind. Her eyes sparkled at his interest. Vivian wondered if Randi was off somewhere engaging a male human.

The conversation progressed. Where are you from? Where do you work? Nice party, How'd you find this place? During the exchange, Michael repeatedly reached into his jacket pocket for an ornate silver flask, taking quick slugs only to replace the cap and stash it back into his garment. Vivian noticed Mark shooting longing glances at the flask when removed from its hiding spot. Michael shot Vivian a pointed glance. She understood.

"What're you drinking?" she asked him, motioning to his pocket.

"Johnny Walker Blue Label. Want some?"

She nodded vigorously, ravenous and eager to get the learning underway. Michael handed her the flask, and she took a draft. The scotch tasted plain to her, like a swig of water.

"*Blue* Label? No way. Isn't that, like, super expensive?" Mark was noticeably impressed.

Michael shrugged.

"Well, if you're going to buy liquor, you might as well buy the quality stuff. Would you like a nip?"

Mark nodded, and Vivian handed him the flask. Mark took a swallow of the scotch and indicated to Michael that he wanted to share it with the girls. Michael waved his hand to indicate his consent. The flask passed to Jenny, who helped herself to a generous slug without wincing. She then passed it to Katie, who regarded the flask with a reluctant expression.

"Go on, Katie. It's only whiskey," Mark cajoled her. Katie looked terrified.

"No, it's *scotch*, and a damn good one," Michael admonished him. He then gave Katie a warm look. "You don't have to, but how often do you get to drink liquor that costs a couple of hundred a bottle?"

"It's OK," Josh comforted her, placing a hand on her arm. "You don't have to if you don't want to."

The men's shallow reasoning somehow reassured Katie. She accepted the flask from Jenny and had a small sip. The full-bodied liquor caused her face to screw up in distaste, and she handed the flask back to Michael blindly.

"Yeah, that'll put hair on your chest," Mark laughed. Katie coughed a couple of times, managing a weak smile.

"Katie reads poetry," Josh announced, trying unabashedly to make Katie feel special. The adoring expression on Katie's face was pitiable. *He is kind of cute, in a short, goofy way,* Vivian admitted, then stifled a flinch, wondering if he had caught her evaluation of him.

"Really? Who are your favorites?" Vivian asked. She loved reading anything, mostly the classics—anything from Shakespeare to Thoreau. She found herself smiling at the shy girl and felt an unspoken kinship.

"Oh, I like all kinds," Katie gushed, forgetting her modesty as she discussed a topic she enjoyed. "I like Maya Angelou, Sylvia Plath,

Elizabeth Barrett Browning, John Donne, all kinds." Vivian didn't know who Maya Angelou or Sylvia Plath was, but she knew and liked the others.

"I told her you and I were poets, and she looked at me funny," Josh said to Michael in mock offense. Katie shot him a 'How could you?' look, but the smile never left her curved cheeks. She gave him a playful slug in the arm that turned into an affectionate squeeze.

"I thought we'd have a quote-off. You quote from yours, and I quote from mine." Josh took Katie's hand in his, wound their fingers together. He might be an odd, skinny, young man, but he worked fast.

"I don't see why not," Michael conceded. "You go first."

Vivian glanced to Michael, who had managed to wrangle his way onto the tailgate. Jenny tottered slightly in front of him, flanked by his legs. She leaned heavily on the tailgate as he rubbed her shoulders. A drunken smirk rested under her nose, and she appeared to be on the verge of passing out. Vivian shot a furtive glance in Mark's direction. He was looking forlornly at his lost conquests, eyes glazed and half-shut with liquor. Vivian nudged Michael over to one side of the tailgate, and waved to Mark to come over. He assumed a similar posture as Jenny, and she massaged his back.

She was sensuously aware of every fiber of muscle. He was so warm, so... human. Beautiful. She saw his breath as he exhaled into the cool night air. He relaxed against her hands as she kneaded. *Yes, that's it.* She manipulated her fingers up to his neck, felt his pulse against her fingertips. It was almost erotic, the way her body responded. This wasn't lust; it was instinct, involuntary. Survival. Her tongue ran over the points on her canines. She was ready to use them. She wanted him, wanted to drink from him.

Josh let go of Katie's hand and assumed a dramatic stance worthy of an old English bard. With a swoop of his long arm, he began:

> "Give me the drug
> Give me the warmth.
> Show me the way.
> Draw me the blood.
> Kindle my soul.
> Forgive my sins.
> Give me the faith.
> Exhume my soul.

Give me the stars.
Inject my vein.
Revive my eyes.
Give me the drug.
Give me the love.
Give me the drug.
Give me the drug."

Mark sank heavily into Vivian's lap as Josh delivered his poem, and she slowly, deliberately worked on the buttons fastening the top of his shirt. He didn't shiver as the cold air hit his skin. Katie appeared dreamy as she made an effort to applaud as much as her foggy mind would allow.

There was something in that drink, Vivian thought. *Or is it that his words can hypnotize them? Yes, that must be it. He put them in a trance, like the snake story.* Josh caught her eye as she reached this conclusion and gave her a wink that confirmed her suspicions. She wondered about the ease with which Josh read her mind. *Is it because he's so near? If Jude was a few feet away, could he read me that easily?*

Michael glided deftly from his seat behind Jenny, who'd fainted in his arms. He rested her upper body carefully in the truck bed and took his position on the outskirts of the conversational circle. In his black trench coat and boots, he cut an intimidating figure. He strolled around the group, one foot taking its time after the other. As he did, he vanished into and materialized out of the shadows like a ghost.

He spoke, his voice barely more substantial than a whisper:

Ignite me. My memory has grown cold.
I want your hands to burn every inch of me,
to cauterize the pain I feel.
Bleed for me once.
Cut open your façade, and bleed.
Pour your life force on my dying soul.
Heal me. Touch me with your hands.
Caress me like a lover.
Revive a flickering ember.
Make me whole again."

It might not have been her preferred style, but a thespian dedicated to Shakespearean theater could not have delivered the prose better.

Vivian found herself shivering, and it wasn't the night chill. During Michael's delivery, Josh had positioned himself behind Katie. Her knees buckled, and she collapsed into his arms as the poem ended. Petite Josh handled her as easily as if she was a doll. Vivian grew impatient as she stared at Mark's closed eyes, his flushed cheeks, and his exposed neck.

They'd succeeded in the hunt, and their game lay before them. Her coconspirators regarded her with confident ease. She found herself stroking the skin of Mark's upper chest. She detected the warm, musky smell of him, so thick it was palpable. No one had to show her now. She remembered.

Josh was right. Any qualms she once had were gone. Instinct took over. Hungrily she leaned forward, sinking her teeth into Mark's soft neck. Her eyes closed in exhilaration as she drank with fervor. *So delicious... so warm.* The coppery flavor rolled over her tongue like a favorite delicacy. She felt divided, as though her spirit floated above her body, and yet she was aware of the tailgate under her, and of Mark's upper body encircled in her arms, his hips between her knees. She was invincible, perfect. Jude's servings of secondhand blood were nothing compared to Mark's unfaded, unspoiled fluid.

"Melody, you need to let him go. We'll find you another. Melody, *don't kill him,*" Michael's calm voice broke into her contemplation. She knew he was right, but the hungry part of her didn't care. Her fingers dug into Mark's chest in an almost protective act, but her desires were far from protective.

"*Now*, Melody," Michael ordered. She stopped, glaring fiercely. She wasn't afraid. Michael did not scare her. She understood what she had become and knew she was fiercely powerful. She could kill Mark, drain his body in seconds. For that matter, she could have killed Michael. She didn't. That last, lingering bit of consciousness, which wanted so badly to be human, did not want Mark to die. She looked down at the limp body in her arms. She still wanted him.

Michael tenderly removed Mark from her arms, his brow furrowed and his movements slow. He laid Mark on the tailgate next to Jenny.

"How do you feel?" he asked.

She licked the last of the blood from her lips, mindful of her sharp teeth. "Hungry."

◌ ◌

Vivian fed three more times that night, and with each time, she discovered a little more about her skill at influencing human minds. Her aptitude impressed Michael. Her victims fell under her spell in rapid succession, and none suspected her motives. In the end, Michael found himself stepping back to let Vivian lead in their game of cat and mouse.

She cut a beautiful figure under the harsh glow of the streetlights. For the first time since her arrival in Savannah, Vivian looked and felt alive as she and Michael prowled through the party in the alley and the streets. She was so titillated, her senses so acute, she wanted to run, dance, fly. She was aware of the smell of the magnolia trees and the tar on the road, the outlines of the ramshackle buildings surrounding the apartment, the moths beating themselves on the streetlights with feverish intensity. It all made sense to her now. She felt as though she had escaped death itself, and, in a way, she had.

As the sun crept over the tops of the lowest trees and shed the first golden rays of dawn into the alley, the party gradually came to a close. Vivian collapsed onto a couch as the final guests said their goodbyes. The slightest hint of a grin still lingered around the corners of her mouth. Within moments, she was sound asleep.

Michael wrapped her under a down comforter, peering at her with affection. Lukas caught sight of his father out of the corner of his eye and sauntered over from the kitchen. He glanced from Michael to Vivian, and back.

"What do you think?" Lukas asked dubiously.

"I think she may be strong enough," Michael responded. "God knows she'd better be."

Ω ♲

Night draped the Atlanta night in a resplendent black cloak. The evening autumn air was crisp and clear. The skyline glimmered with steady and pulsing neon lights, and the residents scurried about their nocturnal activities, oblivious of the bloodsucking beings gathered in a chamber below the city.

The twenty members of the Table—an elite group of the undead—sat in high-backed mahogany chairs in a conference room the size of a dance hall. They all sat quietly and watched as Jude walked back and forth at the head of a polished table centered in the room. They feigned patience as they wondered what crisis had called them all together.

Jude stopped pacing. The gleaming black walnut floor held smudges and scuffs in both directions. Jude grasped the ornate chair holding his place at the head of the table, and leaned on it heavily. His fingernails dug into the wood and tore crescents into the carved top. A few members winced.

This was going to be bad.

Jude's cheeks flushed bright red, in contrast to the icy blaze in his eyes. This evening, he had overindulged himself, leaving five corpses in a dirty Atlanta alley. The *Shévet ha Dam* may have considered his feast excessive, but their opinions didn't concern him, and butchering people soothed his nerves. The longer he thought about her escape—and her ability to evict him from her mind in her weakened state—the angrier he became. And more frightened. It didn't help that early reports from his subordinates told him the witch bitch and her family had vanished.

The assembly became restless, their phlegmatic expressions gradually crumbling under the strain of Jude's silence. Two or three murmured to one another in undertones of speculation. None wanted to be the one to break the silence and risk Jude's wrath. Finally, it was Jude himself that broke the stillness.

"Ladies. Gentlemen. I have an issue that needs your direct attention. One of my females has fled, and we must recover her at once. We will use every means at our disposal."

He used slow, deliberate English and impressed the importance of his words with telepathy, ensuring that they all understood. He paused to let his message sink in. His colleagues were stunned: Jude had called them together to find a plaything? Jaws dropped, and they shot dubious glances in one another's direction. Why would Jude Shepherd need the *Shévet ha Dam* to help recover one of his playthings? The request was irregular, not to mention ridiculous. They had more pressing things to do with their time than to bother with a runaway.

"*Mit* all due respect, Jude, why?" asked Wolfgang Seifert, a dark-haired, Western European representative. He regarded Jude sternly from under his bushy eyebrows, his dark, narrow eyes gazing at him with effrontery. "She *ist* a slave? You should have no problem finding her yourself. Why involve us?"

Jude weighed his following words carefully. He needed to be persuasive while maintaining his impassivity. They needed to be aware that he wasn't merely chasing down his showpiece. The idea of sharing with the *Shévet ha Dam* that she had expelled him from her thoughts was unthinkable. Any hint that she had realized her potential was dangerous: they would fear her. He composed several versions of the truth before deciding what he would tell them: As little as possible. Still, one did not invoke the spirits of the four winds to send them on a personal mission.

"I have reason to believe," he began somberly, "that she has met an insurgent group that will hide her from me until she escapes my pull, and that is unacceptable."

"Don' be *ridículo*, Jude," interjected Paulo Gutierrez, a showy Spaniard whose bawdiness was only outdone by his outrageous dress. He had shown up somewhat conservatively this time—black and steel blue paisley suit and matching tie. "She has no chance. We have been alive for hundreds of years. They have *nada*. Catch her yourself."

Jude inhaled deeply, deliberately, and the Table cringed. Gutierrez wondered if he had gone too far. Jude dealt with remonstrations harshly. He pictured Jude leaping across the Table and draining him of his blood before tearing his head from his shoulders. He had seen it happen before—it was how he had reached his rank of fifth in command. Jude had killed his predecessor, Mr. Adobet, in the chair in which he sat. He caught Jude's eye, wondered if Jude was doing a mental trick.

He wasn't. Jude was too preoccupied with the correct wording of his following remark.

"*She* may have power over *you*," Jude said pointedly. Again, he paused to let his words take effect. The group was bemused by this idea. A young female and a band of tempestuous rebels causing the downfall of a deep-rooted, centuries-old, undead organization? Not possible. Clearly, Jude had lost his sense.

He had no choice. It was time to share the truth.

"The escapee is Vivian. Jerusha. My *only* full-blooded child," he admitted. At last, he had their rapt attention.

Wolfgang started to say what they were all thinking.

"You mean—"

"I mean, the only one of my sons and daughters that I have transformed into my near likeness. The one who has lived solely through the power of *my* blood for many, many years. She is the Second Curse and has much of my strength and capabilities. We must catch her before she realizes it."

No one was inclined to dispute Jude now. Though he had shown a dangerous degree of recklessness, none dared. Not a soul cast a doubt— at least aloud—on Jude's motives. He was immortal, he was their leader, and he was a killer. He was the heart of the *Shévet ha Dam*.

With Jude's blood keeping her alive for all those years, there was no telling the extent of her cunning, the gifts he might have unwittingly given her. Without Jude to supervise her, to control her strength, there was the risk that she could become dangerous to them, especially if she had met some absurd extremists who would poison her mind further. How long before she discovered her potential?

"We must find Vivian and subjugate the vampires who have aided her," Jude ordered. "Kill them if you must, but bring her to me. We start tonight."

Maysun Khatri examined Jude's eyes—wide, black, so similar to her own. She'd known Jude longer than anyone at the Table, but he was as much of an enigma to her as anyone. Was that fear she saw? Or something else? Unlike the others, Jude had the distinction of being the only creature there that baffled and worried her. Had anyone else understood what Jude meant by the Second Curse? Or were they too frightened to ask? She glanced at Charles Dunning, her American counterpart, but his stoic expression revealed nothing. The man hid his expressions thoroughly. She may be the second-oldest member of the Table, but Charles had a viciousness and cunning that had followed him from life to death that she did not have.

There was no dissension or need to put this to a vote. They were aware of one another's judgments without a word. Vivian would be caught quickly, and the group of rebels disbanded by any means necessary.

C� ʓ

Vivian floated away from her sleeping body like flotsam drifting on the waves, helplessly riding the current. Despite this sense of defenselessness, she wasn't nervous. It was, if anything, relaxing.

She rode the wind westward and north, following the path she had come only yesterday. Faster now, her ethereal body accelerated, the wind offering little opposition. She flew effortlessly, impressed with the feeling she had done it before. A sense of power grew in her, and she savored it as the miles passed under her.

A large city loomed in the distance. She sensed Jude's presence there, along with others, bloodsuckers like him.

The Blood Tribe!

Although the city should have looked bright, welcome, and bustling, it had the appeal of a haunted house. Knowing that Jude was here tainted its beauty. She no longer felt at ease. Apprehension set in like a tick feeding on her conscience.

She sensed that Jude was up to something which concerned her, Michael, and her new family, but it felt like the sort of irrational idea that happens in dreams. Still, she needed to see what was happening.

They can't see me, can they? Surely, she was safe in her misty form. A chill swept over her when she considered Jude's intentions. She followed the wind that carried her, now hoping fervently that she wasn't heading into a trap.

She traveled to a large, gothic two-story house that looked misplaced in an industrial neighborhood. She drifted in, then through an immaculately kept corridor, down two dimly lit flights of stairs, and into a vast room lined with bookshelves that nearly reached the ceiling. She floated above an enormous crystal chandelier centered over a conference table. Ten chairs on each side held distinguished-looking vampires dressed in posh clothing. Two chairs stood empty. At the head of the table stood Jude.

The vampires now looked perplexed and alarmed. She strained to hear, and one voice gradually floated through the haze: Jude's.

"We must find Vivian and subjugate the vampires who have aided her. Kill them if you must, but bring her to me. We start tonight."

Anger, frustration, and fear swelled in Vivian. *Kill Lukas and Michael? For helping me leave the twisted life you would have me lead? What kind of creature are you? Why am I so significant that you can't let me go?*

Slowly, Jude turned his head in her direction.

Can he see me? Vivian thought in a panic. *Can he? Dear God, please let this be a dream. A nightmare I can wake up from. Don't let this be real!*

If she'd had eyes, they would have locked. Jude's icy glare penetrated her to the misty core. She felt herself thrust back over the miles in a second, shot like a bullet from a gun.

Chapter 15

She had been there. Jude hadn't seen her, but he had sensed her. He had managed to evict her without a fight, so she hadn't metamorphosed yet. How was she doing this? It was as if her body rapidly absorbed knowledge without her trying. Could that be? Could she remember who she was so quickly?

Jude doubted if bringing in the Shévet ha Dam had been wise for a few hours after the Table meeting. He did not want to risk becoming vulnerable, or exposing his mind to the others, and it had almost happened. Gutierrez had enraged him to the point he had nearly dropped his shield.

Damn fool. Who is he to question me?

But Paulo had been right. Finding her shouldn't be a challenge. She still had his blood in her veins, and as long as she had that, he had a chance to find her, to read her mind. She was his child, and she was weak, at least when compared to him.

She didn't feel so weak last night. Damn that witch woman for helping her to escape. She shouldn't have made it that far!

The more he thought about it, the less confident he was. She had thrust him from her mind her first night apart from him. She had floated—out of body—to Atlanta, and had found her way into a Table meeting without detection by anyone but him. These were not the signs of a frail, dutiful slave. They were evidence that she would be herself soon if he did not find her first.

His original plan had been to catch her and kill her in front of the Table, to let them know that he had no weaknesses, not even for his favorite plaything. It had been too long since he had reminded them of her. He needed to show them once more how ruthless he could be.

Ridiculous, really. The idea that she could bring about Armageddon. What a dated concept.

His hands shook. He clenched them into fists, drawing blood from his palms. The scent empowered him, and he pushed off into the air, rapidly vanishing into the black, a nocturnal scavenger preying on the Atlanta streets.

☳ ☴

Vivian's eyes opened slowly. It was difficult to make out the apartment in the gloom, but she was thankful to be in back her filthy sanctuary once she did. She had been afraid that she would wake up in that eerie gothic house. Had it been only a dream? She could still picture its details so clearly.

Michael had fallen asleep on the couch along the opposite wall. His chest rose and fell heavily. Vivian took in his handsome face and balanced features. He smiled faintly as he dreamed, and she noticed the laugh lines around his eyes and the dimple on his cheek, the cleft in his chin.

She rose from the couch and surveyed the damage. The apartment was dirty before, but it was nothing compared to the state it was in now. Beer bottles littered the floor, some half-full with cigarette butts floating in warm brew. Ashtrays were filled to overflowing. Empty wrappers from various fast-food franchises lay about, some next to the trash bins. Clothes and blankets were strewn over everything. And the floor! Vivian had never seen a floor so filthy. And if anything, it grew worse on the way to the kitchen. She examined the table. *Has someone licked the table?* She winced.

"How'd you rest?"

Vivian turned as Gina emerged from the bathroom. Steam billowed out like an encroaching fog. She toweled her wet hair with a clean, fluffy pink towel.

"Like the dead," Vivian said. It was a lame joke, but Gina laughed anyway.

"Need a shower? I have plenty of towels from home." Vivian nodded and soon was washing off the night's grime in the bathroom. She changed into another outfit provided by Gina—a tight pink shirt that ended over her navel and a pair of baggy jeans. She left the shower feeling like a much cleaner—if atypically dressed—version of herself.

She found Gina resting on the couch next to Michael and heard Lukas rattling around the kitchen talking on his phone. Colorful cartoon characters on the television stood waiting in what she now knew to be a video game. Electronic music emanated from the stereo speakers, a much gentler version of what had been playing last night. Much of the new music sounded the same to her.

Gina leaned over and turned up the volume on the stereo and danced into the center of the living room, writhing to the pulsating beat. Her arms and legs bent like rubber, much like Avery from the previous night, but her movement was much more seductive. If she intended to attract anyone, though, it was unclear whom. Lukas enjoyed the show from the kitchen doorframe, the sandwich he chewed all but unnoticed.

"Let's go dancing," Lukas suggested, his mouth full of ham and cheese. His eyes never left Gina's swaying body.

Michael nodded, paying little mind to the performance.

"Excellent suggestion. I was thinking the same thing. Another good opportunity for Vivian to learn more about finding prey."

Vivian stared at Gina, who undulated her hips as though she was having sex. *I hope dancing that way isn't involved. I'll starve!* "What do you think, Gina?" Michael asked.

"Sounds great," Gina turned to Vivian. "Come on. I'll help you get ready," she said. She offered her hand, and Vivian accepted it reluctantly.

Gina led Vivian back to her room, where she chose an outfit from the handful stored in a canvas bag. Gina plugged in the curling iron and turned to Vivian, a matter-of-fact expression on her face.

"Michael said if we ever have the chance to get you up to speed on what's changed since you were... whatever it was, that we should. I guess it's my turn to play teacher now." She pulled a tight peach shirt over her head and tugged it into place. Satisfied with her outfit, she removed a brightly colored plastic box filled with make-up from her tote bag, and started to apply some of the contents to herself and Vivian. Vivian watched in the mirror as Gina continued.

"I know that gay people existed in the 1940s. I don't know what you called them then, but nowadays, they're called gay. Nowadays, people attracted to a person of the same sex are called gay or homosexual. If you don't care if you get with a man or a woman when you hook up, you're bisexual, or bi. Some girls act bi to turn guys on, but I really am."

"You're attracted to men *and* women?"

Gina nodded. "That doesn't bother you, does it?" she asked concernedly, her large eyes blinking as she gave her blush a few extra smoothing strokes it didn't need.

Vivian shrugged. "Whatever floats your boat." Gina laughed and handed her a tube of lipstick.

In less than half an hour, they were ready to go. To Vivian, everyone looked gorgeous. Lukas had dressed in black slacks and a shiny blue long-sleeve shirt that set off his bright blue eyes. A thin gold hoop hung from each ear. Michael looked breathtaking in black pants and a thin, gray, collared shirt that shifted colors as he moved, and two silver loops dangled from his ears. Gina was dazzling in her short peach top and tight blue jeans. Her trademark butterflies hung from a necklace and belly ring.

"Uh-oh, Michael done got freaked out," Gina laughed. "Lemme see your tongue."

He stuck his tongue between his long eyeteeth, and a silver barbell flashed. Gina did the same, and Vivian saw that hers was pierced, too. A tiny butterfly dangled from Gina's. As ridiculous as it appeared to her, she felt unadorned in comparison.

"Ok y'all, where're we going?" Michael asked, pulling on a coat.

"Déjà!" Lukas yelled.

"Piano bar!" Gina piped up.

"You can't dance at the piano bar!" Lukas argued.

Michael shook his head.

"Here's an idea," he said. "It's ten o'clock, too early for the clubs to be hopping. Let's get a drink on River Street, and then get a drink on River Street, if you know what I mean. Then we'll go on to the clubs. Let's hit 'em all tonight, in order according to location."

The others nodded, eager to be off. Vivian made sure to grab her purse, ensuring the black velvet bag Beth gave her was tucked safely inside. The dream from the previous night was fresh in her mind. *Better to be safe than sorry*. The thought of the *Shévet ha Dam* tracking her and her new family down was almost enough to make her try to convince everyone to stay home. She'd known them hardly a day, but already she felt fiercely protective of them.

Gina's car was around the corner from the apartment, a boxy blue Reliant K in similar disrepair as the apartment. Everyone scooted clothing and CDs out of the way to find room to sit.

"Gina, do me a favor," Michael said after graciously offering the front seat to Vivian.

"What's that, baby?" Gina asked.

"If I'm going downtown, I'm taking *my* car. Could you drive us to the Jones house real quick?"

"Sure."

They drove toward historic downtown with the windows rolled down and slowed down on Jones Street. Gina slowly parked behind a shiny, wine-red sports car. Vivian decided that if she had to choose a modern car, this would be it. It was the most beautiful contemporary automobile she had seen.

Michael exited the backseat, took out his keys, and walked up to the driver's side of the sports car.

"You *own* that?" Vivian said incredulously.

"Yeah," he said with pride. "Do you want to ride with me?"

Lukas took Gina's shotgun seat as Vivian joined Michael. He pulled off with a screech, putting the car through its paces with ease. Vivian sat breathlessly, peering out the window as they passed vehicles on their left and right. They pretended to race Gina at times, but it was clear Michael could have left her behind whenever he wished.

They drove to a parking garage and cruised up three stories before parking in neighboring slots. The clan piled out noisily, laughing and full of nervous expectation of the night, and the hunt, to come.

Chapter 16

Vivian's outing with her new friends was an enjoyable learning experience. They visited a busy daiquiri bar on River Street that displayed their frozen goods in spinning dispensers along the wall behind the bar. Next, they traveled to a piano saloon where pianists dueled on stage with fingers so quick that they blurred. Afterward, Gina wanted to hit up the gay bars—a concept Vivian found amusing. They never stayed in any location for longer than it took for them to all have a cocktail and say hello to the many people they knew.

When they left the second gay bar, Gina decided to teach Vivian how easy it was to snag a victim. Michael and the rest of the family hid in the shadows of a dim alley as she set to work.

"Watch," she said with a smirk. She quickly hid her fangs behind pouted lips.

Three middle-aged men, tourists, judging from their matching "Georgia" t-shirts, staggered in their direction. Their loud, slurred voices confirmed that they were men on the town. Gina started toward them from the alley, shuffling as though she was trying to keep her dignity despite having too many cocktails. She sniffed and shot a penetrating but libidinous look towards the men. The gorgeous damsel in distress immobilized them.

"My boyfriend just dumped me," she pouted, her voice thick with false misery. "I can't believe it. I don't even have a ride home." Her slurred, sobbing speech was drowned out by the men who circled her in a drunken zeal to console her.

Michael pushed Vivian forward to join them from her shadowy hiding place.

Vivian merged with the crowd around Gina, and the entranced men accepted Vivian's presence as a matter of course. Soon the two of them had their prey leaned up against the wall of a riverside candle shop. It was too easy. To the passing crowd, it looked like an undisguised make-out session. To Vivian, it was revitalizing, wonderful blood.

I have to let him go. I can't let him die. But God, I'm still hungry! Vivian released her victim reluctantly, and he slumped drunkenly along the wall, unconscious, but smiling. A thin trail of red blood trickled down his neck and stained his souvenir t-shirt.

She slurped the fluid from her bloodstained teeth and turned around. She wanted more.

A lone, spike-haired punk with an angry expression was slouching by. His downcast eyes intentionally ignored everything and everyone. *He'll do.*

The fresh blood in her veins empowered her, and she reached out for the punk, sending her thoughts easily into his troubled mind. Her message wrapped tendrils around his mind and erased any idea other than obedience to her.

"Come here," she murmured. Her voice was too low to reach his ears, but it didn't matter. The irritation on his pale features dissipated as he met her glassy stare. His combat boots veered toward her as though he were roped. She took his hand and led him into an alley where she kissed his neck, drinking long draughts of his warm blood.

Vivian released her second victim with much less effort than the first. Stunned looks covered Lukas and Gina's faces.

"How did you do that? *How did you do that?*" Lukas barked, impressed. Vivian smiled.

"I told him to come here, and he did," she replied. She turned to Gina. "You can read minds, too, can't you?"

"A little, but I can't reign in prey from twenty paces," she confessed. "That was the ultimate in cool. You looked at him, and *bam!* He came right to you!"

The three headed back to where Michael had been hiding in the alley. Gina made a motion for them to pause as he came into sight. Lukas patted Vivian on the arm and signaled that he was heading to a nearby bar with a jerk of his thumb. Vivian nodded absently before giving her undivided attention to Michael's hunt.

A pretty brunette in a tailored black suit ambled near Michael, eyeing a building with concern as if she was searching for a restaurant or bar. She referred to a piece of crumpled paper in her manicured hand, looked up at the signs hanging from the buildings, and back to her paper again. She didn't notice Michael concealed under a flight of stairs. She came within an arm's reach of him, and he struck.

Vivian had seen him talk his way toward his victims, but had never seen him take one almost brutally. He grasped her firmly by the wrist and spun her around in his grasp, almost like a dance. She opened her heart-shaped mouth as a scream reached her throat, but she never screamed. Michael tilted his head to the side and pursed his lips lightly as if to say gently, "Now why would you want to do that?" He spoke no words, only gazed into her eyes. She complied without resistance. Vivian heard a contented sigh as he sank his teeth into her exposed flesh.

Watching Michael as he drank, Vivian pictured herself in the woman's role. She remembered that first bite vividly, how delectably rapturous it had felt. She found herself thinking about how changed her life would be if Michael had turned her instead of Jude. Only instead of setting her free when he finished drinking, he kept her and turned her into his own. How different the past fifty years would have been if she had spent them with someone caring and thoughtful, instead of controlling and merciless! *There isn't much point in dwelling on that. You can't change the past.*

Michael finished and carried his victim deftly into the shadows. Her face appeared to be in a peaceful sleep.

"She'll be safe there until she wakes up," he told them.

"Well, are we having fun, or what?" Lukas bellowed from behind them. Vivian jumped at the sound. His smile was big and drunken, but happy. His long legs carried him over the ballastones swiftly, despite the occasional stagger. His blond curls looked almost white under the River Street lamplight.

Gina beamed at him and raced across the cobblestones. She jumped onto his body, latching her legs around his waist and her arms around his neck.

"Dance with me, Lukas!" she laughed. Lukas wrapped one arm around her slim body and rocked back and forth, holding the drink high in the other. He sang words to a lewd song Vivian did not know.

"OK, none of that," Michael barked. Lukas dropped Gina quickly to her feet. "Dancing sounds good, though," Michael continued. "Where to?"

Once again, the two friends overwhelmed him with suggestions. He raised his hands, and the suggestions subsided.

"OK, OK, I heard Lizard's, and I heard Reilly's. Since they're right on top of each other, I think that's a fine idea. It'd give Vivian a chance to see City Market. And who knows? One of those weak cover bands might manage to provide us with entertainment."

Gina proposed going to "Teen Night" at another bar last. Lukas shook his head at her.

"Gina, you're not a teenager anymore," he countered.

"Yeah, but they're such easy pickings at that age," she smiled wickedly.

Nothing in downtown Savannah was more than a few blocks away. Soon, they were standing in line for a dance club on the second story of a two-story bar, since City Market had failed to provide a "weak cover band" on the ground floor.

Upstairs, Michael ran into a Veronica—a stunning, dark-haired human friend that taught Vivian how to dance more or less against her will. Veronica said the trick to dancing to the modern stuff was to "pretend to ride a dick." Vivian didn't need a translation. After a few embarrassing tries to mimic Veronica's easy sashay, it started to feel more natural. She figured she must be doing something right when Michael interrupted as she danced with an enthusiastic young man.

Vivian did not miss the look of astonishment on Veronica's face as Michael struggled to keep up with Vivian. Vivian helped him the best she could, and within a few measures, he got the hang of the basics.

The group went to only two more clubs. They might have gone to more, but nothing stayed open after three in the morning. Michael and Vivian never left each other's side. They spent the entire night dancing or talking over cigarettes and drinks so intense they almost had flavor. He told Gina and Lukas that Vivian had succeeded in teaching him to dance where they'd failed.

Vivian wondered how much effort he had put into learning before she came along.

Chapter 17

After the last clubs closed their doors, their little group converged on River Street again. The companionship and the conversation were enough to keep their minds off the annoying drizzle in the October air.

"Normally around this time, if we've harangued a few humans into joining us, we'll take them out for food or let them bring us back to their place to party," Michael told her. "It's part of the bonding. That's the unfortunate thing about being a vampire. You can't help yourself to a bite out of your human friends every so often and expect them to understand. I mean, sure, there's the occasional Goth freak who'd be willing, but we'd prefer not to be known for what we are. So, we have to keep meeting new people and getting to know them overnight. We go out to eat a lot, even if we don't need to. Eating is a bonding activity people can do in a public place to get to know one another. People go out for 'a bite to eat, 'coffee' or 'a drink.' It's a shame. When was the last time you heard anyone say, 'Hey, let's meet up in the park and wander around and talk for a couple of hours?'"

"Never. People like to have something to 'do,'" she responded.

"Exactly. Why is that? Why can't people just say, 'Hey Gary, it's been a while. Why don't you come over, and we'll shoot the shit?' Everyone's gotta have a motive: a movie, a dance club, a party, a barbecue, a birthday. No one ever just hangs out anymore."

"You're a thoughtful person," she observed.

"Thank you, I try."

"I don't know if I mean that how you think. I mean... well, you think a lot. You look for the meaning of things. You enjoy mulling over things that others take for granted."

His brow furrowed briefly.

"Well, yes. Most people don't study life. It's sad. There's so much to learn, but few people can hold their attention spans for longer than the duration of a commercial or a music video."

Vivian viewed his handsome face. It was deceiving; so much knowledge hid behind its façade. In the soft light of the street lamps, he barely looked twenty. She wanted to spend the rest of her life listening to him talk, hearing him ponder life's curiosities as they occurred to him. She sensed if she did, she would learn the meaning of life—human, vampire, any life. If it was out there, Michael would uncover it.

She grinned, shook her head, and squeezed his hand. He squeezed back.

ଔ ଓ

That morning, on their return to the Jones Street house, Vivian was too tired to appreciate her new accommodations. Michael nearly had to carry her upstairs to her room. She had the vague impression of ivory and lace before falling asleep against a downy pillow.

ଔ ଓ

Her eyes snapped open, her vision swam, and her body trembled. *Where am I?* Something was wrong. She had a vague recollection of the room she'd been in, and she wasn't there anymore. *Or am I? Damn it, what's wrong with me?* A mind-crippling swoon of déjà vu overpowered her.

Her arms brushed a lacy twin coverlet. It was a sickening pink, the same shade as the walls. The color was like being swathed in cotton candy. She pulled back the heavy bedspread and sat up, setting her bare feet on a cold hardwood floor. Her stomach gave a massive lurch, and she feared she was going to vomit. Or was she hungry? Her stomach felt as though she hadn't eaten in days.

Jude. Where is Jude? She needed Jude. Her mind reeled, a twisting maze of emotions that ranged from love, fear, dependence, and hatred. But why? This was Jude, her lover, her all. Why should she fear Jude? She shook her head, trying to rattle her thoughts into place. Her head felt like a helium balloon.

She fought off a blackout, blinked until her vision cleared, staggered out of bed, and eased into an ivory robe that matched a gown she didn't recall donning. Leaning heavily on the walls, she steered herself through a lavish home. She found a flight of stairs and crept downward, placing both feet on each step before descending the next. Voices floated up from the foot of the stairs. She recognized Jude's, but the other was unfamiliar.

"...doing fine. Gabrielle is working at a club downtown, making a shitload of money. I don't see sense in it, but hey—if she wants a job, she can work."

"Very good, David. I'm glad to hear it. Did you bring the papers?"

Vivian rounded the last step. A wiry young bald man with unsavory blue eyes—David, she assumed—sat on the plush couch. Jude sat in a matching chair opposite him, his back toward Vivian. The bald man opened a briefcase and handed a sealed folder to Jude.

"Your name is as you requested: Wayne Curtis. She'll be Bettina Curtis, your wife. There are also identification records in there for your other acquaintances, uh, people, with backgrounds on each one..."

The step squeaked like a mouse caught in a trap as Vivian brought her second foot down. Jude turned around and beamed at her with such false sincerity it triggered a new wave of nausea.

"Darling... what are you doing out of bed?" He started toward her, and she suppressed a wince. Her arms rose feebly in a gesture of self-protection, but she had to put them down again. There was no strength left in her.

"Hun-hungry," she wheezed. The room spun around her, and she collapsed at the foot of the stairs, landing heavily on her behind. David tilted his head and regarded her curiously. Embarrassed, she brought her knees together to cover herself and placed her head near them to fight off the dizziness. It didn't work. The room still felt like it was tilted on an axis, pivoting around like a carousel.

Jude crossed the room with quick strides and placed his hand soothingly on her shoulder. He bent down and whispered into her ear.

"I know you are, but I was coming up to feed you shortly. You needn't concern yourself with such things." There was a hint of anger in his voice. She whimpered like a nursing child denied a teat.

"David, my friend, would you excuse me for a moment?" Jude asked. David motioned his accord. Jude lifted her into his arms as though she weighed no more than a kitten. Her head lolled into the crook of his arm. The last thing she remembered was the sight of the thin young man regarding her with compassion as Jude carried her up the stairs to the prison that was her room.

☙ ☘

Maysun shuddered and sat up. Her sweat-covered body trembled like a woman saved from a frigid, watery grave. She laid a hand on the pale man next to her, her lover of over twenty years—off and on—and his slow, sleepy breathing soothed her.

Did the dream work? Will she remember?

It had taken all the strength Maysun could muster to penetrate the mental walls Jerusha did not know she erected as she slept. If not for the enormity of her task, Maysun might have given up, but "Vivian" was becoming too comfortable. Too complacent. Much too easy of a target for the Blood Tribe.

Tapping into her mind as she slept, Maysun had sifted through Jerusha's memories for one that might open the gateway to her deeply buried memories. Most of them had been untouchable, blocked behind emotional barricades so solid Maysun doubted any creature could move them aside. It was the mental equivalent of Fort Knox.

Then, unexpectedly, she found one left unsecured. Or had the power behind the universe had made it available to her? It did not seem like much of a memory—surely, nothing that would trigger an avalanche of history.

Maybe it wasn't time. Perhaps the Source had its purpose for releasing this memory now. Who was she to question it?

When Maysun released the memory, it flew out with the howl of an angry poltergeist. She struggled to flee, but a ghostly hand with the power of a demonic fiend held her in place. She could not escape. Her memories vanished, and she relived the remembrance as Vivian, with Vivian. Once released, Maysun awoke with a start, drenched in blood-tainted sweat. Thankfully, her lover Eoghan hadn't sensed her panic and slept steadily. The man was a rock. He had to be, if he wanted to be a part of her chaotic, unpredictable life.

She laid back down and relived the memory, this time from a detached, unemotional view.

Maybe it will be enough after all.

Chapter 18

Vivian felt as if someone had slipped her a sedative. Late evening sunlight filtered through the closed blinds and lace curtains. She was paralyzed with fear.

Someone had tucked her tightly into bed in a feminine room. Lace covered every flat surface—the dresser, the nightstand—and a few that weren't flat, like the lampshade and the pillows.

Please, God, don't let me be back with him. Anything but back with Jude. Please!

As she took in her surroundings, it sank in that she wasn't in the same room. She wasn't surrounded by sickening cotton-candy pink. This room was feminine but floral with a profusion of chintz. A fern and a tall orchid stood on short Corinthian columns in the corner opposite the bed.

She took a deep breath, sighed, and inhaled again, baffled.

Is that Michael's cologne?

She rolled over and noticed a second pillow beside hers. A telltale impression of someone's head remained in the down, and the sheets were wrinkled where she hadn't been laying. Feeling ridiculous, she lowered her nose to the indentation and sniffed.

Michael!

She clambered to the side of the bed and leaned over. Michael had placed his shoes at a neat right angle next to the bed and had put his shirt tidily on the polished cherry-wood chair.

She touched her arms and legs in a subconscious gesture to assure her clothes were as she had left them. They were. She hadn't been violated unless she counted violation of personal space. Michael had merely slept next to her last night, and she didn't remember. She didn't know whether to laugh or cry.

She got out of bed slowly, trying to decide if she would scold Michael when she saw him. She couldn't see any reason to, other than her momentary discomfort. No, discomfort was too strong of a word, more like... confusion.

She had been exhausted and asleep. Maybe they had a bed shortage at this house. *And maybe you don't mind the idea of sleeping next to him.* There wasn't any harm in sleeping next to him. She only wished she had been awake to appreciate it.

Unsure what to say—scandals were made of less back home—she left the room. She had to go down not one, but two flights of stairs to reach the living area where the family had gathered. Her new surroundings were lovely. After the last apartment, this was a remarkable improvement. The walls were antique brick, the furniture matching cherry antiques. Beautiful paintings with gilded frames adorned the walls. Plants in pretty brass planters stood in the corners.

Lukas and Gina were playing the video game today. Lukas's frame hunched in his low seat as Gina tilted from side to side as if her movements influenced the car racing on the screen. Vivian sensed that Michael was who she heard running the shower. She felt him with her mind now, along with the rest of the family. Gina looked up at Vivian and grinned.

"Where's Michael?" Vivian asked, feigning ignorance. Gina shrugged.

"He's probably in the shower." She scowled as the car she drove crashed into a brilliant explosion on the screen, and she put her controller down. An idea occurred to her, and her face brightened.

"Hey, you want to come to work with me? I could introduce you around, and you could maybe meet some new people. It's a good place to get a drink—our kind of drink, you know?"

Vivian didn't know what to say since she didn't make the connection.

"I work in a club," Gina explained. "I'm a dancer."

"A dancer? What sort of dancer?"

"Don't lie, Gina. She'll die of culture shock if you don't tell her more than that," Michael reprimanded lightheartedly. He entered from the other room, still toweling off from his shower. He was shirtless and wore nothing except a loose-fitting pair of athletic shorts. He had an appealingly developed chest. Beautiful legs, too. Vivian strove not to stare but failed. He caught her gaze and winked. Her mouth twisted in a bashful smile as her eyes dropped to the floor. No one else in the room paid any attention that he was, well, gorgeous. *They must be used to it.*

"I'm an exotic dancer," Gina offered.

"She's a stripper," Michael said.

"Oh," Vivian replied. The idea of going to a club to watch women remove their clothes, and being left to herself in a bar full of rowdy men, wasn't tempting. She looked at Gina. The expression on her face was so hopeful it was heartbreaking.

Well, why not? If she was going to be a part of this group, not to mention this decade, she had to get used to things.

"Are you going, Michael?" she asked, knowing she would feel less awkward if he was with her.

He weighed his decision for only a moment before conceding.

When it was time to go, Michael looked even more handsome than the night before in a tight black short-sleeve shirt and slacks. Gina wore a shiny pink dress with strategically placed holes up the sides that accentuated her generous breasts and thin waist. Vivian managed to borrow a much more conservative green dress but settled for what she deemed tacky shoes. She fussed with her hair and make-up for what felt like an hour, but nothing looked just right. She gave up on it when Gina knocked on the door and told Vivian that if she didn't get out, she would make her late for work.

With a final glower at her imperfect updo in the mirror and a resigned sigh, she left the bathroom. It was worth the preparation to see the appreciative look on Michael's face when he saw her.

The old historic homes graduated into a modern section of town. Michael weaved his sports car through traffic like a racecar driver until they pulled into the parking lot of a flashy, neon-lit building with black tinted windows hidden off one of the side roads by large trees. Above the door was a neon sign that read "The Pink Peacock."

Vivian climbed out of the backseat. Traffic buzzed by and a thumping bass line radiated from inside the building. Gina appeared adrenalized by the atmosphere, tapping her feet and wiggling her hips, ready for the dance floor.

"Time to go make money!" she chirped.

Michael slipped one arm around Gina and the other around Vivian as they approached the club.

A blast of music erupted from inside as soon as Michael opened the door to the building. Vivian's eyes focused swiftly on the smoky interior. The inside of the bar was more garish than the outside. It looked as though a neon outlet had held a clearance sale, and the owner of the Peacock had bought the lot. What he hadn't stuck haphazardly outdoors gave the interior a tasteless, brassy feeling. Most of the lights embellished the bar, leaving the back shadowy and dim. Nearly naked showgirls added to the vulgarity more effectively than the neon. They writhed in four tiny cages in the corners of the club. The shadowy rear held a DJ booth and a catwalk ending in a stage with a pole in the center. Men with half-empty bottles or glasses occupied tables, glazed eyes staring luridly at bare-breasted performers.

"You work here?" Vivian asked Gina once she got them past the bouncer.

"No better place to get drunken men alone to expose their body parts," Gina said. "You should try it; it's ridiculously easy."

"No," Vivian replied, "I don't think I'm ready for that."

"You get used to it," Gina explained with an absent wave. "It took me a while, too. Well, gotta tell the DJ what I want him to play for my set. Catch you later."

Vivian and Michael took a table toward the back. Vivian eyed the chair primly before sitting. A waitress in a halter top and short shorts asked them if they wanted anything to drink, and Michael ordered a single malt scotch. Vivian, not knowing what else to order, asked for a beer. When the waitress offered the name of an unfamiliar brand, she shrugged and nodded.

A hard thumping song began, a man singing about a woman called "Mustang Sally." A vampire Vivian recognized from the party sashayed onto the stage wearing a short, baby blue velvet dress and thigh-high white boots with perilously high heels. Gone were the teacher glasses and the demureness Vivian remembered. She worked the stage with confidence, going so far as to put a boot heel on the forehead of an over-zealous patron who tried mounting the stage on all fours.

"Are all the dancers vampires?" Vivian asked.

"Not all of them," Michael said. "But the ones who are like it. They watch the men drinking, pick out a real smashed son of a bitch, and lead him to the back room for a private dance. They help themselves to some blood and leave him there. Come closing time, the bouncers take them out to their cars. The owner's a vamp. He's in on the whole thing."

"Do you come here a lot?" Vivian asked, uncertain she wanted to know the answer.

"Sometimes I give them a ride to work and stick around for a couple of drinks. They know me here, so I get 'em cheap."

"Do you like it? I mean, does it turn you on?" Vivian found herself saying, not sure she wanted to know the answer.

Michael regarded her solemnly.

"I like a woman who knows the right time to take her clothes off," he responded. Their drinks arrived, and they sat back to survey the show. Vivian sipped her beer with a small smile.

03   80

Outside, in the inky shadows provided by the trees hiding the club from the road, stood a thing called Jacob. Not human and not vampire, Jacob's sole purpose for living was to please his master, Lily. Lily was not his lady's true name any more than his was Jacob. She gave Jacob his name, and he worshipped her too much to question her. It did not matter to him. To him, she was always Milady.

Jacob could not have been more devoted if he was Lily's son. The blood ties that bound them were not biological, at least not in the conventional sense. He was addicted to her blessed blood. Jacob was more adoring than any son, more loving than any spouse. One day, if he proved himself Lily's finest servant, she would drink from him and give him her gift of eternal life. She had promised.

Jacob scratched his dirty skin, cocked his head, kept his eyes on the club. *She* was in there—the runaway. Jacob knew the *Shévet ha Dam* was on a search for Jude's runaway slave. He had felt it the moment his master knew. He followed that telepathic connection through the minds of the other vampires. Lily had spoken to David, who had spoken to Paulo, and he quickly leaped through these connections until he reached Jude. From Jude, he detected what she looked like, smelled like, felt like. He did not have the intelligence that other vampires had, he was often a source of ridicule among the bloodsuckers. His insight, however, was far better than theirs. It was the one trait he had over any of the undead. His simple-mindedness made him exceptionally open to reading the thoughts of others. That's what they called him. Simple-minded.

He knew she was in there, and he would stay put until she came out. Then he would kill her. He would be a champion, a hero in the eyes of the *Shévet ha Dam*. After that, Lily would have to give him her power. He would have proven himself. He would do whatever it took to prove himself to his love, his Lily. She was his queen.

03   80

At ten minutes to three, the bartender announced last call. By three-thirty, Gina had split her tips, said her farewells, and they were on the way out of the musty, smoky bar.

The cool, clean, outdoor air was a striking contrast to the stale air inside the club. Temperature is odd to a vampire: it is sensed, but not felt. Vivian knew the air was cool, but it didn't make her cold. She inhaled a deep lungful of the fresh, crisp air and donned her jacket. As she did, she caught a sour odor. Something off. Unusual.

Her eyes moved up to the gossamer silver and white clouds passing over the bright moon. A large, dark object flew in front of the moon. An owl, maybe? It was big, whatever it was. Her nostrils flared as she took a few short, focused sniffs. The sour smell grew.

Michael's eyes darted about, and his body looked tense as if he'd sensed a threat and was prepared to pounce. She inhaled deeply again and tried to figure out what it was she smelled. It reminded her of the walk through the plantation after her awakening. No, it was more specific than that. It reminded her of—

—someone grabbed her brutally from behind—

the cemetery.

She wrenched her arm away painfully and turned to face her attacker. Drool hung from the corner of a scowl, and his eyes hid behind a curtain of greasy hair.

He wasn't vampire. He wasn't human.

What is *this thing?*

In that watery, half-hidden gaze, she swiftly discovered two things. One was the disparity between her new family and the creatures of the *Shévet ha Dam.* The malice in this beast's gaze was ferocious, hateful, and preternatural. He snarled as he glared at her in grim determination, his glassy eyes screwed up with more resolve than a kamikaze pilot. Her second realization was that it was bent on killing her in the parking lot in the presence of humans, damn the rules of the *Shévet ha Dam.*

The rules? How would I know—? Don't be stupid, Vivian. Pay attention!

He shook his dirty hair back and pounced toward her with extraordinary strength, covering three parking spaces as if they were only a step. He maneuvered deftly behind her and pinned her arms at her sides with one Herculean arm. Vivian froze in shock, immobilized by uncertainty. She tried to step back and wriggle from his grasp, but he held fast.

Michael moved behind her assailant, pulled the two of them backward to separate them, but the creature, powered by a maniacal force, would not let go. Vivian felt her attacker's free arm reach back and heard it punch Michael's head. Michael fell with a heart-sickening thump.

With his free arm, the creature reached into his coat. Vivian continued to jerk and fight, but his grasp on her restricted her like a straitjacket. She tried to kick with her feet, but in her panic, failed to reach his shins. He pulled out a large bottle and opened the flip-top lid, and Vivian smelled gasoline. The vaporous fumes polluted her lungs.

He was going to burn her alive.

Her eyes widened in terror. The stench of gas cleared her head quicker than smelling salts. He spouted the noxious fluid on her, either unaware that he was covering his arm with it at the same time or not caring. Vivian gagged, reached up, and dug her long fingernails into her attacker's hand, dragging her claws into his soft flesh and exposing the meat underneath to the gasoline. He strove to remove his hand from the dripping, stinging fluid while struggling to retain control of her. She picked up her right foot and, wincing from the fumes, took aim and drove it into his instep. Instinctively, he lifted his injured foot and was caught off-balance. As Vivian wrenched free, she thrust her attacker to the ground with a sudden burst of strength she didn't know she had.

Driven by anger and fear, she stomped down hard on his chest. She heard ribs crack, but the unholy creature did not die. He attempted to get up, writhing like a wounded animal. She kicked him in the chin with all the force she could muster. His head made a hollow thud on the pavement. This time he appeared unconscious, but Vivian was doubtful.

"Vivian, here!" Gina shouted. She threw her flip-top lighter to Vivian, who removed her gasoline-drenched jacket, covered her assailant with it, and set it on fire. He ignited at once, burning in a paradoxically merry way like a pile of dry kindling. The stench was nauseating. Vivian would have rather inhaled a hundred bottles of gasoline.

Her mind reeled. *How did this thing find me?* The *Shévet ha Dam*, or maybe Jude himself, must have sent him.

It was too bizarre to be a coincidence. *What about the dream? Maybe it wasn't a dream at all. Dear God, what if Jude has convinced the entire* Shévet ha Dam *that I am some crazy target, a criminal to capture?*

Michael staggered to his feet, and the three friends viewed the dying creature as though he was nothing more harmful than a campfire. Vivian shot her eyes about, but there was no one around watching them as the beast died, and the trees shielded them from the road.

"Can't we leave?" Vivian pleaded.

Michael removed the pack of cigarettes from his pocket, placed one in his mouth, and bent down to light it on the blazing corpse. He righted himself, never taking his eyes from the burning thing before them. He looked as though he wanted to spit on it in disgust.

"Not until we know he's nothing but ashes. I don't want him coming back and finding us again."

The burning beast crackled loudly, and Vivian jumped. The wind stirred, and she caught another atrocious whiff of burning flesh.

"Why? I mean, how...?" She started, but Michael interrupted angrily.

"You know why. How? I have no fucking idea." He caught her eye. "You have to get out of town. Tonight."

س ش

He had failed. Because he had failed, he did not care that he was dying. It was excruciating, yes, but not as painful as disappointing his Lady. He would never be the god he strove to be, never rule the earth by her side, never experience the heavenly bite that would have kept him alive eternally. He was nothing, a pitiful excuse for a servant. He deserved to die, to be nothing but ash.

His last fleeting thought was to please her in any way. Jacob would never be her hero, but perhaps if she knew he did not die in vain, but in performing an act of heroism, it would bring her a sense of pride in him. His last breath, thought, action, was for her, to let her know how much he adored her.

He reached out. It took everything he had to get past the pain, but he reached out with everything left in him and sought Jude. Normally, this would be as effortless as using a light switch. Dying was complicating things.

There. He felt Jude. It was like sending his mind to hell to connect with the vampire father. He received the typical preliminary reaction of those whose thoughts he impeded on, the familiar mental self-defense. Anyone who knew how usually blocked him out in seconds, but Jude sensed his desperation, identified the creature he was dealing with, and he accepted the image Jacob was sending. That picture was the last sight Jacob had—the gloomy look on Vivian's face as she watched a pitiful creature burn to death. Palm trees framed her, and behind her was a sign that read "White Bluff Road."

Chapter 19

Michael tried to call Lukas once they reached the car, but his cell phone battery died as he waited for his son to pick up. He swore and threw it into the backseat, narrowly missing Gina, who called him a name Vivian hadn't heard before.

Michael put his car into gear and peeled out of his parking slot with a squeal of tires. They raced back to the house on Jones Street. No one spoke. Michael clenched his jaw so hard Vivian was convinced he would be chipping teeth soon. She didn't know if he was angry or scared.

They entered the house in a flurry and found Lukas seated on the couch in front of a small TV, calmly watching a movie. When they saw the look on Michael's face, he jumped to attention quicker than a soldier.

"Lukas, are you set up yet?"

"Almost. I thought we'd have time—"

"You should've known better. This is Cartaphilus we're dealing with this time. I need you to get me a ticket to wherever you can, preferably out of the country, to*night*."

Vivian was so busy wondering why they'd referred to Jude as Cartaphilus that she nearly overlooked the significance of Michael's words.

"*A* ticket?" she interjected. "Whoa, hold on. I'm not going alone. No way."

"Look, you'll be fine. We'll arrange—"

"I'm *not* going alone. Forget it! You know I'll never make it alone out there. I don't even know how anything *works* anymore. And I'm not just talking about machinery."

Michael attempted to match her gaze, but his glower faded after only a moment.

"Fine. Lukas, check that. Get me two tickets."

"Who will the other be for?" Lukas asked.

Michael's steely gaze bore into hers. "Me." He pivoted, his eyes shooting around the apartment. "Where's Gina?"

"Back here!" sang a voice. "In the kitchen!"

Michael strode to the kitchen, where Vivian heard him bark, "We need your keys. Now."

"Hold on, I'm coming with," Gina replied as she licked the last of a pastry from her fingers.

The three drove south to the local shopping mall and parked in one of the first slots outside a department store. Michael's flashy Mitsubishi was the only car around, which made Vivian nervous. There was no doubt that what they were about to do was illegal, and she guessed she was due for her luck to run out. After all, she had managed to survive so far.

Michael scanned the area and motioned with a nod for them to follow. They sprinted from the car to the door, at which point Gina produced a large key ring and inserted the proper key.

They dashed inside like the criminals they were. Gina locked the door swiftly behind them and punched a sequence of numbers into the alarm pad with experienced ease. The pad beeped, and the light changed from red to green. They were in, and none too soon. A white Jeep Cherokee with "Mall Security" emblazoned on the door in turquoise blue letters drove by only seconds later.

"Mall security doesn't check inside the department stores. They only roam the halls," Gina explained as she reached under the checkout counter to collect a handful of large plastic bags. "Whenever we need things like clothes or kitchen stuff, we come here. Saves us having to go out during the day when it's less healthy for us." She handed Vivian several of the bags and gave the rest to Michael.

"How'd you get the keys?" Vivian asked.

"I bit the manager and stole his spare set while he slept," Gina laughed. "He was sooo cute. But dumb. He not only told me that they don't run the cameras at night but that he set up the code as the last four numbers of his phone number, which he gave to me that night. He'll probably just think he lost the keys. He's not the brightest color in the crayon box."

They quickly collected luggage, clothes, and other essentials for the trip. Since Vivian had no idea where she was headed, she tried to grab a selection of clothes that could be layered for warmth if necessary. She took a pair of comfortable running shoes, a heavy black jacket, and some toiletries, including several bottles of sunblock from the make-up counter. She met Michael and Gina at the door in less than forty-five minutes.

Michael put his finger to his lips and brushed Vivian behind him as she came within reach. He and Gina were worriedly watching someone outside. A mall security truck had pulled up near Michael's car, and a slim-built security officer was peering around inside with a flashlight.

"Shit. Shit, shit, shit," Gina whispered. The mall cop strolled around the car with cocky steps, sticking his light into every window like a customer shopping at a car lot in the middle of the night.

"Damn mall cops," Michael said. "You'd think he believed he wore a badge. Doesn't he have doughnuts to eat somewhere?"

"No, Krispy Kreme saves those for the real cops," Gina quipped. "Don't worry. I got this. Let me hold your car keys for a second."

Gina righted herself from a crouch, accepted the keys that Michael grudgingly gave her, and unlocked the door. She strolled out as if she were the mall owner in for a late-night stroll. Her hips swung back and forth like a pendulum.

"Hey there," she drawled. "That's my car. Do ya like it?" The honey-sweet Savannah accent went to work immediately. The young cop blushed so red Vivian saw it from several meters away. Standing together in the quiet store, she and Michael listened as Gina slyly convinced the young night guard that she was a store employee checking to make sure she hadn't forgotten to lock the safe. She persuaded him to relax in the passenger's seat of Michael's auto while she showed him the car from the driver's side. The two of them disappeared from view.

"If she gets blood on my seats, I'm gonna kill her," Michael growled.

Gina's head and bloodstained lips bobbed up only moments later. The three of them removed the officer from the passenger seat, placed him into the backseat of his vehicle, and loaded their stolen goodies into Michael's trunk. The whole trip had taken less than an hour.

"Well, I guess it's time to see where our little unplanned vacation is taking us," Michael said. "Let's hope Lukas got us someplace nice."

C5   80

When they arrived at the house, Lukas was staring fixedly at his computer, set up on the desk in a living room corner.

"What's the word, Lukas?" Michael asked.

"First flight I could get was two electronic tickets, leaving at six twenty a.m. from Savannah International. You'll land in Newark and catch a connecting flight that arrives in Frankfurt. From there, you have a rental that you can take to the Weilerbach house. Secure, secluded, and, most importantly, a long way from here. Doyle said he can hook you up with military IDs once you get there."

"Good man," Michael responded with a pat on his son's shoulder. "What kind of car did you get?"

"Opel Astra," Lukas said. "It was all I could get on such short notice."

"Not bad," Michael said with a nod. "Vivian, go pack and don't forget your passport. Think cold weather. We're leaving here in half an hour."

"Oh, one more thing," Lukas said. "You should see this first."

Vivian and Michael came around to the desk.

Lukas pulled up what he called a website. It was for a small news publisher and contained several articles, but one headline dwarfed them all: "Young Woman Implicated in Assassination Attempt." Next to it was an unflattering artist's rendering of Vivian's face.

"How bad is it?" Michael asked, scowling as he scanned the article.

"Pretty bad. They're claiming that Vivian tried to kill some delegate from a foreign country and that she's part of a small-time terrorist group. The positive side is that this is not a well-known site, and the image is only an artist's sketch. The downside is that it's probably only a matter of hours before the *Shévet ha Dam* has it on CNN."

"Fuck. Well, we're going to have to risk it. Chances are, the story won't be hitting Savannah until later today. Better to leave this morning before the whole East Coast wakes up and sees her face over their morning coffee. By this time tomorrow, she won't be able to go anywhere without being spotted. They'll post her picture in every airport in the country."

Vivian shivered at the sight of her likeness on the screen.

The *Shévet ha Dam* had influences she hadn't grasped. They probably owned the website. What else did they control? Would anyone believe the phony story about her? The whole thing sounded ludicrous. The only person she wanted to hurt was Jude.

She saw Michael looking at her out of the corner of his eye, and she suspected that he had read her thoughts. She wondered if she could do the same.

Michael turned and looked at her full on. She looked back, genuinely *looked* back, burrowed through his eyes, and pried into his thoughts. She surprised herself at how easy it was, like diving headfirst into the deep end of a warm swimming pool and discovering she knew how to swim.

A vampire had stolen his wife from him when Lukas was only two. The killer had fed on Michael, drained his wife, and then gave him enough blood to live until sunrise. Then the vamp had left Michael for dead with Lukas sleeping by his side.

He had raised Lukas alone for years, all the time wondering what kind of life he was giving him. She saw how difficult it was to explain to a young Lukas why they'd had to move once Michael's appearance started to reveal his secret, why he was poles apart from other fathers, and—most problematic—why he refused to turn his son and force him to live a cursed life as an "immortal" who feared the sun.

Now she understood why he fought them so vigilantly. They'd shattered his existence, taken his wife, and forced him to watch his son grow up while he stayed young off the blood of humans. In all probability, he would have to watch his son die. He loathed them for that. And she knew that he felt she would help him achieve his objective, that she was key to the downfall of the *Shévet ha Dam.*

She left his mind. He blinked but otherwise appeared impassive.

"Better pack your bags," Michael murmured. "We've got a long way to go."

∛ ∜

Vivian tucked herself away in an upstairs bedroom and packed her stolen clothes and incidentals in one large suitcase. She dressed in a pair of comfortable blue jeans, a warm long-sleeve shirt, her jacket, and her new shoes. She checked her purse for her passport and made sure the velvet bag Beth gave her was still there.

She took in her surroundings with a sigh. The bedroom looked the way she would have decorated it if she lived there: knitted afghans, colorful flowers, like a young woman's room should be. She wondered if she would ever see it again. It was a shame she had to leave.

When she finished packing and made her way downstairs, Michael was set. Gina agreed to escort them to the airport. They put their suitcases in the trunk of Gina's car, and Michael drove, his grip whiteknuckled on the wheel the whole way. The night was almost over.

Vivian stared out the window at the bleak, fog-shrouded darkness in morose contemplation. She was exhausted, but her mind was running a marathon fueled by fear-induced adrenaline. Fifteen minutes into the trip, a gusty autumn rain began, somehow suited. Michael and Gina respected her silence and said nothing.

When they arrived at the airport, Michael steered the car through the tangle of streets and up the ramp to the second floor of the two-story red brick airport where friends and family dropped off departing travelers. They checked to make sure their passports were readily available, removed their luggage from the trunk, and said their goodbyes to Gina.

"You keep that boy of mine in line, OK?" Michael directed her. She nodded and wrapped her arms tightly around her friend as though she thought she might never see him again. Then she moved to Vivian, who accepted her embrace though it was accompanied by an expression that made Vivian feel guilty.

"You take care of him," Gina whispered. Vivian agreed without a word.

They collected their luggage and headed inside. Vivian took in the ambiance of the airport with detached indifference. Not even the technology amazed her anymore. Everything left her with a strange, dull feeling that she had lost something, and she was pretty sure it was her soul.

Michael guided her through procuring their tickets and checking their luggage with a fresh-scrubbed, robust woman behind the counter. Vivian noticed that his passport was under the name Dillon Moriarty. He kept up a friendly dialogue as the agent processed their tickets. Vivian neglected to contribute.

After receiving the boarding passes, she and Michael walked toward the center, where various small, cozy-looking restaurants circled a large old-fashioned clock. Travelers relaxed on park benches around it, reading or talking with other vacationers. The atmosphere had been arranged to give it an outdoorsy feel. Only one restaurant was open at this hour, but she heard voices of cooks preparing for the busy morning in all of them.

How long before we're safe? What if that crazy news story becomes widespread before we board the plane? Although she and Michael were the only ones of their kind there, she felt wary of everyone now. Every person who passed looked menacing. Even the humans were a potential threat. It was one thing to suspect that Jude would come for her—she was prepared for that. It was another to grasp his ability to harness the potential of hundreds, maybe thousands, of others.

"Coffee?" Michael asked. Vivian grimaced.

"You don't have to drink it. We can sit over a steamy cup and talk," he said encouragingly. She shrugged.

They ordered coffee from the cafeteria-style restaurant and sat down in a booth. Michael was right; the smell of coffee was scrumptious, even if it had no flavor.

"Where are we going?" she asked once she found her voice.

"Germany."

Vivian's eyes grew large as eggs, and she nearly spilled her coffee when she jerked in astonishment.

"Which side?" she asked uneasily. Michael looked confused for a second and then laughed. Vivian wasn't amused.

"No, no, no. Germany is one country, a republic. The wall came down around 1990, and the US hasn't had problems with them for years and years. It's safe, I assure you."

"Germany's... cool?" she asked, struggling to use a portion of the vernacular she had picked up. Michael bobbed his head to affirm her guess.

"Very cool. I think you'll like it. It's quaint, very clean, and the people are nice. You'll be safe there. *We'll* be safe there," he corrected himself. He cocked his ears toward a speaker to hear what was playing overhead and tapped his fingertips on the table in time.

She smiled. Passenger jets were new in the 1940s, and the idea of boarding one made her nervous—going to a new country only doubled her worries. But Michael was, without a doubt, the most charismatic person she had ever met. Even more suave than Jude, who'd swept her off her feet decades ago with a dance and an expensive, fancy date. She felt caught up in his enthusiasm, that the weights anchoring down her psyche were slowly letting go.

After staring at their coffee and exchanging lighthearted conversation for about half an hour, they did a little shopping in the souvenir store. They stocked up on what Michael called "time-killing apparatus," incidentals like books, magazines, and puzzles. The magazines were for Vivian, to get her caught up on the latest "paparazzi bullshit."

Michael explained the procedure for clearing the metal detectors as they moved toward the terminals. Although he insisted it was nothing to worry about, she still felt nervous under the scrutiny. She was more worried about boarding the plane when Michael told her that the purpose of the detectors was to ensure no weapons made it aboard. Her stomach was a flurry of butterflies as they walked the jetway to the airplane.

They sat in a row of uncomfortable metal chairs with pancake-thin cushions near their gate. Putting the glossy magazines to the side, Vivian tried to absorb herself in a novel. It helped to take her mind off her problem, but she still found herself looking around for an evil pair of eyes glowering at her with the intent of killing her, or maybe another vampire assassin sent by Jude. What would she do if someone spotted her? What if one of the humans thought she was a terrorist?

"Don't think about it," Michael admonished from the seat next to her. He hadn't read her mind, and yet he had. Vivian bit her lip nervously, cautious not to expose her eyeteeth.

"I can't help it," she said. "I've never been through anything like this before."

"Well, you've never been to Germany. Think about that," he offered. It was helpful advice, and she did.

Shortly before six, Michael handed her a tube of sunblock and directed her to cover all of her exposed skin. When she finished, he did the same. If anyone in the terminal thought what they were doing was odd, they didn't show it.

She fidgeted on the narrow cushion. Her knees bounced up and down with impatience. Michael rested his hand on her knee in a fatherly fashion, his look pleading with her to stop. She tried to read again but lost her place too often when her eyes scanned the lines as her mind wandered. Her eyes drifted from the book to the clock on the wall that was creeping all too slowly. She removed her tickets from their resting place in the rear of her novel, checked the departure time for the umpteenth time, pulled her passport out, opened and read it. Time moved so slowly she thought the clocks must have been stung with a tranquilizer dart.

"Attention, Continental Airlines flight 3596 with nonstop service to Newark International Airport will now begin boarding at Gate 2..."

"That's us," Michael said. He stood up and stretched, and Vivian followed suit. The flight attendant droned through a well-rehearsed speech regarding people with special needs and families with small children. Before long, they were aboard the plane, leaving the only country Vivian remembered.

Chapter 20

Vivian tried to settle in on the flight from Newark to Frankfurt without much success. It had hit home that she was leaving the US when the instructions for flight safety continued in German. She thought of a few questions she wanted to ask about international travel, but Michael, unfortunately, had wasted no time falling asleep once the plane reached thirty thousand feet and was unavailable for consultation. She struggled to watch a movie on the tiny seat-mounted screen but could not work out how to hear it. She made an effort to read her book again, but the turbulence made her queasy.

She resigned herself to sleeping, but had a hard time settling down. Her stomach lurched with every dip as the jet rode the air currents, and the thought of spending hours flying over the ocean with no land for miles and miles disturbed her. Nevertheless, exhaustion, triggered by the flurry of the past few days, finally set in, and her eyes closed as the plane flew over the vast Atlantic.

 CB BD

She's leaving. Excellent. Looks like my suggestion to advertise her departure with the news media may have helped.

Maysun felt Jerusha's parting in the rising airplane as a lurch in her stomach. She clenched her jaw against the impression that she was going through a swift ascent. Maysun hated flying unless it was under her power.

And Jude thinks she's in Savannah. Even better. Now to stir up things a little more.

Maysun smiled an angelic, bright, white smile and reached for Jude's sociopathic right-hand man, Charles Dunning.

"Attention passengers, the pilot has lit the fasten seat belt sign as we begin our final approach of the Frankfurt Am Main Airport. Please lock your trays and return your seats to the full, upright position..." The flight attendant continued with instructions in both languages. The plane was about to land.

When the fasten seat belt light switched off, she and Michael stood. He took her hand protectively and led her past the herd of people dislodging their carry-on bags.

They followed the crowd through the massive airport. Frankfurt Am Main would have been a glorious airport if it weren't so dreary. Unfortunately, it was almost clinical in its drabness. Everything was in tones of grey, from the flecked floor to the grey scaffolding ceiling stories above their heads like drably-painted dinosaur bones. The only relief was the brightly lit blue directional signs and the occasional green exit sign depicting a person running to a door.

Michael directed Vivian through the passport checkpoint with its austere attendants and down the escalator to the baggage claim. She tried to read the colorful billboards above the baggage carousel. Some were easier than others. She knew what Lucky Strikes and American Express were, but the German ones baffled her.

"This way. He's meeting us here."

Vivian didn't ask who this friend was, but she wished she had when they cleared the glass doors leading through customs to the reception area. The bulky jacket concealed his slender frame, and the rectangular sunglasses hid his piercing blue eyes. He still had his bald head. Michael's German contact was none other than Jude's friend David, the man she had seen in her dream.

❧　☙

She choked back a scream. Her voice babbled a steady stream of random words, and none made any sense. All that came out were garbled, vague whimpers and half-structured sentences as Michael continued walking the short distance in David's direction. The small group of folks waiting for disembarking passengers waited behind a fat velvet rope. Not much of a barricade for anyone on a mission to kill.

She had to act fast. The waiting area was only about fifteen steps long, and they were closing in quickly. David expressed no shock at seeing her, if he had noticed her at all. She grasped the sleeve of Michael's jacket firmly, but when he turned to look at her, all she uttered was an unintelligible stammer.

"Michael... I... he's..."

"It's OK," he said reassuringly, but Vivian wasn't convinced. She knew that David was *not* OK, he was in thick with Jude, and she did not intend to let him help her. He would tell Jude where she was, and then Jude would find her again with no effort at all. She had to take action to protect herself against him, and if that meant leaving Michael, so be it. She would not endanger him to save herself. She had to get away.

She decided a split second before she reacted. She released her hold on Michael's sleeve, dropped her bag, whipped around, and ran back in the direction they'd come, jostling travelers out of her way in her haste. She ignored their indignant looks, ignored Michael's voice beckoning her to come back, and reached for the door...

At first, she thought someone had pushed the door from the inside. She prepared herself to weave around someone as they came through, but no one was there. The door had leaped into her hand, which was just as well: there was no handle on her side. Vivian was stunned.

Did I do that?

The brief pause was all Michael needed to catch up. He grasped her firmly around the shoulders and forced her to turn around and face him. His voice droned with crazy talk about David, who he was calling Doyle, how he was there to help them while they were in Germany. She was so frightened none of his jabbering sank in. She wouldn't let him look her in the eyes, wouldn't let him tell her that it was fine. She knew that David, or Doyle, or *whoever* he said he was, was one of Jude's cronies. She *remembered*. She remembered being trapped for decades, recalled how she existed for years to satisfy Jude's sick whims, remembered how Jude had *used* her, *lied* to her. And this "friend" of his, this *vampire*, had helped him!

Her breath came in shallow gulps as Michael tried to console her, his soothing words unable to penetrate her fright and desperation. He hadn't figured out what had triggered her, exactly, and had assumed that seeing a vampire as soon as they'd disembarked the plane had meant the *Shévet ha Dam* had found her. But it had. Didn't he know that? She wanted to grab him and run. Was David—Doyle—thinking Michael was a threat, too?

She tried to maintain a façade of calm, attempted to hide what she was considering—anything to get moving. People looked too intently at them.

Her plan wasn't much, but it was all she had.

She relaxed her breathing until it no longer bordered on hyperventilation. As Michael loosened his grip, she coaxed his hands down from their firm post on her shoulders. She covered Michael's hands with hers, behaving as though she had come to her senses and praying he wasn't prodding her mind for answers. She was aware her eyes still darted around like a caged animal that had been prodded too many times, but either Michael didn't notice, or he believed her other actions more than her eyes. When she was confident he was convinced she was okay, she put her hands squarely on his chest and shoved him.

The thrust didn't need much effort, and it achieved much more than she had hoped. Michael flew nearly four feet before colliding with Doyle, taking the velvet rope down behind them as they fell. The look on his face would have been comical if not for the circumstances—a combination of surprise and what might have been pride. She had caught them both off guard, and they fell like toppled trees.

Vivian pivoted around and dashed for the door again, covering the distance in two steps. Her way cleared easily. The handful of people who saw her display of strength and frantic behavior wanted no contact with her. The handle didn't leap into her hands as it had before. She grabbed it from someone's hand as they passed through and jerked it open to enter the spacious customs and baggage claim area beyond.

You have no plan... you have no plan. Where are you going to hide? They'll know where you are. Doyle might be able to read your thoughts. Her feet kept running no matter what her mind told her. She would not let her pessimism keep her from trying. As long as she put distance between herself and Doyle, she could worry about a plan later. She didn't turn around to see if they were in pursuit; she had no doubt they were. She could practically smell them.

She picked up momentum. Running was effortless. Her feet moved at superhuman speed. Her visual acuity swelled with her increase in pace. Her breath came easily, as if she was out for a brisk walk. She zigzagged around pedestrians in an attempt to dislodge Michael and Doyle's visual lock on her. In her rush to escape, she captured the glance of everyone she passed, including that of a woman in a green uniform with *Polizei* stitched on the vest. She did not need a translator to understand that, or to interpret the stern tone the officer used as she called into the device mounted to her vest.

Vivian tried to block her pursuer's view of her by ducking behind a large, dark-skinned family. A man, presumably the father, was barking orders to his highly vocal, argumentative relations.

She circled to the backside of the group unnoticed and tried to keep her back close to the wall so she could locate Michael and Doyle without fear of them coming up behind her. Unfortunately, the family was tall and impossible to see over.

To the right, a women's restroom was down a corridor and semi-hidden. Perfect. She hurried down the passage and entered the brightly lit lavatory. It was small, drab, and divided into separate toilet and hand-washing areas by a heavy door. There was an oblong mirror over the sink, and only five stalls. Five vacant stalls. She was alone, but for how long?

She didn't know she had been holding her breath until it burst out in one large exhale. She looked around for a window, a large ventilation shaft, anything that would provide her with an escape route besides the door. There was nothing. But the stall doors reached nearly to the floor.

She knew that it was a ridiculous measure considering the nature of her trackers, but she pulled the door closed behind her. She fumbled with the flimsy, unfamiliar lock until it was secure, which wasn't saying much. She sat on the commode, put her face in her hands, and prepared to wait. She guessed if they knew she was in here, they'd appear shortly. If they didn't know she was hiding in the women's room, it was an ad-equate hiding place until they gave up on her. *If* they gave up on her.

Vivian cleared her head and focused on black space, hoping that do-ing so would give Doyle nothing to home in on. She hated knowing that he might be telepathic.

She heard women come in and out to use the restroom and tried to block the distinctive bathroom sounds out. She contemplated her shoes, the white-black-grey flecked tile, anything mind-numbing and dull to keep any mind-readers from discerning where she was.

Time passed. She waited for what felt like hours, but knew that her concept of time was distorted after a long flight, lack of blood, and a heavy dose of fear and paranoia. She had no watch to keep track of the passing minutes. The absence of a timepiece on her wrist made the fact she had abandoned everything she owned firmer. And not just every-thing she owned. She had left the only person who she was starting to trust. She wondered what Michael thought of her now.

Are they still after me? How would I be able to tell? She didn't know how to judge if they were still in pursuit. That was the most disturbing part of waiting. She knew it was likely they were hunting for her, but had no clue what they were doing or where they were. With a bit of luck, they had no idea what she was doing, either.

She tried to formulate a plan to keep herself alert. *If it's daylight, I'll stay hidden in the airport until dark, and then... then I'll drain someone and steal their car. No, I don't know how to drive here. Do they drive on the other side of the road? Or maybe that's just England. Hell, I can't speak German, much less read the road signs. OK, bad idea. What else can I do?*

Gradually the traffic in and out of the bathroom subsided. Vivian supposed that there might be a lull in air travel during nighttime or between busier flights. *It should be safe to leave the airport, right? Please, God, let it be safe.*

She was starting to feel spacey. At the very least, she needed blood before leaving the airport. She knew it was beyond time to leave and find sustenance when she found herself drifting off to sleep with her head cradled in her hands.

She took a deep breath and unlocked the flimsy catch on the stall, cracked the door, and peeked out. All the stall doors were open, and the stalls were empty. She was alone. She released her breath in an exhausted sigh.

She crossed the narrow bathroom and stood in front of the sink. The faucets were unlike any she had seen before and took a little figuring out, but soon she was splashing cold water on her face. It revived her, but water wasn't what she needed.

She tried the water again. This time as she bent down, a cold hand grabbed her wrist firmly from behind and pinned it behind her back. She stood up and saw Doyle's reflection staring back at her from the mirror. He looked furious.

"Whatever you do, don't scream," he snarled.

Chapter 21

Jude descended onto Victory drive as a pearlescent fog that coalesced into flesh and blood when the roads were bare. He set his polished black shoes onto the sidewalk and strolled west as his mind reached out for a dark being familiar with the target of his search. He found one and adjusted his course.

He only closed his eyes for a moment, but that was all it took for the final ephemeral thought of the Renfield, Jacob, to resurface. He had engraved the image in his mind; it was his most recent clue to the whereabouts of that insolent bitch, Vivian. White Bluff Road. He knew it was only a few miles away, and that she wasn't there now. His best course of action was to follow this lead. All the better to surprise her.

He tried to focus on Vivian. She had to be close—he knew this with a bit of personal effort and help from the *Shévet ha Dam*—which should have made it simpler. Yet, she eluded them.

He cursed under his breath. *She must have discovered how to block. She's learning fast. Too fast. This could be dangerous.* His pace quickened, but he didn't notice.

For two millennia, Jude had been unafraid of anything. His power had been substantial at first, and had only grown stronger through the centuries. So had his confidence. Two thousand years of corruption and death, and he could not be happier. How many vampires had he created? Hundreds? Thousands? Enough to populate a small country with generations of his offspring. He believed that Yeshua had made an enormous error. Cursing the man he had been—Joseph Cartaphilus—to walk the earth until Armageddon had had the opposite effect from the one Yeshua had planned. Jude had no reason to believe he would die, or that the world would end. Until now.

I still don't understand how she got away. I know I left her weakened. She should not have been able to walk—much less made it past sunrise.

The *Shévet ha Dam* had made little progress in tracking her down. Jude had learned about a stir among the Savannah small group—a party—which tied in with the impression he had received. They would find her soon, and he would kill her in front of the entire Table. She had gone too far.

You'd better kill her this time. You know you're losing control where she's concerned. Why in the hell else did you take her so quickly last time? And you didn't let her awaken for fifty years.

You didn't let *her awaken at all.*

He squelched the thought. The land below flew by at a comfortable pace. While his mind was preoccupied, his body had assumed control and brought him to his search's focal point. His feet touched down in the sand outside a grubby two-story, redbrick house. He inhaled deeply as his eyes darted around as quickly as a fly, taking in everything from the sandy driveway to the collapsing porch.

She had been here. He felt her in the very air he breathed.

He took the failing stairs and pondered the identical doors a moment before choosing the one on the left. The lock released effortlessly under his grip. He climbed the stairs, assimilating himself to the area, the smells of mold, beer, stale cigarette smoke, the worn green carpet covering the steps, the chipped paint, and jasmine. Something smelled delightfully of jasmine. A second door at the top of the stairs also accepted his grip as a key, and he entered a grimy apartment.

"Lukas? Is that you?" a surprised voice asked.

He scanned her mind rapidly and found the expected vocal fluctuation, tone, and phraseology.

"Yeah, it's me," he replied in a voice matching whoever Lukas was. He heard the rattle of cans and bottles inside a plastic bag coming from the other room. Evidently, the unseen female had decided to clean the filthy place up a bit.

He walked through the kitchen and entered the living room. He heard and sensed no one else in the apartment but the jasmine-scented woman. She had her well-shaped backside turned toward him as she stooped to collect the bottles in front of her.

He crossed the room and trapped her in his arms before she had a chance to turn around. He sensed her confusion, the brief exhilaration, then the fear as she recognized that he wasn't the man she expected. His powerful hands on her slender arms were more than enough to hold her in place. Though she, too, was a vampire, he was profoundly stronger. He spun her around. The fear on her face was beautiful.

"I need to ask you some questions," he said, "and I know you have the answers, so don't try any of that 'I-don't-know' nonsense, OK?" Her lustrous blonde hair waved as she shook her head violently up and down. Her brown eyes, enormous to begin with, looked to be on the verge of bugging out of her head as she took in his features—his eyes, lips, jaw, and chest. He also noticed that she wasn't wearing a bra. Her large nipples pointed in sharp contrast to the soft curves that comprised the rest of her body. Was she cold? He became aroused. If she noticed, she wasn't distressed by the complication.

First business. Then pleasure. He could have prodded her mind for the information, but this was much more fun.

"What is your name?"

"Va-Virginia." She paused. "Everyone calls me Gina."

"You have a new little friend, don't you, Gina?" he asked in a sweet growl. Her eyes flickered to one side for a moment as she contemplated a lie, but whatever she dreamed up died with his vice-like clamp on her tiny arms.

"Y-yes." But she offered no more than that.

"Vivian Black?"

"I... I don't know her last name." Jude gave her a demoniacal look that would have withered an oak.

"Where is she?" His voice was too calm, unsettling, and it had the desired effect.

"She... she's gone. She l-left town."

He blinked. *She isn't blocking—she ran. Why hadn't I considered that?* But he knew why. This was supposed to be simple. He had taken significant steps to ensure she could barely think, much less walk, talk, or escape. She wasn't supposed to be able to envision life without him, existing on her own. But she had. He had assumed that if Vivian found somewhere she felt was safe, she would sit there, helpless, until he arrived to take her back.

But you knew better than that. She kicked you out of her mind mere hours after she had escaped from your crypt, you idiot! She astral projected herself into your little meeting. And she knows you're after her, along with all of your little friends. And now she's gotten away again!

But did that matter? No matter where she went, the *Shévet ha Dam* was close. Every vampire across the globe was a part of it, whether they knew it or not.

"*Where?*" he commanded.

"They didn't say. They left yesterday—" Gina caught herself in the slip and bit her lip.

"They? Did someone go with her? Who?" *And why does that piss me off?* He slipped his hands to her wrists, gave her arm a little twist to convince her of the gravity of her predicament. She winced and moaned in pain, and Jude felt his erection harden. She wasn't thinking about fighting back; he would have felt it if she was. She believed that her life hinged on her ability to satisfy his curiosity.

"Michael. She left with Michael." It was barely a whisper.

She left with someone named Michael. Who in the hell is Michael?

She said no more, and Jude presumed it was because she only knew his first name. It didn't matter. He had faith in the *Shévet ha Dam.* If it meant tracking every Michael on earth, they would find him.

"Do you know how to reach them?"

Gina shook her head regretfully, beautiful eyes downcast. Her large breasts swung in an unintentionally seductive way.

"Do you know someone who does?"

At this, she hesitated, and her eyes remained turned away from him. Her lack of response said volumes.

"Look at me," he ordered. Her eyes slowly turned upward, shining with tears. Her bottom lip trembled. He could hardly wait to finish the interrogation. His erection was so hard it was painful. He remembered the name she had used when he arrived.

"Lukas? Is it Lukas?"

She swallowed hard and said nothing. He drew back a hand and slapped her left cheek. She fell to the floor with a choked cry, hands flying to her face. The blush where his hand connected was faint, his handprint barely perceptible despite the force he had used.

She hasn't fed tonight. She's young and weak.

"You need blood, don't you?' he crooned. "You're feeling tired." His hands went to work as his voice soothed and mesmerized her. He tore her shirt off as easily as shredding paper. Her breasts hung heavily on her chest, and her torso was darkly tanned. He noted the navel piercing with amusement.

"I can help you," he murmured as his finger traced a path along her jawline. "If you take only a sip of me, you'd be stronger than you can imagine." *And you would be mine.* He cut a small gash in his forearm with his index fingernail and dangled the bleeding limb in front of Gina. Her faraway eyes grew large, and her gaping expression reflected her hunger. His hypnotic voice took effect, and the smell of his blood, irresistible to vampires, reached her. She hesitated only a moment before accepting, gripping his arm as if it was the only thing saving her from falling from a cliff.

"That's right," Jude said, crouching next to her as she sipped. His hand encircled her right breast and flicked the nipple. She barely noticed as he single-handedly unclasped his pants and withdrew his hardened member. He withdrew his arm from her desperate grasp, but it was enough. She was hooked. Her expression was that of a junkie denied a needle full of their substance of choice.

"Do you want more?" he asked tauntingly. She nodded, all thought fleeing in a desperate attempt to get more of the newfound drug, this powerful chemical in his veins.

"Not yet," he said, his voice deep and soothing. He turned her onto all fours and unfastened her pants with experienced ease. He yanked them down around her hips to her knees and found her feminine parts were swollen and wet. His blood had aroused her as she fed. He slipped a finger in, then a second. Gina groaned.

Perhaps it was because he knew he was befouling someone who had helped Vivian escape, but he had no patience for foreplay. He pulled her hips roughly toward him and thrust his cock inside. Then again. And again. Gina cried out. He didn't know if it was from pleasure, pain, or fear, and he did not care. He gripped her hips aggressively and pulled them forcefully to him with a fierce rhythm until he could not hold back any longer, and he exploded inside.

Finished, he pushed her over and pulled his pants back over his cock. Gina looked at him plaintively; a junkie denied her fix. Her gaze went from the front of his pants to his dripping forearm and back.

She wants both again, he thought with a satisfied smirk. Sometimes being the father of all things evil had its benefits. His blood could turn even another vampire into a sniveling Renfield.

"Want more?" he asked. Her eyes went from his arm to his cock again, unsure which he referred to and ultimately not caring which he meant. She nodded and reached for him, weak with need. He knocked her hand from his arm and then from the fastener of his pants. She sat down hard, her eyes filling with tears.

"I'll give you more of both, love, but I need something from you first. Here's what you're going to do..."

Chapter 22

Screaming wasn't what Vivian had in mind. Fear made her oblivious to the pain Doyle inflicted. She didn't care if she broke her arms off to get away. Spinning around with more fury than a cyclone, she caught him on the defensive and pushed him forcefully away from her. He broke a stall door, fell into the stall, and wound up straddling a commode hitting his head on the tile behind him. She didn't stick around to ensure he was unconscious. He was a vampire. His injuries wouldn't last long.

She cleared the tiny bathroom in three long strides and burst out the door.

Without warning, Michael appeared at her side and firmly grasped her arm. With his touch came a mental message as audible to her as if he had spoken: *Don't worry. He's on our side.*

A jumble of thoughts went through her head at once. How much the world had changed since she was last aware. Everything around her had evolved: cars, music, telephones that did not plug into walls. Things existed now that hadn't been conceived of fifty years ago. The US had established civil rights. The country she stood in had united only a handful of years ago. Was it plausible that Doyle had changed too?

Can a leopard change its spots? Or even more difficult, could a friend of Jude's?

Michael raised one dark eyebrow in her direction and gave her an unsteady smile. She gave in, or at least deigned to be coerced for now. Michael could convince a queen into handing over her throne. *But if Doyle gives me one good reason to doubt his intentions, I'll kill him. I'll never go back to what I was. Not for anyone.*

Two women entered the restroom and came out frantically muttering in a language Vivian didn't understand. Translation wasn't necessary.

"I'll get him," Vivian offered and strode off before Michael said anything.

She entered the women's room and found Doyle sitting where she had left him. His head was in his hands, and he appeared to be wincing.

"Sorry," Vivian said without feeling.

"Goddamn it, woman, when you push, you *push,* don't you?"

"I um... I thought you were a friend of someone I don't trust," she explained.

"Jude. Well, he went by Jude to me and quite a few others. You, I suspect. Lord knows how many names he's had over the years." Another woman entered the restroom and, unperturbed by the male voice, went about her business unburdening her bladder. "I don't see him too often these days. By choice. I'll explain it all on the way, if you don't mind waiting until then."

Vivian nodded and offered him a hand. Doyle shook it and then used it to help himself up.

They gathered their bags—which Michael had collected while they waited for her to emerge from hiding—and headed out to a multilevel parking area by way of an elevator. Vivian kept a wary eye out for the polizei, but their efforts must have been called off when she had hidden in the restroom.

It was disturbing to Vivian not to be able to read the signs as they headed to the car. A portion of them were obvious, but other meanings eluded her. For instance, *Ausgang,* hung on the wall pointing in a direction, but to what she didn't know, and another door was labeled *DRÜCKEN.* Illustrations didn't accompany these signs, and she hated not knowing what simple instructions meant.

They paid for parking and settled the luggage into the tiny rental car. Doyle took a moment to apply a liberal amount of sunblock, sunglasses, and a hat. Michael also covered his pale exposed skin with a visor, sunglasses, and another layer of sunscreen. Vivian noticed that both of them looked like they'd spent an unplanned day at the beach. Their complexions glowed pink, and fair-skinned Doyle was peeling. She looked at her skin and wondered why she alone was unblemished. Doyle looked at Michael and glanced at Vivian, who had only put on sunscreen because the others had.

"Ready?" Doyle asked. He peered resentfully from the underground parking space at the bright sun beyond. Michael nodded. Doyle did not bother to confirm Vivian's vote before he steered the car out of the parking lot.

She spitefully wished she had hidden a little longer. If she had come out from hiding three hours later, the sun would have been at its peak. She glared at Doyle's peeling neck. If he was still friends with the *Shévet ha Dam,* why didn't he have photoprotection?

Vivian's first impression of the autobahn was that most of the cars careened down its roads as if they were shot from a wobbly cannon. Doyle joined them confidently, weaving in and out of traffic as swiftly as a land-bound jet.

Vivian hunkered down in the backseat and tried to pay attention—when she wasn't cringing at the many near-miss traffic accidents—as Doyle chain-smoked cigarettes and babbled over the radio. Doyle had worked hand in hand with the *Shévet ha Dam* at one time, he said, but had left their employment fifteen years ago. His job had been to slip other vampires into human society through job placement, name changes, relocation, and so on. Through the *Shévet ha Dam*, he provided them with money, identification, housing, and other basic needs. He made personal deliveries when trust was a concern from time to time, but those were rare. He had been second in command for US relocation, directly under a vampire who then went by the name of Charles Dunning. To his knowledge, Charles still sat in on The Table.

The Table, Vivian learned, was an expression for the selected members who ran the *Shévet ha Dam* at its highest level. It consisted of an elite group of twenty, plus Jude, who met to discuss influential subjects on occasion.

That sounds like my dreams, the personal deliveries, all those vampires around a table. It must have really taken place.

Doyle went on to say that he had gotten tired of all the politics involved with the Tribe, not to mention his dislike of the way they treated humans like cattle in a slaughterhouse. He said he had backed out of his job, pleading mental exhaustion. It seemed the most plausible excuse, he claimed.

"I'm still close to Charles and a few others. I've always found it a good idea to live by that saying, 'Keep your friends close, and your enemies closer.' Who said that first? The Godfather?"

"I prefer Sun Tzu," Michael said.

"Who?"

"*The Art of War?* 'If you know the enemy and know yourself, your victory will not stand in doubt; if you know Heaven and know Earth, you may make your victory complete.'"

"Yeahyeahyeah," Doyle said dismissively. Vivian already noticed that one of Doyle's annoying habits was repeating words three times in close succession. "Well, it's a great saying, whoever said it. And true, too. It's always a good idea to know where your enemies are."

Is that why you're helping us? Vivian thought. *So the* Shévet ha Dam *knows where* its *enemies are?*

Doyle continued babbling, but Vivian tuned him out. By now, she had decided he was a manipulative, faithless blowhard, but if Michael found him helpful, she would use him, too. But no matter how necessary he was, she would not trust him. Who would turn his back on the *Shévet ha Dam* after being a vital member? It didn't add up. Doyle was about as steady as quicksand.

As Doyle continued his self-adulatory tirade, which involved knowledge about anything from German traffic laws to the upcoming Euro currency, she stared out the windows.

Daylight arrived quickly, and with it came vibrant color. Bright fall hues painted the fields. Rounded grey and blue mountains loomed distantly, topped by tall, white windmills, their triad arms rotating in the gusts circling the peaks. Hills and valleys swelled and dipped, and the autobahn curved to accommodate them. The land was a stunning quilt of vineyards and fields. Groves of trees came to dramatic stops where towns began, and more than one village wound down the side of a hill.

The architecture reminded Vivian of fairy tales. Homes were cinder block and stucco, often white, but sometimes earthy hues, with red or brown tile roofs. Although it was autumn, windowsills boasted flower boxes with bright flowers.

Doyle swerved off the autobahn and never stopped talking.

Here, towns and countryside merged. Clusters of houses ended in fields or pastures with horses or cattle. Streets intertwined with no noticeable pattern. It felt to Vivian that they drove in circles, except the scenery kept changing.

Doyle turned off a primary road into a small neighborhood. The road, barely wide enough for two cars, wound up a large hill and past a small fountain. At the top of the hill, Doyle pulled into a drive barely long enough to accommodate a car.

"Need any help?" Doyle offered.

"Sure," Michael accepted. "I need to ask you a couple of questions, anyway. Come on in."

They gathered their bags, and Vivian followed as they backtracked down the sidewalk to the gate.

She hadn't gotten a good look at the house from the road. White, one story, with a brown tile roof, it resembled many German homes. The walkway led under an impressive ivy-covered lattice at least ten feet tall. Some of the leaves were as big as her hand. Tall evergreen trees lined the walkway. To her right was a small garden, not in bloom, but a garden gnome stood proudly among the withered plants. Three small rosebushes dotted the yard. Along the porch, planters held shrubbery growing with healthy abandon. A five-foot-tall rosebush jutted from the planter, held in place by an ivy-laced trellis.

The men continued into the house. Michael was asking Doyle about obtaining new identification cards, and could he get them some military ID so they could go to the Air Force base and enjoy some entertainment where English was spoken? Doyle said it shouldn't be a problem and asked for a method to reach Lukas to match up the IDs Lukas had made.

The three walked through a closet-sized entryway into a large foyer, where Doyle and Michael set the bags onto the floor. Vivian waited a moment to see if Michael would offer her a tour. When his conversation continued, she proceeded alone.

The first two rooms to her right were small, square, and beige. One was an office, the other a spare room filled with individually labeled boxes. The master bedroom was comfortable, with lush grey carpet and grey and steel-blue wallpaper. The furniture was cherry, and touches of gold were everywhere, from the clock to the silk comforter.

She wandered alone through the house, which was surprisingly homey for what was clearly a gentleman's retreat. Brown tile, beige carpet, and colors of brick, green, and gold gave the house a relaxed but carefully decorated feel.

She paused after she followed the dining room into a family room. Not as large as the bedroom, perhaps fourteen by sixteen, it made up for its smaller size in ornamentation. On the right was a large sandstone fireplace. On the mantel stood various statues and works of religious art. In the very center was an eighteen-inch statue of Shiva, to his right, the head of the Green Man. To Shiva's left, statues of Anubis, Toth, and Horus, and a fat, smiling Buddha. Ahead was a picture window. Brick red velvet curtains hung from golden hooks with matching tassels. Next to the curtains hung a painting of the mythical Icarus after his fatal fall.

She left the family room and walked to the living room. The dark green couch was comfy. A rustic golden oak armoire across from the sofa held a television and stereo, and next to the armoire, a matching stand had a plethora of CDs.

She reentered the foyer and was about to see what room lay behind yet another door when Michael stopped her.

"That's the basement," he said. Doyle had taken his leave during her exploration of the house.

"There's a basement, too?"

He nodded, and an amused smile crossed his face. "Washer and dryer, paneling, tile. Dartboard." He grasped her hand and led her to the couch.

"Now, let me show you one of the things I love so much about Germany," he said. At the window, he loosened a cord that looped through a hole in the wall. Heavy blinds, constructed of plastic and aluminum and built into the window frame outside, rumbled down on tracks. Once shut, they let in not a splinter of light. It reminded Vivian of the lines from *Romeo and Juliet: Away from the light steals home my heavy son, And private in his chamber pens himself, Shuts up his windows, locks fair daylight out, And makes himself an artificial night.*

"All the windows have them. So, we can be out of bed whenever we want, and we don't have to worry about sunblock as long as we stay inside. Pretty cool, huh?"

Together, they lowered all the blinds in the house and met back in the living room. She reclined on the sofa, this time with Michael by her side in the dark.

"How do you feel?" he asked.

"About what?"

"About being here. About the house. Can you feel Jude reaching for you?"

"No, not at all." She looked from the textured white wallpaper to her fingernails, which were too long again. Michael rested his feet on the sturdy coffee table. She ran her tongue over her pointed eyeteeth and wished she had something—someone—to bite. How long would she have to wait before they hunted again? Concern shadowed Michael's face, and he leaned forward and put his hand on her knee.

"What's wrong?"

"Nothing. Everything. Oh, hell, where do I start?" She rolled her eyes in frustration and searched for the right words. She knew she needed blood when her thoughts became as muddled as this. She picked a piece of lint from her jeans and sighed.

"I know that my life can't go on with any real quality until I face Jude," she explained, "And I don't know what tools I need to face him. I don't know what it's like to be a vampire or anything about fighting. I've been a wimp, and suddenly I find myself running for the life I *do* have, which is, as I pointed out, completely unfamiliar. And to top that off, I don't know a damn thing about how the world has changed in the last fifty years."

She stopped and took a breath. Michael cocked his head to the side.

"Are you finished?"

She nodded.

"We'll work on all of that together. I'll give you a crash course on the latter half of the twentieth century so thorough you'll feel you were there for all of it. I'll answer any questions you have, and if I don't know the answer, we'll hop on the internet or go to a library and find out. I'll teach you what I know about vampirism, what I've experienced, what I've heard from others like us. As far as the wimp thing—that's up to you. I can't turn you into someone you're not. But if you can think of anything you feel will help, I'll do whatever I can."

Vivian looked at him gratefully. He took her hand in his and clasped it firmly, but gently.

"Oh, and one more thing," she added.

"Yes?"

"There's only one bed."

Michael chuckled and shot Vivian a guarded glance. His smile died when he saw her stern expression. Clearly, he had known this was coming but hadn't prepared a response.

"Yeah, well, this is more often than not a one-person hideaway. Mine, usually. The landlord and his wife, well, they're nice Germans who don't ask too many questions, and they maintain the yard and everything. He's a carpenter or construction worker or something—"

"Who's. Sleeping. Where?" Vivian demanded. "You didn't think I'd sleep with you, did you? I mean, you didn't think...?"

He cleared his throat a little and shifted awkwardly.

"I'll sleep on the couch. We have blankets and pillows inside the coffee table. There's a casket downstairs—"

"What?"

He laughed.

"It's part of a joke—a long story involving a Halloween party with some guys from the base nearby. I'll explain it later. Right now, I think it's time for us to get some sleep."

Chapter 23

The next night was educational, but frustrating.

First, Doyle knocked on the door at three in the afternoon to deliver supplies—temporary passes onto Ramstein Air Base and human food. The food threw Vivian off, but she didn't ask. She didn't have the urge to start Doyle on one of his know-it-all tirades. He stood in the foyer for a few unpleasant moments, reapplied his pasty-thick sunscreen with fervor, adjusted his wide-brimmed hat, pulled his gloves up to meet his shirtsleeves. His cheeks were the only skin he exposed to the sun, and they were still pink and peeling.

"From yesterday," he explained. As if she had forgotten.

After Doyle left, Vivian was restless and hungry. She put the groceries neatly away in the cupboards where she felt they belonged and wandered through the house again. She made the bed, took a shower, and trimmed her fingernails, which seemed to grow almost overnight. *Or over-day. Oh, whatever.*

She left Michael undisturbed on the couch and headed into the family room. He needed a library. The shelves overflowed with books. She scanned titles for something to read. There were several titles of varying genres. The last two looked like children's books, and she smiled, amused that Michael would have a hidden childish side. *Well, he did have a child. Hmm. He must like Stephen King quite a bit.*

She was unfamiliar with most of the titles, and although she could venture a guess about a book's genre by the way it appeared, she knew the adage about judging a book by its cover.

Finally, a title caught her eye.

Interview With the Vampire? *That can't be right.* She took the paperback from the shelf and peered at it curiously. Well, right or not, it was a book. She took a seat opposite the fireplace and read.

By the time Michael stirred, she was several chapters into the book.

"Hungry?" he asked. She nodded vigorously. She was past hungry and would have been grateful to drink from Michael himself to stave the hunger off, but the thought of cold blood made her shudder. How long ago had it been that she had sucked the blood from unknowing party-goers? It felt like weeks.

He asked her to wait until six o'clock. By that time, full darkness had settled, assisted by a sky heavy with storm clouds. Vivian rolled the blinds up partway on the living room picture window and watched impatiently as the wind blew through the trees. Finally, at twenty after six, he was ready.

The two took the walkway side by side, and Michael began to teach.

"I know I didn't mention it last night, but humans aren't going to be our prey here. Not often." They walked through the gate, and he pointed toward the right where their road ended, and a broad, paved path picked up. He spoke quietly, though it appeared that nearly all of the village of Weilerbach was in for the night.

"We're taking that bike path. You see, not many folks around here venture out at night during the week around here now that the weather's turning cold. We also don't need anything drawing attention to us—like a bunch of unconscious people lying around the neighborhood."

Michael chuckled to himself. Vivian was too hungry to talk.

"For now, we live off animals," he continued. "We'll use another bike path from time to time. I'd hate to be too predictable; you never know who's watching. Oh, and I can't take you into public until I hear more from Doyle. We may be stuck for a while. We can't risk another vamp seeing you. And we'll need to make sure you're fed so you can ward off Jude if he tries anything."

A single streetlight illuminated the start of the path. Darkness surrounded them like a curtain once they passed the small circle of light on the wet blacktop. To the right, a forest loomed, dark and unexplored. To their left, a vast expanse of freshly-turned fields permeated the air like an organic perfume that complemented the smell of decomposing leaves and rainfall.

In the distance, Vivian saw seven tall, straight objects aglow with brilliant red and white lights

"What's that?" she asked, pointing at the glowing spires.

"Ramstein," he answered. "A runway on the airbase."

She nodded, and they continued walking. Though the climate was cold, her breath did not fog.

They walked for a mile or more—or rather, Michael walked. Vivian trudged. She scanned the area for animals to chase, but she saw and heard nothing. Michael walked on assuredly, so she continued to follow, hoping this wasn't an exercise in futility.

Another half-mile, and forest surrounded them. On their left was a steep plummet into dark woods. To the right, a hill climbed beyond a screen of trees. Michael touched her elbow and cocked his head to the hill.

"C'mon," he beckoned and dove into the woods without preamble. Vivian heaved a frustrated sigh and followed. Her senses, heightened by the hunt, reveled in the scents of the night woods. She thought if she tried, she could determine the types of trees around her by dividing the scents that permeated the air. Pine, for sure, but what were the others? Elm? Oak?

Tracking animals in the woods at night proved much harder than hunting people. Unlike humans, they could not be induced to approach by hypnosis. The slightest snapping twig or footfall sent their prey scampering, climbing, or hopping away. If it hadn't been for her vampiric speed, eyesight, and agility, she doubted she would have caught any. Michael taught her how to stand still until an animal came within range, but nocturnal creatures were attuned to the slightest movement, and they too had exceptional nighttime vision.

It was exasperating. It started raining, and as the heavy drops landed on the forest floor, it became tricky to discern the footsteps of what little potential prey came along. It also seemed like far too much work for a little blood. She found that human and animal blood did not taste alike, and not in a good way. She gagged on the first rabbit she caught and handed it over to Michael without finishing it.

Then she caught the squirrel.

If anyone had told me when I was a child that I would be chasing squirrels in the woods at night and drinking their blood to live, I would have called them harebrained. She bit into the furry creature, larger and much redder than any in the States, and proceeded to drain it of its life-giving fluid. She told herself that it was like eating steak or chicken, just alive, but it disconcerted her as the creature writhed in her hands and fought for its life.

Without warning, a shudder passed over her, and with it, a feeling of euphoria. She released the dead squirrel in a daze, sucked in the cold night air. Her skin crawled, but it felt fantastic. She felt as though she were floating, flushed from her head to her feet, and wonderfully alive.

Michael stood an arm reach away from her, and finished off the squirrel's companion. He shuddered and seemed to share in her euphoria, judging from his half-smile and the glassy look in his eyes. He caught her intent look, and respectfully set down the dead animal.

"It's called a 'Death Rush,'" he explained. "It's what most vampires like the best about killing. It only happens once you drain the life from something. It's been said by many who would know better than I that it's the best, if most short-lived, high they've ever known—with the exception of the moment they were turned."

Vivian exhaled, blinked, and shook her head as the brief high left her. She hadn't realized her mouth was open in amazement until it snapped shut.

"Some say when you feel the high, the animal impresses into you some of its abilities, or even its soul," he said. "I don't know about that. I've killed quite a few rabbits, but I don't feel as though I run any faster because of it."

They hunted until they were filled, which took most of the night. Vivian grew adapted to the chase—the tracking, the stalking, the feel of the animal as it struggled against her palms as she bit. Most of all, she learned to enjoy the Death's Rush. She felt more animal than vampire that night. There was no elegance in the hunt, but the reward was worth it.

As dawn turned the wood shades of greys and blues, they headed home sated, flushed, and full of life. She felt every hair on her head, heard the birds chirping their morning calls as loudly as a roar, heard each car as it sped down the road, she felt the cold of the night air. She felt full of life again but more animated and whole than when she was mortal. *In moments like this, I can understand why vampires want to continue their cursed existence. Who wouldn't want to feel like this every night if they could?*

She and Michael smiled at an early morning jogger as she passed. She eyed them warily, and Vivian smelled her fear. It was then that she grasped how horrible she must look. Blood on her chin, hands, and clothes, dirt from tip to toe. She didn't care. They were only a few steps from the house, and she was euphoric.

"Going forward, we should leave for home about half an hour earlier," Michael suggested. Vivian took in his mottled, leaf-covered blue jeans, his blood-spattered shirt and face, and his unkempt hair and nodded. There was no point in sneaking off to find their prey in the forest at night if they came home covered in blood and filth in the morning. They may as well hang a sign around their necks that said "Vampires."

"I always thought vampires flew," she remarked.

"I've heard that, too, but I've never seen one do it," Michael admitted. "But most of the vamps in Savannah are young and have been vampires for under thirty years. Like me. It's surprising for such an old city."

They neared the end of the bike path, and he looked both ways before he crossed the street. Vivian almost laughed at his involuntary habit. If there had been a car approaching, they'd have heard it a mile away.

Once inside, sleep was far from her mind. She was too full of life to think about lying down and doing nothing. She expressed this feeling to Michael.

"Well, that works. I have a lot of teaching to do, and it'll start right now."

He took her room by room. If there was an object in the room she did not recognize or know how to operate, he told her what it was and showed her how it worked. They began with the digital clock in the bedroom and continued to the microwave, the stereo, and the food processor. What challenged her most were the remote controls on the stereo equipment. She had no problem identifying which remote went to which object—it was easy enough to match brand names—but when the time came to choose the sequence of buttons to push to exact the correct response, she became confused. When she finally conquered the process of selecting a CD from the rack, inserting it into the player, choosing a song, and making it play, she was so happy she jumped in circles.

She stopped jumping and peered at Michael through squinted eyes.

"What're we listening to?" she asked with distaste.

"The Dead Kennedys. It's a punk band. We'll cover the evolution of music another time. Oh, wait! I might have something you know." He strutted over to the CDs and scanned the titles.

"Go ahead and eject that one. Put this in, instead."

She did, and as she hit the "play" button, a crooning voice filled the room.

"Recognize this guy's voice?" he asked. Vivian shook her head.

"I like the style, though. That's much better."

"Frank Sinatra," he told her.

They let the CD play as they continued to the kitchen, where Vivian discovered the reason for Doyle's visit. Nearly everything in the bags was an ingredient for a gourmet meal. Evidently, Michael fancied himself a chef and had decided to teach Vivian what he knew. That night she learned the function of the blender, the mixer, the bread machine, and the juicer as they prepared Cracked Alaska Dungeness Crab with

Spinach Dipping Sauce, Dill Wheat Bread, and King Crab with Mushrooms. He said dinner parties were a great way to entice humans to their home for drinks and to eventually surrendering their blood. From the smells coming from the kitchen, she could see why people enjoyed Michael's parties.

"I don't think that these are Alaskan Dungeness Crab," Michael informed her as they removed the meat from the crab legs with the crackers that Doyle had brought. "But that's the title of the recipe in the book, so that's what I call it."

"May I ask you a question?"

"Sure."

"Why are we cooking if it won't taste like it used to?"

Michael smiled, and his crow's-feet crinkled.

"Aren't you having fun?"

"Well, yes."

"Are you learning?"

"I'm learning how to use crab crackers pretty well." As if to prove her point, the shell she worked on separated perfectly, and the meat slid from the shell with ease.

"Isn't that the whole point? To have fun? It's the main reason I cooked before I was changed. It's fun. And besides, it makes you look more human to those around you."

It was a valid point. When the CD ended, she put the second of the 2-disc set into the player. Frank Sinatra made her feel at home because his music was strikingly close to what she remembered. It was as if she found a vortex in time that transported her back to Michigan, 1943. It was almost enough to make her want to open the blinds and let in the gorgeous, wintry sunlight from outdoors.

Almost.

Chapter 24

What's happening to me? Gina wondered. *Why am I lying on this filthy futon?* She tried to lift her arm. Useless. Only her eyes moved. She scanned the water-stained ceiling freely but could not turn her head to see if Jude was there. Everything else on her slender frame was immobilized, except—she suspected—when Jude willed her to move. She almost wished he would never will her to move again. Not after last night.

Gina wouldn't have thought that a vampire could have that much control over another vamp. She had found herself performing the most depraved acts, things beyond imagining. *What did I expect? He's Jude Shepherd, for Christ's sake.*

She attempted to dislodge herself from his grip last night, reminding him that if she didn't show up at work, someone would know she was missing. He had simply laughed and taken her to the Pink Peacock. Only she didn't work. Not for long, anyway. It pleased him to watch her dance through two sets, removing her clothes in a perfunctory fashion as Jude surveyed the club. Her moves had been robotic, her tips lousy. After her second set, he motioned her to his side.

"Yes?"

"The one who calls herself Vanity. Her, or Diamond."

She didn't have to ask what he meant.

"Why don't you get them yourself?" she shouted. Her eyes opened almost as wide as her mouth once she realized what she had said, and she pulled her jaw shut before any more words leaked out.

He peeked at her from under his dark brow and continued stirring his untouched vodka tonic. Gina glared at him, clenched her fists, and turned on her heel. He had her by the wrist before she had a chance to stalk away. She turned back, her glare replaced by an attempt to conceal her pain.

"And if the rest of these little girls mean anything to you at all, you'll obey me without tantrums. Do you understand?"

She nodded and hurried off like a reprimanded child.

Diamond joined them that night, and although sleeping with another woman had never bothered Gina before, the things he'd had them do... It was unnerving, and more often than not, disgusting. Everything he dreamed up, they did, anything to satiate his sick, sadistic whims. They never stood a chance.

Poor Diamond. She and Vanity were the only two human dancers at the club. *He* would *choose one of them. Asshole.*

"How is my pretty?" a familiar voice asked. She winced before she realized she had control of her facial features.

"Oh, surely it's not all that unpleasant. Are you hungry?"

She hadn't thought about it, but now that he mentioned it, she was ravenous. *Was I hungry before he said anything, or did he do that?* She couldn't remember.

Jude plopped down on the edge of the dirty futon. His expression reflected childlike guilelessness.

"I think you'll find that you can move if you like. Enough to sit up. I'm not going to move you from this apartment yet. After all, you like it dirty, don't you?" His libidinous look was almost more than she could stand.

Jude reached out a hand and slid it under the stained comforter. She hadn't realized until then that she was still naked. Sexual fluids had dried and crusted on her body in numerous places. He glided his hand across her exposed flesh, unheeding of the filth that covered her. His hand cupped her below the pubic bone. She became aware of warmth spreading to her nether regions. He touched her, and she throbbed against her will. Her nipples grew pert instantly.

"Don't—don't you—"

The words formed in her mind but disconnected en route to her mouth. Jude smirked.

"Don't what? Don't stop? I think that's what you meant to say, isn't it?" His hands stroked her. Her breath came in short gasps. He unzipped his pants and removed his shaft. She eyed it hungrily.

"No, dear. Not there. There," he removed his hand from her crotch and pointed to his neck. She mewled like a kitten for his touch, her back arching with her need.

"More?"

She nodded eagerly. *Why am I acting like this?* He snaked his arm under the comforter again and found her center effortlessly. She panted and reached for her breast, but he knocked her hand down forcibly before directing it to his penis. He leaned down and bit her breast gently, drawing a trickle of blood. She sat up, making an effort not to hinder his fondling her, and started for his neck.

Then she saw the body.

Diamond lay unmoving on the floor just out of reach, her neck and right arm twisted in an unnatural direction. Her eyes stared with an empty gaze at the ceiling. Her skin was white as paper. A huge gash had been torn from her neck; it was the only sign of blood. Two fang marks surrounded by Passion Pink lipstick on her breasts bore witness to Gina's participation.

I didn't... I don't remember.... Oh God, Diamond!

Gina screamed.

C3   80

In Houston, Charles Dunning sat alone in the dark of his Tudor mansion, his fingers tented in front of his outwardly placid face. Only the slight downward turn of his lips belied his tranquil façade.

He always thought best in the dark, and it was unquestionably time to think.

How had Joseph—Jude, Joseph, whatever name the bastard chose to use this century—lost a slave? Especially *her*. It was so irresponsible and contrary to Tribe standards it seemed unthinkable.

Could Maysun be right? More importantly, could Jude? Why had Maysun reminded Charles about the Second Curse? What would happen if Jude and Jerusha were brought together under the wrong circumstances?

Was it conceivable that the destruction of one creature might bring about the end of the world?

Maysun's contact with him earlier had been anything but typical. He felt the shield she'd erected around her thoughts like an impenetrable forcefield. Although he prodded her verbally and mentally, her resolve and the barrier remained firm. Maysun had never been forthright, but she was being exceptionally careful this time. Why? Was she hiding from Jude, or did she have secrets she needed to hide from him?

He didn't have the stamina to go up against Jude, but he often wondered if he could defeat Maysun in a confrontation. He had never risked it before, but the end of the world was an excellent reason to find out. Besides, he had never cared for Maysun's life of secrecy.

He didn't like where things were heading. Jude had gone too far when he had inadvertently let Jerusha go. It was one thing to rule the nation of vampires with an iron fist. Charles could tolerate that. He understood why Jude exerted mind control to keep those closest to him in check and slew those who disobeyed. He recognized the need for secrecy and control. It was imperative to keep the existence of their kind hidden from the world. For all their power, vampires could be killed just like any other creature if someone knew how.

This, though... this was too much.

What disturbed him the most was the impressions he had received from Maysun and Joseph as he heard about this "Second Curse." True or not, *they* both believed it.

That won't do. I haven't lived this long only to die because of Joseph's idiocy.

೦೪ ೞ

Vivian and Michael left sooner and returned much earlier from their hunt the next night, though it meant only sleeping three hours. When they returned to the house, they discovered that Doyle had brought over several older movies. She glanced through the titles. *Bringing Up Baby, Guess Who's Coming to Dinner? A Streetcar Named Desire*, and *Arsenic and Old Lace.*

"I asked him to bring "*Hush, Hush, Sweet Charlotte*, too, so you could get used to the idea of horror movies a little better, but I guess he loaned it to someone else. I thought we'd start with *Casablanca*. He didn't bring that one; it's mine."

Vivian did not have the heart to tell him that horror films were nothing new. She had seen Bela Lugosi as Dracula with her mother at the Flynn Theater back home.

Michael explained to her that movies depicted the changes of an era—beliefs, styles, and so on—more thoroughly than his descriptions would, and if she had any questions at all, not to hesitate to ask.

Three movies later—they decided to save a couple for the following night—Michael said that her education wasn't complete until she learned some new technology. She had conquered all the entertainment center and kitchen equipment yesterday, so using them tonight hadn't counted. He led her into the office and familiarized her with the phone.

Telephones were nothing new, except for the button-pushing instead of rotary dialing and not talking to an operator first. She listened with half an ear. What interested her was the computer.

On her first night in Germany, she had determined that the only way to beat Jude was to be at least one step ahead of the *Shévet ha Dam*. Unfortunately, she was over fifty years behind. It scared her that false reports about her were available through that machine. She desperately wanted to learn computers, dared to hope she could become as proficient as Lukas.

Michael noticed her distracted glances at the computer.

"You want to learn that, too?"

She nodded.

"That'll take a while, but I'll teach you. I taught Lukas. Hell, I built that computer myself."

Vivian's eyes glowed. He had *built* the computer? Who better to learn from than one who'd assembled the equipment?

"It's going to require several lessons."

"I don't mind."

He looked at her eager face and smirked.

"No, I reckon you don't."

"What was that thing Lukas was using that had that article about me on it? The intra-, enter..." she trailed off as the word failed to come to mind and shrugged in embarrassment.

"Internet," Michael completed. He bent over to turn on the computer. It clicked, and a fan blew noisily as the machine came to life.

"The internet is a modern way people can access information. It's made public in the form of websites. A website is like a digital flyer or newspaper. Not all the information put onto the Internet is accurate—"

"No kidding," Vivian interjected.

"Yeah, I guess you're familiar with that. A lot of it's trustworthy, though, and comes from businesses, schools, or other reliable or semi-reliable sources."

The computer finished booting, and Michael wheeled out the chair for Vivian. He told her the names of each component, starting with the mouse and ending with the scanner.

To Michael's delight, she was a quick study, absorbing knowledge with diligence and enthusiasm. It seemed that as soon as he threw a concept her way, she assimilated it and moved on.

He introduced her to pointing and clicking the mouse and showed her some of his favorite websites. However, what captured Vivian's interest was an icon she glimpsed on his homepage. Next to a cartoon of faceless but somehow friendly-looking stick figures were the words, "Find People." The words triggered an idea, and although she attempted to sit patiently through her lesson, she tapped her foot restlessly.

Michael noticed her agitation.

"Want to try something?"

She nodded. He rolled the mouse in her direction, and she took over, asking questions when necessary until he directed her to what he assured her was the most effective people-finding website he and Lukas used.

She had no problem with the name, birth date, and last known address, but she peered at him uncertainly when the site asked for a social security number.

"Don't worry about that. You don't have to fill in all the fields, just the ones you know." He took a second look at the name she had typed, "Rose Black," and asked if she was looking for Snow White's cousin. Vivian shot him a brief glare as the computer searched. He had forgotten that Black was her surname.

"Who are you—?"

His question ceased as the computer pulled up a website. Vivian couldn't have been less responsive if she were a stone.

She leaned in impatiently as it scrolled from the top to the bottom of the screen. Vivian licked her lip, ran a hand through her hair, beat a tattoo on the desk with her fingernails. Her nose waited inches from the monitor.

The web page was a terrible purple-pink with pictures "stuck" on with black corners to resemble an old-fashioned photo album. The snapshots were of older adults engaged in various activities. The top of the page gave the name of a business in bold black letters: Bender's Nursing Home. In the bottom left-hand corner of the screen, a frail, white-haired woman in a wheelchair watered a healthy chrysanthemum. The caption read, "Rose Black waters her favorite flower."

Vivian's eyes grew moist as she rasped, "Still gardening, Mom?"

Chapter 25

Sex was only satisfying when accompanied by debasement, and there was only so much he could do to her alone. After a few more hours of painful intercourse, Jude allowed Gina to taste another dose of his addictive draught.

"Happy?" he asked.

Her face went blank, and she hastily lapped at a ruby droplet before it slipped down her chin. He smirked and blocked her attempt to prod his mind for the desired answer.

"Ye-Yes?" she replied.

He tutted and shook his head. If he'd had any remaining urge, the childlike look of pain and fear that crossed her face at his disapproval would have brought him around again.

He enjoyed Gina. Her ability to convey fear and desire to accommodate him was the most arousing he had found in centuries. It was even better than with Vivian in many ways. Of course, with Vivian, the need had never been sexual. With her, it was about control. His ability to dominate her against her will was the ultimate aphrodisiac.

"Gina?"

"Hmm?" she replied. She was so pliable, so ready for anything he wanted.

"I need something from you."

She bit her lip and began to play with herself with a look that bordered on guilt. He chuckled and moved her hand.

"No, no. Not this time."

"No?" Had he heard disappointment in her voice? His lip curled into a leer.

"No. I have something else for you to do. A favor. A little errand, you might say."

☙ ❧

"So, what was your mother like?" Michael asked once they'd relaxed on the couch facing the fireplace. A healthy fire crackled in the hearth. Vivian stared into the flames expressionlessly. Michael had torn her away from the desk several moments ago, but she still appeared soulless.

"She was great," she murmured. "Independent. She swore she didn't need anyone except me. Father had left us quite a bit of money when he died, so she didn't need to work. She loved to garden, though. God, she loved to garden! She'd spend all day out there and come inside smelling like dirt and plants, and her cheeks would be pink and beautiful. We canned and pickled so many things we never had to buy vegetables."

Vivian sighed and curled up into a tight ball, seemingly reminiscing about happier times.

"What about your childhood? Your father? What was he like?"

Vivian blanched and cringed. Michael regretted the question. When she spoke, her voice was a monotonous whisper.

"I don't remember him... or my childhood. Mother said that it's normal after a trauma to block things out. All I know is what she told me about him. That he was devoted to us and his work. And that 'He couldn't have loved me more if he'd given birth himself.' Her words, not mine."

Her voice never changed pitch, and her eyes never left the fire. After a few moments, she blinked. Her posture relaxed, and her fists released her feet. Her eyes flickered to the mantle, to the statues of Shiva, Buddha, Anubis, and the outstretched hands of the Virgin Mother.

"Do you believe in God, Michael?"

"Depends on what you mean by God, I guess," he said. "If you mean do I believe in the traditional Judeo-Christian Father, Son, and Holy Spirit, I'd have to say... Well, I'm not sure what I'd say. Rumor has it that it was Jesus who cursed Cartaphilus—Jude—to walk the earth until His return. Well, Cartaphilus is still walking, so Jesus had great power, that's for sure. I just don't understand why He did it."

"Why do you call Jude 'Cartaphilus'?" Vivian asked.

Michael paused. "Vivian, you should know Jude was the first vampire. There's a story about how it happened. Some say it's a myth, but I've never heard another explanation that makes sense. You know the story of the crucifixion?"

"Jesus' crucifixion?" Vivian asked. "Of course."

"The day Jesus was crucified, there was a man... he's had various names in various myths... Longinus and Ahasuerus are two. Some say he was a cobbler, others a Roman soldier. But the story that prevails most often is that he was a gatekeeper of Pontius Pilate. He struck Jesus and taunted him for pausing in his trek to Golgotha—the place where Jesus was crucified. Jesus then cursed Joseph to walk the earth until his return. Ergo, Jesus created the first immortal. The first vampire."

Vivian was stunned.

"But Jesus was God. He had to be God to have that kind of power. Why would He do that?"

"Why'd God make Satan?" Michael countered.

"Isn't it hard to believe in a god after all that's happened?" she asked, her eyes brimming with tears. "I mean, your wife is dead, your son is aging before your eyes, and you survive on the blood of others. You're a *vampire*. Doesn't that make God hard to accept?"

He reached for her hand and was a little relieved when she didn't pull it back.

"On the contrary. Why would I need to believe in a God if my life were simple? So many people only turn to God when they need help. They expect God to make their problems vanish. That's like asking for someone to help you move and then standing by while they carry it all in for you. Others believe God is a tyrant up in the clouds, giving you pass/fail tests, allowing evil to enter our lives for mystical reasons, waiting to judge us all on some apocalyptical day. I believe if there is a God, it's someone close to us. Not someone we turn to in 9-1-1 prayers, but one we thank for wonderful things and ask for help during the difficult times."

"If you don't believe in Jesus or Buddha, why do you have these statues?" she asked, waving her free hand at the mantle.

"I believe in a balance. Life is a balance. What would happen if nothing bad ever happened to you?"

Vivian shrugged. "It would be great."

"Would it? Would you be able to recognize good for what it is if you never experienced evil, never had challenges or sadness or any doubts? No questions as to where all your blessings come from?"

"You mean—"

"There *has* to be evil for there to be good. Otherwise, there's no contrast. We wouldn't *need* a God if evil didn't exist. It helps us to acknowledge the existence of a balancing force in the universe."

"It sounds to me like you *do* believe in God."

"I don't have a favorite. I don't believe there's a religion that understands for certain what God is. Ever hear the story about the blind men and the elephant?"

Vivian shook her head.

"Well, it goes something like this: Five blind men approach an elephant. Well, he's in their way, so they try to figure out what it is to decide the best way to move it. Each man grabs a separate part. The first one grabs his leg and says, 'It's a tree,' the second finds his ear and says, 'No, it's a fan.' The third one runs right into his side and says, 'It's a wall,' and the fourth man finds its tail and says, "I think it's a rope." The last guy finds its trunk and says, 'You're all crazy. It's a hose.'"

Vivian giggled. Tears broke and trickled down her cheeks. He dried them with his fingertips.

"The moral of the story is, I feel God is like the elephant and religions like the blind men. They each have it a little right, but they don't get the whole picture."

"In other words, to understand what God is, is to understand the mind of God, and as humans, we're all blind men?"

"That's beautiful. I couldn't have said it better myself."

Vivian beamed. "What else do you believe?"

"I believe there's a power struggle involving the balance of good and evil in this world. Some things affect it only slightly, and others can severely tip the scales in one direction or the other. Jesus was one. Jude is another, and he's been tipping those scales very heavily for a long time."

"How long?"

Michael raised his thick eyebrows.

"I was hoping you could tell me."

ك ل

"Control, Alt, Delete. Done," Lukas said. The computer fan died as he reached into a shirt pocket for a soft pack of Marlboro Lights. He fished the last one out, rested the unlit butt in his mouth, and looked around his office for a lighter.

"Lighter... lighter...." His eyes scanned the desk. Blank zip disks, full zip disks, burned CDs, unburned CDs, blank paper, overflowing ashtray. No lighter. *Goddamn Attention Deficit. I can't remember where I put anything.*

He took the butt out of his mouth, set it on the desk, and took a moment to dump out the ashtray as he mentally retraced his steps. Grey and white ash fluttered like malformed snowflakes and clung to his flannel shirt. He brushed them in the general direction of the basket, picked the butt up, and put it back into his mouth.

"Let's see.... Came in here, booted up, searched..." *and didn't find squat.* That his search revealed nothing was unusual. A skilled hacker like Lukas had little problem overcoming the hurdles the *Shévet ha Dam* used. What concerned him was the lack of information in the last few days regarding the search for the missing "female vampire slave" or the unknown assassin that had flitted through the news and disappeared into obscurity. For the first time, Lukas seriously doubted if he was looking in the right places. But he had no idea where else to investigate.

At least Dad and Viv don't need money. He ensured that their account was in ridiculously good standing. It hadn't been touched. *Wonder what they're doing? They sure haven't gone out.* A thought crossed his mind, and he winced. Even though his father looked his age, there was still something gross about the fleeting mental image of him having sex. He resumed looking for his lighter.

"I searched the net for a few minutes, and then I... *aha!*" Lukas exclaimed. He placed the cigarette back into his mouth and started to stand, his hand heading for the small pocket of his Levi's, where he stowed the lighter. Before he rose halfway, a familiar Zippo flashed in front of his face, held by an equally familiar, well-manicured hand. The pink-tipped fingers rolled across the lighter expertly, and a flame danced just beyond the tip of his Marlboro. He tilted forward, puffed, and suppressed a flinch.

Gina looked like shit.

She looked worse than any vampire was entitled. Her hair drooped, listless and dull, and dark purple half-circles stemmed from the inner corner of each eye. She also smelled foul, which was very un-Gina-like. Shabby clothes hung from her slender frame. It was as if she had been living in squalor for weeks, though Lukas knew it had only had been a couple of days since he had seen her last. She smiled, and a flake of what could only be dried blood drifted down from the crook of her lips.

Damn. She looks pissed. He grimaced at her dismal expression and unkempt appearance and wondered what the impetus was for her sudden change. *She looks like one of the crackheads downstairs at the Waters place. Worse. She looks like Vivian did when she first got to the house.*

Gina straightened and gazed at Lukas with what bordered on disgust, and he was glad he knew Gina couldn't read minds. From her expression, he would have almost guessed she had.

I'd say she almost looks mad enough to kill me.

Chapter 26

"*N*o. No. No. A thousand times, *no!*"

They'd had the same conversation several times over the past few nights with varying degrees of passion, but he refused her request every time. It wasn't easy. Vivian had gone so far as to accuse him of denying her because she hadn't slept with him. The implication made him so furious he'd stormed off without a word.

He paused in his march away from her. His feet chilled on the cold brown tile. *Why do I feel like I'm losing ground here?* He turned and faced her. She had a determined set to her jaw, just like he did when he was hell-bent on having his way.

"Because Jude will undoubtedly have some of his cretins hanging around the nursing home waiting for us to do something just that stupid. You'll be putting both of us and your mother in danger!"

Vivian glowered at the implication that her notion was stupid and stared furiously at the foyer wallpaper. Michael waved his hands around as if trying to get his message across using sign language since the words coming out of his mouth hadn't convinced her.

"I don't *care*, Michael! You saw how old she was—she's got to be close to a hundred. She won't live much longer. I can't take the chance that she'll die before I see her! I need to tell her that my disappearance wasn't her fault. That I didn't leave her."

"Vivian, how do you know that seeing her will help either of you? She might be senile. She might not recognize you."

"She'll know. I'm certain of it. She was always a fighter. She fought against everyone who said she was silly for raising me alone, who said she was too independent. She fought against the church, who said she set a bad example by not looking for a father to replace mine. She fought them *for* me, *because* of *me*. I have no doubt she's waiting for me, and I won't give up on her!"

Michael's hands dropped to his side. All the fight had left the moment he saw the look on her face. *Rose Black taught her well. Or at least,* somebody *did.* He searched for the words to counter her argument, but the attempt was half-hearted. She had won.

"I'll call Lukas and have him work with Doyle to get us some tickets. We'll leave as soon as we can."

CB   BD

Charles Dunning pressed *end* on his cell phone. His arm pulled back, but he caught himself before he launched it across the dining room and into the beveled glass mirror.

He crossed the room with long strides and surveyed his crystal menagerie in the corner cabinet. He had meticulously placed hundreds of pieces to generate myriad prisms using the tiny bulb in the top of the cabinet, and the effect usually soothed or at least distracted him. Today his collection of little homemade rainbows offered no solace. He doubted anything would.

That bastard. Where in the hell has he been?

Charles had failed to get in contact with Jude for two frustrating weeks. He had lost track of the number of messages he had left. He hadn't gotten one call from Jude. Not a single response. Only reports from the Tribe that all said one thing: no progress finding Jerusha. Every day she lived apart from her creator and diluted his blood with new, her bond with him lessened.

Unless she's out there killing humans to live. We might stand a chance then.

Jude had ensured Charles knew what he was working on in the past, even when he excluded the rest of the *Shévet ha Dam.* Dunning's years of seniority and loyalty to Jude—not to mention his willingness to slaughter anyone when ordered—had assured that he was privy to Jude's secrets. And, of course, the ever-present Jude was aware of anything Charles thought, much less did.

Out of habit, his eyes flitted to the corners of the room, but Jude wasn't there. Charles would have known. Jude's presence was like an oppressive heat; he turned the very air around him into a powerful, spirit-crushing force.

I knew that woman would prove to be trouble. She was a weak spot for him from the beginning.

Charles had never forgotten the day Jude had introduced him to

Jerusha. She was beautiful, graceful, elegant, regal, and powerful beyond belief. Only Jude surpassed her in strength. She was oblivious to what an ungodly creature Jude Shepherd was, and it was apparent he had no intention of showing her. When he thought about the preternatural glow in Jude's eyes as he explained the things he did to her, Charles shuddered. Of course, he had nothing against the killing; murder was often a source of entertainment for him, but that was twisted.

He headed from the dim dining room into the bright billiard room. The fully stocked wet bar boasted golden spouts and faucets, shining walnut panels covered the wall, heavy curtains thwarted any trace of sunlight. Everything down to the pool table was gilded. He worked hard for the *Shévet ha Dam*, and Jude ensured that Charles was generously compensated. Every room in his mansion boasted rooms of equal splendor.

Was it all worth it if the world is on the line?

Once known as Oisian Drummann, Charles Dunning was one of the founding members of the *Shévet ha Dam,* and most of the original edicts had been his. He lived for its laws, preserved its order, and had no problem cutting out or slaughtering those who saw differently. His brotherly relationship with Jude ensured that his commands were followed either out of respect or fear. He had appointed himself into the highest echelon. He had formed the Table over a thousand years ago. He lived for the Blood Tribe

Now nothing I've worked for may matter. That woman will be our undoing if she remembers what she is. She could kill even me.

The Second Curse was Jerusha. With every passing minute, he grew surer that the rumor was true. And if someone didn't do something soon...

Damn it all to hell.

He poured himself a glass of single-malt scotch and raised it with a trembling hand to his lips. He could not taste a thing.

CS BO

Michael placed the phone down distractedly. His mouth formed a thin line. His eyes clung to a corner of the far wall, avoiding hers.

"Still no answer?" Vivian prodded. He blinked and focused on her.

"No."

"Doesn't he have a—a—whatdoyoucallem? A cell phone?"

He looked at her as if she had reminded him of some unwelcome news.

"Yeah, I've tried it, too. No answer." He reached into a kitchen drawer, found his cigarettes, and headed outside to smoke, not bothering to put on slippers or a jacket, not caring if the neighbors wondered why he wasn't freezing in the cold. His face was tight-lipped and stormy. Vivian followed him, anyway, surprised he pulled the cigarettes out after several days without touching them.

Michael rested with his rear on the concrete window ledge, his back against the picture window. The icy rain that had been pouring for several days showed no sign of stopping. Fat drops splashed in ankle-deep puddles in the streets. The wind had blown in gales, drenching the entire porch. Vivian paused to put on fleece-padded slippers before joining Michael past the threshold.

He spotted her as he pocketed his lighter. An appreciative look crossed his face. His feet fidgeted on the concrete, and he stared at them as if he expected them to do tricks. He removed the cigarette from his mouth.

"I don't know why I smoke these damn things," he said, attempting to sound offhanded but failing. He continued to stare at his now still feet. "I never quit. Not even when I knew they didn't do a damn thing for me." Another drag. "I guess I'm psychologically addicted," He looked at her and shrugged, took another drag, and stuffed his free hand into his pocket.

Vivian didn't interrupt, joining him on the window ledge. Michael motioned to his pocket, offering a cigarette, but she shook her head. He took another drag, noticed that he was down to the filter, and flicked the remaining ash into the wet bushes. He lit another.

"Nancy hated that I smoked," he continued. Vivian guessed he meant his wife. "She quit when she found out she was pregnant. Didn't want Lukas around the smoke. She knew it was bad for him. I tried to quit, but after a while, I thought, fuck it. If she doesn't want Lukas around smoke, I'll smoke outside. That way, the house won't smell like it. I still smoked in the car, though. I was an asshole about that." He took the time to inhale another lungful. He faced Vivian, and his gaze seemed heavy, appraising. He looked away.

"I was a bad father at first," he said. "I wasn't ready for it. Just out of the service, wanted to get a house and stuff first before we had kids. It wasn't planned, and she was afraid to tell me. I commented to her that it had been a while since she... you know... had her time. Then she confessed. I was mad, but I tried to hide it." He shook the last bit of lit tobacco out from the end of his second cigarette but made no move to head inside. Now that he had started talking, the words poured out, though the effort seemed painful.

"I should've known better. She knew me better than I knew me. She even insisted on naming the baby after my father, like she thought it would make me love him more. Lukas Dean." He raised his head, stared into the rain.

"After she died, I didn't know what to do. Here I was, a single father, and I'd hardly changed a diaper. I loved him, but I didn't father him, you know? Not like I should've. I was scared. I think Lukas was more frightened than me. He didn't understand about Nancy being gone all of a sudden. He had nightmares. He'd been almost potty trained, and he acted as if he'd never seen a toilet. He cried at nothing at all. On top of that, I was going through so many changes, and trying to figure out what in the hell had happened to me."

He took in a shaky breath. Vivian put her arm around him, and he gave her a self-effacing smirk.

"Now, I don't know what I'd do without him," he said. "He's so fucking smart he makes me feel slow, and that's not easy."

"Tell me about it," Vivian quipped. They shared an awkward laugh.

"Yeah, I raised one hard-nosed kid. But I had to, you know?" She nodded.

His eyes burned, and he fought to hold back tears. Vivian took him in her arms and embraced him. Michael placed his hands on hers, and she reveled in his touch. He returned it with feeling. After a moment, they separated and stared into one another's eyes, each reading and feeling the other's thoughts. It came so easily, words without speech, profound feeling without explanation, understanding, and caring without fear.

They embraced again, stronger this time. It seemed only natural, their bodies pressing against each other, their hands caressing each other's back. They relaxed the embrace without letting go. Michael breathed a sigh.

"Vivian..."

"Hmm?"

"Ha! You *are* home!" A third voice barked. Doyle sauntered up the walk, his arms toting plastic bags of supplies. Michael tried to preserve the embrace, but she pulled away.

"I was wondering what was up. I tried to call on my way over, but first, it was busy, and then there was no answer."

Michael met him halfway up the walk and shot him a resentful look. Doyle's glance darted from Michael to Vivian and back to Michael. A guilty expression crossed his face, and he mouthed, "Sorry."

Michael took some of the bags. Vivian had already opened the door, and she waited in the foyer.

"You should've seen this girl on the way over here," Doyle confided to Michael. "She couldn't have been more than fifteen, but my God, she was fuckin' hot! Blonde, big titties..." his hands cupped in illustration in front of his chest, and his voice trailed off for a moment. Michael and Vivian shared a dry look over Doyle's head as Doyle continued. "*Man,* I would love to tap that. Her pants were on so tight. I was thinkin' about taking that fresh grass and runnin' my fingers through it." He illustrated graphically with his hands. "I wish I could've. It's so hard to be good sometimes, you know? Sometimes I wish I was still one of them," he confessed. His tirade ended, and his hands dropped to his sides dejectedly.

"One of whom?" Vivian asked.

"*Them.* The Tribe. To be going at it with a bomb body like that, and tear into her neck and time it so right as you blow your load you have that... that Death Rush." He shuddered and looked at the other two to see if they shared in his enthusiasm. Michael and Vivian were wearing similar but unsympathetic expressions. The three of them stood in awkward silence for a moment. Doyle stood slumped-shouldered, his eyes downcast in embarrassment. *To look at him, you'd think the* Shévet ha Dam *rejected him instead of the other way around,* Vivian thought.

"I thought you had a girlfriend," Vivian said. Doyle's head snapped up, and a self-satisfied look crossed his face. Vivian suppressed her disappointment. She had meant to drive home his stupidity, not give him a means of escape from his shame.

"Shit, Gabrielle don't care. She *likes* girls. She'd have been like, 'Just save me some, honey.'" He looked at the bags still in his hands. "This one's movies, this one's more food." He indicated which was which by lifting the bags slightly with each sentence. "Where do you want 'em?"

"Movies in the living room, food in the kitchen, dipstick." Michael chided.

After dropping off the new movie supply, Doyle joined them in the kitchen.

"I don't know why you keep asking me to bring food. You can't tell me you're eating it." Doyle's disdainful tone revealed his attempt to earn back some of his dignity by belittling Michael. Vivian smiled a smug smile. His sophomoric behavior was amusing when it wasn't irritating as hell.

Michael looked into one of the cloth grocery bags and, finding a means to illustrate his point, and asked Doyle to close his eyes.

"Why?" Doyle asked suspiciously.

"Trust me," Michael said. Doyle grudgingly closed his eyes.

Michael removed a large orange from the shopping bag and peeled it deftly, unraveling the skin in one long peel.

"What do you smell?" he asked. Doyle's nostrils twitched a moment.

"An orange," he said, unimpressed.

"Doesn't it smell great? Sharp? Sweet? Maybe better than they did when you were alive? Can't you just smell how it used to taste?"

Doyle shrugged, but his bobbing Adam's apple belied his cavalier act.

"Yeah, I guess."

He opened his eyes. Michael's dexterous hands had peeled the entire orange. He separated a segment and held it in front of Doyle's mouth.

"Open," he ordered. Doyle rolled his eyes and opened. He chewed uninterestedly.

"Doesn't taste like much."

"Don't taste it," Michael instructed. "Feel it. Feel the texture. Be aware of what part of the orange is soft, which is fibrous. Feel the juice as it rolls down your tongue."

"This is stupid," Doyle said, swallowing the orange.

Vivian shook her head. *He can picture having sex with a dying woman and can't remember what it's like to eat an orange. I guess it's all what's important to you.*

ଓଃ ଃଡ

Charles made more phone calls that night than he had in decades. Usually, he delegated phone calls to Doyle, but for some reason, Doyle was unreachable. Another complication? He put the thought aside. He had enough on his mind.

He would not resort to using telepathy. He had gotten the impression from Maysun that secrecy was crucial, and his belief only increased after he spoke with her again. He approached her first with his idea. As his only elder in the Tribe, aside from Jude, she deserved that respect.

Besides, he was curious what her reaction would be. Thankfully, she had agreed.

His calls were met with a combination of resentment and amazement. Another meeting so soon? Tonight? Where? The idea of holding two meetings in such close succession was more than unusual—it was unparalleled. No one questioned the need for secrecy, either, which relieved him. He had no prepared response, for any deceit would be spotted in an instant.

Ten members. Only ten. He hoped he had chosen wisely.

Chapter 27

Charles was at a loss for words. It wasn't wise to open with a joke; the humor would be lost on this group. None of them looked in the mood for wit, anyhow. He had been listening to them grumble for several minutes while he lingered, concealed toward the back of the cave. Some heard him. Others smelled him, just as he heard and smelled them now. He'd never had to give a speech as momentous as the one he intended to deliver tonight. His life depended on it.

He put off entering the room for forty-five minutes, pacing back and forth over the uneven ground as he went over what he believed were the most convincing arguments. Meanwhile, he ensured that his servants made his guests as comfortable as possible in their unusual surroundings. He was sure that a couple of the members felt put out at being unable to assume their typical ranking positions around the table in Atlanta. Servants had arranged enormous silk pillows as makeshift chairs around the tiny cavern, with only one remaining at the back of the room for him, the vampire who'd called them together for the second time in as many months.

He had tried to ensure that Jude would not catch wind of this meeting. He had invited only half of the Table, the half that held most of his trust. The half who had shielded their minds at his request. The half who—he hoped—viewed Jude as nothing short of a deity.

He stepped with vampire grace and silence into the lantern-lit cave and assumed a seat on a plump silk cushion. Ten dark sets of eyes swerved in his direction. It took all of his belief in his position to keep a resolute front. Inside, he was cringing from the blow their eyes delivered.

"Good evening," he said.

"I don't need you to tell me what kind of evening it is, Charles," Errando Medina broke in, his Spanish accent thick with agitation. He drew up his short, stocky frame as tall as feasible and glared at Charles boldly from behind a pair of ridiculous, not to mention unnecessary, wire-rimmed glasses. He leaned forward and rested his chubby hands on the back of his knees. "What in the hell is going on? Why the Bohemian accommodations?"

A look passed between Medina and Maria Perez, and they nodded their concurrence. Charles sighed. This was not going to be easy, but he had hoped that it would start better than this.

"Right," added Peter Ford. "Like I've had to pull resources from my operations to go looking for Shepherd's girl in airports and seaports after that last conference." His Outback accent was so thick that those who did not usually speak English pinched their faces in concentration as they tried to understand. Peter, oblivious that his articulation caused trouble, plodded on, "I know he said that she's important—his child and all—but... I mean, I'm losing money having to sink manpower into a search-and-destroy mission that probably won't come to my continent."

"Search and destroy?" cried Zivon Duscha. "I thought we were supposed to find her and bring her back!" He ran a small, pale hand through his mousy-brown hair and shifted his weight on the pillow. Duscha was forever getting facts mixed up and, as a result, doubted himself even when he was right.

"Where are the others?" questioned Perez. "I thought this was a Table meeting. Let's not start until we are all present."

A chorus of opinions erupted, and the volume grew into a roar as everyone tried to drown out their neighbor. Charles stood raised his hands to achieve quiet.

"I called you here to speak to you privately. The other members of the Table were not summoned."

If he thought he had reached silence before, it was nothing compared with what surrounded him now. No one blinked. Every eye was wide, and all ten sets rested, unmoving on him. Charles Dunning, the leading Table member, had gone against regulation. It wasn't that the other members could not, would not, or refused to make it. They had not been asked. By association, every member present was guilty of breaking a major statute. Furtive glances shot about the room. One younger member under five hundred years old appeared ready to flee. Some of the older seemed to be ready to kill Charles if it meant saving their own lives.

"Hear me out," Charles said. To his relief, his voice sounded composed. "That's all I ask. Give me two minutes of your time. After that, anyone who wishes to leave, may."

More eye contact. If possible, their expressions were more ambiguous this time.

It was at times like this Charles felt most human. His heart had jumped to his throat. If only one person left, the group would be at a political disadvantage. Everyone knew that it would take all of their votes to turn the Table. If one of them left, they would all have to leave, or they would die.

That he hadn't asked the other members to attend left no doubt in their minds what Charles was proposing. A mutiny. If the meeting adjourned and word got back to Jude—and it most certainly would—chances were that Charles alone would die. If they merged, though, the future held an uprising. A revolt against Jude Shepherd, whose leadership they hated and scorned, whose power they resented, and yet respected out of fear.

No one left. They looked terrified, but none left.

Charles cleared his throat and spoke.

ɢʒ   ଓ

Doyle, unfortunately, decided to stick around for a few hours. He had "accidentally" delivered the wrong collection of movies—all vampire flicks. The unlucky outcome of this oversight was that he felt his presence was necessary and critical for Vivian's education.

"You see, Michael's only been around for about fifteen years as a vamp."

"Seventeen," Michael corrected.

"Yeahyeahyeah, seventeen, whatever," Doyle waved in Michael's direction as though he was a pesky bug, "He's only been around a little while. Me, on the other hand, I've been around for about a century. My friends in the Tribe, they've been around for a coupla centuries. I've learned a lot from them. I can tell you what's true and what's bullshit better than Michael."

Doyle placed his hand in the small of Vivian's back as they headed into the living room, but Vivian marched beyond his reach and sat on the couch nearest Michael. Doyle trudged to the love seat.

They never got around to cooking anything that night, as Doyle played movie after movie in rapid succession. Vivian suspected that he was afraid if he let too much time pass between, they would come up with a reason for him to leave. It was the most astute judgment he made all night.

Nosferatu, Blade, From Dusk 'Til Dawn, The Lost Boys, Bram Stoker's Dracula. They hardly left the couch all night. Between the movies and Doyle's not-too-infrequent pauses to dispense his sagacious advice and alleged knowledge, it was daylight before they finished. According to Doyle, one could sire vampires through hypodermic injection of vampire blood and a feeding, vampires burned easier than humans, and yes, many vampires can fly. Vivian's head swam. She did not know what to think. When she peered into his thoughts, it seemed that Doyle believed what he told her.

"But *how* do they fly?" she asked. Doyle looked at her strangely. It was as though he hadn't believed the night had been devoted to teaching Vivian, but Michael.

"You mean, you don't know?" he asked. "God, I'd have thought for sure if anyone knew, you did."

Vivian looked at him quizzically. "Why would *I* know?"

Doyle chuckled. "Well, because you're so much older than I am."

She gave him a blank look. "No, I'm not."

Doyle's expression reflected unfeigned surprise.

"Wasn't that you at that place in England? Cambridge?" His narrow eyes grew smaller as he scrutinized her. "I thought for sure that was you."

Vivian remembered her dream. Jude *had* been speaking to Doyle, but England? *No, it couldn't have been. Could it? I don't remember being in England.* Maybe Jude had dragged her there sometime in the last fifty years, but no longer than that. Doyle must have his dates confused. She struggled to remember, but it seemed the harder she tried, the farther out of reach her memories became.

Unaware that she was interrupting Doyle, she looked at Michael and said, "I think you should try to call Lukas again."

"Vivian, it's three in the morning there."

"Michael, it's Lukas."

"Good point."

He sat up and headed to the office. She heard the speakerphone dialing the thirteen digits to Savannah. As it rang, she redirected her attention to Doyle.

He was staring at her.

"What?"

He flinched.

"Are you *certain* you were never in Cambridge?"

"What the hell is the big deal with Cambridge?"

"I would've bet money that you were the same girl that Jude had there around eighty years ago."

"That's ludicrous. I've only been a vampire for fifty."

Doyle shook his head and muttered, "I would've sworn it was you."

Michael emerged from the office, shaking his head.

"No answer. Not at the house, not on the cell, and not at Waters." He regarded Doyle with hesitation.

"Doyle? I need a favor, man."

"Name it." Doyle sat up and gave Michael the most earnest look Vivian had ever seen—on Doyle's face, anyway.

"I've been meaning to ask you... do you have anybody you trust over at the Tribe? Somebody who can get us airline tickets ASAP?"

"Just tell me where you want to go," he replied confidently.

Michael sighed. Vivian put her hand on his and looked at him imploringly, her head shaking subtly back and forth. He shrugged as if to say, *What choice do I have?* She didn't move her hand or break her focus. His face reflected his hesitation, and his shoulders slumped.

"Lemme think on it overnight, OK?"

"Anything you say, bud," Doyle replied sprightly. "Can I crash here? I don't want to get any exposure today. I've been out way too much the last couple of weeks. Starting to look like a lobster."

"Sure, bud. You can sleep—"

"On the couch," Vivian finished, making sure she spoke over Michael's offer of the casket in the basement.

"Let me get you a blanket," she offered with a meaningful look in Michael's direction. "I'll just make sure Doyle gets all set up, and I'll meet you in the bedroom." Michael only blinked a moment before following Vivian's instructions.

"OK. Do you need any help?"

Together they lowered the blinds around the house and settled Doyle with blankets and pillows on the couch. Once in the bedroom, Michael asked, "OK. What's up?"

"Nothing. I just don't like the way he looks at me, and I thought he might stop if he thought we were... together."

"Aren't we?"

"I don't know." They looked at each other. They looked at the bed. They looked at each other again.

"Should I sleep on the floor?" Michael offered.

"No, don't be ridiculous. You don't have to do that."

"What about changing. Do I change here?"

"I'll use the bathroom."

After ten minutes of blundering through their nightly preparations, they settled on opposite sides of the California king-sized bed.

Vivian stretched her legs and retracted them. Michael fidgeted with the pillow. Vivian adjusted her hair, and Michael scratched his back. They both kicked the blanket until it lay just so, and then they kicked at it some more.

"Are you comfortable?" Michael asked.

"Well, I'm not used to sleeping on this side," Vivian admitted.

"You usually sleep on the other side?"

"Yes. Well, no. Usually the middle."

"Aahh. Well, don't feel bad. I usually sleep in the nude."

Vivian laughed, and it came out hollow and nervous.

"Are you comfortable?" she asked.

"As comfortable as I can be, knowing you're way over there," he said. The comment was met with silence, and Vivian heard no sound at all from Michael's side of the bed for a moment, not even breathing. She pictured him cringing, regretting his words.

"I guess we could both sleep in the middle," Vivian offered.

The sound of shifting blankets told her that Michael was rolling over, and she turned to meet him halfway. They laid that way for a moment, facing each other, half-smiles on both of their faces as their gaze met and locked. He reached forward and tucked a long strand of hair behind her ear; his hand caressed her jaw as he pulled it back. He leaned in and gently touched her lips with his. The heat between them ignited swiftly, like a suppressed fire that suddenly finds a source of oxygen. They drew each other close fiercely, pressed against one another as if a molecule of distance was too far.

The strength in his arms and hands quickened the heat in her body, and she wrapped a leg around him, twining them together. Lips and hands caressed and explored previously untouched parts. Vivian felt like her world was on fire. She could hardly believe that Michael had been holding back the passion for her he showed now. They shed their clothes as they discovered one another, and when their bodies came together, it felt natural, breathtaking, incredible. She closed her eyes as he entered her, and with her hands on his back, she urged him deeper inside. Complying eagerly, he drew her to him, kissed her ardently. She ran her fingers through his close-cropped hair and pulled his face toward hers.

Their vampiric teeth scraped one another and drew a trickle of blood from their lips. The smell heightened their desire, now for one another's blood as well as bodies.

As Michael drove himself into her, Vivian raised her hips to meet him thrust for thrust. He seemed driven like a man possessed. Just as she thought he was about to finish, he rolled over and placed his back against the headboard, pulling her with him. As she straddled him, lifting and lowering her hips, which were cradled by his hands, he buried his face into her neck. She felt his gentle bite and remembered her tinge of jealousy at seeing the way Michael had bitten the woman on River Street. After he took a sip, he sat back, giving her the chance to dip to his pale neck and draw from him as well.

It seemed that the taste of her was enough; Michael shuddered and groaned, pulling her toward him as he released deeply inside of her. The taste of his blood, combined with the sound of his orgasm, was enough to push Vivian over the edge as well, and she cried out, wrapping her arms around his head and shoulders as she finished.

They sat that way, tangled together, exhausted, content. Michael buried his face in her breasts and kissed them. Vivian giggled.

"Good God, woman. What is *in* that blood of yours?" he exclaimed.

She shrugged. "I don't know. What I'm wondering is why didn't it taste gross this time? I've always had super gross dead blood before. That wasn't gross at all."

"You're right," Michael said. "I've heard that as well."

"You've never had a drink from another vampire before?" She thought of how long he had lived with Gina, and all of the parties hosted with the Savanah vampires. Did that mean he had never been with any of them before?

"Never have," he confirmed.

They disentangled their bodies, reclined, and wrapped their arms around each other once more.

"Maybe it's because of how we did it," Michael suggested.

"What do you mean?"

"In caring. In, um, passion."

Was he about to say love? Vivian wondered. "A lot of caring and passion. Maybe that's it." She ran her fingers through the patch of hair on his chest and drifted off to sleep.

03 80

Lukas swam in a river of red a handful of meters from the surface. He was quickly running out of air. He saw the glow of the sun through the murky liquid and turned toward it, using it as a point of reference in the never-ending crimson stream. He strained for the surface, paddling through water that felt heavier than mercury and every bit as deadly. He reached a meter from the surface and realized that he was swimming parallel to it instead of toward it. He cursed himself for his stupidity. His lungs ached for air, his legs felt weighted as the muscles cramped and refused to move. He felt his body sinking. *No, I won't die. Damn it, I can swim!*

His arms pulled toward the surface with all his might. Air bubbles erupted from his lips and floated to the elusive surface. He struggled to force his cramped legs into cooperation with his feverishly flapping arms, but they barely moved.

He heard a melodic laugh.

That sounded like Gina. Something about the voice pulled a final effort from a reserve he wasn't aware he had. His legs kicked, and he swam in the right direction, toward the bright light beyond the water.

I'm not going to make it. My God, I can't! I'm going to die! His lungs burned hotter than a steam locomotive, and as he reached the air, his mouth opened, and he took a lungful of thick, red water. Metallic water.

Holy shit, I'm swimming in blood!

He coughed up blood and sucked in air. He looked up and discovered the sun wasn't a sun at all, but a brilliant full moon. His feet touched the ground, and he realized that he could have touched bottom all along. *Why did I think I was drowning?*

Gina stood barefoot on the left bank, casually playing with a walking stick. She wore a lightweight white gown that glowed as brightly as the moon reflecting in the unholy river.

"Shhhh," she said. Her voice sounded preternatural, childlike, and it sent gooseflesh down his spine. "Gina's baby is going to be OK. Don't worry. You won't see that mean old sun again." She threw the stick into the river as Lukas reluctantly approached his friend, who was acting nothing like his friend at all. He took her outstretched hand and allowed her to lead him, staggering and confused, onto the bank. Her large eyes were red-ringed, and they glowed eerily. His legs wavered, painful reminders of his recent, bizarre swim. The rest of his body felt like it had been hit with blunt instruments, exhausted and sick.

"I never wanted it to be this way," she whispered.

What does she mean?

She looked like Gina. She sounded like Gina. Her fingers felt like Gina's fingers. But she wasn't acting at all like Gina. The Gina he knew was boisterous, impetuous, fun-loving. The Gina before him was shy and withdrawn, a beaten woman.

She smiled a wan, but libidinous smile, which he found himself returning. Gently, she pushed him down onto his back on the soft, dry sand. Her long, blonde hair tickled his cheeks and bare shoulders.

"Shh," she cooed, though he wasn't about to speak. She pushed the bloody locks away from his forehead. "Lukas, I love you. I'm so sorry."

He felt himself getting aroused despite his exhaustion. He knew she wanted him, and he found himself wanting her as well.

I shouldn't let her do this. She's my friend. My father will banish her from the family. I... Oh my God, what is she doing to me?

Her long, tan legs wrapped around his, and she climbed on top of him. She plucked at the fasteners on his pants and reached inside. Lukas felt the stirrings of desire through a fog of confusion.

Take him, a voice bellowed from somewhere inside his head. Gina shook her head stubbornly, and it occurred to Lukas that she heard the voice, too.

What the hell's going on? Where's that voice coming from?

Her hands lovingly removed his clothes, and his body simultaneously felt feverish and cold. She slid her gown past her ample breasts, and he reached for them as voices quarreled in his mind. He felt her guide him inside her, and her warmth surprised him. He wouldn't have thought a vampire would feel so warm inside.

Lukas closed his eyes as waves of pleasure enveloped him. His tired muscles complained, but the rest of him relished the feeling. He took deep, shuddering breaths and reached for her body. He wanted to see her face, wanted to see if she wanted this as much as he did....

When he opened his eyes, he saw her beautiful face streaked with tears of blood.

"Gina." he gasped. He stopped bucking under her. *Why is she crying?* He reached to her face, brushed away the tears. Gina took his hand in hers. She held it forcefully.

"Oh, Lukas," she sobbed. Her teeth sank into the flesh of his wrist. He cried out in pain. Without warning, he was drowning in the red river, the moon far out of reach above.

Chapter 28

Lukas awoke in darkness with his throat so dry it hurt to breathe. The impenetrable blackness made it impossible to see where he was or if he was alone. His head felt like it was on a carnival ride, and he was afraid to stand. The symptoms were similar to his nastiest hangover, but worse.

His dreams had been nightmares from a twisted, unknown segment of his subconscious, and Gina featured in them all. Gina and some malevolent, Machiavellian vamp he had never seen before. Gina treated the stranger like an angel, but Lukas knew he was no angel—unless it was Lucifer. He reeked of evil and death like a hellish garden. Lukas remembered how she gaped at the dark vampire with reverence, and he burned with jealousy.

She shouldn't act like that toward him. She's my girl, isn't she? I mean, didn't we...?

But he didn't remember. His head swam with blurry half-impressions, and he wasn't sure what had happened.

He tried to sit up, but a wave of nausea washed over him. He gagged, dry heaved, and felt for the edge of his bed. He found it and retched over the side. Bile rose in his throat. He knew the feeling from when he was young, when Michael was out of work, and there was no food. He was violently hungry—hungrier than he had ever been. He retched again, and nearly fell forward.

Head swirling like a whirlpool, he lay back down, too weak and light-headed to stand up and seek food.

A single, 40-watt bulb clicked on overhead, and Lukas blinked, temporarily blinded. Gina strode into the room with a peculiar smile on her lips. She was well fed. Although the light was dim, it was easy to see her flushed cheeks.

More importantly, he smelled blood.

He let out a yelp and tried to shove her away, but his dizziness made him lose his balance. He crumpled into an ungraceful heap on the floor of what he now knew was the Waters Street apartment. Gina laughed, her familiar giggle gone, replaced with a demonic cackle.

He pushed himself up from the floor and back onto the futon. Gina's eyes were overly wide and innocent. It gave him the creeps.

"What've you done to me?"

She wrinkled her nose. He used to adore it: now he wanted to bash her face in.

"What your dear old man didn't have the balls to do himself."

"You didn't."

"Oh, but I did. Too easy." She shook her head back and forth and plopped down on the futon beside him, ignoring his glare.

"Bet you're hungry."

He was. If he'd had the strength, he'd have made her his first kill.

ʘ   ʘ

"I'm not sure I understand. Are you proposing that we overthrow him but let him live? Are you *suicidal*?" Errando Medina cried. His voice reverberated off the cave walls.

"Of course not, Errando," Charles said. "We may kill him in the process. We've all heard the likely consequences of that. You all know I have no compunction against killing, but Shepherd's death may be cataclysmic."

His two minutes of preaching from a proverbial soapbox were over. Now, it was up to his unlikely congregation. Heads shook. Eyes dropped to the floor in ashamed silence. Charles searched each face for a hint, a flicker of deliberation. *They're terrified. It's like asking a child to kill his parent. Only this parent has been running their lives for hundreds of years. Not to mention that his death may mean the end of them, too.*

"It's futile to try to kill him. You know that," Wynda Moireach murmured. "Even if we do this, there's no assurance that he'll die. And we may die trying." Her wavy auburn hair covered her icy blue eyes like a veil as she lifted her head to turn them toward Charles. "He is stronger than any of us, stronger than anyone on this earth."

"Not anyone," Charles replied assuredly. "I believe I know a way."

ʘ   ʘ

Vivian pondered the barrage of vampire representations from the movies she'd seen. Vampires with contorting faces, eyeteeth elongated into rattlesnake fangs, their hunger for blood turning them into gruesome demons. Vampires turning into rats, bats, or smoke. Vulnerable vampires unable to withstand a hint of sunlight. Vampires who flew.

The room was absent of light, save the tiny rays let in near the top of the blinds. She heard the clock ticking on the nightstand on Michael's side of the bed. It sounded loud as a church bell.

Look how humankind views us. We're monsters, denizens of the dark, unholy beasts from hell. It's no wonder we live like we do, hidden into dark corners, barely daring to show our faces.

She wondered if the *Shévet ha Dam* had anything to do with people's impressions about vampires. Most of *them* were butchers, just like the movies. It would make sense. After some consideration, she decided probably not. People were capable of jumping to those conclusions without any help. She thought of *Nosferatu*, the vampire from the silent black-and-white movie, his bald head, and talon-like claws. She sniffed in disdain.

Michael sighed and rolled to the opposite side of the bed, withdrawing his arm from across her body. She studied his shape in the shadows. How often she had considered this very thing—having Michael next to her in bed.

Beautiful, intelligent, urbane Michael. How had he learned so much about vampires without years of experience and insight into the *Shévet ha Dam*? And yet, despite his knowledge, he hadn't managed to teach her what Doyle had. Like about shape-shifters assuming human form by drawing in their eyeteeth. Others grew claws as sharp as razors. A smaller number had the power to change into animals—wolves, giant cats, things of similar size. It was said that Jude could become anything he wished.

"What determines the extent of one's power to transform?" Vivian had asked.

Doyle shrugged, his finger on the Pause button. On the screen, Dracula had just collapsed into a pile of rats.

"Some say age. Others say experience or drive. Me, I think it has to do with how damn evil you are."

She rolled over and faced the window. Her eye wandered to the light at the top of the collapsed blind. *Doyle said that the oldest vampires wander about in the daylight as well as humans. I'm not as old as Doyle, but I haven't burned once.*

She tried to stop the thoughts that turned over and over, like a record with a skip. The curious look Doyle shot her when she said Gary Oldman looked a lot like the historical Dracula, Vlad Dracul II.

How would you know that, Vivian?

Oh, he must look like a picture I saw once.

How would you know that, Vivian? How would you know?

Damn prodding Doyle. Broken record, over and again. She sighed.

I miss playing records. And I miss my mother, and I miss Ruth and Wesley and Phillip.

She hadn't thought of Phillip in so long. Just the thought of his blond hair and handsome face brought a tightness to her chest. Poor Phillip, sent to Europe to fight for his country only days after mustering the courage to say, "I love you." He had come close to tears when he told her he was deploying, had babbled about how he knew she was a girl who would pray for him and wait for him. And for so long, the airmail letters came regularly, and she treated each onionskin arrival as if it was part of the Good Book itself. After a time, the arrivals tapered off, and in time she was sure he was dead, or in terrible conditions he couldn't bring himself to write about. He wouldn't lie and say he was alright if he wasn't. Phillip was too honest.

Too honest. Too good. And I left him for the worst being on earth.

She rolled over again and held her hand up to view it in the dim light. Phillip's hands had been so lovely. He was avid about grooming and always smelled like soap and hair oil. And he would polish his shoes until they gleamed. He was an extraordinary dancer, forced to learn against his will by his two older sisters, and he could whip her across the floor with such finesse that she looked like a practiced dancer. She smiled fondly.

Ruth had been such a devoted friend when he left, but then she always was. Jude had killed her. She knew that now. He had killed her best friend, thus directing her down a one-way path to depression, confusion, and, eventually, her change into... into...

God, I'd have thought for sure if anyone knew, you did.

Why on earth would I know?

Well, because you're so much older than I am.

No, I'm not.

Are you certain you were never in Cambridge?

She let out a sigh of frustration. Michael stirred briefly and settled again. What was Doyle thinking? Was he confused, or was this his way of upsetting her? *He'd like that, wouldn't he? Upset me, so he can catch me off guard and... and...*

But she had no idea what he would do. What if he tried the same trap Jude had used, the sickening, hypnotic trance that made her feel like she was drowning? Did he have the strength? She didn't think so. Vivian had the impression that Doyle rubbed shoulders with evil, hoping that some of the stench would rub off on him. He didn't have the same taint, the same corruption to him. He was like the boys in school who tutored the football team to be seen with them but didn't have the strength to get on the team.

She sat up and headed to the adjoining bathroom, feet silent in the pile carpet. She closed the door carefully after her so she wouldn't let in any of the hazy bathroom light. They rarely bothered to lower the blind on the bathroom window since it let in so little light. She crossed the white tile, dropped the lid, and sat on the toilet.

Head in her hands, she willed her mind to stop reeling. Then, she became aware of Doyle's harsh whisper coming from the office.

"Yeah, no shit. I understand you're uneasy with the whole thing, but you've gotta trust me on this one. Just do it."

She sat stone-still, straining her ears to hear above her pounding heart. What in the hell was Doyle doing?

"I know you say it's done, but I'm looking at my screen here on the computer, and it's not done. I don't have anything."

What time is it? What is he doing up? Her breath caught in her throat. *Has he been reading my thoughts?* She struggled to remember what it was that she had been thinking.

"Kyle, just listen to me, will you? This is really important. They can't know what we're doing here—"

Who? Who can't know? Is he getting us tickets for the plane? Or something else? Why is he whispering?

"...so just do it, get it over with, and go on with your pitiful existence."

Silence again.

"Fine, fine. Don't do me any favors, asshole."

She heard the phone settle into the cradle with a bang. A second later, there was the sound of a lighter and an inhale.

She heard the office door open as Doyle headed outside, closing the door behind him. Vivian rose. As she tucked back into bed, she pulled Michael's sleeping form close to her trembling one.

Chapter 29

Jude pressed the *play* button on the tiny stereo, and Albinoni's Adagio for Organ and Strings filled the room. Speakers positioned just so around his newly acquired office on Jones Street sang in perfectly equalized sound. He smiled as the strings took up their melancholy melody and eased himself into the leather chaise. He took in the apartment, which he had learned from Gina was Michael's favorite: its elegant pieces of art, impeccable decor, and classical music offered near the stereo. *Michael, I find myself respecting you the more I learn about you. If only you hadn't interfered with Vivian.*

He reclined and let his mind wander to Gina, entering her thoughts without her knowledge. He lingered only long enough to ensure that she continued to struggle with her newly transformed vampire, Lukas. He relished her inner turmoil about turning the boy she loved into a bloodsucker. He paused long enough to let her know of his presence, which brought about a whole new wave of torment. He smiled.

He raised a wineglass of cooling blood to his lips. He appreciated Michael's taste in leaded crystal.

A French phone rested on a marble-topped table nearby. He lifted the receiver and halfheartedly dialed the well-known numbers to Dunning's home. No answer.

Undiscouraged, he tried Charles' cellular phone. Also, no answer.

He replaced the receiver and tried to reach for him. Nothing. It was like Charles no longer existed.

His brow furrowed. There were certain situations where his reach for one of his offspring would not succeed. If Charles had blocked Jude, he might not be able to pierce his defenses without considerable effort. Jude wasn't sure. Charles had never had reason to block him before.

Jude knew, though, that Charles had begun to question Jude's station in the *Shévet ha Dam*. Jude frightened him—had for centuries—but he had been able to put his feelings aside. This facade was crumbling fast under Charles' skepticism, which had increased to unprecedented levels after Jerusha's escape. Jude also knew that Charles believed Jude to be ignorant of his mistrust. Combined with the frantic tone of voice in the messages Jude had found on his voice mail, he knew that Charles' desertion was imminent.

Jude snapped his fingers and placed the wineglass on the rug. The trembling, pale body of a naked college boy shuffled to him on its knees as fast as his drained body allowed. Jude focused on the retracted talon on his index finger and seized the boy's arm with his right hand. The nail grew nearly four inches and sharpened as it extended. The stunned boy stared blankly, as if viewing himself from out of his body.

Jude deftly positioned the wineglass under the boy's arm with his foot and sliced the arm open. Blood gushed from the wound as muscles and tendons were exposed, and the boy looked as though he wanted to shriek, but his mouth drew open soundlessly. He watched as blood spurted from his arm and poured onto the carpet and into the glass. He lurched back and forth as if he was about to be sick and collapsed forward. Jude lifted his filled glass and kicked the boy backward with his foot. The boy's eyes stared at the ceiling, his blood and his life drained from his body. Jude shook his head in disgust. *Bloody humans.*

He lifted the glass to his lips. *Yes, bloody, bloody humans.*

03　80

Lukas was barely conscious. His breath came in deep inhalations, paused, and left so slowly Gina barely saw his chest budge. His eyes darted back and forth under their lids. Judging from their rapid movement, she was amazed his breath wasn't coming in short gasps. It was the eye movement of a rabbit pursued by a determined fox.

She tried to enter his thoughts the way Jude invaded hers, but the moment Lukas sensed her, he forced her out and blocked her from coming back in. It was the first vampiric talent he had displayed, summoned out of sheer hatred. For a moment, though, she saw his thoughts and his feelings about her. Lukas hated her more than she loved him. It was no meager comparison.

She sighed and leaned in to speak into Lukas' ear.

"Lukas, where's Michael?" she asked gently. "Where's your father?"

Lukas' head lolled to the side drunkenly, and she jumped back. He sighed, and his features took on an open, innocent look.

"Bye baby bunting, Daddy's gone a-hunting," came the reply. He smiled feebly, tried to laugh, and coughed on his saliva. His eyes opened, bulged for a moment as he hacked, and then settled back down. Gina sighed again in frustration.

"Lukas, where's Vivian?" she prodded. Lukas' head wobbled from side to side.

"No!" he retorted, his voice childlike.

"I need to know, Lukas. Please. Where is she?"

Lukas paused, licked his lips. His tongue trickled with blood from where it had pricked on his new fangs. The taste set him off like a finger squeezing the trigger of a gun. Without warning, he sat bolt upright. He seized her by the throat, lifting her off the bed and twisting her body painfully. Her feet dangled inches from the floor. Her neck felt surrounded by steel cables. She silently cursed Jude for making her turn Lukas after he had drained her of her strength. *He should've known this might happen. Now I'm defenseless. Oh, God, he's going to kill me!*

Lukas stared into her eyes and cocked his head to the side. His lips peeled back malevolently, tongue playing on the canine fangs that part of Gina refused to believe she saw although she had given them to him. He lunged almost playfully at her, effortlessly bringing her body toward his mouth and snapping his teeth at her neck. Gina wondered where he found the strength when only moments ago, he was, to all appearances, incapacitated.

"You want me to talk? Feed me, you fuckin' bitch," he growled, and cast her aside. She landed on the floor with a solid thump and winced.

He collapsed back onto the mattress. Gina wasn't sure if he was spent or had nothing more to say. She didn't want to stay and find out. Nevertheless, she found herself staring for several seconds, dumbfounded.

Lukas was as still as a corpse. His breath had returned to indiscernible inhales and exhales. Gina curled up into a ball and rubbed her worried brow. She didn't dare take her eyes off him.

God, she loved him so much! And it took having to kill him to realize how much. *At least he's not dead. Not really. Just undead, like me. Like Michael.*

As she rose and brushed herself off, she decided that she didn't care what Jude had told her; she was going to feed Lukas. Not from herself. After that outburst, she knew she had to build her strength to cope with him. No, something small would do. A rat, maybe.

I can't wander too far, she thought, descending the stairs. Apart from the danger of daylight, she couldn't give Lukas any chance of escape if night should fall before she returned. She would find a meal for herself from the ragtag crowd that gathered at the gas station and bring Lukas an animal from the alley. There were always stray cats and rats. If all else failed, there was the neighbor's dog.

She froze, her hand extended halfway to the doorknob.

He didn't take me.

He'd had the strength to overpower and drain her. Why didn't he? If he was as hungry as she had been—as every vampire she knew had been when they awoke for the first time—he should have drained her on the spot.

Why hadn't he?

He loves me! He hates me so much because he still cares, and he doesn't understand what I've done to him. He doesn't know that I didn't have a choice.

She was so heartened by this thought, she skipped out of the apartment. She crossed the alley to the gas station where some unwary customer or homeless drunk would soon be her feast, a smile of hope stretched across her weary, fanged face.

ᘏ ᘒ

Doyle was gone when Vivian rose much later than her usual dusk. He had left a note on the counter next to an orange drained of juice through two puncture marks.

Be back later.
Don't leave.
—Doyle
P.S. I didn't taste a thing.

Vivian crumpled the note and picked up the withered orange to examine it. Michael padded up behind her, scratching his head and flat stomach sleepily. He wrapped his arms around her from behind and peered at the orange over her shoulder.

"Cute," he observed. Vivian chunked the orange into the trash and threw the note in after.

"I knew he had a weak sense of humor," she remarked. She turned around in his arms and gave him a kiss, which he returned with fervor.

"What'd the note say?"

"Be back, don't go anywhere. No reason."

"What d'you wanna do?" he asked.

She shrugged. She supposed she should tell Michael about the conversation she had overheard, but Doyle and his secretiveness had pissed her off. She wanted to inconvenience the cocky, bald-headed bugger.

"To hell with Doyle. I'm hungry," she replied.

He took her hand. "Let's go hunt."

They drove through a light, drizzling rain to a bike path about three kilometers away from their usual hunting ground. The wipers screeched in protest against a sprinkling of water, and it set Vivian's teeth on edge. Everything was getting on her nerves. The orange. Doyle. The rain. The way the tires splashed through the occasional puddle. Her thoughts were haunted by portions of dialogue overheard through the bathroom door.

I understand you're uneasy with the whole thing... This is extremely important... They can't know what we're doing here.

Her mind twisted with possibilities. *Why would someone be uncomfortable doing a favor for Doyle? What is he asking of them? And who can't know what they were doing?*

Michael parked the car in a lonely gravel parking lot. With one hand on the door, he turned to Vivian.

"Ready?"

She hesitated. Now would be the perfect time to tell him, before they felt the exhilaration of fresh blood flowing in their veins, before they became giddy from the hunt and the moment for serious conversation passed. If Michael knew what she had overheard, maybe he would know how to make sense of it. Perhaps he could put her mind at ease. If not, she would be on edge the whole night. When he returned, her behavior towards Doyle would be highly annoyed at best and suspect at worst. She couldn't risk that. Not if Doyle still had the connections with the *Shévet ha Dam* he claimed to have.

She licked her lower lip carefully and brought it up to moisten the upper. She smiled at Michael's concerned expression, his furrowed brow, the lines around his eyes.

"How much do you trust Doyle?"

He started to answer, but she cut him off with a pointed finger. "And none of that macho bonding crap. I don't care if he's your hunting buddy from way back or if you've gone chasing girls together. I mean, do you count on him? Has he lied to you? Would you trust him with your life?"

She ran out of wind and paused. Michael blinked and looked down, his heavy brow still furrowed.

"I hadn't told him you were coming with me, if that's what you mean," he admitted. Vivian's eyes popped.

"Why?"

"Because he could've easily told me over the phone that he was okay with it, wouldn't tell a soul, and then turned around and let it slip to one of his Tribe buddies. I had to see his face, had to look him in the eye as he told me, or I wouldn't have known for sure if I could trust him or not."

"You risked my life?"

"No! Absolutely not. If he'd reacted strangely, there are other places in Europe we could've gone. I would've told Doyle that we'd stay here, and we would've hightailed it to London or Prague as soon as he turned his back. I wouldn't put you at risk."

She blinked, not sure what to think. So far, Doyle hadn't turned them in, though he knew where they were staying. They *had* been there for weeks. From what she had learned of the Blood Tribe, her presence in Europe would not have wrinkled their plans to kill her or bring her back to Jude.

"What about Lukas? Don't you think the fact that we can't reach him might be a sign that something's gone wrong?"

"Why do you think I'm going back to the States?"

"Just you?"

Michael sighed.

"I told you I'm not going to put you at risk—"

"I'm not going or staying anywhere without you, Michael."

"Vivian, if Jude is behind what's going on with Lukas, then you're in danger—"

"So don't go."

"He's my *son*. Vivian, I love you, but *he's my son*."

Two thoughts hit her with equally heart-wrenching force. One, that Michael had said he loved her. Two was that despite that fact, there was a chance they'd be separated before long.

"Don't leave me," she whispered. She hated herself for pleading, for sounding so needy, but the words tumbled out of her mouth. "Please. I wouldn't know who to trust. I'd be terrified to go anywhere, do anything..." she let her words trail off, unsure how to continue. Then she knew.

"I love you, too."

He smiled, leaned in slowly, took her hands, and kissed her. His lips were gentle and warm.

Damn fangs. I wish there was a way to get rid of them for a while.

After a blissful moment, they parted slowly, neither one wanting to cut it short. Vivian grinned flirtatiously. Michael began to respond, but his smile faded on his lips.

"Vivian. Your fangs. They're gone!"

Chapter 30

At seven-thirty, Doyle arrived at A-6, a club directly off Autobahn 6 for which it was named. He knew letting Sabine decide where they met was a mistake as soon as he entered. A-6 was doing minimal business for a Thursday night—mostly an after-work executive crowd—but it didn't stop the disc jockeys from spinning piercing music over an extravagant sound system. The volume wasn't set for anyone with supernatural hearing, and the effect was like putting his ears near a pair of tuning forks and letting a toddler strike them at will.

A round bar about two and a half meters across stood centered in the first room. The bartender, a blond who looked cut out for the job of looking handsome for tips, bopped back and forth to the rhythm. His ears clearly did not feel assaulted. The center bar was the only well-lit portion of the club, and the overabundance of fluorescent overheads reminded Doyle of daylight. Four rooms branched off from this core. To the right, rump-shaking R & B and European Top-40 rooms. To his left, a shadowy Techno area screeched and boomed next to a restaurant playing clips from each club in turn at decibel levels tolerable to a vampire. It was there he was scheduled to meet Sabine.

He ambled up to the bouncing bartender and looked around for an idea. Above the bar, red, silver, and blue cans of Red Bull formed a pyramid, above which hung a sign: "Red Bull *mit Wodka, 8 DM.*"

"Lemme get a Red Bull and Vodka."

The bartender stopped dancing.

"*Was?*"

Doyle paused, agitated. He wasn't sure if the volume of the music or his use of English had confused him, but he decided to play it safe and speak German.

"*Ich möchte ein Red Bull mit Wodka.*"

The barkeep nodded, which set his entire body into rhythm overload again. He danced, this time possessed by Michael Jackson, as he prepared Doyle's drink. Doyle searched the nearby restaurant for Sabine, but, as usual, she had made herself hidden.

"Acht Deutsche Mark."

Doyle snapped back.

"Was?" His turn to look like an idiot, he supposed. The bartender smiled a toothpaste-ad smile and held up four stout fingers.

"Acht Deutsche Mark."

Doyle nodded and gave him the required funds, then added an extra as a tip. The bartender nodded again, and danced to the next patron.

Doyle loathed the idea of arriving first. It would add to Sabine's suspicion that he was desperate.

He picked up his drink and trudged to the restaurant, keeping an eye peeled for Sabine. Unless she was hidden around the corner of the L-shaped room, she hadn't arrived yet. It would be just like her to force him to search for her. He swore under his breath.

She had refused to give him the electronic tickets he requested. It didn't take a Phi Beta Kappa to figure out why she demanded personal delivery this time. She wanted to make sure Doyle wasn't doing what he wasn't supposed to be doing. That is, exactly what he *was* doing. Why was it that every time someone wanted to see if he was lying, they tried to look at his face? He knew he was skilled at veiling his thoughts. Was his face that transparent? *Jesus, I hope not.*

He and Michael, although not close, had always managed a level of businesslike professionalism that he valued more than he let on. Michael spoke to him as an equal, an act that Doyle held more valuable than all the money the *Shévet ha Dam* paid for his less than honorable jobs. The higher-ups in the *Shévet ha Dam* always treated him like a weasel. And not without reason. The ways and means he used to acquire some of his trickier items weren't always scrupulous or close to legal. Never mind that it was the Blood Tribe who'd formed him into a virtuoso of unlawful acts. Although the *Shévet ha Dam* consisted of cold-hearted killers, they considered themselves, if not law-abiding, at least dignified. They prided themselves on class, for the most part. On the other hand, Doyle Christy wasn't a man of class and had long ago shed his last shred of dignity. The organization he had debased himself for would never consider him an equal, and for that very reason.

As for Vivian, he liked her, too, because she didn't like him. Crazy as it sounded, he respected her for disliking the sides of his personality he had shown her. She had a proud, moral character that he admired because he lacked it. She was the kind of woman that made a man want to better himself. And for her, even if it was only for a handful of days, he was doing just that. He would show Vivian and Michael that Doyle Christy was a vamp to be trusted and hope to earn their continued friendship.

The restaurant was awash in the amber glow of bulbs covered with tinted lampshades that colored everything yellow and brown—the walls, the tables, the bartenders. His Red Bull and vodka had assumed the shade of muddy urine.

Sabine was there, resting comfortably and patiently in the corner booth. Polished, as usual. Her pale, unblemished complexion contrasted starkly against the jet-black of her glossy upswept hair, giving her the appearance of a china doll. Her rounded cheeks and lacy clothes completed the likeness. An untouched bloody Mary rested on the table before her. A hint of a smile rested on her lips.

Ok, Doyle, just get through this without making an ass of yourself, and get the tickets. Don't let Michael down. Do something right, for once.

〜　〜

Lukas awoke to the stench of garbage, wet fur, and blood. Something wriggled and scratched against his pillow. He opened his eyes and nearly jumped out of his skin. The only thing keeping him from doing so was that he didn't think he had the strength.

Dangling by its tail from Gina's hand was a fat, filthy rat. It wriggled and tried to bend itself in half by its meaty tail to attack her, without success. Gina giggled like a kid with a new toy. Lukas groaned.

"Get that disgusting critter away from me," he said, gagging. She did.

"I thought you were hungry."

"I... well, I..." the thought of bringing the reeking vermin near his vampire-sensitive sinuses nearly made him gag again, but his hunger overcame his nausea. He reconsidered the wriggling rat with the expression of a man offered castration without anesthesia.

"Give the bastard over," he said, sitting up slowly and extending a long limb. She complied. It promptly bit him in the webbing of his right hand.

"*Oww!* Fucker."

Gina giggled. Lukas glanced at her and found himself smiling.

"Guess you don't have to worry about rabies, huh?" she offered timidly.

He shook his head. Dirty blond curls bobbed above slumped shoulders.

"No, guess not."

Gina bit her lip and wrinkled her nose, managing to flinch at the same time.

He took a deep breath, staring at the writhing rat in its panicky eyes.

"Well, here goes nothing."

He almost held his nose like his father had shown him to do when taking a teaspoon of vile-tasting medicine. When his fangs sank into the rat, he wished he had. It could not have been worse if he had gone swimming at Chatham Waste Disposal on the hottest day in August after a downpour of acid rain precipitated by a generous helping of air pollution from the paper mill. That was the image that came to mind as he sucked his first helping of blood from the rat.

The next sensation was one he had never been able to appreciate fully.

Growing up the child of a vampire, he had tried to imagine thousands of times what drinking blood was like. He used to play games with the neighborhood children, where he tackled them to the ground and forced them to endure bites and hickeys. When his victims were little girls, they thought he was silly and playing at kissing. The boys quickly ostracized him from games of make-believe. He remembered wishing as he lost each baby tooth that maybe, this time, one would grow like Daddy's fangs, and he would get to go hunting with his father when he disappeared nights. He had cried when he realized his canines had stopped growing. Any bleeding nick or cut his body suffered, he had put to his lips. He would suck the blood and try to envision the sensations his father felt as he drank. And there was no debate about his costume every Halloween.

The experience put every fantasy to shame, even from a putrid rat.

His eyes rolled back in his head, and he shuddered, draining the rodent quickly to avoid inhaling the stench. Within a minute, the ecstasy reached its pinnacle, and it overshadowed the best orgasm a hundredfold.

The rat was dead. He threw it to the floor, disgusted with both the rat and himself.

"Death Rush. That last part."

"I know."

"Oh. Yeah, I guess you would."

They didn't speak for a minute, their eyes dropping to the floor, then to separate corners of the room. Every so often, they stole a glance at one another. Each second passing made conversation that much more challenging to begin.

She moved to a corner of the mattress. He didn't turn.

"Are you draining people?"

Although he avoided using the word "killing," she refrained from answering for a beat. Was almost too ashamed to answer.

"Sometimes," she murmured

"Only sometimes?"

Now her downcast eyes looked at the same nothing on the floor as Lukas.

"It wasn't my idea. None of it was my idea. I'd forgotten about what it was like. The rush. Living every night with death and enjoying it. Staring it in the face and not fearing it... "

"Everyone fears death."

"Not if they're old enough. Not if they're like Jude—"

"Jude? Is that what this is about? Is he—" Lukas began to say, "Is he the man from my dreams?" but stopped short when he realized how ridiculous it sounded.

"Is he behind all of this?"

"Didn't you know?" Gina asked, genuinely surprised. Lukas slumped over farther. He had known. Of course, he had known. Taking Vivian in was like handing Jude Shepherd an open-ended invitation, but he and Michael had decided it was a gamble worth taking. He was reminded of campy flicks in which a vampire stood outside a door or window and waited for someone to invite him in. According to superstition, it rendered humans powerless against vampires. He and Michael may as well have stood at the door and invited Jude inside their lives.

"Oh, Christ. Oh, man. He's got you, and he used you to get to me. He needs me to get to Dad and Vivian. Shit. So much for the rebel alliance."

She gave him a blank look.

"But he won't touch us. He only wants her."

"*Bullshit*. Don't tell me you believe that. He'll use us to get to Vivian, and then he'll kill us. He hasn't been the leader of the *Shévet ha Dam* for centuries only to let a tiny group like our family go when he's through using us."

Gina tried to interrupt, but he dismissed her with a wave and continued.

"How do you figure a group of twenty or so vampires controls the *entire global* vampire population? He kills anybody who stands against him. What's one of the things that can kill a vampire? Give up? *Another fucking vampire! They* control the identity scams. *They* control the population growth. *They* try to tell us how and where to live. And, in case you've forgotten, they're *extremely* against individual groups cropping up, especially ones that stand against the Tribe. I'm surprised they've left us alone as long as they have. No, he won't let us go. He'll kill us as soon as he has what he needs."

They stopped staring at the imaginary spot on the floor and shared a matching, panicked stare.

"He'll know if we lie."

Lukas shook his head, bewildered.

"If we tell the truth, *all* of us die."

❧ ❧

Vivian blinked, disbelieving. Her fangs were gone? She remembered the mirror on the reverse side of the sun visor. She flipped it down, pulled back her cheek with her index finger, and stared.

They *were* gone. She checked both sides. In place of the fangs, normal eyeteeth stood in their place.

"You're right! Oh, no. How will I eat?"

It seemed so odd. The evidence of her undead life was gone. She could walk among humans, smile as broadly as she wished, and no one would stare. But she wasn't one of them. She was a vampire. The fangs she resented as a symbol of her change were also the means of her survival. What had she done?

Michael took a firm hold of her arm until she calmed down.

"Vivian, stop. It'll be OK."

Easy for him to say. He didn't just lose his fangs.

"If need be, I'll help you hunt tonight. We'll find a way. It's not that hard, I'm sure. Better if you start thinking about what might have generated the change."

"I don't know. I was just—" She paused, retraced the events preceding the change. They'd been kissing.

Yes! Of course! She should've made the connection. She had been thinking about how complicated it was to kiss with her fangs in the way, and they must have retracted then. And then when she knew they were gone, she had panicked, and...

She felt with her tongue. They were back. She had simply wished them gone and back again.

"Holy moly. That's just too easy."

"What?"

She smiled, exposing her magical disappearing/reappearing fangs. Michael choked on a laugh.

"What did you do?"

"I just *thought* about them. When we were kissing, I wished they'd go away for a while, and they did. Then when you told me they were gone, I regretted it and wished they were back. And abracadabra."

Michael cackled with relieved laughter and gazed at her with admiration.

"Damn. You're the first shape-shifter I've met. This is wonderful! I wonder what else you can do."

Vivian paused and thought about it but couldn't think of anything she wanted to try. She was too excited.

"I don't know where to start. What else have you heard of vampires doing?"

"Let me think. Ummm, claws. Can you do claws?"

She almost didn't want to try, but she was too curious not to. She thought of Nosferatu, and the hideously long, taloned fingers of Max Shrek. She stared at her fingers and pictured them growing into grotesque claws.

Nothing happened.

"Are you trying?" Michael asked after a moment.

"I thought so. I mean, I'm not sure what the difference is or why it worked the first time. I guess it's because I don't *want* claws growing out of my fingers."

Michael laughed.

"Well, I guess we'll just have to wait and see what you want to grow next."

Vivian pondered this a moment.

"Maybe I can wish myself a fuller bosom," she laughed.

Michael leaned in, and took her hands again.

"I *like* your bosom," he said sincerely.

They kissed again, and she would not have wished for anything else.

C(3   &)

Sabine left A-6 empty-handed and smiling. She could have used telepathy, but she suspected the mental lines were running hotter than the satellite-based ones. Outside the bar, she removed a cell phone from her pocket and pulled out the sticks holding her hair in place, allowing it to tumble past her shoulders.

She dialed a familiar number and raked her fingers through her hair. The other end picked up as soon as she reached the tips.

"Hello?"

"Hey," she crooned. "It's me. He picked them up. They're headed to Savannah."

"We'll be there. Thanks."

She hung up.

Chapter 31

They returned to the house after an exhilarating hunt. Vivian's body thrummed with energy. The combination of the blood, the rush, and Michael's taut body were magnificent. The drizzling rain did not spoil her mood. If anything, it left her more invigorated.

On the drive home, her hands reveled in the feel of Michael's body. His muscles looked so defined under his wet clothes. She ran her hands over his thighs, reached under his shirt, caressed his broad chest, and stroked his short, wet hair. He did nothing to hinder her, casting delighted glances in her direction. Both of his hands were on the wheel, which Vivian knew was unlike him. She worried only briefly—long enough to realize he was racing the little rental car home as though the country roads were the autobahn.

He didn't park in the garage but instead drew the car to a halt directly outside the gate. The two rushed through it and for the front door.

They found Doyle sitting in a patio chair waiting for them. He greeted them with a glower, and they stopped.

"Where. The fuck. Have you been?"

"Out. Hunting," Michael replied. It was the second time she had seen him unsettled, and she hated that it was Doyle who'd caught him off guard.

Doyle nodded with exaggeration and glanced back to where she and Michael had been so frisky only moments before. Vivian had had enough of Doyle's attitude.

"Who the hell are you to tell us not to go anywhere and not tell us why?" she demanded. Michael shot her a shocked look, Doyle doubly so. Then he caught himself.

"*I* am the one risking my neck to get you plane tickets back to the States. *I* am the one trying to make sure that Michael gets back to find out what's been going on with his son. *I* am the one who lied to a beautiful vampire tonight who'd just as soon kill me as look at me if she knew who I'd gotten these tickets for. *That's* who the fuck I am."

"He never said to get the tickets!" she exploded.

"Well, they're here. It's done," Doyle snapped.

Michael's head swiveled between the two of them. Finally, he accepted the tickets from Doyle. "Thanks, man." And he meant it. Doyle gave him an "Aw shucks, 'twernt nothin'" look in return.

"Wanna come inside?" Michael offered. Doyle shook his head.

"I shouldn't be underfoot while you guys get ready." He reconsidered as soon as the words left his lips. "But I guess you'll need a ride to the airport."

"How soon do we leave?" Vivian asked.

"Like, now."

Michael and Vivian packed in silence and haste, their trains of thought traveling in separate directions. Doyle, meanwhile, spent his time acting as the house DJ. Unfortunately, his taste in music leaned toward the most nerve-rattling available.

Michael tried to reach Lukas, but, as he predicted, there was no answer. Gina's number sent him straight to voice mail, which he didn't bother to use. He was beginning to think he would have no luck getting a hold of anyone trustworthy, but he managed to get through to Josh on his cell phone. Vivian could clearly hear the young vampire's voice as she threw her clothing into her suitcase.

"Michael? Hey, dude. How have you been? What's up?"

"I need you to be at Savannah International in about ten hours."

"Well, yeah. Sure. You sound freaked, man. What's wrong?"

Michael's voice tensed as his throat constricted.

"Have you seen Lukas lately?"

There was an elongated pause on her end of the line, and he sat down on the floor. He almost thought Josh had hung up on him, except for the staticky sound of his breath.

"You haven't been able to reach Lukas?" Josh asked. His voice was flat with poorly hidden concern.

"Josh, what's going on? What do you know?" He strove to keep his voice level, but the anger and frustration came through. He regretted the accusing tone, but didn't want to interrupt to apologize. Apologies could be made after he knew what had happened to his son.

"Nothing. I mean... It's just too weird to be a coincidence. Randi sad that Gina hasn't been to work in about four days now. Gina never said anything about quitting, and you know that's not like her. She won't answer her phone, either."

"Shit," Michael breathed. "Josh, man, don't go to any of our apartments anymore."

"Michael, are you saying what I think you're saying?"

"If you're saying I think Jude's found us, then yeah, that's what I'm saying."

"Fuuuuck."

"Just be at the airport in about ten hours. Rent a car if you've got the cash. Week, month, whatever you can get. A national chain, OK? Nothing local. I want to be able to return it wherever it winds up."

"You got it."

They made hasty good-byes and hung up. Michael shook as if he had stepped into a sub-zero refrigerator. He had heard stories of the merciless Jude Shepherd, tales about vampires begging for clemency who died in gruesome ways: impaled on spikes and drained of their last drop of blood, dismembered, hearts ripped out, locked into coffins, and burned alive. And those were vampires he kept *close* to him. What cruel death would Shepherd envision for the human son of a tiny vampire family who refused to bend to the will of the *Shévet ha Dam*?

Lukas, if anything has happened to you, I'll never forgive myself.

ೞ   ೲ

"Block your mind. Act on instinct. Don't use words in your thoughts, like 'I hate this bastard.' Hate him all you want, but don't put the thought into words. He might read it, he might not. He might not bother, but in case he does, dwell on something that prevents whatever crosses your mind from becoming words. Like song lyrics. Something easy, like maybe just one line from a favorite song or a rhyme."

"And this will keep him from being able to read my thoughts?" Lukas asked for what was probably the tenth time. Gina shrugged.

"You did really well with me," she said. "But I'm..." she trailed off, unable to state the obvious thought which filled them both with terror.

"You're not Jude Shepherd," Lukas finished.

They shared a reflective moment. Gina took his hand.

"Why can't we run away again?" he asked. Gina laughed softly and shook her head.

"He has a link with me. Sometimes, I can feel him poking around inside my head, reading my thoughts, and tracking how I feel. Through me, he has a link to you. He has a link to all vampires, supposedly, but with me..."

She shook her head. She didn't want to tell Lukas about what had happened to her, but she felt pressed to explain why she had betrayed him. At first, with her head filled with Jude's coaching and her veins burning with his blood, she was helpless to resist. Now, hours later, Jude rested easy, knowing that he had complete control over both. It was compliance or death, and even with the former, there remained the possibility of the latter.

"I'm addicted," she said. "He's doing to me what he did to Vivian. I'm worse than a junkie, and he's the drug. Even though my blood's diluted with other people's now, I *can't* leave him. I couldn't tell him 'No' to anything. Not even for you."

Tears burned, and she turned away. He knew her well enough to know she wanted no comfort, only a chance to compose herself, but he put a hand on her shoulder, anyway. She didn't turn around, wouldn't let him see her red-ringed eyes.

"If we run, he'll be on us before we reach South Carolina, and he'll kill us."

Lukas put his head into his hands. Every answer to the questions he had posed was as he suspected. He'd hoped that Gina, with her new insights into Jude's mind and methods, would have uncovered some flaw, some Achilles' heel that would allow them to survive. So far, Jude's armor appeared unchipped.

"And you think deceiving him is the only solution?"

Gina shook her head and sniffled loudly, turning it to face him before she answered.

"I think either way, we're dead. But at least this way, we tried."

Chapter 32

Gina steered her Reliant K onto Victory Drive through a swiftly descending fog less than an hour later. An enormous palm leaf swooped down from one of the trees bordering the street and landed on the windshield with a loud thump. They cried out in alarm, each expecting the shadow to be Jude, the doors of the car to be ripped off the hinges.

But it was only a leaf. Gina pulled to the side of the road. Lukas rolled down his window and hurled it onto the roadside. Conversation, which had been slight up to that point, stopped during the rest of the trip.

Gina pulled into their usual parking spot across the street from the apartment on Jones Street. It was the only thing ordinary about the night. Lukas stepped out of the car with trepidation and stared at the apartment door. Fond memories assailed him. Christmas with Michael, the apartment redolent with pine. The day he and Michael discovered that Lukas was the taller of the two—he was eleven. More than any place he had known, this was home. It was his father's. Jude had desecrated it.

He and Gina shared an encouraging glance and crossed the cobblestones. The door, typically lit by a dim bulb when the apartment was occupied, remained in the shadows.

Gina extended her arm to knock, but the door opened before her first rap. Jude Shepherd held the door, his full height nowhere near Lukas's. Nonetheless, he dominated the occasion. His eyes were every bit as wide, dark, and threatening as Lukas recalled from his dream. His black, wavy hair shone, despite the dim light. His left hand held one of Michael's crystal wine glasses, drying blood crusting inside.

"Do come in," Jude said. His voice was genteel but restrained as he waved a hand graciously into the apartment like a host welcoming company. *Dinner guests*, Lukas thought, and dismissed the subsequent idea with a shiver.

He had chosen a song lyric to recite mentally as the three of them conversed, but it flew from his mind the moment he heard the false politeness in Jude's voice. He caught a flickering glance in his direction from the corner of Jude's eye as he led them past the naked corpse of a young man and into the sitting room. Jude's eyebrow arched in amusement at Lukas's expression.

Lukas struggled for a new verse to focus on, anything to try to block Jude's telepathy. The only one that came to mind he had learned years ago from one of his babysitters and was so inauspicious he nearly laughed. "Now I lay me down to sleep, I pray the Lord my soul to keep, if I should die before I wake, I pray the Lord my soul to take."

Maybe it's not that bad an idea. Jude will think I'm scared silly. Which, of course, is true.

He focused on the verse, tweaking it with a shrill, infantile pitch that would curdle milk and would also—hopefully—deter any mental intruders.

Gina, he noticed, trailed behind Jude like a scolded dog. Her head was down, staring at her folded hands. *Not a good sign, not a—No! Focus on the verse. I pray the Lord my soul to keep...*

Jude did not bother sliding the door closed behind them, but crossed the room and sat behind Michael's desk. Lukas scanned the room. Four sets of paned windows lined the wall behind Jude's seat, each nearly reaching the ceiling. Closed plantation blinds. Other than the single door, the windows were the only means of escape. Lukas had no clue if the garden behind those windows was filled with Jude's minions.

He's probably alone. He wouldn't think he needed help disposing of two baby vampires, even if we're his descendants.

A wave of fear and love washed over him—love for his father and fear for Michael's safety. *Dear God, please let Dad and Vivian be safe. Don't let anything... If I should die before I wake...I pray the Lord my soul to take.*

"So," Jude began, hands pressed together before his rigid mouth. His voice was as hollow and poisonous as rattlesnake fangs, "I assume Gina's told you why I insisted you become one of the family." His sneer belied the implication of Lukas's acceptance into his fold. Lukas braced himself, struggling to suppress words for the thoughts that came to mind. He already had a family. How dare Jude assume Lukas would wish to be part of his "family!"

Focus. He's trying to distract you by belaboring the point. So far, I don't think he's done the mental thing, but it's only a matter of time. Now I lay me down to sleep...

"Yes."

Jude flexed his palms back and forth. The effect was like watching a spider mate with its reflection in a mirror. *I pray the Lord...*

Not using words to think was much more complicated than Lukas imagined. Although he struggled against them, vocabulary jumped into his thoughts. It was an act learned in childhood that was difficult to unlearn in less than an hour. He focused on the verse. He wasn't sure if it was becoming a mantra or a bona fide prayer.

Jude's eyes arched up, and his head lowered. The effect was a contemptuous glare that weakened Lukas's knees.

"And?"

"Oh. And..."

Now I lay me down to sleep...

"They're in Costa Rica." *I pray the Lord my soul to keep. If I should die before I wake...*

Unseen fingers massaged his mind, searched for a sign of untruth.

Here comes the mental shit. Oh, Christ. Don't let me... I pray the Lord...

"Where in Costa Rica?" he prodded.

"Oh. Um, a place called *Vista del Mar.* Near San Jose." Lukas forced the memory of their Costa Rican safehouse to mind.

"Mmm." Again, the mating spiders.

The idea that Jude was mulling Lukas's answer to his questions was asinine, but some part of Lukas hoped just that. More than likely, Jude contemplated the most efficient means of killing them. He continued with his mantra-prayer, trying like hell to keep his eyes from flickering to the corners of the room to search for a formerly unseen means to escape.

"Gina," Jude barked. Gina held fast to her position on Lukas's left. Jude fixed her with a stern, reproving look.

"Gina," he cooed, his voice that of a loving father dealing with a stubborn child. She gasped, and her hands flew to her temples. Judging from her agonized expression, the torture she felt was excruciating. Lukas winced in sympathy, and he wished for a way to share her pain. Her knees weakened, and she staggered on hobbled legs to Jude's side, where she crumpled.

Jude grabbed her roughly by her hair, forcing her mouth within centimeters of his forearm. Although healed, Lukas noticed an area pinker than the rest of his arm. He had broken the skin there lately, and often. Her mouth opened instinctively, and he withdrew her head with a cruel smile, depriving her of the blood—his blood—that she desperately craved. Her eyes bugged, those of a junkie eyeing an out-of-reach fix.

"He's lying, isn't he, Gina?" Jude queried, his voice filled with rancor. She held out, trying desperately not to betray her loved ones, but the struggle pained her. He yanked her closer. His skin was a hair's breadth from her dry, cracked lips. She looked willing to let him rip the hair from her head if only she could sink her fangs into his arm.

"Gina?" he prodded.

"I... I..."

She didn't reply. Lukas knew Gina well enough to understand her grimace. She was undergoing an intense internal battle. It pained him to see her like this. His heart wrenched in anguish.

Why is he doing this to her? Why doesn't he just get what he wants from me and leave her alone? The questions were rhetorical. He was a vampire in more than one sense. Jude lived to inflict pain; he lived to torment every creature he encountered. He drank the blood of the living and drained them of life, and he lived to drain the joy, hope, and love from any being, living or undead.

Gina didn't answer. Lukas only hoped that he would be as strong when it came to his turn.

Jude lifted Gina's body like a pile of limp rags. He buried his face into her neck, and Lukas heard a sickening sound as he tore her neck open and drained her blood. A burbling sound emerged from her throat.

Lukas bolted for the front door, stretching his long legs in the opposite direction. His fight or flight instinct had kicked in, and his mind had wisely chosen flight without considering the alternative. He made it halfway across the house when Jude glanced up from his prey and tossed her down.

Jude stood in front of Lukas before he blinked.

Lukas skidded to a halt on an area rug that slid on the polished wood. At first, he thought Jude was an illusion, his mind playing sick tricks on him. There was no way *any* creature could move so swiftly, not even a vampire. He almost started for the door again, but the "illusion" blocked the way.

Jude lurched forward. Leathery black bat wings burst through his silk shirt and unfolded. The claws on each finger were five inches long, with deadly points. Jude's face twisted grotesquely, his nose protruded upward, exposing wide, bat-like nostrils. His corneas clouded and grew black. His clothes strained to contain him as his muscles expanded. His body extended until he looked Lukas in the eye. Lukas had no doubt his height was a conscious decision, as was his grotesque appearance.

Lukas froze, consternation overriding rational thought. Jude's nostrils flared tempestuously.

His prayer-mantra escaped him now. All he could do was look Jude in the eye, and hope that he would kill him quickly, so he did not have to withstand torture. He had no confidence in his stoutheartedness, and more than anything, he did not want to endanger his father.

Jude tilted his head. Lukas got the impression that all of this entertained him; the way he and Gina had entered the apartment with their hearts in their throats, their attempt at deceit, Gina's unflinching death, and now... now, whatever he had in mind for Lukas.

He likes *all of this conflict, thrives on the chase. He wants fear in the hearts of his victims. He wants them to challenge him, knowing they'll lose.*

Lukas made the mistake of catching Jude's black stare. It felt like shrinking, being sucked through a short distance without his consent. In an instant, the house, Gina, Jude, and his body disappeared. Then he saw, no, *was* Jude, saw his thoughts as Jude's thoughts, saw his pale, terrified face through Jude's eyes, and knew what Jude knew.

Jude had already known about Michael and Vivian. He had known they were coming back to Savannah. He had not needed Lukas or Gina at all! Jude had known he and Gina were coming, had felt their arrival as easily as fingering his pulse, and had let—no, encouraged them—to follow through with their plan for his entertainment that evening.

Entertainment? Lukas thought as he felt shoved back into his body. *We were his fucking toys?*

Lukas hadn't been raised in a religious home. Michael had abandoned formal religion after Lukas's mother died. Still, maybe it was his informal learning in the basics of most religions or how his babysitter used to compel him to pray before meals and bedtime. Perhaps it was the effect of the mantra-prayer in this hopeless situation. Most likely, it was because this was the first time Lukas was aware that he would probably die.

He prayed.

Dear God, I don't know if you're out there or if you can hear me. I've never prayed before, and I don't have the time to say much now. But if you're there, I only ask for one thing. Don't let Jude use me to betray my father. Please, God, don't let me do anything to harm him.

Jude spoke with a voice summoned from hell.

"There is nothing you can do. Your battles are pointless. She is mine."

Lukas had to think before he understood Jude. His concern for his father had overridden his worry for Vivian, and in his frantic emotional state, only one of them monopolized his thoughts.

Jude misinterpreted Lukas's confused expression for resistance. With the deafening shriek of a monstrous rodent, he effortlessly enveloped Lukas in his leathery wings.

Everywhere Lukas looked, Jude encompassed him. His colossal wings might as well have been concrete for all they moved under his shoves. In the other direction were Jude's blood-drenched jaw and fiery glare that promised death. The wings felt disgustingly slick and furry simultaneously, like a short-haired dog covered in motor oil. Those oily wings made his stomach churn. Lukas flinched, revolted, and fought with every ounce of effort in his body. He smelled death and Gina's blood on Jude's heavy breath.

Jude toyed with him, nicking his cheeks and neck with sharp talons, smiling maliciously at the blood it drew. Lukas frantically pounded on the unyielding wings and refused to look at Jude's jaw, dripping with Gina's blood. He heard his throat emitting high-pitched woman-like shrieks, but he didn't care.

Jude tightened the circle, trapped Lukas closer, forced him to face him. Lukas drew hyperventilating breaths. Jude's chin no longer dripped, but he caressed the remaining gore onto Lukas' face, painting his cheeks with his friend's blood.

"I could do the same to you, you know," he taunted. His voice was a smooth, growling, finely-tuned engine. "I could make you mine for ages. Turn you into my slave. You'd do things for me you've never—ever—considered doing with another man."

Jude's wings surrounded him in an indestructible embrace. Prayer was out of the question. Words escaped him. His thoughts spun like a whirlpool as he looked without blinking into Jude's jet-black eyes. Lukas tried to dream up a way to infuriate Jude so he would kill him in a blind rage, save him the pain of living and betraying Michael. But violence, spiteful words—none would work. They were Jude's fuel and would only amuse him. He tried to fast-forward his mind, to will some grand scheme into being. Nothing came.

What else was there? He didn't have to worry about using his mantra-prayer anymore in his panic. His mind was blank. His eyes clamped shut, burned by the heat and stench of Jude's hellish breath.

In his deliriousness, he pictured his father with all the perfection he'd attributed to Michael in his youth. Michael Graves; strong, handsome, and intelligent. The man who chased away the bogeyman from his closet and assured him that vampires were more powerful than anything in the world. The smartest man he knew, who gave him anything his heart desired—but only after he earned it. Michael, who always knew just what to say and when to say it. His father, whom he loved more fiercely than anyone else.

Jude's mind wrapped around Lukas's, and he knew for an instant what Gina had fought against before her death. Jude made a sickening sound when his mind connected with Lukas's love for his father, and his grip weakened.

Don't be stupid. Jude will never weaken. You're as good as dead.

The clamp on his mind gripped more firmly. Lukas opened his eyes wide in pain, only to discover that his vision was snowy. He was on the verge of unconsciousness.

Dad! Oh, God, Dad! Forgive me.

To his shock and amazement, he heard a response as clearly as if Michael were standing next to him.

Lukas, if anything has happened to you, I'll never forgive myself.

Lukas felt strange, as though a small part of him had moved hundreds of miles in an instant. He felt at one with Michael, and he knew that Michael felt the connection, too. The love that bonded father and son merged psychically and spiritually. Lukas felt the presence of his father inside him, all of Michael's strength, his paternal passion, his love for Lukas that was born the day he saw his son for the first time. Lukas understood how his filial adoration of his father had grown into love and respect, that his father wasn't merely the man who gave him life but had grown into his closest friend.

The grip was gone.

Lukas was released. He had no recollection of landing on the floor, but his smarting buttocks told him that he had been dropped without catching himself.

He shook his head, dazed, and noticed that Jude seemed to have been clobbered. His mouth hung open stupidly, and one hand clutched his head while the other searched blindly for his lost prey.

Lukas didn't waste time trying to understand his sudden good fortune. He scuttled backward across the floor like a crab until he was beyond Jude's reach, at which point he righted himself and dashed away.

He reached the sitting room without looking back, and as he crashed through both the blinds and the windows with the ease gained from panic, he remembered wondering earlier if Jude had any friends in the garden beyond.

Chapter 33

Michael leaned his head into the bedroom. "I hope you're about ready, 'cause we gotta go," he snapped.

Vivian nearly retorted with the first thing that came to mind—exactly where *he* could go—but she stopped short at Michael's stormy face. He was not in the mood to quarrel. She glared back and zipped her bag in reply.

"Doyle!" Michael barked. Doyle turned down Metallica's pounding drums and screaming guitars and peered at Michael like a diligent servant.

"Get her bags. Let's get the hell out of here," he commanded with a thumb jerk towards Vivian's luggage. Doyle's open trap snapped shut, and he turned off the stereo and meekly obeyed Michael.

They marched to the car and threw the luggage in the hatch without regard to safety. Michael tossed a set of keys over the hood to Doyle.

"Mind?" he asked.

"Return your rental? Yeahyeahyeah, not a problem, man," he agreed.

Doyle threw the car in gear and whipped out onto the tiny road without looking, nearly sideswiping a passing auto. Michael glared at him furiously, his eyes tearing him limb from limb.

"Sorry, man," Doyle apologized.

"Don't kill us, please," Michael pleaded dryly, "I'm in a hurry, but I won't do anyone any good dead."

"Of course," Doyle agreed. "You know I'm usually more careful," he observed, to which he received a dubious glance, but no further comment.

The ride to Frankfurt Am Main Airport was the usual hour and a half duration, but it seemed to take days. Doyle tried a few times to start a conversation, but after too many lukewarm responses, he showed unprecedented good judgment and didn't pursue it.

They parked, unloaded, and entered the busy airport together. Michael checked his watch, checked the tickets, and nodded with approval.

Doyle took this as a sign that he was forgiven for nearly killing them.

"Yeah, don't worry about your car. You'll get to Savannah International soon enough, and I'm sure everything's alright. Got your sunblock?"

Michael nodded and shot Doyle a meager smile.

"I hope you're right."

Surprise crossed Doyle's face. He'd forgotten the absentminded comments he had spoken only moments before. Vivian watched him retracing his conversational steps, remembering what he had said to provoke Michael's response and then nodding with enthusiasm.

"Yeahyeahyeah. Don't worry, man."

Michael extended his hand, and Doyle shook it with pride.

"Never do," Michael responded. It sounded to Vivian like a lie.

⚃　⚂

The wait for the flight was much shorter than last time. Vivian counted only twenty minutes once they reached their gate until takeoff. She and Michael stood impatiently in the terminal as they waited for their flight to board. Vivian half stared, half glared at Michael, who looked unaware of anything but his inner monologue.

"Sooo, we're flying to Savannah, right?" she asked. Michael jerked from thought and turned to face her.

"Yeah, supposedly," he responded.

She dismissed the questions *this* comment provoked.

She'd had an idea on the trip to the airport and decided now was the time to ask for Michael's input.

"Since we're going back to the States, don't you think I should try to.... change? In case anyone's still looking for me?" Michael blinked. It was as if he was trying to pay attention to Vivian while lost in thoughts so heavy, they would not allow a disruption.

He only paused about for a moment before replying, "Sure. Why not?"

Vivian stormed off to the restroom closest to their terminal. In the state of mind that he was in, Vivian would not have been surprised to find that Michael had entered the plane without her if the flight boarded before she made it back.

Thankful for the seclusion provided by the privacy doors, she locked herself in the first available stall. She tried not to think about how similar this restroom was to the one where she and Doyle had had their first confrontation. Like before, she seated herself on the toilet and focused. Only this time, instead of emptying her mind, she concentrated on her body.

What would I like to look like? It wasn't a line of thinking she had pursued before, having never had a reason to consider it. Now, when confronted with the likelihood of going to jail, a change of appearance had definite appeal. She did not have time to weigh all the possibilities; redhead, blonde, brunette, tall, short, stout, or thin. She needed a quick disguise—one that fit into the clothes she currently wore. Most importantly, she needed to want it to happen.

An image repeated in her mind. *Dark, wavy hair, thick as a bird's nest, but glossy and beautiful. Dark skin, long, tapered fingers. Shapely, swan-like neck. Smaller breasts. Large brown eyes. And no fangs. White, even teeth.*

While she lingered on these images, she felt the shifting in her body. The image blurred, and pain racked her muscles and bones as they contorted to meet her requests. It took an effort to continue the change once the pain hit. She had to want the change more than she wanted the pain to stop. She ached from her toes to the follicles of her hair. She bit her lip to keep from crying out and felt her fangs shrinking. Her jaw cracked and narrowed slightly. Her joints snapped loudly. She watched in grotesque amazement as her fingers darkened and elongated, the nails became more oval.

When it was over, she stood on legs as wobbly as a newborn giraffe's. Her shoes were about half a size too big, and her pants were too short, but not enough that anyone would notice. Her bra cups weren't as full, and a strap fell down a narrower shoulder like a wet spaghetti noodle. She adjusted the straps the best she could.

She took in her overall appearance with apprehension. Her legs were flush. Her hands and arms matched. Her torso looked normal. From what she saw of her lower back, it had changed the way she had hoped.

What about my face? Her fingers reached up and, like a blind person familiarizing herself with her features, touched her cheeks, lips, and forehead. Everything seemed in place—nothing protruding or misshapen. The real test would be the mirror. She took a deep breath and let herself out of the stall.

She caught her breath as she stared back at a reflection precisely as she had imagined. The short red-haired woman at the neighboring sink looked at her with concern.

Vivian scanned the woman's mind more quickly than she could snap her fingers without realizing it. She found just what the woman was hoping she would say.

She looked into the woman's worried blue eyes with her new brown ones and said clearly, "*Es tut mir überall weh.*"

The woman nodded.

"*Ich hatte einen langen Flug,*" she added.

Vivian had no idea how she knew to tell the woman in German that she ached all over and that she'd had a long flight. She didn't dwell on it. She had a plane to catch.

⊗ ⊗

Gina blinked and tried to open eyes weighted down by coagulated blood. It hurt to blink, and the trace of light seared her eyes like dual hot pokers. It hurt to concentrate. She tried to remember where she was. All she remembered was Jude's sharp teeth closing in on her neck, and then, nothing. Nothing but pain and the sensation of suspension in warm water.

From somewhere far away, yet internal, she heard the sickeningly sweet crooning of Jude's voice.

Gina. Gina, come back.

Come back from where? Where am I? Why do I feel like I'm dying?

She heard an evil chuckle, and she wished it would stop. The sound pounded in her ears like a bass drum.

You won't die, Gina. I can make the pain stop, or we can go on like this for as long as you want.

She tried to move, just a finger. Her body was immobile, not an eyelash budged. She floated on an ocean of pain, and every wave, every ripple racked her body with new suffering. She felt skinned, every nerve exposed and rubbed raw, every ligament torn, and every sinew stretched nearly beyond physical limits. She wanted to cry out in distress but couldn't bring herself to open her mouth, having no doubt the slightest sound would multiply to the pain. Her head ached with every thought. Her stomach wretched involuntarily, sickened by the intensity of her torture. The motion caused an avalanche of agony. The closest she came to relief was to remain perfectly still, but her body reflexively twitched, seeking a way to ease her pain. Nothing worked.

I want to die! Death can't be worse than this.

You won't die, Gina. I can do this forever. You know it, and I know it.

She did.

Just tell me what I want to know.

Her resolve dried up and crumbled. She found that she didn't—*couldn't*—care anymore. The synapses of her nerves exploded like dynamite. Her mind felt as though he had wedged an ax through it crossways. Jude finally had her exactly where he planned, and her torment probably turned him on more than anything she had done for him.

The greatest disadvantage to being damn near immortal was the possibility of an eternity of torture.

Despite a tremor of pain, her jaw opened, which eased the moment Jude sensed her intentions. Her parched mouth nearly forced a cough as she inhaled a shallow breath.

Her voice rasped, "Germany. They're in fucking Germany."

"Not *that*. I *know* that. And I know they're coming back." The sadistic confidence in his voice made her queasy. He continued:

"What I need for you to tell me is that you'll do what I ask of you. That your mind, body, and soul are mine."

She said nothing. There was nothing to say. He owned her thoughts as surely as he owned her body. Besides, the silence would save her some pain. He heard her thought, tainted with what little sarcasm she dared muster.

As if I had a choice.

☙ ❧

Vivian left the restroom and marched to the place she had left Michael. His expression was the same. Blank. Michael hadn't been himself the whole night. She longed to find out what had upset him so badly.

Wondering how long it would take him to notice, she resumed her place next to her carry-on. Michael turned his head, most likely because he had seen movement out of the corner of his eye. It was almost comical, the way he took in her feet in their too-big shoes and panned upward to her dark face and wavy hair. Vivian guessed it was the familiar way she looked at him, not her attire, that helped him see through her disguise.

He nearly leaped out of his skin, and she grinned with even, white teeth.

"Vivian?"

She shrugged and nodded. Inside she quivered. What if he didn't like it?

"Of course," she said, her voice straining to maintain her nonchalant charade.

"You look so... so..."

On the one hand, she was proud of herself—she had never stupefied Michael before. On the other, she hoped her drastic change in appearance wasn't a turn-off.

"That's the point, isn't it?" she prompted.

It was Michael's turn to shrug.

"I guess it's a pretty good idea." Her heart broke. Then he continued.

"No, lemme correct that. It's a damned good idea, and I'm ashamed I didn't think of it. But..."

"Yes?"

"Your passport. You don't match your picture anymore."

She hadn't thought of that. Her first instinct was to turn on her heel, run back to the bathroom stall, and change her appearance back to the old Vivian and pray that no one noticed. Then she remembered the woman in the bathroom, how easily she had read her mind, said what was expected.

Could I...? I wonder...

"I think I may have that covered."

"Okay." His voice revealed no doubt, and she appreciated his confidence. The conversation was going well, but he hadn't shown any sign that he found her attractive.

"What do you think?" She stood and turned a pirouette to give him a view of all sides. Her concern was obvious. He smiled, and raised his eyebrows appraisingly, scrutinizing her new guise with one hand on his chin, the other stretched across his broad chest. He added a pointed "Hmm" worthy of a puzzled doctor as he strolled around her lackadaisically, his brown eyes panning her from her newly dark hair to her feet, loose in her shoes. Vivian didn't know if she should laugh or smack him but found herself smiling. He wrapped a strong arm around her waist and smiled, amused at her frustration.

"I think it's you," he said, "and I'd love you no matter what shape or size or color." He emphasized his point with a fervent kiss.

C&8   80

Lukas didn't stop running until he reached River Street despite the strange looks from the few pedestrians he saw. He supposed it was unusual for a person to be out for a morning run clothed in jeans and a sweater, but he didn't care. His only thought was to put as much physical distance as possible between himself and Jude.

He wandered the streets, delirious with panic and hunger, until his legs threatened to buckle. He hunched into a shallow doorframe for protection from the wind. The cool morning breeze was too extreme a sensation for his newborn vampire skin. He shivered like a hypothermic drowning victim saved from an icy lake.

Only two pedestrians passed as he rested, and neither showed any regard for his well-being. He wanted to attack, but his body wasn't listening. He needed to rest a moment and try to think, try being the operative word. He had never had such a hard time stringing together a coherent train of thought. He was reminded of a small poster his father had hanging from a corkboard in his office. One humorous "word" in bold rainbow letters: THIMK.

Dawn was approaching rapidly, and he needed to find shelter soon. A two-day-old vampire has no tolerance for the sun.

The moment Lukas was turned, his immune system mutated, and he became deathly photoallergic. Just a few seconds of exposure to ultraviolet rays would violently damage his connective tissue. He would rash and blister. Within minutes, the congested capillaries supplying blood to the skin—which cause a normal sunburn in humans—would swell, forcing his skin to stretch. This skin would become dry and scaly. His nails would rise from their nail beds. His skin would shed like a snake's but with no underlying layer. It, and the rest of his body, would crumble instantly.

He needed to find shelter quickly, but had no idea where to go.

Chapter 34

Their flight was called. Vivian checked her passport and the picture that no longer looked like her, grasped her ticket, purse, and carry-on.

They got in line toward the rear, and her nervousness only got worse as they waited. She studied the flight attendant checking the tickets and passports. Could she look into her mind as easily as she had the woman in the bathroom? More importantly, could she *influence* her thoughts?

Don't let yourself doubt this. It's got to be done.

Her options were simple: invade the woman's mind, or go back to Weilerbach with Doyle. Not easy choices, but her preference was clear.

They reached the front of the line. Michael assertively handed their passports to the flight attendant, who looked at his first. Vivian almost jumped the gun and tried to influence her to believe that she was Michael, then caught herself. When the flight attendant opened the passport to her picture, Vivian was there, penetrating her beliefs, not understanding the foreign words she heard but grasping the content. The attendant was tired, indifferent, ready to board the plane and get the long flight underway, and unwilling to deal with complications. Vivian dropped the suggestion that the flight attendant did not notice the discrepancy between Vivian's picture and her person. The flight attendant grasped the idea as a good one and handed her the passport back with a smile.

"*Danke,*" she said. Vivian and Michael continued down the jetway, Vivian forcing everything from her thoughts to her stride to remain inexpressive.

They stowed their luggage except for her purse, which Vivian kept by her side, and settled into their seats. She decided to wait for the plane to be safely in the air before starting any serious dialogue. This wasn't a courteous measure on her part. Takeoffs were nerve-racking enough without complicating things by maintaining a serious conversation.

She checked her watch. Michael did the same, sighed, and fidgeted in frustration; the plane was running behind. He looked anxious enough to jump into the cockpit and try to fly the jet himself if he thought it would get him where he was going faster.

Ten, fifteen minutes passed. A few passengers were already attempting to sleep. Vivian fastened and unfastened her seatbelt and flipped through the informational packet in the seatback just to give her hands something to do. A couple of rows ahead of her, a woman read a book. A boy in a baseball jacket and cap played with a handheld video game.

Twenty minutes after Vivian estimated the flight should've been in the air, the pilot's voice came over the speakers. First in English, then in German, he explained the flight was delayed as they waited on a tardy incoming flight that held passengers holding tickets for their flight. He apologized for any inconvenience.

"Figures," Michael mumbled, followed by something garbled.

"What?" she asked, leaning in and touching his hand lightly.

"I said, 'Figures. They probably aren't worried for their sons' lives.'"

Vivian leaned back, took back her hand.

"You're more worried than you were before. Why? What's happened that you haven't told me?"

Michael studied her face for a second, broke eye contact.

"You'll only think I'm crazy."

Vivian choked down a hollow laugh and leaned back in.

"Michael, we're vampires," she whispered. "Have you *considered* the insanity of our everyday lives? I know it's probably something you take for granted after so long, but if anyone on this plane knew what we do to survive, they'd be chasing us with crucifix necklaces and stabbing us in the hearts with umbrellas. Think about *that* for a second, and then tell me what's bugging you, for God's sake."

Michael smiled, and his weighty conscience lifted a little. He took her hand. Vivian didn't know if it was for strength, or to make sure that she did not run away when he told her what was on his mind.

"Have you had an out-of-body experience?" he whispered.

She nearly asked him to define the term, but the explanation dawned on her slowly; a spirit traveling while the body remained elsewhere. She didn't know how she knew this but told herself it was simple logic. The expression provided its explanation, didn't it?

Without waiting for her answer, he continued. "I haven't. Until today, that is." He was serious and frightened, and it scared her.

"You had an out-of-body experience? When did you have time?" She hadn't intended it to be a joke, but it was worth the slip-up to see

Michael laugh, however shallow it sounded.

"Earlier today, when I got off the phone with Josh. I was worried about Lukas. I was just thinking, 'Lukas, if anything has happened to you, I'd never forgive myself,' or something along those lines, when I *felt* him. I mean, I felt myself *in* him, sort of. He was scared to death, like he knew he was about to die."

He paused, and Vivian gripped his hand tighter when she saw the tears about to fall down his handsome face. Her intent focus encouraged him, and he continued.

"I don't know how it happened. I've always read there had to be a lot of physical and spiritual preparation. Nowhere have I seen where it happens spontaneously. But that wasn't what frightened me, and it wasn't what scared Lukas. What got to me was this: I knew, through him, that Shepherd was *right there.*"

Vivian gasped, and some of the passengers turned to see why. She gave them all a reassuring glance and then turned back to Michael.

"Jude's in Savannah?"

Michael nodded.

"And we're flying to Savannah," she added. Michael self-consciously tongued a fang, then shook his head as he snapped his mouth shut.

"We're flying to Newark, then Savannah," he corrected. "Only now, I'm not sure Savannah is the best course of action."

"What do you mean? What about Lukas?"

His eyes closed. The suspended tears dropped onto his slacks, forming blacker spots on the dark fabric. Vivian's eyes riveted on the tearstains. She didn't want to hear what Michael was bracing himself to say and was angry at herself for putting him in a situation where he had to say it.

"It's probably too late for Lukas—"

"You don't know that!" she said, hating herself for interrupting him while he stumbled over the painful words.

"I'll try to find out," he continued. "If the worst has happened, we have to be prepared for it."

It's probably too late. If the worst has happened, he can't bring himself to say he believes his son is dead.

Determination and bravery showed in Michael's smile. He kissed the back of her hand. She closed her eyes, but the thought of Lukas' smiling face would not go away. She didn't have to use her imagination to know the torture he would suffer in Jude's hands. *How Michael must hate me!*

If not for me, his son would still be alright! It's my fault. I never should've put them in danger.

The passengers from the overdue flight finally showed up and filed into the remaining seats. Michael was again lost in thought, oblivious to the jostle and noise.

She laced her fingers through his. He turned and gave her another sad, but heartfelt, smile. She knew then he wasn't upset with her at all, and she wondered why. If she were in Michael's shoes, she didn't think she could be so gracious. She resolved then that she would find some way to repay him for his sacrifices.

ڇβ

"Doyle?"

The voice on Doyle's cell phone caught him so off guard he nearly swerved into a passing Mercedes minivan.

Fuck. I knew I shouldn't have answered this. Now I gotta pull over.

"Charles, is that you? Hold on, I'm turning into a *parkplatz*."

Doyle tossed the phone into the passenger seat as he pulled off the autobahn and deftly swerved the tiny Opel into the nearest parking spot. The rest area was abandoned, save his car.

Charles' voice had made him wary. It was too nice. Too chummy. He gripped the steering wheel tightly with his left hand and stared at the phone, now back in his right. He felt as if God Himself had dialed him up and asked if he would like a rundown of everything he would burn in hell for. He considered hanging up with the intention of blaming it on a faulty connection later. He didn't, but he took a long time before he put the phone back to his ear.

"Charles. I'm back."

"Don't you know not to answer the phone while you drive?" The fatherly reprimand didn't ease Doyle's mind a bit. He tried to make himself relax. *Maybe he just wants a favor. Maybe he doesn't know.*

"Yeah, I suppose you're right," he said, forcing himself to speak casually. "What's up?"

"Doyle, I need to speak to you. It's urgent. Where can we meet?" Still, the fatherly tone, stern and patronizing. It turned Doyle's stomach sour. He recalled the time he drank from a young woman he thought was only asleep. It turned out she had tried to commit suicide by ingesting poison and was dying. The poison circulating in her bloodstream had given him an upset stomach similar to the one he had now.

That Charles wanted to speak to him was distressing. That he wanted to meet was worse. It meant there were things he did not wish to speak of over phone lines, things he didn't want to be overheard by the wrong person. Doyle had a sneaking suspicion Charles had caught wind of some wrongdoing on his part—for instance, his recent purchase of plane tickets for an unnamed couple.

Fuck. They find out every goddamn thing.

"Doyle?"

Doyle snapped back into the present.

"Oh, yeahyeahyeah. Um, I'm thinking."

"You don't need to think. Meet me at the *Café Wiedmann* in half an hour."

"So soon?" Doyle exclaimed. "Hey, don't you think you'll stand out? I mean, it's a really hip place." He cringed as the awkward words left his lips. *OK, so I'm grasping at straws. I don't want to see this motherfucker tonight. Hell, I'm not sure I want to see him again, ever.*

Charles let out a low chuckle.

"Since when, Doyle, have I not been able to blend?"

Doyle heard the smirk in his voice. *Condescending bastard.*

"Yeahyeahyeah, OK. Gimme forty-five, though. I'm on the road."

"I know. Knowing how you drive, I'm surprised you're not in Kaiserslautern already. Did they make it alright?"

Doyle blinked. There was stunned silence as Doyle struggled with what to say, or, more precisely, what he *should* say. A wrong answer could mean death. He paused for a moment, and when no ingenious replies came to mind, he squeaked, "Who?"

Charles laughed a deep belly laugh. Doyle wasn't sure if it meant he sincerely wasn't upset or if he was having one of his more sadistic moments.

The wind picked up, and with it came the soft patter of fat raindrops. Doyle rotated the key, switched on the auxiliary power, and turned on the windshield wipers, ensuring that his field of vision was clear. His paranoia had escalated quickly. Charles knew he had helped her escape. Doyle knew it was likely that the Blood Tribe knew where he was— sitting in his car, waiting like a convicted criminal with his neck in the noose, just waiting for Charles to open the trapdoor under his feet. He scanned the shadows for any flicker of movement indicating a minion of the *Shévet ha Dam* sent to kill him for his part in Vivian's escape. He tried to calm his accelerated breathing so Charles would not pick it up over the phone.

"Be there, Doyle."

The line went dead.

ᚴ ᚴ

Shortly after takeoff, she realized that her jaw hurt from clenching. The flight was a turbulent one, and the constant bumping and swaying of the plane frazzled Vivian's nerves. She periodically looked out of a window to her left that gave her a view of the wing. On many of the stomach-wrenching dips, she glanced over and ensured it was still attached. After roughly an hour of this, the young man in the window seat caught on and dropped the plastic shade.

They announced an in-flight movie selection, and this time Michael was awake to show Vivian how the headphones attached to the seat. She chose a Pixar film, finding it difficult to believe that the plane would fall out of the sky while she was laughing at a computer-generated cartoon. It was foolish logic, she knew, but it was something.

She tracked the progress of the plane on the monitors over the aisles. It did little to alleviate her fear to know that if the plane dropped from the sky, it would most likely be a water landing. She guessed that if dropping from thirty thousand feet and crashing in an enormous ball of twisted metal and jet fuel didn't kill her, the sharks would. Not even a vampire could withstand that. If the flight didn't kill her, thousands of vamps in the U.S. waited to do the job.

Vivian, with logic like yours, who needs pessimism?

After the movie, she tried to sleep under the too short, too thin airline blanket, but the skies refused to calm, and sleeping upright had never been easy. She gave up.

She grasped Michael's hand and stole a glance at his face, hoping to find solace. Silent tears streamed down his pale cheeks as he slept.

She checked her watch. Any minute now, they'd be circling Newark International Airport.

ᚴ ᚴ

Snap.

The neck of the Renfield broke like a dry twig, and the body fell from a pair of strong, black hands, collapsing in a heap on the thin airport carpet.

God, these motherfuckers are too easy. Blood Tribe, my ass. Sending their little fucking henchmen to catch this super powerful vamp. Were they too scared? Why couldn't they come themselves?

Grey-blue eyes peered from behind thick dreadlocks and marked another vampire lurking in the crowd near terminal B-58. He was one of the few full-blooded vamps there, and his power was equal to ten Renfields. He was an old one, probably over four hundred years. Long, frizzy hair hung to his neck and framed a pale, equine face. Tan duster. Cowboy boots.

Hmm. He'll be tricky. Ugly and tricky.

Soundlessly, he stalked the vampire from shadow to shadow, ninja-like, until he was within luring distance. He paused, considered his options, and went for the obvious.

"Hey, you!"

The vamp looked up in surprise, obviously not expecting a confrontation in the center of the terminal.

Good old Blood Tribe rules.

He shot him an impish smile, winked, and ran. The vampire sped after him. He dodged among tourists, the cowboy in pursuit.

Fast, but not too fast. Can't let them give up.

He ducked down a corridor marked "Employee Entrance Only" in bright yellow letters. The vampire behind him lunged and caught the door before it closed. He turned and grabbed the cowboy by the lapels of his duster. Using his opponent's weight to his advantage, he brought the vampire's neck to his lips and bit, attaching himself like a starving tick.

The blood was cold but filling. The cowboy vampire struggled, but his hold was secure as he drained the cowboy of strength, then life.

There was blood splattered all over his clothes. He wiped his mouth and wished for a mirror so he could see if he had made a mess. He ripped a corner of the cowboy's thin plaid shirt off and wiped his face. He removed the jacket and used it to cover his clothes.

There. Ten down, probably two to go. Then I find the girl.

Chapter 35

afé Wiedman was the only bakery in Kaiserslautern with tables outside in the winter chill. Doyle understood, now, why Charles made the choice he had—he wanted to meet away from listening ears. *Table outside in the freezing cold it is, then. That'll look normal.*

Doyle walked up to the counter more out of habit than an urge to drink. The young woman behind the counter smiled broadly.

"*Un café, bitte.*" he said. They exchanged drink for Deutsche Marks, Doyle accepted the tiny cup of bitter black brew, and headed outside to a table.

After an unsatisfying sip, he turned around and tried to appear casual. The cold did not bother him, but he felt odd sitting alone outdoors.

An attractive, if slightly effeminate, Euro-gay vampire strolled up to him. He perused Doyle with blue eyes framed by impossibly long lashes. Doyle looked away. The Euro-vamp pretended not to notice.

"Want to talk?" he asked. It should have been impossible to lisp saying those words, but it sounded lisped. His question was part vocal, part psychic. It also insinuated that talking wasn't what he had in mind. Doyle didn't know what to say. "Eww" came to mind.

"No thanks," he responded, increasing the bass in his voice. He raised the coffee to his lips, drained it, and stood to go, indicating that he was blowing the vamp off. As he headed back to the café, he hoped the dude wasn't staring at his ass. *Man, why is it that just because I'm in shape and have style that—*

"I think you do," the vamp said in clipped tones, the staid voice of a man with a gun to someone's back.

Doyle froze. He hadn't felt anyone trailing him, but the Euro-vamp couldn't have been more than two feet behind him.

Charles, the sanctimonious asshole, had sent this Euro-vamp to kill him. If he weren't so frightened, he would have been slightly amused at the notion of dying at a gay man's hand. He set the drink down on the counter, ready to battle, if necessary, but he knew the rules: *Shévet ha*

Dam was exacting about public altercations. It wasn't allowed. The woman behind the counter eyed them both warily, not understanding the conversation but preparing for the need to react nonetheless.

"Where?" Doyle asked. The vamp smiled serenely, and there was a darkness behind his hooded eyes. It gave him the creeps.

"Right here, if you like." He stretched his hand out, indicating where they stood.

Doyle paused. Something was amiss. He studied his opponent, took in the tight jacket and tighter black pants. He scrutinized the vampire's face; high, European cheekbones, dark brown eyes, and tousled, golden hair fixed in elaborate curls with gel. Tasteful platinum rings with precious stones drew attention to long, manicured fingernails.

Wait a minute—those eyes.

"Charles?" he gasped.

Charles gave a dramatic bow. His eyes never left Doyle's, and his leering smile unsettled him.

"In, as I like to say, the flesh," he replied.

Doyle wasn't sure if he was thankful or disappointed. If Charles had sent one of his cronies, there would have been a slim chance of dueling skillfully enough to escape, however bruised. Afterward, he might have been able to stay alive long enough to talk his way out of his predicament—whatever it was. It would not be the first time he had thrown himself a lifeline after a heinous blunder. This was another story. It would take more coercion to fix a problem with Charles and, most likely, a lot of lying and pointing fingers.

Doyle had never seen Charles in a shape-shifted form before, and the reality of it was weirder than his imagination. Charles had been turned in his forties, but because of his centuries as a vampire and experience as a Tribe leader, he carried himself like a much older being. Now, in his shape-shifted form, he looked young, and vital, and—Doyle hated to consider the word when pertaining to Charles—attractive. But why had he chosen to appear gay? It unnerved him.

Say something, you idiot.

"Glad you could make it," he mumbled half-heartedly.

"Pleasure," Charles responded. Again, with the smirk. It was starting to make Doyle sweat. Charles would have made a magnificent detective. He was skilled in flustering people. He was even more skilled at killing them.

"What was it you needed, Charles?"

Charles' smile never wavered. *Damn him to hell.* He turned to the nervous woman, who hadn't moved, and signaled that he desired two more coffees. She nodded, understanding that they'd drawn a truce, and poured two more drinks.

Once their orders were filled, Charles coaxed Doyle out of the café and back to his empty seat.

"I need your help, Doyle." In Charles' voice, there was no question of Doyle's cooperation. In Doyle's mind, any dispute ceased. He might have been willing to battle a Renfield, but resisting Charles, at least to his face, was a death wish.

"Not with finding the girl," Charles continued, "Thanks to Sabine, we know where she is and where she's headed. It wasn't easy getting it out of her. Hell, it wasn't easy getting *her,* what with her being Jude's little harlot. *Prost.*" He lifted his petite cup jauntily, and Doyle mimicked him in a limp toast with his cup. After a sip, Charles screwed his face in distaste. "Not very good, are they? Well, they never are."

They know where she is already. He cursed himself for using Sabine. That he hadn't divulged his clients to her hadn't mattered. He should've known better, but what choice had he had? None. Despite his claim to have vast resources at his disposal, the truth was that Doyle's ability to get what he needed was based on his ability to play both sides against the middle.

"You know that if *we* know where they are, then *they* certainly do. Or will, shortly." Charles added. He eyeballed Doyle like a fascinating bug and mimicked Doyle's pose of leaning back, legs crossed at the ankles. His long, manicured fingernails flickered subtly in the sunlight. The implications of Charles' statement sank in as slowly, like water easing into saturated ground.

"Hold the phone," Doyle said. "*We? They?* What're you talking about?"

The irksome smile faded, at last, from Charles' lips.

"Of course. You haven't heard," Charles said as if the matter were common knowledge. "There's been a division. The Table is disunited. Jude's long-held tenure as leader of the *Shévet ha Dam* is, for the first time, subject to change."

Doyle blinked, his mouth agape. Jude would never volunteer to surrender his position while he lived. Charles implied a mutiny, an attempt to kill Cartaphilus, whom no one knew how to kill. Judging from Charles' composure, the latter part of Doyle's assumption was no longer true.

"But won't that—"

"Hush, boy, and listen," Charles snapped. It struck Doyle as unnatural to be called "boy" by a creature that hardly looked older than himself, but he obeyed.

"Doyle, you're one of the few of our kind that Michael Graves speaks with. We've known this for a time, but have chosen to leave it alone. The tiny tribe of vampires in a hick American town was of no real concern. That is, until they intervened with Vivian."

"You want me to talk to Michael? Why?"

Charles finished his coffee with evident distaste and peered at Doyle with the fascinating bug look again

"*I* need to talk to *her*," he explained. "I need her to understand the role she plays in this. I don't think she understands how important she is. I don't think she knows *who* she is."

For a brief moment, Doyle considered denying any knowledge of Vivian's whereabouts, but he knew it would be pointless. Charles knew more than he was letting on, and what Charles knew tended to get people killed.

Chapter 36

A flight attendant announced their approach into Newark International. They'd land in about ten minutes.

Michael opened his heavy lids and gave her a strained smile. Vivian wondered how long until she believed him when he said he was fine.

The plane landed with a stomach-lurching thump, and Vivian loosened her grip on the hand rests. *If there's a way for vampires to fly without using a jet, I'm going to find out how. This is torture.*

They grabbed their carry-ons and meandered down the aisle, weaving their way among less eager travelers. Michael moved forward in stiff half steps, and it wasn't from sleeping too long in an airplane seat. He was nervous. She smelled it.

He's expecting trouble.

She followed him through the Jetway, ears perked, eyes scouring the area, half expecting one of the passengers to turn without warning and attack. She was ready to defend herself but wasn't looking forward to it. Especially not in front of an airport full of people.

They rushed through customs and entered the terminal, where friends and family awaited travelers, not stopping for their bags. Michael anxiously scanned the crowd for someone awaiting them, someone vile and hostile.

"Car rental," he muttered to her under his breath, and she nodded.

Her suspicions were right. They would not be catching their connecting flight. Her heart felt like lead in her chest. She wondered if he had a plan or if he was improvising. She desperately hoped he had a better idea than she did about what to do next.

She kept a lookout as he used an ATM at the first opportunity and withdrew an obscene amount of money. She couldn't believe no one had attacked yet. As they waited for their cash to dispense, Michael explained that their arrival was most likely known; their change of plans might not be.

"If they know we're here, then why haven't they—"

"Turn around," a voice bellowed. "Slowly."

Vivian stiffened. A shocked looked crossed Michael's face, then the slightest trace of a smile. They did as ordered.

Before Vivian stood the strangest, stockiest vampire she had ever seen. His face was strikingly handsome, his hair twisted into thick, deliberate cords that hung to his waist. His eyes were grey and cheery. His smile looked ostentatiously bright in the heart of his dark-skinned face.

"Y'all were too easy to find. You're lucky I was here."

"Blu!" Michael cried. He forgot about the cash and embraced his friend. Vivian removed the money from the ATM and pocketed it. She had no idea who this man was, but judging from the blood she smelled on his clothes underneath a jacket two sizes too small, they were indebted to him for arrival without incident.

There was a quality about him that struck her as familiar, but she couldn't put her finger on it. She shook her head, dismayed that daily confusion had become her norm.

The men hugged and exchanged pleasantries. Michael's grin appeared frozen in place.

"I suppose I have you to thank for the absence of, shall we say, conflict?"

Blu smiled with pride.

"Oh, man, you should have seen it," he said. "I mean, no, you shouldn't have. They were after *you,* but jeez. I haven't seen more obvious thugs since... Well, I've *never* seen more obvious thugs. It was pathetic. Like the big Table vamps were afraid to be here in person."

Michael patted his friend on the shoulder with affection.

"They didn't know what they were up against, did they?" he asked. Vivian wasn't sure, but she believed she saw a blush under the dark skin.

"Well shit, Michael, I mean you'd think they'd have sent out there best to pick up Princess Katerina instead of some burned-out vamp wanna-bes."

"Who?" Vivian asked.

Blu paused and licked his lips. He appeared nervous.

"I guess... No, I..." he stammered. His voice betrayed his uncertainty. "But if she ain't Princess Katerina, why does Shepherd want her back so badly?"

૏   ૐ

River Street's population dramatically increased as dawn approached Savannah, Georgia. Lukas's option of sneaking into one of the deserted warehouses on the less-visited end of the street narrowed as busy laborers drove down the cobblestones on their way to work.

He forced himself to stand on shaky legs and walk. He tripped as his long feet struck protruding cobblestones. His eyelids drooped as he remembered when he went to the hospital because of an allergic reaction to a spider bite. The doctor had given him an antihistamine through an IV tube, and it had put him to sleep as he reclined safely in the doctor's office. He wished he was in a doctor's office now, stretched out on a soft table covered in butcher paper. At least there, he would be safe.

All I need is a little blood, and I'll be better. I won't die as fast, and I'll be able to think clearer. I think. The redundant thought triggered a chuckle.

Although his logic was sound, his method was not. He knocked on a shop window to get the attention of an attractive young woman inside, hoping she would open the door long enough for him to snag her. No luck. She peered at him with furrowed brows and pointed to the sign on the door that showed the store would not open for another hour.

"Then why are you there?" he slurred at the crack in the door. She shook her head again and wandered away.

Damn. So much for that idea. He started back down the sidewalk, his brow fretted. *Maybe I can find a cat.* But he knew that idea was ludicrous. He hadn't the energy or the time to chase feral strays.

Dawn turned the sky from black to concrete gray. His skin grew warm.

Anger supplanted his frustration. He needed to throw something. He reached down to pick up a pebble, but he tripped over his feet and landed with a pronounced thud face-first on the sidewalk in front of a candy shop. From his height, it was quite a fall.

He let out a long string of colorful vocabulary, mainly of the four-letter variety. He eyed his scratched hands—the smell of his blood drove him wild. One knee of his jeans had torn, and the fabric hung down in a bloodstained flap. He had hit his chin. *Great. Now I'll lose what little blood I have.*

He slouched resignedly, laid his elbows on his knees. He could not get up, nor would he. He would sit there, and wait for dawn, and he would die in front of God and River Street. It would be better than waiting for Jude to find and kill him.

"Are you alright?"

The voice from behind sounded like an angel. He turned around and discovered he was right. She certainly *looked* like an angel.

He gave her a lopsided, drunken grin. *Maybe I'm dead, and heaven looks like River Street.*

The young woman came closer, wary. Her brown, almost red hair ruffled faintly in the breeze.

She's probably used to finding party leftovers on her doorstep.

He hadn't realized that he hadn't responded until she repeated herself.

He nodded, inhaled deeply, straightened his posture, and tried to put himself right.

"Oh, yeah. Just tripped, you see. Long feet." He held one up for her to examine, and she nodded politely. *Shut up, you idiot. Shut. Up!*

"I see."

"Yeah, well, I guess I'll be getting out of your way," he said. He tried to stand by resting one hand on the door frame and lifting his weight slowly, but his bloody hand slipped, and he was down again, to his immense embarrassment.

"Oh!" the angel exclaimed. "You're hurt!"

"Nonsense," he replied, trying to summon up every ounce of masculine courage he had left. "Just a scratch."

"Well," the young woman replied, digging into her pocket for the key to unlock the iron gate barring the door, "I can't have you bleeding on my stoop. It's bad for business. Guess you'll just have to come in and let me bandage it."

Lukas eyed the dawning sky anxiously. *Guess I will.*

Ψ Ψ

"Why do you want to talk to her?" Doyle asked. He felt Charles prodding his thoughts, and it was, as usual, unnerving as hell. He was willing to risk Charles' amusement for the opportunity to gain some knowledge.

"Ahh... She's touched you, too," Charles observed with condescension. He eyed his empty cup and tilted it from side to side, watching the dregs of espresso as it swirled around the bottom.

"Touched me?" Doyle asked. A small laugh escaped. *Vivian wouldn't touch me with a ten-foot metal dick.*

"Vivian. The girl. How did she make you feel?"

Doyle contemplated the question, unsure of the connection.

"She... she made me feel bad about one or two things. She made me feel like I wasn't living up to my potential."

"And you are not," Charles said. He set the cup down on the bistro table with a clank loud enough to be heard over the children playing loudly nearby. The server scooting by picked up the cup and motioned his willingness to refill it. Charles dismissed him with a wave.

"I still don't get it. What's the point?" Doyle asked.

"Vivian is a unique kind of vampire," Charles said. "To the same extent that Jude is evil, Vivian—I believe—is his opposite. Jude is wicked. His thoughts, emotions, and conduct, all motivated by the urge to kill and destroy everything he touches and everyone he contacts. In every thought, every word, in total. Vivian, on the other hand, is the yang to his yin."

"How?" Doyle asked. "I mean, I thought only gods and demons were completely good or evil."

Charles shrugged.

"I cannot explain why, and I will not philosophize. Perhaps it is not them, but powers—supernatural beings or elements that use them—that are good or evil. That would be my guess. That is what I'm wagering on."

"They're just chess pieces in a game of the gods?"

"Yes. That's what I believe."

"So, Jude wants her back so badly because he—or this thing driving him—hates her—or whatever's using her—for being good?"

Charles smiled. The age that had seemed absent from him was subtly noticeable once more. He was an old vampire in an eye-catching, young body.

"On the contrary. I believe *Jude* wants her back because he loves her."

"I don't understand," Doyle said. "How can a being incapable of good love anything?"

"That's my point, and that is why we need the girl."

"Huh?"

"He doesn't *know* he loves her. Jude has deluded himself into believing that her capture was motivated by hatred, that he took her to dominate the one thing he could not understand or be. I believe that if we prove to Jude it is love, it will be his undoing, and, ultimately, his destruction."

"But the curse—"

"The curse was placed on him because of a force that coerced him to abuse a righteous man. If I'm correct, it was not he who was cursed, but the evil in him. If we change the nature of who he is by removing this force, he becomes, in a sense, a new being—or at least the being he once was. He becomes merely a sinful man, but the evil driving him is exorcised, and the curse lifted."

"But what if it isn't?"

Charles shrugged, but the gesture was heavy, his shoulders burdened.

"Then you and I, along with the rest of the world, are going to be kissing our collective asses goodbye."

Chapter 37

Jude was stumped. It was a sensation he had forgotten, and he re-membered now why he did not like it.

Sabine had tried to contact him, but her message had been so confused and panicked he could not make sense of it. She had tried to convey a message to him about Vivian and Germany, but her transmission was broken, and then suddenly: nothing. As if she had died. He received a vague impression of a running young woman, but instead of running *from* something, she was running *to* it.

Could Vivian be returning to him? No. She would never return to him or fight him. It was not in her character. She was a beautiful crea-ture, and powerful, but she was also afraid. Centuries as his slave had honed her fear to a sharp knife that would cut her deeply with every thought of returning. But if that wasn't what Sabine had meant, then what?

Jude stretched out on the long couch near Gina's sleeping figure. Sabine's death was no great loss. Replacing female companions was easy, except for one.

Perhaps Vivian had killed Sabine. It would corroborate the impres-sion he had received. Sabine had found her in Germany and had tried to capture her for him. She had no idea of Vivian's power and was over-come. That would explain the female running toward something: Vivian had run toward Sabine and attacked her.

Although this explanation made sense, Jude knew it wasn't true. Sab-ine's message may have come through broken and confused, but it wasn't Sabine who was pursued. Although the running female was most likely Vivian, it wasn't Sabine she was running toward. The timeline of her flight back to the United States did not line up. He looked at his watch. If she caught her connecting flight, she was scheduled to land in Savannah in a few hours. If the minions at the airport conducted their job correctly, she would be his soon.

He put the mystery out of his mind. There were more pressing matters to contemplate.

His children were on the move; he felt them crossing the globe, descending on the city in which he now stayed. He felt it like the pressure of a pending storm, thought they veiled their thoughts. He had felt it earlier as he spoke with Wynda Moireach. She pressured him to hold an emergency meeting of the Table, but became unclear when he pressed her for a reason. Something was going undeniably wrong, and for the first time, Jude felt powerless to prevent it.

Damn Vivian! He should have killed her years ago. She was a threat, and he had always recognized her potential for disaster, but still he waited. It had been so much fun keeping her on a leash, heeled at his side.

She had the power to wreak havoc, to destroy everything he knew. He had been aware the time would come for her to die, but he delayed that for years. Whenever he convinced himself the time had come, he saw her delicate face, and his resolve washed away like silt in a rushing river. He believed that he had her spirit and body diminished, that she was under control.

Is that the genuine reason? You thought you had her beaten?

It was time to end it. This time had proven it. She was a hazard to him and everything he had worked two thousand years to build.

◕ ◖

Lukas watched his angel's quick-thinking eyes as he sat across from her in the cramped bathroom behind the candy shop. Her eyes were a fantastic, beautiful combination of blue and gold. She paid him no mind as she dabbed his knee with cotton balls drenched in alcohol. He wanted to hear her voice again.

"So, what's your name?" he asked. It was the only thing that came to mind.

"Megan Jameson," she replied.

"Like the whiskey?" he asked. She stopped patting his knee and frowned at him.

"Now, don't be one of those," she said in a brook-no-nonsense tone.

"One of what?"

"'Like the whiskey?' As if it's not bad enough that my name is probably the most Irish you could find in this Paddy McO'Somebody-or-other town. Yes, like the whiskey. Like the *Irish* whiskey. Now drop it."

Lukas regretted mentioning it and told her so. She paused, and a grin crept across her perfect features. He noticed she had laugh lines around her eyes and mouth, making her look older than he had initially guessed.

"I've got an Irish temper, too," she admitted ruefully. She grasped his right hand with gentle hands and painted it with alcohol.

"You also have beautiful eyes," Lukas observed. They both froze. Her grip on his hand loosened. He sensed that she was uneasy and didn't doubt that it was frightening to be alone in a locked store with a giant of a man she had just met. Inwardly, he admired her strength.

"Did I just say that out loud?" he quipped. The apologetic tone in his voice loosened the tension, and they laughed self-consciously. He started to smile but caught himself. *The fangs.*

"Thank you," she murmured, accepting the compliment. Her lovely smile returned, as did a brief, appreciative glance.

"Lukas," he said, changing the subject to alleviate any lingering awkwardness. "My name is Lukas."

"Bandage, Lukas?" She offered.

"What do you think?"

"I put bandages on anything that bleeds. I've heard it helps the healing."

I don't reckon I've gotta worry about that anymore, he thought, but he nodded. He could not stop staring, kept in rapt attention by the endless beauty of this woman; her reddish hair, her unique eyes, her short but perfect fingernails.

She put two bandages on each palm and a large, gauze-and-surgical-tape dressing on his knee. After finishing, she gave it a playful pat.

"That's gonna hurt coming off with all that leg hair," she observed. He grinned, curling his lips in an unpracticed way to cover his teeth.

God, he was hungry.

☙ ❧

There was an awkward silence as Blu stared at the ground, discomfited.

There go the somersaults again, Vivian thought as this new puzzle piece tried to find where it belonged. Blu believed her to be Princess Katerina, and maybe her new appearance held a similarity. But how could she be the person he remembered? She had conjured her looks from her imagination. Hadn't she?

"Blu, this is Vivian," Michael said. "Vivian, my fine friend Blu."

They shook hands. Vivian eyed Blu evenly and smiled. Blu's eyes opened wider when he saw her even teeth.

"Damn," he said. "The likeness is stunning."

Vivian shrugged. There was an awkward silence.

"Did you rent a car?" Michael asked, attempting to get the conversational ball rolling again. Blu ticked his tongue in disdain. He withdrew a key ring from his pocket and dangled it in front of Michael's eyes. Vivian noticed a bright rainbow dangling among the keys.

"No, honey," Blu said, "I brought my own."

They made a rapid exit from the Newark airport. In the parking lot, Blu proudly presented a rebuilt 1988 Ford Crown Victoria.

"It's an old cop car," he joked as his two passengers stretched out on the comfortable seats. "Can you imagine me in the *front* seat of a cop car?" he asked Michael, who shook his head with amusement.

"Check out this system," he said. He inserted a CD, and music blared from the speakers in an equalized sound system that handled the treble-heavy disco well. Blu bopped up and down in his seat like a man possessed.

"Blu, only you would still be listening to gay club music like this," Michael teased.

Vivian ignored them as they bantered back and forth and caught up on things. Exhausted after a long flight and a long night, she stretched out on the backseat and fell asleep.

γ   δ

Blu maneuvered the car through the parking lot with experienced ease and paid the small parking fee with a fifty from Michael. The attendant glared at them and tried to point out a sign that spelled out his inability to accept anything greater than a twenty, but the friends ignored him. The attendant handed Blu their change in a huff.

They swept out of the parking lot, and Blu steered them to the highway.

"Where are you heading?" Michael asked.

"New York. It's the closest city to get lost in, and a useful one, too. Speaking of which, Michael, if you ever make me set foot in New Jersey again, I'll kill you."

"The airport isn't that bad or that far from your apartment. Don't give me that shit. But don't bother heading to New York. We're going to do the unexpected, for once."

"How's that?" Blu asked with the unease of a friend who is familiar with his companion's wild tactics. He pulled a pack of Newports from a pocket on his bloody shirt and offered Michael one. He accepted, and lit his cigarette skillfully.

"By doing exactly what they expect us to do."

"Michael, what the fuck are you getting me into?"

"Head to 78 or 95 South."

"Where in gay hell are we going?" Blu asked with a flick of cigarette ash out of the window.

"Michigan."

"Detroit?"

"No, the southwest corner. A little town called New Bridgeport."

"Oh, no. Oh *no*. Michael, are you *serious*? Do you know what they do with large, gay, black vampires with butt-long dreads in Podunk, Michigan?"

"Admire you from afar?" Michael wagered.

"Admire you from the dull end of a big, pointy stick is more like it!" Blu retorted. He took his eyes from the road long enough to give Michael a look that bordered on a glare. "Jesus, Michael, you're lucky I love the hell out of you. First New Jersey, now Michigan, and every hick-ass town and every hick-ass state in-between. God, *why* did I leave New York?"

He addressed the last comment to the sky, his hands leaving the steering wheel to raise them to the heavens as he pleaded. Michael smiled and gave his friend an encouraging pat on the arm.

Blu smirked, or maybe it was a grimace, as he replaced his hands on the wheel. Michael wasn't sure.

Blu glanced in the backseat to where Vivian slept quietly, and a troubled expression shadowed his face.

"Michael, I need to ask you a question. And I need you to be honest with me," he said. He threw the butt of the Newport out of the window and rolled it up.

"Have you known me to be any other way?"

Blu shook his head. "No," he admitted. "Okay, here goes: I *know* her. I met her years ago in Russia. I'm sure of it. You know how I am, Michael. I don't forget a face. I have a photographic memory when it comes to that, like those kids who are good at numbers or art or—"

"Autistic savants," Michael interrupted.

"Yeah. I'm like that with faces. It was *her*. Her hair was a little shorter, and she was nowhere near as timid, but it was her. And she was with Shepherd. Only he was Duke Something-or-Other at the time, and he told me that she was centuries old."

Michael sucked deeply on his Newport and reached the filter. He exhaled, looked at the butt with disgust, and threw it out the window. He pulled his pack out of his pocket and lit two new cigarettes. He handed one to Blu, who accepted it with a nod and rolled his window back down an inch.

"Michael?"

"I don't know what to tell you, Blu. I don't know anything about her. She wound up on our doorstep, but at the time, she was shorter, blonder, and curvier. Lenny brought her—"

"Atlanta Lenny? How is he?"

"He's doing well. So's Beth and Arnold. You know how they have that crypt on their property they can't exterminate and how they refuse to move off the property because it's been in Lenny's family since abolition? Every once in a while, one of the crypt's inhabitants will wander onto the grounds. Sometimes they can help them, and sometimes they can't. Beth usually has an awareness about those things, you know?"

Blu did know, and he indicated his agreement.

"Well, I guess Viv meandered onto their porch one morning, and it surprised her. Usually, if they're found at all, it's way before daybreak since Beth wakes up from one of her dreams in the middle of the night and rouses the whole house. She and Lenny and Arnold search the property for the vagrant, but if they find one, it's usually young and dying. If she can, Beth feeds it a couple of chickens and sends it off with Lenny to us, or to another safe house that keeps them away from the *Shévet ha Dam*."

"But Viv showed up after daybreak?"

"Yep. Beth had pretty much given up on her, but she sent Lenny out to call Lukas just in case. She said she heard Vivian thumping about like a cow doing a tap number on the porch. She had put on the clothes Beth laid out for her and was about to try to leave when Beth caught her."

"But it was after daybreak."

"Blu, she's had *his* blood."

"Does she remember anything about being taken? About what happened after?"

Michael was silent for a moment. "Not really."

"She hasn't had a chance to build up a tolerance to sunlight? That we know of? Less than a hundred years or so?"

Again, momentary silence from Michael. "Right."

Blu shook his head and switched off the headlights. Daylight had broken, and the day promised to be a sunny one. He pointed to the glove box.

"I have a bottle of photoprotection in there if you want to freshen up."

Michael opened the glove compartment and dug around through a stash of CDs for the tube of sunscreen. He found it under a box of condoms. He gave Blu a mocking look of surprise.

"What?" Blu asked with an innocent smirk. Michael shook his head. He rubbed photoprotection on his exposed face, neck, and hands, and pulled his sunglasses from the pocket of his jacket.

"Michael, I have an idea. But you've got to trust me on this one."

"What's that?"

Blu glanced in his rearview at Vivian. She hadn't moved since he last looked.

"I'm positive she's the woman I remember, and there's one sure way to find out. Let's conduct an experiment."

Chapter 38

His doctoring done, Lukas saw no reason for him to hang around the candy store. Megan had mentioned when they first entered that the other employees would be arriving shortly and that his presence would jeopardize her job.

Sure enough, after she assisted him—with no small effort— to his feet, she led him to the wooden front door. He staggered, swaying within inches of perilously balanced displays of saltwater taffies and caramels. When they reached the door, she placed his hands on the wall to ensure he held his balance. As she fumbled through her keys, Lukas saw the deadly bright rays of morning beyond the cracks in the antique door. *Shame for her to have doctored me up only to have me die on her door-step the second she opens the door.*

She found the key. Her hand stretched for the lock.

I've got to stop her. I don't care how much of an idiot she thinks I am. I'll make her understand somehow.

He reached for her with his long arm and gently grasped her hand. She hesitated, her expression a combination of fear and uncertainty.

"I can't leave," Lukas said, his voice more somber than a preacher at a eulogy. "I can't go outside."

She didn't move.

He didn't doubt if his voice had been any less sober, she might have shaken off his grip. Luckily, he had piqued her curiosity with his grave tone. *Or maybe I've hypnotized her. Wouldn't that be cool?*

He didn't know why he thought it was cool, other than that it would be the first conscious vampire talent he displayed. He was drunk with hunger.

Get it together, Lukas. This is important.

"Why not?"

The lock clicked. For a feverish moment, Lukas had the impression Megan had somehow freed her hand without him knowing and was once again at the lock. He cringed, ready to brace himself for the sunlight, when he noticed her hand was still in his. The click had come from outside.

"Come *on*," she grumbled. She dragged him by the hand back into the depths of the candy store. She dodged expertly among barrels filled with the stuff of a dentist's nightmares. He nearly made them both fall more than once, and they narrowly avoided toppling more displays as they twisted their way through the large shop. Lukas doubted he could find his way back out. *It's like I'm lost at Willy Wonka's,* he thought.

She led the way to a darkened storage room. They crouched together behind commercial-size bottles of corn syrup and pallets filled to chest height with ten-pound bags of Dixie Crystals sugar. He heard her shallow breathing as she caught her breath. If she thought it odd that his came normally, she didn't say so.

She squatted in front of him, listening, he guessed, to see if they'd been followed. He could have told her they hadn't.

She was so beautiful it hurt him to watch her. His hand reached for hers instinctively. She twitched at the unfamiliar touch and peered at him with uncertain eyes. She looked ready to kiss him or scream for help, depending on his next move. He saw her pulse dancing in her jugular. His stomach felt both sick and depthless at the same time. His mouth flapped open and shut, and he fought desperately not to do what his instinct begged him to do. He struggled to focus on other things, on noble, safe things, but found he had no power over his thoughts.

You need to drink. She's right here. Her blood is warm and good. Take her.

His hunger had reached a breaking point, and Megan was caught like an insect in a web.

Don't cry out. I won't hurt you, would never hurt you. The thoughts crossed the short distance from his mind to hers easily and calmed her. He knew he was in her mind when he felt her thoughts start to swim like his and heard her think, *What's happening?*

"This won't hurt, I promise," he whispered. He closed in and took her easily into his arms. She didn't resist. His amorous kiss to her neck deepened as he quenched the hunger consuming him.

I'm sorry. I'm so, so sorry.

C8 ЄO

Maysun's body lay rigid and cold. Away from her lover and buried deep in the earth where she felt most in touch with herself and the world, she strained to keep in contact with a myriad of minds. It wasn't easy to reach several powerful psyches across the globe at once.

Two—an important two—were close, easier to touch. Charles had left his walls up, which was good. It wasn't time for him to know. And Doyle. If he knew, then Charles would as well. Damn. How many of the old blood did Charles plan to kill? If he had both Jude and Jerusha killed, he would be after her next to ensure he was the oldest alive.

Jude—he was tricky. How much should he know? How much had he deciphered? There was no way for her to hide the arrival of hundreds of his demonic children. What if one decided to drop in on Daddy? She scanned the minds of those around him, but they were doing their damndest to keep her out. This wasn't going to be easy. Her mental tensile strength was near the breaking point, but she didn't dare stop. There was more on the line this time than most.

God, this was such a balancing act.

α ѳ

"How much longer, do you think?" Michael asked.

"Hell if I know. It would help if I had any idea where in Michigan we were going."

"Southwest corner," a voice said from the back of the car. Both men jumped. A feminine laugh followed.

"Just north of Indiana and about five miles from Lake Michigan. That is, if we're going where I think we are."

They were on Interstate 80, heading west after the occasional wrong turn and some guesswork from Michael and Blu. The landscape was mostly empty fields, the trees oak, elm, and sassafras. Judging from the abundance of leaves on the ground, they'd just missed seeing a countryside bejeweled with autumn.

"Good morning, princess," Blu grinned. Vivian scowled.

"I'm not Princess Katerina," she said.

"Whatever. You still look like a princess to me," he said. "Anyhow, I'm glad you're awake. Otherwise, I would've had to stop in Toledo and figure out where we're headed. Now I can stop in the sticks somewhere to get gas and scare the fuck out of someone."

Vivian laughed.

"Just head like you're going to Chicago, I think. I mean, we're going to have to get off the highway well before there, but that's the best route I can think of," she said.

Blu nodded.

"How'd you sleep?" he asked

"Really well. This backseat is almost like a small couch."

Blu wagged his eyebrows up and down. "Why do you think I like this car so much? Saves me in motel fees."

"Where are we?" she asked, rubbing her eyes.

"Somewhere outside Fremont, Ohio. In other words, BFE."

"BFE?"

"Butt Fuck Egypt."

Vivian thought about asking him to explain further but decided against it. She reached into her pocket for her sunglasses, rubbed the lint from the lenses, and put them on. She turned to watch the scenery go by, but there wasn't much to see, so she faced front again and wished for her book.

"How do you feel?" Michael asked. His voice was tainted with poorly hidden concern.

"Fine. Why?"

"Is your skin warm?"

"Michael!" Blu barked. Michael frowned at him guiltily and turned back to Vivian. She sat up and rubbed her arms, feeling for warm patches of sunburn, blisters, or red patches.

Her skin was fine. There were no telltale red or pink spots—not a freckle. Her skin was unmarred.

"What are you trying to do, Michael? Give me a heart attack? That's not funny!" she snapped with more force than she intended. Michael's sheepish expression became, if anything, more shamefaced.

"It was my idea," Blu interjected.

"What've you done to me?" Vivian demanded. She shivered despite the warm sunlight flooding the car.

"Relax, Vivian," Blu said. "It's what we *didn't* do to you that you would've had to worry about."

"What are you talking about?"

"Sunscreen. Sunblock. Photoprotection. Long sleeves. Sunglasses. You've been bare of the basic defenses against sunlight, and you haven't had a single problem. The sun didn't wake you up. It didn't faze you. You're not burned. I'm a five-hundred-year-old *black* vampire, and my happy ass still wears sunblock whenever I'm out for a day."

"How... what...?"

"Vivian, you shouldn't have been able to tolerate the sun for so long. Not if you're as young as you claim. Don't worry; we've been keeping an eye on you to make sure you're alright. Well, Michael has. He's worse than a mother freaking hen. And you've been fine, although we've been out in the sunlight since we left the airport over four hours ago."

"Four hours?" Vivian murmured.

"Four hours, and not a spot," Michael agreed, eyebrows raised.

"What do you think it means?" she asked. Only one thing came to her mind, but it didn't make any sense to her.

"I think it means your mother has a lot of explaining to do," Blu said.

Chapter 39

Lukas panicked.

Megan lay unconscious in his arms. His sharp ears picked up the sounds of a store filling with employees conducting their morning duties, oblivious that a coworker was dying only feet away.

He hadn't meant to rob her of so much of her blood. He had been so ravenous he couldn't stop himself. And now that he was sated and rational thought came easier, he knew that Megan would not live if he didn't take action to help her.

But what? If he emerged from the stockroom with her limp in his arms, her coworkers would freak out, maybe try to kill him. It wouldn't be difficult—a shove out the door into broad daylight would clinch the job.

He considered making a loud noise to draw one of her coworkers to the back, but he couldn't guarantee they would not stumble on him first. On top of that, if they found her, they wouldn't have any idea what was wrong with her. They would probably assume from all the blood that she had been attacked. The ambulance team summoned by 9-1-1 wouldn't understand what had happened. No. He couldn't risk it.

He rose from her side and looked for a back door. He wondered if he had the stamina to withstand the shade in the alley behind the shop long enough to locate another hiding spot, like a trash dumpster. Surely, there had to be a fire exit or an alternate route out of the shop. And there it was: right behind a pallet nearly chest deep in ten-pound bags of sugar.

Don't they know that's a fire hazard? Lukas asked himself, but he already knew the answer. The candy shop likely caught wind of Fire Marshal inspections from an inside source and cleared the space when someone tipped them off. Meanwhile, it was a convenient storage space. Or, in Lukas's case, inconvenient.

He would never get the heavy pallet unloaded before someone found them, and he couldn't squeeze into the space between the bags of sugar and the door to freedom.

Now what?

He went back to where Megan lay dying on the floor. Her skin was pale, her mouth open as if to receive a kiss. Her breathing was shallow and short, and with every exhale, he thought her breathing would shudder to a halt. He'd never felt so awful for anything he had ever done.

He took off his shirt, ripped off the sleeve, and pressed it onto the bruising punctures he had inflicted to slow the blood loss, then wrapped the rest of his shirt over her torso to ward off shock. He felt her heart pounding rapidly through the fabric in a frantic attempt to circulate what little blood she had left. Her skin was growing clammy. She groaned almost inaudibly.

This is stupid. She's lost enough blood to die, and keeping what's left isn't going to do a damn good. What she needs is more blood. Like a transfusion. Or...

A thought struck him. What if he gave her some of his blood? He could let her have just enough to help her regain consciousness, and then...

And then she'd be a vampire.

It would spread to her as surely as a virus. Then the two of them could sit in the dark together and wait to be discovered. If someone found them after he turned her, what would she do? Go to work? The customers would open the door and let in the sunlight. It was that, or hide with a stranger who'd come close to killing her before giving her fangs and explaining she has to drink blood for eternity. *Not to mention the whole Jude thing.* He shook his head. *No. I won't do that to her.*

But if she died... If she died, he would gladly walk into the sunlight and die with his guilt.

He studied her face, her flawless complexion. The freckles scattered across the bridge of her nose looked painted on by the hand of a god. *I must be in love. Even dying, she looks beautiful.*

The idea of sinking his teeth into his wrist or arm made him cringe. He searched for a sharp object to aid him. He found a box cutter lying on a carton of jelly beans and took it back with him to Megan's side. He crouched beside her.

Let me take it back.

He depressed the blade, which, luckily, was a sharp one, and cut a shallow trench into the soft part of his forearm. It was surprisingly easy and less painful than he imagined. A narrow strip of red came into sight. He pressed the blood to Megan's lips.

She fought him at first. She muttered unintelligible sounds as he held her head stubbornly in place and refused to let her pull back. Eventually, she had no choice but to swallow.

She coughed and sputtered, and he let her. Once she began breathing, he placed her mouth back over the deep scratch. She swallowed again. Her eyelids fluttered.

That's it, Megan. Come back.

⌓ ⁊

Jude reclined into the soft chaise and closed his eyes. Every ounce of energy he could have used to move, he redirected to his psyche. In this position, he embodied the vampire of legend: pale body limp with death, chin stained with the blood of his recent kill, his fangs visible in a death grimace, arms crossed on his chest.

He focused, spread his consciousness outward with sharp mental hooks. He pierced the minds of the undead everywhere. He reached the sinister, those with a lust for killing and blood, strength, eternal vitality, and power. To every dark vampire created. It was easier to enter minds with thoughts so similar to his. The good...

He cursed the good. The words *good* and *vampire* were incongruous. Vampires thrived on death, and they lived to corrode the lives of those around them. They lived to kill. The handful of "good" vampires were an aberration, a powerful gift gone awry. Like Vivian. His blood should have contaminated her, should have made her imperfect, unclean.

His Table had failed him in finding her. It was time to recruit them all. He stopped the dreams of those who lived where it was daylight and the actions of those walking the nights. Across the globe, vampires everywhere became in tune with Jude Shepherd.

He pried into their minds. So many vampires so close, and he hadn't been informed why. Now, he knew.

War.

Someone had called everyone to a battleground, and he had no idea who or why. Charles, maybe. It was likely.

War! What an excellent plan. Death, violence, bloodshed. Jude's blackened heart sang. He didn't care who'd called the battle, as long as the troops were ready. War of the magnitude he sensed awaited only came around every few hundred years. Who cared how many died? Progenies were easy to spawn. War, now that was hard to come by.

You idiot! Vivian's declared this war! She's coming after you!

His excitement melted in the light of this notion. Facing a battalion of compassionate vampires didn't strike as much fear in his heart as the likelihood of coming head-to-head with the only child who stood a chance against him.

He had to do something.

It would take too much time to speak to them using individual languages. He impressed only images upon them: her face in its many forms, her scent, her voice, the way her skin felt, and with it, he instilled the need to kill. He stressed the importance of stopping a vampire so powerful.

For the one or ones who killed her, he offered the ultimate accolade: to be one of the Table, second only to him in the vampire hierarchy, the right hand of evil incarnate. Authority, privilege, security, and a promise to live up to the "eternal" life they were aware wasn't a certainty.

All they had to do was find and kill her.

☙ ❧

Maysun sighed. Her grip on many minds became tenuous; on others—those farther away—it slipped.

Damn. Damn Damn Damn.

She clenched her hands into tight fists. Her eyes disappeared into folds of tightly clenched flesh. Her fists tightened, and the tendons in her forearms tensed. Her mind stretched to the point of exploding. She felt she must surely be on the verge of what humans called a stroke. Sweat mingled with the dirt over her and ran into her hair as salty blood.

I've got to get them back. How am I going to get them back? And I have no time to do it now. Damn. Damn Damn!

☙ ❧

Blu's car crossed into Vernon County. Vivian was impressed by how much the area had grown. It was still predominantly farm country, but small villages had sprung up where the occasional feed store and grocery used to be. Places that hadn't been considered proper "towns" now boasted respectable communities. Factory work had replaced farm work as the leading local trade. The growth of the hearty community impressed her.

"Where to, Princess?" Blu asked.

Vivian replied, "New Bridgeport."

There were plenty of new roads, and most of the old ones were now paved and branched into new routes. The changed landmarks turned her around three times.

She directed them onto what she'd known as Broken Arrow—now Broken Arrow Highway—and they drove the newly paved road through New Bridgeport.

There was no Bender's Nursing Home.

"Are you sure we're in the right place?" Michael asked. Vivian shook her head.

"No, but I know it's on this road. It said so on the website."

"Nothing personal, Princess, but I'm sure this is a long highway," Blu added. "Maybe we should stop and ask for directions."

"Just keep going!" Vivian cried. "We're going the right way. I can *feel* it."

She turned and faced the window so closely she could have kissed the glass. Blu gave Michael a look that screamed, 'I told you so.' Michael faced the direction opposite Vivian and kept an eye on the other side of the road.

They drove for what felt to Vivian like an hour but was probably more like fifteen minutes. They passed a sign that read, "Welcome to Lakeshore." She remembered Lakeshore. Their high school had competed with hers in various sports. Hadn't they? *Why can't I remember details that should be so clear? High school should seem a handful of years ago.* It was impossible to remember the most trivial details; her school colors, teachers, and classmates. *What's he done to me?*

Daylight was fading, and with it faded Vivian's hope of finding the nursing home before dark. She knew it was close, she hadn't lied about that, but she wasn't sure how close.

Just as she considered suggesting they turn around, she saw it. Past a small copse of trees stood a two-story building constructed of bricks painted a dirty yellow. The large sign above the door, lettered in the same black block letters as the website, read Bender's Nursing Home.

Blu turned on his blinker, cut from his place in the left lane in front of a rusted Dodge pickup truck, and swerved into the parking lot. The Dodge gave an angry honk and sped past. Blu swerved into a parking spot and cut the engine.

Michael and Blu unfastened their seatbelts. Vivian folded her hands in her lap. After panning the parking lot for vampires lying in wait for them, Michael turned and faced her.

"You don't have to do this if you don't want to," he said, his brown eyes full of concern.

Vivian's head moved up and down as if stirred by the wind. She sniffed.

"Yes. I do," she replied. She unfastened the belt holding her in place, aware that she had to hurry. It was growing late. Chances were good that visiting hours would be over soon if they weren't already.

She closed her eyes and concentrated. Focusing with the two of them staring at her was unnerving, but she was determined to try. Slowly, before their eyes, she metamorphosed into the blonde, blue-eyed Vivian that Michael had met.

"That's the creepiest thing I've seen in a long time," Blu murmured. "Why'd she do that?"

"That's Vivian," Michael explained. Blu shook his head in disbelief. They exited the car.

Michael took her left hand as they approached the glass double doors, and Blu took her right and gave her an encouraging squeeze. Grateful for the strong hands that held hers, she squeezed back.

Blu let go of her hand and opened the door for them. Vivian's knees shook violently as they approached the reception counter. Her resolution was weakening, and she was glad Michael held her hand firmly. Without it, she would have been tempted to run away.

A friendly-looking nurse with heavily frosted hair and large brown eyes sat chatting on the phone behind the desk. She saw the three friends and put the person she spoke to on hold.

"Yes? Can I help you?"

Vivian felt about to collapse. Her mouth opened, and what came out sounded like a combination of a squeak and a croak.

"I'd like to visit Rose Black, please. What room would she be in?"

The nurse eyed her curiously for a second, and for that long second, Vivian was certain she was going to tell her that she had arrived too late, that Mrs. Black had died last week, and she was so sorry. Instead, she heard, "Room 116. Down the hall and to the right. I'm glad you're here! Miss Rose doesn't get many visitors. Are you a granddaughter?"

Unprepared for the question, Vivian almost slipped and corrected her, but instead, she just nodded.

"Melody. Melody Lewis," she said. "This is my husband, Stephen, and our friend, Arthur."

"Very nice to meet you, Melody," the nurse said with a sincere and beautiful smile the old widowers probably adored. "Go straight down this hall and take the first right, and it will be about halfway down on the right."

"Thank you so much," Michael replied. Together they walked down the hall like prisoners headed to a communal cell.

"Arthur?" Blu whispered. His attempt at humor sounded grave, and it gave Vivian the creeps. She only shrugged in reply.

The walls were yellow-beige cinder blocks with framed bulletin boards posted regularly. Although curious about her mother's life, Vivian ignored the pictures, menus, and the schedule of "Senior Activities." She had the crazy idea that if she paused for a moment at any of the boards, she'd find herself rooted to the spot.

That's silly. What do I have to be afraid of?

But part of her *was* afraid, and she couldn't shake it. Blu's large hand embraced her shoulder in a half-hug, and Vivian knew, then, that she was trembling.

The door to room 116 was halfway open, and Vivian heard the sounds of a television host smoothly coaxing a game show contestant with the practiced ease of a door-to-door salesman. She saw a window ledge and a bushy yellow chrysanthemum.

Beyond the door, her past awaited.

Chapter 40

Megan sat up and retched, but nothing came up. Her stomach felt alternately hot and cold, and her eyes watered. Sharp stomach cramps flared and died, and her skin crawled with the feeling that she was covered in palmetto bugs.

"I'm going to be sick," she whispered. Her hand flew to her mouth as she retched again.

"You'd better not," a voice said. "You nearly died until I gave you the blood in your stomach." A vaguely familiar face framed in blond curls came into the light of the dim stockroom bulbs. *Damn, he's tall. Who is he? Should I remember?*

"Blood in my stomach?" she echoed. "Don't be stupid. I'm no vampire."

A somber look covered the man's face. He crouched down, and she saw his powder-blue eyes. He took her hand in hands as cold as hers.

"You are now," he said intently.

Megan would have laughed if she weren't so sick. A vampire. How stupid did he think she was? There were no such things as vampires. She didn't read vampire books, didn't like vampire movies, and she sure as hell didn't appreciate vampire jokes.

Then she examined what she had thought was dirt on his stubbly chin. It wasn't dirt at all.

Blood. And some foreign part of her brain told her it was her blood.

She drew a sharp breath, but he'd seen the thought that crossed her mind and covered her mouth with his hand. She did the first thing that came to mind. She bit him.

Two shallow puncture wounds appeared on the side of his hand, which he pulled away and put in his mouth. She started to scream again, but the shuddering breath she pulled in left her without a sound. She started hyperventilating.

"Shh, shh, shh." He tried to take her into his arms, but she backed away, scuttling crablike across the floor. The look of pain on his face at her reaction almost touched her, but terror quickly won out.

"I'm sorry," he said, shaking his head. He looked like he was about to burst into tears. "I didn't know what else to do. I didn't mean to hurt you. I never..." His hands stretched out in an effort to communicate, then collapsed to his sides.

"I never meant to hurt you," he concluded.

"What—?"

The question was cut short. As her lips formed the first word, she felt an odd protuberance on her eyeteeth.

No. It couldn't be.

Her tongue flicked forward. Sharp, pointed fangs hung where her canines used to be.

"*NO!*"

"Damn it, woman!" he said, forcing her to stagger to her feet. "They'll kill us!"

He dragged her, stumbling, around the furthest corner of the stockroom and pulled her down behind a stack of yellow boxes. Together, they squatted in the dark and cobwebs. Footsteps pattered in their direction.

"Listen to me," he hissed. "If they find us, they'll know the minute you open your damn mouth. And they won't care if you're Megan, their friend from work. You'll be a bloodsucking vampire, just like me. And all they have to do to kill us is shove us out the door. Poof. A quick and painful death."

Megan didn't believe him, but his face reflected a conviction in what he said.

"Hello?" a voice called.

It's Karl. He's had a crush on me since high school. Karl wouldn't kill me.

In the darkened shadows where they hid, she saw the stern look on Lukas's face, and she knew he wasn't kidding.

That's his name. Lukas. That guy I found on my doorstep.

Could she afford to make a mistake?

He's probably right. People wouldn't view you as the person they knew once they saw you as an undead monster—a bloodsucking undead monster at that.

Karl peered halfheartedly around a few dusty palettes. Megan realized she was nervous, and didn't want Karl to find them.

Goddamn it. I can't believe this. It must be a crazy nightmare. Oh,

God, I don't know anything about being a vampire. Oh! I do know I have to kill people to eat. I don't want to kill anyone!

Then the strangest thing happened. Lukas looked right at her and shook his head as if he had heard what she'd been thinking. He placed a finger on his lips and then on hers. He had read her mind. How did she know that?

"Who's there?"

She didn't say anything. It went against everything that she thought made sense, but she did it anyway. A quiet, exasperated sigh escaped her lips, but that was all.

"That's fuckin' weird. I could'a sworn I heard someone," Karl muttered. His footsteps faded away in a defeated shuffle. Megan found she could breathe again.

"Now what?" she snapped.

"Now I have to ask if you know of a better hiding place," Lukas answered.

Ψ Ω

"He's not answering his phone," Doyle said, his voice almost relieved. He placed the phone back into its clip and reclined. Charles' place in Kaiserslautern was posh. Why hadn't he seen it before?

Charles blinked, and his face screwed up as if he was straining to hear a conversation from behind a thick door.

"Charles?"

Doyle snapped a finger in front of Charles' face. Charles pressed his lips together in an impatient grimace, and Doyle shivered, afraid he might have angered him. After another minute of consternation, Charles finally shook his head as if clearing it.

"What's wrong?"

"I don't know," Charles replied. "And that's what's bothering me."

It was the most heartfelt sentence Charles had ever uttered in Doyle's presence, and it scared the hell out of him.

"Can you explain something?" Doyle asked. "Jude made Jerusha. She's super strong, but he's kept her subdued until now. Every time I've seen her over the last century, she's been like a human on Thorazine. What's the big deal? Can't we arrange for him to have her back, and then things go back to normal? I mean, I like her, but..."

"You would turn her in for a profit?" Charles asked. Doyle cast his gaze to the floor, licked his lips. Shrugged. Charles said, "I thought not."

"Tell me about Vivian. What's her story? Jude took her back in the day because of a grudge with God, and..." he trailed off, prompting Charles to pick up where he left off.

"Joseph Cartaphilus seduced Jerusha, then became her vampire father. He starved her, weakened her, and then dominated her. He took pleasure in forcing her to do anything he wanted, so her virtue was never defiled, only her body.

"He spent centuries performing the same test. He wiped her mind clean of memories, and he would make her fall in love with him. He did this repeatedly over the centuries. Sometimes he would leave her for years, decades at a time, but he always came back for her. It was a game to see how long he could stay away. You see, the longer she had to become integrated into her surroundings, the less her faded memories recalled her involvement with him. That way, when she ultimately fell for him, the greater his victory. What he didn't realize was that her love for him was part of a bigger plan."

"I don't get it," Doyle said. Charles' expression said he found that easy to believe.

"Those who can wield the Source are a small part of God on earth. They reflect God in a small way. What Cartaphilus doesn't realize is that he loves Jerusha. And in loving her, he loves God. As the saying goes, God is love. That is true."

"So? He loves her. So what?"

"What happens when something evil falls in love?"

Doyle shrugged.

"That love becomes a part of him and changes his nature. Now we help him to realize it."

"Why?"

"If he loves Jerusha, he loves the Source, for that is what she embodies. Thus, he is no longer evil, at least not entirely. Cartaphilus is the strongest embodiment of wickedness walking the planet, but he is motivated by a stronger force than jealousy or anger—the Maleficence. Our job is to help him realize his love, thereby casting out the Maleficence. If we can do this, he will be changed, weakened. Also, if he is no longer the person he was, the curse is lifted."

"And he can be killed," Doyle said. For the first time, he understood.

"Exactly. No more Joseph Cartaphilus."

Doyle didn't know what Charles had in mind for the Tribe after he dispatched Jude, but the dark, preoccupied stare on his face told Doyle it wasn't good.

ೞ   ೧

The door to room 116 swung open silently. In a wheelchair, facing away from the door, facing a window and television, was the frail, white-haired woman Vivian saw on the picture on the web page. She was wrapped in a frayed, pale blue robe, her feet in worn blue slippers.

"Mom?" Vivian breathed. The woman perked up. Her head turned around slowly, and her expression changed from boredom to astonishment.

The face was lined and freckled, the skin and lips old and dry. Her hair was white and shorter, and bald spots showed through in places. But it was the same small nose, the same proud blue eyes, same high cheekbones. A smile parted the parched lips, revealing store-bought teeth. But it was her. It was Rose Black.

"Vivian?" she gasped. She started to laugh, coughed, laughed again. Her arms reached out, and Vivian flew to her arms.

"Vivian, Vivian, Vivian," Rose muttered as her lined hand combed Vivian's long blonde hair. "Oh, my precious Vivian. How I've missed you."

"I missed you, too," Vivian sniffed. Tears streamed down her face freely now, but she didn't care. She buried her face into the weathered terrycloth robe and cried like a child. "I missed you so much," she murmured. "I'm so sorry. I never meant to leave you. I never wanted to leave you alone. I'm so sorry."

"Oh, I know. I know."

They held each other wordlessly for several minutes. Vivian cried helplessly as Rose sniffed gently and clutched her daughter. They laughed. They sobbed. They sniffed and laughed some more. Finally, they separated. Vivian perched on the edge of the hospital bed. Her mom smiled proudly at her, clinging to her hand like a lifeline.

"So," Rose said. She swung the hand that held Vivian's out and examined her daughter in admiration, but her face reflected no astonishment at her daughter's unchanged features.

"You look beautiful. You always have."

Vivian's free hand flew to her mouth. Michael grabbed some tissues from a box on the nightstand and handed some to Vivian, some to her mother. Vivian dabbed her tears absently.

"Mother, aren't you going to ask me how I look the same? I haven't changed in fifty years, Mother. *Fifty years*!"

Rose Black shook her head, a wan smile increasing the wrinkles at her eyes until they almost disappeared. She touched her face with the tissue, completely missing the tears, but she didn't notice.

"No. I've never asked. I was only grateful for a chance to be your mother."

Vivian crumpled the tissues in her hand. She sat up, a puzzled look on her face.

"I don't understand. You know as well as I do that I should be nearly seventy years old. Don't you know how old you are?"

Rose Black nodded.

"I know. I've known every day for ninety years, or at least the last eighty-five of them. I feel it every day as I wake, and I think about it every night before I sleep. Darling, sometimes I think you're the reason I am alive today," she said. "I clung to the hope that one day you'd re-member me and the time we had and would come to see me." She beamed with a pride Vivian didn't understand.

"Of course, I remember you. You're my mother," Vivian sobbed. Rose clenched her hand, and Vivian was surprised at the strength in her wrinkled, spotted hands. Rose sat up and straightened her robe with a frown. She took in Vivian's friends with a glance and a nod, but no welcome. Her laugh lines deepened, and she tapped her foot as she searched for the proper reply.

"Vivian, it's past time I told you the truth," she said. "Maybe we should be alone."

"You can talk in front of them," Vivian insisted. "They're my friends."

Rose nodded and eyed Michael's mouth with a knowing look. She straightened up again, and released her firm grip on Vivian's hand. Shame replaced resolve. She frowned again and looked warily at Viv-ian, unsure how to proceed.

"After Matthew died, I was a mess. I fell apart. All those years we had tried to have children without success... They didn't have ways to help couples like they do nowadays. I felt that if we'd just been able to have children, I would've at least had that child to remember him by. I didn't care about his money. I was willing to work. I *wanted* to work. What I didn't want was to sit around the house thinking about all the things that might've been.

"It wasn't hard for a woman to work back then. Jobs were available for women during the war. I got a job in a factory. It kept me busy, and it helped me, knowing that I would be able to live without using too much of Matthew's money. But every night I'd come home to the house we bought together, sleep in the bed where we'd tried so hard to conceive children. I couldn't bear it. I put up a "For Sale" sign, but the housing market was so slow, I could hardly give the house away."

The war? Vivian thought. *That doesn't make sense. I was a young adult by then.*

"One night, I left work late, and on the way home, I decided to visit Matthew's grave. I stood there pouring my heart out about how much I missed him and still loved him, how badly I'd wanted to be the mother of his children, how I cried myself to sleep every night because I was so alone.

"Then I looked up, and this handsome dark-haired man was standing over me. He looked so disheartened."

"Jude," Blu stated. Rose nodded.

"He called himself Joseph, but I learned later... He said he'd overheard me talking to Matthew and that he wanted to help. I told him I didn't want another man to replace Matthew. That's what I thought he meant, that he wanted to marry me there on the spot. Maybe he wanted to help me conceive a child. What man wouldn't offer that to a woman if given a chance? He said no, that he wanted to give me a companion. A daughter."

Vivian gasped as the truth dawned on her.

"You mean, he—he *gave* me to you?"

Rose nodded.

"At first, I thought he was crazy. He quickly explained what he meant. He carried you to Matthew's grave from his car—a LaSalle sedan; I'll never forget it. You didn't look like you, then. You had dark, curly hair, and you were taller and darker-skinned, and beautiful. I couldn't move. I didn't know if I was happy, or scared, or what."

"He has that effect on people," Blu told her.

"Oh, I learned that," Rose said. "I saw him countless times after that, and every time it was like someone stroked my spine with an icicle, but at the same time, I was exceptionally calm. Almost drugged, you know?"

They all indicated they did.

"Anyway, he told me to take his hand and think of Matthew, all the features about him that I loved the most. I couldn't believe I was doing this, but I took his hand and thought about his blue-green eyes. Out of all of his features, those eyes were my very favorite. I developed this perfect picture in my head, and as soon as I was done, he told me to open my eyes.

"There was a beautiful young woman lying on top of his grave. You were perfect; dark blond hair, beautiful figure. You could've been his daughter. Most importantly, you could have been *our* daughter. And when you opened your eyes…"

Rose sighed. Vivian thought about how she described Matthew and her likeness to the man in the pictures. She thought she was going to scream, but it was choked, stuck somewhere around her voice box. She felt confused, betrayed, and profoundly disturbed, but she didn't interrupt. There were still a lot of unanswered questions.

"He told me to tell everyone you were Matthew's niece, but if I wanted to, I could tell you I was now your mother, that your family had passed away. He would be coming to visit, every night or every other night. I was not to question this.

"I did as he told me, and he did as he promised. At least twice a week, he came after dark when you were asleep. I knew. How could I not know? I saw blood on your sheets, your clothes. But you never—you thought they were dreams."

Rose paused. Two large tears broke off and trickled down her spotted cheeks. She wiped them away with a tissue.

"I am so sorry, Vivian. I should've told you sooner. But he said he'd kill me."

"He would have," Vivian confirmed, running a hand through her hair. Michael and Blu concurred.

"I know. But I shouldn't have let him do that to you. Vivian, you're the closest thing I've ever had to a daughter, and I loved you from the start. I should've tried to protect you."

"Mrs. Black, there wasn't anything you could've done," Michael interjected. "He would have killed you and taken Vivian away. And he would've wiped her mind clean like he did before."

"Here's what I don't understand," Blu said. "If he had her under his thumb, why put her in with Rose at all? Why'd he go through the trouble to separate himself only to visit every night and keep her alive?"

"Every night for three years," Rose said.

"I don't understand it, either," Vivian said. "But I'm going to find out."

☙ ❧

After Karl left, Megan took Lukas by the hand and led him through the stockroom. Judging from the sound of things, the candy store was open for business. Lukas heard the *ching* of the old-fashioned register, the rattle of a jelly bean dispenser.

"What are you doing?" Lukas whispered, his voice squeaking with near panic as she neared the swinging doors.

"Shhh," said Megan.

She raised a large wooden door with a horizontal handle tied with a rope. Behind the door was what looked to Lukas to be a spacious, dusty cupboard. She climbed inside.

"Come on," she said, beckoning to Lukas and peering anxiously at the doors. Lukas climbed in after, feeling all knees and elbows.

"Shut the door," she hissed. Lukas extended a long arm and pulled the door shut with the rope. It closed with a thump, enveloping them in blackness.

"What is this?" he asked.

"Dumbwaiter," she replied. "The shop used to be part of—"

She shut up as they heard a door bang against the wall as someone entered the stockroom. There was a slight bump and shuffling as whoever it was found what they were searching for and left.

"Used to be part of the Cotton Exchange. You know how Savannah exported a lot of cotton back in the day? Well, to expedite the processing from Bay Street to the ships on River Street, this building used dumbwaiters. We're sitting in a part of history."

He thought she was trying to be funny, but her face was hidden in the dark. He yawned and wished he had just a bit more room to stretch out. He heard her shuffling uncomfortably in the dark. Somewhere in the distance, he heard the thrumming of some large machine—an industrial-size mixer, he decided. Probably blending batter or icing, or maybe chocolate. It was a relaxing sound.

"Lukas?"

His eyes opened with a jerk. He'd fallen asleep without realizing it. "Yes?"

"We're not going to have to hide in dumbwaiters every night, er, day, are we?"

He almost laughed. He knew she didn't mean what she said literally, but he wasn't sure how to answer. He could have responded with more conviction if he knew where his father was. As it was, he had no idea how Michael or Vivian was doing, and Gina was dead.

"No, no dumbwaiters," he said. "No coffins, unless that turns out to be a preference of yours. Regular beds in very dark rooms."

"Good," Megan replied. She startled him by resting her head on his shoulder. He smiled in the dark, and they fell asleep.

Chapter 41

It was difficult acting normal. Her head was awhirl with contact, her mind tangled in the thoughts of vampires across the globe, and here she had to sit, behaving as if everything was normal!

For the first time in centuries, Maysun worried.

Not for herself. With what felt like an eternity of living comes an eternity of knowledge and wisdom. With knowledge and wisdom came the assurance that if things didn't go as planned, creation struggled forward, with or without her.

This, however, was beyond the help of all her knowledge and wisdom.

Her telepathic connections were more tangled than a barrelful of snakes. Her messages, her taps on others' consciousness, and her blocks on those she needed to protect were a clutter of incoming indistinguishable voices. She *had* to straighten this out soon, or events would get out of control. If they weren't already.

Some followed Jude and searched the world for a trail leading them to the vampire goddess. Others followed Maysun's instruction, descending on Savannah. Some struggled with doing both.

The only way out of this is to tell them the truth. Let them know that if they come to Georgia, they will be where she *will be. And then, I have to get her there.*

She set about picking her connections apart as delicately as a spider reweaving a web.

;<

They sat in stunned silence for several minutes. Vivian was unsure if she felt frustrated or angry. Part of it fit into her puzzle. It explained why her childhood memories were broken and distorted. How long had she lived with Rose Black? Three years? From the time she believed she was seventeen until she "turned" twenty-one. Why hadn't she noticed that she didn't blossom like other young women? That her maturity had never allowed her to bond with others her presumed age?

The answer was obvious. Jude. It was Jude who'd visited her both in dreams and life. He had washed away any memory he didn't want her to keep, replacing them with superimposed ones.

"What else can you tell me?" Vivian asked.

Rose's eyes darted to every corner as if she expected a legion of the undead to crash through the windows and doors at any moment.

"Not much. He never told me where you came from or gave me any clue how long you would stay, except to hint that it would be 'A long time.' He said that any time I expressed concern about losing you." Rose fidgeted in her wheelchair, cast a concerned glance at Vivian as if she waited for her to contradict or berate her for what she had done half a century ago. "Lies, of course. I knew he was... evil... as soon as I saw him, but I would've done anything to have a daughter like you, and he preyed on my weakness. It wasn't as if *you* were evil. You were perfect, the perfect daughter."

She sobbed softly into a disintegrating tissue, and Blu patted her on the shoulder.

"No one blames you for any of this, Mrs. Black," he said. "You were as much a victim as Vivian. We understand why you did what you did."

Rose placed her pale hand on top of Blu's dark one. Her expression regained some of its composure.

"Thank you," she breathed.

"So, you can't tell us anything else?" Michael asked. "Anything at all? Sometimes the most insignificant detail may turn out to be a clue."

Rose shrugged and inspected the flaking tissue in her hand. She turned it over a few times, wavering between telling them what was on her mind or dismissing her secret. Vivian leaned forward on the bed across from Rose Black.

"Only this," she whispered. "As he carried Vivian's body to Matthew's grave, he was murmuring words to her in a language I didn't understand. The language was guttural, but at the same time, it flowed. Romanian, maybe. Maybe Russian. I don't know, but you know the sound I mean. And although I didn't understand any of the words, I did pick up a name. He said it several times."

She stopped as if someone had interrupted. Her ears pricked up like a dog's, and she tipped her head to the side as though she'd heard a noise. This woman had kept her secret for fifty years, most likely under the threat of death. Now, she feared that death was coming for her.

"Did you hear something?" Rose asked. No one responded. No one had.

"The name, Rose," Michael prodded.

"Yes, the name," she muttered. "He called her Katerina."

Vivian blinked. Blu's head shot up, and he looked at Vivian with a smile.

"You *are* her," he said, his voice triumphant. "*You are Princess Katerina.*"

Ψ ؃

Lukas heard a sharp intake of breath as Megan awakened. She extended her head from side to side and tried to stretch. Her feet made a loud *thump* as they hit the side of the dumbwaiter.

"This is real, huh?" she asked. Although Lukas was the only one present, it didn't sound like she asked him. "I didn't just dream I was stuck in a box with a vampire."

"Or about being one. No," Lukas replied.

"Damn."

They sat in uncomfortable silence. Lukas's guilt about changing her resurfaced. He wished he had some consolation, but he had none. He had taken a young woman he barely knew and forced her into a life she knew nothing about. On top of that, he was still sought after by the most powerful vampire—the most powerful being—on earth, and it was liable she'd be captured, tortured, and killed just for being with him. She would not live long enough to appreciate any of the positive aspects of being a vampire. The *Shévet ha Dam* would tear her to pieces.

"Is it dark outside yet?" she asked. Lukas nodded, then realized that even with their heightened senses she could not see him in the lightless dumbwaiter.

"Yes," he replied. "Vampires have very keen senses. If anyone were walking within fifty feet, we'd hear them."

"In other words, the candy store is empty, so it's probably after close, which means dark."

He nodded again, caught himself, and replied, "Yes."

She nodded, too. He heard her hair moving, and he smiled.

"So... why aren't we leaving?"

Should he tell her? *Could* he? He envisioned the conversation: *Hey, no prob. We'll leave, and Jude Shepherd will descend on us and shred us like a bloody block of cheddar cheese. You don't know who Jude Shepherd is, so let me tell you. He's the head of this gigantic organization of the undead called the* Shévet ha Dam, *and I kinda pissed him off.*

Megan awaited his response, indicating that she hadn't heard his thoughts. Small consolation.

They couldn't stay trapped in a dumbwaiter forever. If Jude was pursuing them, he would wait until they came out into the open, where the pursuit would be more of a game, but that was no reason to prolong the inevitable. If nothing else, he had to know if Jude was out there. He had escaped once, and he could do it again. Right?

The idea of telling Megan, though, was tough. She may not live long enough to forgive him for what he had done to her.

"Megan?"

"Yeah?"

"I need to tell you something."

"Shit!" she said explosively. "I can tell by your voice that this is really bad. Oh, shit. You're *kidding!* You mean the last twenty-four hours aren't going to be the worst of my life?"

Damn, she's making this hard.

"I'm on the run. Somebody very powerful is angry with me."

"What'd you do?" she interjected.

"It's not what I did. It's who I know. My father and Vivian."

She paused, trying to process what he'd just told her.

"Your father? He's still alive? I thought vampires always lived a really long time. You know, outlived their kin."

Lukas contemplated how to word his story.

"He's still alive. My father is a vampire too."

"Vampires can have children?"

"No. He was changed the day my mother was killed. I was two years old."

Megan fidgeted in place for a moment and searched for a comfortable way to sit. There wasn't one.

"Look, this sounds like a touching story and all, but can we have it on the other side of the door? My ass is numb."

Lukas felt in the dark and found the rope. The door went up with a protesting squeak, and he eased himself into the darkened stockroom. Megan followed, and they both stretched tense muscles. Megan was shocked at how her muscles, now released from the position that cramped her, quickly relaxed.

"Much better," she said. "So, you changed to be like them? Or he changed you?"

"No. I was changed 'cause the guy after me wanted information."

"He changed you to find out where your father is? Is he that important?"

"No, but the woman—vampire—who's with him is."

"Wait. This sounds involved. Start at the beginning."

He did, starting with the moment Vivian arrived at the apartment on Waters to the adventure from the night before. Megan listened almost without blinking, often interrupting for details on the finer points. She appeared almost sympathetic when he explained why he had taken her blood and how his guilt had caused him to change her.

As he wrapped the story up, Megan asked, "So, you've only been a vampire for a day yourself?"

"Pretty much, yeah."

"And you needed a drink that desperately after a couple of hours?"

"The way I understand it, young vampires drink much more often than the older ones do. A decade makes a big difference in the amount and frequency of blood one needs."

Megan mulled this over for a moment. "The way I see it is, we'd better go ahead and get out there. We're doing okay now, but we'll need blood soon, and I don't want to be caught by this Shepherd guy when we're vulnerable. Besides, you need to teach me how to do this. I don't want to kill anyone by mistake."

Lukas was proud of her courage and common sense. If she was angry with him, she seemed to see no point in arguing it while she needed his counsel. He was grateful for that. Perhaps she'd forgive him. He hoped.

☙ ❧

"My daughter—a princess?" Rose gasped. Vivian's brow furrowed as she struggled to recall what should have been a significant piece of her past. Her memory of Katerina was nothing—less than nothing. Surely, if she had been royalty, she'd remember.

"Not necessarily," Michael interjected. Vivian's brow dug deeper trenches.

"What do you mean?" Rose asked. Michael shrugged, unsurprised by the news that Vivian hadn't always been Vivian.

"Well, yes, Vivian may have been a princess. Or she may have had documents showing that she was royalty. Vampires have been forging documents for centuries. It's a requisite when you never age, along with a nomadic lifestyle. It keeps humankind from suspecting what we are.

"For centuries, Jude has been treating himself to the best life that money and power can afford. If you were his companion, it only makes sense that he'd have given you the same privileges."

"I wasn't a princess? Then was I Katerina, or was it just another name? And if I'm not Katerina, then who am I?" Vivian shrieked.

Michael shrugged, his expression pinched in pain.

"I'm not saying you weren't. I'm saying chances are better that you were a normal vampire claiming to be royalty and living like a royal."

Vivian hadn't realized that she was half-standing until her body buckled back onto the bed.

She squelched resentment at Michael for supplying puzzling answers to her myriad questions that only raised more questions. He was like the sage at the end of a long pilgrimage who, when asked the meaning of life, merely responds, "The answer is within you." The worst part was that the answer *was* within her, buried somewhere under... under what? If she knew, maybe she'd be able to end her journey and start being herself again. Unless...

A freakish possibility crossed her mind. Until now, she had always been Vivian, always knew who she was and where she came from. Now that her history stretched for untold lengths into the past, a new, horrible possibility loomed before her. The longer she sat on the bed and thought about it, the more this terrible likelihood made sense.

What if I'm like Jude?

What if she was a horrible, bloodthirsty killer capable of torture and pleasure in the suffering of others? What if, when she remembered who she was, she reverted into this monster and joined Jude for a reign of terror on humanity? *What if she was evil?*

Could she forget if she was a murderer?

She knew that Blu and Michael most likely heard her thoughts, as they practically screamed inside her head, bouncing around her mind like some demonic toy. She stole a glance towards them, and the look of sympathy on their faces was more than she could stand.

"I'm sorry Rose," she whispered, and she fled the room before anyone spoke another word.

Chapter 42

Megan wanted to leave her key to the store behind for the store owner. She said if she left the deadbolt unlocked and slid the gate closed, the store would look locked. Lukas dissuaded her.

"If we make it through tonight, we may need to use the dumbwaiter again when dawn comes. There's no telling where we'll wind up at the end of the night. If you keep your key, they'll just think you flaked out and quit without leaving a notice. It'll probably take them a couple of days to get around to changing the locks, if they change them at all. Meantime, we have a place to hide."

Megan saw the logic and locked the store securely. She still looked a little guilty when she pocketed her keys. Lukas smiled at her, taking his eyes from the street only momentarily.

"You can mail it to them in a couple of days, once everything settles down," he said.

Together they walked the street as quietly as moccasin-shod Indians on the hunt. So far, the bar-lined walk looked like a typical Thursday night after sunset. Die-hard Savannah bar-hoppers staggered over the cobblestone street alongside dating couples and businesspeople on an extended happy hour. They saw nothing crouching behind the shrubs, heard no one whispering their names. Nothing lurked in the shadows around the corners of the timeworn buildings.

Then Lukas remembered a comment his father often made when they watched movies. At the critical point in a search, when a hero is looking for the villain in a darkened room, they always forget one thing:

They never look up.

Lukas hesitantly tipped his head to the sky. Inky, swollen clouds hid a thumbnail moon and stars. The absence of celestial light could not disguise the flight of what would have appeared to anyone else as large, nocturnal birds. Lukas knew better. Those wings weren't feathered, but black and slick, with talons capable of ripping apart a body in seconds.

At his best estimation, there were at least two hundred of them.

The *Shévet ha Dam* had found him.

"Megan?" he mumbled. He was afraid one of the circling predators would hear him and somehow recognize his voice. If any of the vampires hovering above were a couple of hundred years, they'd most likely be able to listen. The fact that they flew implied they were at least that old.

"Yes?" Her voice sounded like a shout.

"Shhh. Not so loud. And don't look up."

She looked up. Lukas nearly slapped himself in the forehead.

"Are those—?"

"Yes," he interjected.

"Holy shit," she whispered. "Why haven't they attacked?"

"They can't. Not while we're in public. It's one of the strictest rules of the Blood Tribe. No exposing our existence to humans. They can't swoop down and take us somewhere else if there's a chance someone might see us."

"We need to stay in sight of people."

"Yes."

"Doesn't sound so hard," she replied.

Lukas let out a long sigh—hard to do with his heart in his throat.

"It's harder than you think. All it takes is one second. And we haven't fed yet."

Megan tilted her head to give him a curious look. She didn't get it.

"We have to drink tonight," he said. "We can't grab anyone with all of these people watching. And we can't duck into an alley, or the vamps will kill us."

Megan's eyes darted from corner to corner as if peering at their predators from under her eyebrows would reveal an answer, or at least a weakness. To Lukas's amazement, she didn't appear deterred, but challenged. He knew he was right when a childlike grin crossed her cherubic face.

"I've got it," she announced.

<

Vivian still felt the need to be outside in the fresh air, in the crisp darkness. Part of her felt guilty for leaving Ruth without a good-bye, but in light of recent events, the strength of any lingering bond between them had shattered.

Once outside, she paused. Fat November snowflakes fell, an army of tiny angels descending double-time from some heavenly brigade.

She had no coat, having left hers in the car, but she wasn't cold. She crossed her arms more out of habit than need.

Alone in the dark, facing the highway, she absorbed her surroundings like a sponge. It was an inclination now, developed in Germany during weeks of hunting animals in the forests. Anytime she stepped outdoors, her senses perked up, and she sought a life to hunt.

There was little activity. The snowfall had discouraged the few travelers that might have ventured into the night from leaving their homes. The night was dark and peaceful, and...

Wait. *What was that?* Her ears perked like a bat's, and her radar scanned her surroundings. She drew in a sharp breath, separated the odors as a scientist divides kingdom from phylum. There. The sound of a running animal. And the smell of...

of a graveyard.

Vivian spun in place and faced the nursing home. Three vampires bounded like clumsy mountain lions through the snow: one on the roof and one on each side of the nursing home. Two females and a male. The male crossed the roof heedless of the ice and snow that threatened to dump him down the steep slope onto the lawn with every step.

Vivian didn't move. Her muscles tightened, but she felt no fear. Her mind had crossed into some forgotten territory she didn't know existed.

She remembered how to fight. She saw the motions to use when they attacked. Her mind scanned the thoughts of the three hunters. She knew that they'd take her alive if possible, and they were scared of her. *They* were scared of *her!* Her confidence soared as a mind-dump of adrenaline sang through her blood-starved veins. She could do this. She was a vampire, an ancient being. Dead blood didn't sound bad right then. She was famished.

The clumsy pursuers came within eight feet of her and stumbled to an awkward stop, unsure how to proceed. Vivian laughingly thought that they might as well have strolled to her side for all the time they spent deliberating. One shivered, although they, like she, felt no cold.

They were scared of *her!*

She saw their plan as she read their minds, from the taunting words they'd planned to throw at "Vivian," to the seduction-like hypnosis one had dreamed would work well on her because it had worked for Jude.

Then she saw a name. A name the *Shévet ha Dam* had told them. The name Jude had delighted in, as it was the Hebrew word for "possession."

Jerusha.

Her knees weakened. A floodgate in her mind cracked under the weight of centuries of suppressed memories. Her sympathetic nervous system kicked into full gear, working with all its strength to force the flood of memories back. *Not now. Not now! Fight now. Remember later.*

One thought slipped through the crack: what if her memories and her need to survive cooperated? The memories of battling the vampires had to have come from *somewhere.* What else did she know?

The lead female struck. She crossed the eight feet as if they were inches, landed in a crouch, swept Vivian's feet out from under her with her leg, and deftly leaped eight feet to the opposite side. Vivian fell onto her back with a heavy thud onto the snow-covered asphalt.

Vivian paused, her thoughts clicking in rapid succession now. She was unconcerned about her safety as memories trickled through a mental crack. Snow fell on her face, but she didn't feel the icy flakes. *They fear me because I am Jerusha. I am...*

The other two took her hesitancy for weakness and descended on her like ravenous hyenas. Before they reached her neck, she stretched out without thinking and grasped them both, breaking the skin on the sides of their necks and threatening to rip out their throats if they budged.

Her captives, the dark-haired male and the other female, peeked at each other as best they could without turning their heads. Vivian—Jerusha—smelled their fear, and her thoughts tumbled faster with the scent. Her eyeteeth, which had remained retracted with her Vivian disguise, grew as her body contorted to her proper form: the dark-haired vampire Blu had known as Katerina, the body the Creator had given her. Jude's favorite version of her, which he returned to repeatedly as he shaped her appearance. The body she had occupied nearly two thousand years ago in Israel, which Joseph Cartaphilus had transformed into the second vampire humanity had ever known.

He had been the first.

The two vampires she held effortlessly made strange gurgling sounds. A dark trickle of blood ran down her arms. The blond vampire who'd struck her first paced back and forth, afraid to interfere for fear of harming her companions.

Vivian let the flood of memories wash over her. Her thoughts were discharging now more quickly than a machine gun.

Jude had approached her as Joseph Cartaphilus, a man who worked for Pilate until an unfortunate incident during the crucifixion of a young teacher from Nazareth. Parts of Joseph's behavior had disturbed her. As stories of Jesus grew, he would spit on the ground and say that Jesus was a blasphemer who taught the eating of human flesh, and anyone who followed him must be a cannibal. He cursed him at every opportunity, and when Jerusha asked why, he said, "He has placed a curse on humanity, myself most of all."

He seduced her quickly. As a vampire, she understood that his desperation grew with his new thirst for blood, but at the time, she didn't know what motivated him to pursue her so desperately.

She was a grown woman then, married once but barren. Her husband had died of fever less than three years after their marriage, and she had been considered unlucky by the townspeople. She thought no one would want her, but Jude—Joseph had. He treated her as if she were a precious jewel, as if her childlessness didn't matter. He behaved as though he loved her, and she thought he did.

They were never married. His thirst overpowered him, and he took her blood and her mortal life. He forced her to drink from him, the ultimate act of violence and betrayal, and she became a vampire.

But her nature didn't change. Her loving heart didn't allow her to become a killer as Cartaphilus had become. And he hated her for it.

One of her captives wiggled. They grasped at their throats in disbelief. Vivian gave her a smirk and tossed them away.

"Go," she bellowed. "Go and tell the *Shévet ha Dam* that I—we— are coming for them. Be sure that Joseph knows I remember."

She saw Blu and Michael exiting Bender's glass double doors cautiously, prepared to back her if needed. The commanding look she gave them stopped them in their tracks. The unfamiliar vamps leered at her.

"Why should we?" the female growled. Her eyes darted behind her long enough to notice Michael and Blu before fixing on Vivian again. It was easy to see she was weighing her odds of getting away.

Vivian rolled her eyes in an exaggerated pantomime, and she let out a throaty chuckle. The young one's eyes grew large.

"You're right," Vivian said. "You're dead, anyway. What would be the difference if you die here or after you report your failure to your superiors? Except that here, we might kill you less painfully." She shook a head heavy with pity. "It took three of you to muster the confidence to battle me, and you barely touched me. You may as well lie down and let us drink your blood. You're nothing but Renfields."

Her words wove themselves into the minds of the young vampires and convinced them. Their eyes brimmed with shameful tears.

"You're right," the male said. They positioned themselves before her like dogs exposing their bellies. "We're not worthy of living."

Vivian didn't revel in the idea of killing them, but it was true that they were dead if they returned to the Table without her and Michael in tow. At least this way, they would not go hungry. It was cold blood, but it was blood all the same.

She smelled human death on the two Renfields. *Vampire Renfields. How pathetic.* Full-blooded, but still subservient to authority, hoping someday that authority would be theirs. They weren't only power-hungry but stupid.

"Michael," she said. It was more a statement than a question. He and Blu stepped forward, and they relieved the Renfields of life.

"What do we do with them?" Blu asked once the "undead" were dead. They were full, but Michael had a small problem with vampire blood. His face twisted with disgust.

"We'll put them behind the building, in the copse of trees," Vivian answered. "They're young, and they'll ash in the sun."

The two men nodded and lifted the bodies with ease. Vivian stood in silence as they walked away. Tears crystallized on her cheeks like diamonds.

After they returned, Blu smiled at her with uncertainty. He shifted his weight from right leg to left and brushed the bloody front of his shirt and slacks.

"Vivian?" he asked. His tone was so unlike him, so subservient she nearly laughed. Blu was, if anything, more royal than she'd ever been. She would know. She had met him over a century ago.

"Babu Latif Ubora," she said with a laugh, rediscovering the name with every syllable. "No wonder you go by Blu. And don't you dare address me like that. You've got more money than a Pharaoh."

An enormous grin split Blu's face in half. He appeared on the verge of leaping for joy, accosting Vivian with a ferocious hug, or both.

"You remember!" he laughed.

Vivian nodded.

"I remember everything," she exulted.

"And?" Michael prodded, noting that she appeared ready to burst with the knowledge. Even Blu was eager to hear the whole story.

Vivian sighed, and tears poured down her face in relief. She knew. She really knew.

"My name is Jerusha," she began. It felt like "Once upon a time."

Chapter 43

After a quick tally of their cash, Megan led Lukas into a riverside shop. She walked around racks of clothes and other displays with the ease of someone familiar with the layout. The dark-haired woman behind the counter addressed her by name. Megan smiled—lips closed, thank goodness—and asked her if they still carried capes. The dark woman directed them to a remote corner of the store.

"What're you doing?" Lukas asked as Megan removed two black velvet capes from their brass hooks.

Megan didn't seem to hear him at first, holding up the voluminous cape and noting how it still dangled well above Lukas's knees.

"It's an extra-large, so it's the biggest one they have. Damn, you're tall."

"Six foot ten," he informed her. "But I don't see how that has any–"

"If there's one thing I know about Savannahians, they all want to be famous."

"But what...?"

"We're holding auditions, my friend, for the latest vampire flick, to be filmed right here in Savannah, Georgia."

Lukas's mouth flapped. It was a bold move, but it just might work.

Megan chatted with the woman behind the counter for several minutes. Before Lukas knew what he was doing, he was volunteered to carry two borrowed capes and a folding sign to the following shop. There, Megan bought poster board and black pens, talked with the owner of *that* shop, and persuaded a student of the local art school to fashion a sign: "American Vampire auditions, 9:00-11:30 p.m., River Street pavilion." The only catch, the student stipulated, was that she be the first in line to audition.

If you only knew, Lukas thought with wonder. It appeared that Megan was right about Savannah's Hollywood fever.

After that, Megan borrowed a microphone and amplifier from another shop owner who did karaoke Wednesday nights at her bar. She also nabbed a clipboard and blank sheets of paper.

She's an excellent person to know in a pinch, Lukas thought as they headed, burdened with borrowed treasures, to the brick pavilion across from the daiquiri bar. *She knows everyone in town. And I thought my father was social!* He was mystified about the purpose of a couple of the objects, but she was so self-assured she inspired confidence in him.

Megan deftly assembled the equipment. She unfolded the sign and attached the poster board with a roll of electrical tape—also borrowed. She connected the amplifier to an extension cord she trailed across the cobblestones to the bar. She waved at a few passersby she knew. Some of them stuck around for the audition. When they were fully assembled, a small crowd gathered, exclaiming excitedly. Megan gave her friends a broad smile, and they chattered animatedly over the authentic appearance of her "costume" teeth.

Lukas knew now that he must still have a beating heart—if not, what was sticking in his throat? He glanced periodically at the skies that roiled with demons just out of sight of human eyes. *Megan, I sure hope this works.*

She handed him the larger of the velvet capes, and they costumed.

"Well, folks," Megan said after testing the microphone, "I know you can read, but this is our official kickoff. I've been asked to hold open auditions here for an independent film called "American Vampire." It's only for small parts. We don't have scripts here, just doing improv. But if you want, here's your chance.

"What's gonna happen here is that my assistant, Luke, and I are playing the part of vampires. Y'all are the humans. You'll notice that we have the teeth, and you don't."

Lukas grinned, and Megan matched his grin, exposing their eyeteeth. This received a nervous titter from the audience and one shout of "No fair!" but appreciative smiles, too.

"We're going to wing a couple of scenes, and judging by the response we get from the crowd, we may or may not take your name and number for callbacks."

So that was what the clipboard and pen were for, Lukas thought, admiring her foresight.

"Who's making the film?" one of the spectators asked.

"A new company, Runaway Productions," Megan replied without missing a beat.

"Who's first?" Megan wanted to know. The art student jumped into his assigned spot. A line quickly assembled at the steps, and the first actor stepped forward.

Cß   ℂ

Cartaphilus clenched his jaw. Hours had passed, but still no word from any of his children. Jerusha was still alive.

The *Shévet ha Dam* had failed. His minions had failed. Where in the hell was she?

The one thing he had counted on was his Renfields, his demon dogs. He wasn't lying when he'd told them her blood was better than gold. He had put them at serious risk by siccing them on her. If her memory was restored, she would cast them aside like toy soldiers. But wasn't that what they were? He smiled despite his grim contemplation.

They'd probably die in their eagerness to capture her. Collateral damage. It would be such a delicious vision to see through their eyes as the blood flowed from their body at her hand. She would probably cry as she took their lives in self-defense.

As he focused, he sensed the loss of three somewhere northeast... three wretched lives dying in a parking lot... blood... the aged stench of elderly humans. They had one thought on their weakened minds as they passed: Jerusha. The scent of her had reached them, and they'd attacked. Now they were gone. Jude frowned. If Vivian had killed three vampires, she must have her memory back. *Damn.*

But they'd found her. She was in Michigan. Near Lake Michigan.

Near where she met me as Jude. Un-fucking-believable. She's been awake for only a couple of months, and she's homesick for a place that's not her home!

She must have found the old crone that used to be her "mother," confronted her, maybe asked her about the past. Ask her if anything looked, acted, or smelled funny way back in '43. At her age, Rose probably looked, smelled, *and* acted funny. And if Rose remembered anything—and how could she forget?—she would tell Vivian now and divest her soul in time to free herself of her worldly burden and maybe earn a "Get into Heaven Free" card.

Nosy old biddy. He should've killed her fifty years ago.

Judging by the number of vampires making an inexplicable commute to Savannah, Jude had a new opponent in the Tribe. If he wanted to stand a chance defending himself, it was time to withdraw the troops from their search to use them in the upcoming battle.

He'd worry about Vivian later.

೫ ೮

"That means you're..."

"The world's second-oldest vamp. Holy shit, girl. I knew you were one of the old ones, but..."

Jerusha smiled at their reactions. She was a little hesitant to share her newfound knowledge at first, afraid of the feedback from such a mammoth revelation.

"So now what?" Michael asked. She smiled at his trepidation, the sudden reversal of roles that had taken effect. Now she was the one with the knowledge.

"Now we have two choices," she replied. "We can go to Savannah and try to save Lukas and the others, or we can try to track down the *Shévet ha Dam* without them, but—"

"Lukas is..." Michael let out a shuddery breath that revealed his relief at the knowledge that his son lived. "I don't want Lukas involved," he said. "He needs to stay clear of this. I don't want him—"

"He's been changed, Michael," she said.

This comment was met with silence. Blu bit his lip and studied Michael from the corner of his eye. His hand went out to soothe him but stopped short. Jerusha stared straight-faced, expressionless.

"How do you...?" He paused, knowing the answer but having to ask nonetheless. "Are you sure?"

Jerusha nodded.

"How?"

She shrugged almost dismissively, as if he'd asked her how she knew the sky was blue.

"It's a feeling I get when I think of him. I can contact him on a level that I can't with humans. You're both telepathic, right?"

They nodded.

"You know how vamps and humans are different? How it *feels* different, and yet the same, like how putting your hand in icy water almost feels hot? I can *feel* that about Lukas. He used to be icy, but now he's hot."

Michael took a deep breath. His eyes refused to meet his friends. He tongued his eyeteeth irately, and his jaw took on a determined set.

"Michael, I know you're pissed. But we've got to move," Jerusha said, her voice soft and coaxing. "Those sycophants were easy enough to dispose of, but we might not be so lucky next time. It won't be long before the next member of the *Shévet ha Dam* shows up. Someone might die."

Someone, Michael thought, *but not you.* Vivian heard the words as if he had spoken them aloud.

"At least Lukas isn't dead," Blu said, his voice thick with sadness. Michael set his jaw and said nothing.

"We need to move," Jerusha reminded them.

"Move? Where?" Blu asked pointedly.

She sighed, stamping down feelings of urgency. "It doesn't matter. Can you fly?"

"No," Blu responded with shame.

"Well, plenty of them *can*. Come on."

ϣ Ϣ

They flew from across the globe, mental ramparts in place, descending on the ground appointed for battle. Some used wings. Others, those more ancient and in tune with the unseen ways, moved without visible support, levitated by the powers which fueled them.

They spoke not a word to each other. The lines had been drawn, but it was not time for battle. The impetus had yet to arrive.

They flocked to abandoned homes and darkened factories, dug graves, hung from rafters, and waited.

The Blood War was only hours away.

ϣ Ϣ

Lukas set his fifth victim down on the red brick floor of the pavilion. He gave Megan a look that said thumbs-up. She reciprocated.

"Now just lay there a minute, act tired," Megan coached. "Pretend that we've just drained you of blood, but not enough to kill you. Think of how it feels to be anemic, to be just so exhausted you can hardly move." Both humans did as she directed.

"We've got some excellent method acting going on here tonight,"

Megan observed with a satisfied nod.

From the onset of tonight's proceedings, Lukas felt that he was an observer in some twisted play instead of an actor in it. He ad-libbed his lines almost cockily, imagining himself as Jude Shepherd, the blackest of dark souls. He smiled as Jude smiled, walked as Jude walked. He took the aspiring actress in the folds of his velvet cape. As he did, he recalled the inky, slippery feel of Jude's wings against his hands. He shuddered and struck her neck, and the audience shuddered with him.

Then his teeth pierced the skin of his victim.

Not too deep, he told himself. *No scars, no death. Just blood.*

He concealed a gasp as the warm, thick fluid moistened his lips. He lifted the tiny woman's body in one arm and draped the cape over the two of them with the other. He found heaven in her neck, a bliss more powerful than any reached during sex, and he wished to enjoy it with a modicum of privacy.

Just a few draughts. Remember to stop.

It was like going through withdrawal, but he forced himself to stop with the knowledge that the next victim was waiting in line only moments away.

Now, as the drained woman lay exhausted on the bricks at his feet, a victim of his somnolent kiss, he felt a slight twinge of guilt. And a tinge of something else, too. A voice from a great distance made his ears vibrate like the ting of a tuning fork. The words were almost audible, but they reverberated until it sounded like a buzz. He knew the voice. Oh boy, did he know that voice. He'd heard it in his nightmares. It had taunted him from within a leathery embrace. It was Jude.

Why can I hear it? He wondered. *Shouldn't that be a power only the dark vamps have? I'm no member of the* Shévet ha Dam.

As the buzzing continued, shadowy images flashed through his mind, like images of an out-of-focus camera. War. Close. Soon. He swayed where he stood, and he stabilized himself.

Megan was beside him, and the humans were stirring. "You okay?" she asked. She put a concerned hand on his arm.

Lukas swallowed hard, blinked, and stared at this young woman he had thought an angel, still thought was an angel.

"Yeah," he said. "You hear that?"

"You mean that buzzing? I thought it was the amplifier," she replied. Lukas shook his head. She didn't hear it as clearly, which made sense. He was second-generation from Jude, and Gina was the first. Megan was the third. With each successive generation of vampires, the voices grew fainter. The only reason he heard it now was because he'd drunk from Gina, who had imbibed from Jude. More than likely, Jude had consumed some of Lukas's blood, which would only increase their bond.

My God, I'm probably more powerful than my father!

He thought more clearly with the fresh human blood flowing through his veins. How long had it been since Gina changed him? He had long since lost track of time, having been in a fog while she toyed with him. Who knew how long he was unaware? A week, maybe? He recalled the dreams, how she cried, how she used him physically in every way a vampire could, how she died.

Above, in the inky black clouds, the flapping grew incensed. Human ears could not hear it, but Lukas and Megan exchanged worried looks. An earsplitting screech came from the cloud of black wings, attracting the eyes of humans and vampires alike.

"What the hell was that?" a voice asked.

"Splat," Lukas said. It was an expression his father had used, and he'd picked it up over the years.

"Splat?" Megan asked.

"The shit just hit the fan," he explained.

They stood side by side and watched as the cloud took flight, heading north and west. The humans on River Street strained to see what they watched, but only he and Megan beheld where the inhuman bat-like cries came from.

"Where are they going?" Megan asked.

"We're about to be at war," he answered.

Chapter 44

Blu pulled onto Broken Arrow Highway, headed back toward the interstate, and asked, "Where now?"

Jerusha shrugged, her posture weary. "Someplace with lots of people and an airport."

Blu shook his head as he contemplated the criteria she gave him.

"The nearest decent size city is South Bend, and in this weather, it's an hour and a half away. A lot could happen between now and then."

Michael turned to face her. "Do you think we have time? Can you feel them the way you can Lukas?"

"No. The only reason I can feel Jude at all is that he's my sire, and I fed on his blood alone for two thousand years. Normally I shouldn't be able to feel vampires who are that ingrained with Jude's dark power."

Blu turned the music down to its lowest setting, and Michael faced front.

"There's a truck stop nearby," she said as she sat up, her vigor instantly restored from an unseen reserve. "Blu, we need to go there. They're open twenty-four hours, there are plenty of humans milling about, and they sell phones. Michael, can you please try to get a hold of Lukas again? You may have more luck now."

"How can you know all of this?" Michael asked. It was like Vivian had become a psychic, a frighteningly skillful one. Being a born skeptic, Michael needed reassurance.

"There's one of us there. A decent one, like one of our family. He works in a cellular phone center, and he's preparing a phone for you." She laughed a brief, caustic laugh. "He says it's got a good rate plan, too."

The other two chuckled, dry, short laughs that spoke of stress and uncertainty.

"How do we get there?" Blu asked.

Jerusha leaned forward and placed a hand on his shoulder, tapping into his thoughts with a touch. He saw the route to the truck stop whiz by him. Then Jerusha formed a bridge between Blu and the young man risking his life for their cause. For a brief moment, he saw the inside of the truck stop: painfully bright fluorescent lighting, chest-high shelves stocked with overpriced gizmos, sugary foods, and atlases. He heard the beeps of the video games in the corner and the conversation of truckers satisfying their late-night cravings in the diner. He saw the bright red and grey phone in the palm of the young vamp's hand. He blinked and shuddered, and it receded swiftly in reverse. Then he saw only the road. She lifted her hand and broke the link.

Blu said. "If you could never do that again, I'd appreciate it. Next time, use words. You're lucky I didn't run us off the road."

She smiled. "Sorry. It was just easier that way," she apologized.

Blu swallowed the lump of fear in his throat and tried to shake the images lingering like sunspots on the back of his eyes.

"You okay, bro?" Michael asked, leaning forward.

Blu nodded. "Vivian?" he asked.

"Yes?"

"If you can do all that, then why don't you talk to Lukas for us?"

"I could, yeah. He'd probably rather hear from you, though."

"I'm still not clear why we need to involve him in this," Michael said.

The corners of Vivian's lips turned up at the paternal concern in his voice, but it twisted her guts like snakes in a bathtub. She hated having to explain. "Michael, Lukas is a connection to Jude."

The implication sank in slowly, and as it did, Michael's expression changed from perplexed to alarmed.

"How? What happened?" he demanded. Vivian put up a hand, and his interrogation ceased.

"Don't worry, he's fine," she said. "At least, as fine as you or I or any other vampire who isn't *Shévet ha Dam*. I can't pick up the whole story, but I received the distinct impression Gina and Jude were involved. He's second-generation descended from Jude. He's a link."

"So are you," Blu observed. Vivian shook her head.

"You don't understand. I shouldn't get into Cartaphilus's mind right now, and neither should Lukas. It would pinpoint us too easily. But without trying, Lukas can feel him in ways I can't."

"Why can't you?" Michael asked.

Vivian blushed, not wanting to say. It sounded too much like bragging, too incredible. Only when their glares refused to let her go without an answer did she speak.

"Because I'm connected to the Source."

They exchanged a confused look. Blu shrugged at Michael's raised eyebrows, and Michael frowned, his brow furrowed with thought.

"The Source of what?" asked Blu.

Vivian tried to think of a way to explain without sounding pompous. Nothing came to mind, so she just spit out the first thing that came to mind. "Jesus wasn't the only person pure of heart walking around Israel around two thousand years ago," she sighed. "He just... he knew something I didn't. Or... someone." *That was real genteel, Jerusha. Why don't you just cut down a tree, fashion a cross, and nail yourself to it?*

"But you're not—"

"No, I'm not a virgin. I wasn't born from a virgin, so far as I know, I don't perform miracles. I'm not perfect. It appears that something, some power, somewhere thinks I'm close enough to use me.

"When Jesus cursed Joseph to walk the earth until its end, he tipped the scales in evil's favor. They—Jesus and Cartaphilus—aren't the only beings able to change the balance of good and evil, but as time has proven, they're two of the heavyweights. God also knew there would be someone there to help correct the balance when the time came. That person was me."

"So, you're sort of like Vishnu right now," Michael observed. Vivian nodded.

"What the fuck is a Vishnu?" Blu asked.

"One of the beliefs of Hinduism," Michael explained. "Vishnu takes on an avatar, or physical form, when humankind is in crisis to save the earth from destruction."

They all sat silently for a moment.

"Wait a minute, are you telling me the earth is about to be destroyed?" Blu asked.

"I hadn't thought about it in those terms before, but it might be," Vivian answered. "Jesus cursed Joseph to walk the face of the earth until his return, which is understood to mean Armageddon, the end of the world. The final battle of good and evil. The end of the world as we know it."

Another moment of solemn contemplation.

"Isn't there any other way?" Blu asked.

"If there is, and you see it, I'd appreciate your input," Vivian said. Blu and Michael merely stared—Blu at the highway ahead of him, Michael at a point in space.

"Well, fuck," Michael said.

"*That's* why we need Lukas," Vivian said. "He can probably give us a good idea what Jude is up to now, like a radio antenna tuned in to Jude's thoughts."

"So, you hold the fate of the world in your hands?" Michael asked.

"Not directly, I don't think," she replied. "That is, I think I'm involved somehow, but I also believe this was due to happen with or without me. The Table has been unhappy with Joseph, and it was only a matter of time before they tried to kill him." She regarded her long fingernails thoughtfully. "I guess I started it."

"But don't they know what'll happen?"

She frowned.

"Just because Yeshua put a curse into action two thousand years ago doesn't mean vamps still think it holds weight. Maybe they feel they've found a way around it. Or maybe it's been so long they don't believe anymore."

Her voice cracked a little bit, and she stopped speaking. Michael turned back in his seat and studied her beautiful features, but she would not face him. She watched the world fly by from the backseat window and said nothing.

"I believe," he whispered.

Chapter 45

B lu steered into the truck stop parking lot and pulled into the slot closest to the door.

The truck stop was a painted white brick building the size of a mini-mall, a brightly lit oasis in an otherwise gloomy night. It had stopped snowing, but the moon and stars hadn't emerged from behind the thick clouds. Vivian paused as she stood, sensing how near the closest of her stalkers were.

"We don't have much time," she told them. They nodded solemnly.

They followed her brisk walk inside. She paused again after the double doors, looked around rapidly, and headed right.

"She's like a psychic detective," Blu joked. "She just *knows* shit."

Michael nodded with a grimace-like grin. They hustled after Vivian through aisles of gizmos, maps, and the wide assortment of junk food only available in gas stations. She headed directly to a wisp of a young man behind the counter of a cellular phone stand. *He can't be a vamp,* Michael thought. *He looks about fifteen years old!*

"Mark?" Vivian asked. The young vampire nodded shyly, and she joined him in his stall. The way he gawked at Vivian with wide brown eyes, Michael would have thought he was a Catholic having a vision of the Virgin Mother.

"Do you have something for me?" Vivian encouraged. Mark nodded shyly.

"Yes, ma'am," he said. He reached under the counter and pulled out the same phone Blu had seen through Vivian's eyes.

Vivian took the phone, and Mark explained its capabilities. She nodded as if she understood, and Michael was sure she did. She probably saw everything through Mark and assimilated it all effortlessly.

"Thank you, Mark," Vivian said. Mark beamed like a child told his report card would be posted on the family fridge. She turned to go.

"I—I have this, too," he said. Vivian stopped and turned around. He pulled another object from under the counter. Michael gaped. Plane tickets. Three of them.

Vivian took them, her eyes grew, and her body shuddered as she shared contact with Mark and the tickets.

"How did you get these?" she demanded. Mark blushed, his cheeks flushed with the blood of a fresh kill.

"I—Well, they were going to Savannah. Three of them. It seemed too auspicious to be a coincidence, so I... I took them."

Auspicious. Good word. Michael couldn't help but think of the phrase he used so much with Lukas whenever his son used unique new expressions growing up.

"You didn't steal the tickets, did you, Mark?"

If possible, he blushed darker. His head dropped as if weighted. "No. Not exactly."

"Did you kill them for these tickets?" she prodded. Her voice was that of a disappointed mother, stern but loving. Mark responded in kind.

"Yes." His eyes intently studied the toes of his scuffed running shoes.

"Don't ever do that, Mark. Not even for a good reason like ours."

He raised his head and looked Vivian in the eye. A tear dropped from his doe-like eyes. "I'm sorry," he said. "I'm so sorry."

Vivian enveloped him in her arms. He sobbed, sniffling quietly. Patrons of the truck stop paid them no mind as Blu stared at them intently, one by one. It was the best trick in his repertoire: a psychic nudge that said, "Nothing to see here." To the people in the truck stop, the spectacle taking place behind the counter was no more interesting than a boring sitcom, and they paid it no more mind than that.

Vivian let Mark go and kissed him on the cheek. She picked the tickets up from the counter.

"I understand where your heart was. Thank you." It was sweet and heartfelt, and it touched Mark to the core of his soul. He was beaming again.

"You're welcome," he said. He buried himself back in her arms and then finally let go.

Vivian moved in Blu and Michael's direction. "Let's go."

They left the truck stop as quickly as they came and settled in the car, Vivian in the front seat now, Michael in the back. Michael tapped Vivian on the shoulder.

"Yes?" she asked.

"Remember when we were back in Weilerbach, and you expressed such disappointment at being such a wimp?"

She laughed a short, surprised laugh. "Yeah?"

"Well, I don't want to hear that shit anymore."

☃ ☃

Lukas and Megan watched the dark shapes retreat until they disappeared into the black storm clouds. When they faced the audience, Megan provided them with an off-the-cuff explanation of actors needing a moment of meditation to maintain the wonderful flavor of the method acting they'd seen tonight. It sounded like a crock to Lukas, but they accepted it readily enough.

A handful of auditions more, and Lukas had to fake his attacks on the necks of his wanna-be actresses. He couldn't drink anymore.

Eleven-thirty came at last, and they thanked everyone for their cooperation and said they'd let them know. They received a smattering of applause. They disassembled the equipment, returning it all with a Thanks and an I'll see you later.

"I don't believe I will see them again, will I?" Megan asked. Lukas shrugged.

"Maybe. Maybe not."

Megan clenched her hands into angry balls and frowned.

"How can you live like this? Not knowing from day to day where you'll sleep, how you'll eat?"

"It's not usually like this," he said. "Well, let me be honest. It's *never* been like this. Sure, we moved around a lot, but it was closer to every three or five years. Not every day. We avoided the *Shévet ha Dam* out of dislike—not because they were trying to kill us."

Disbelief painted Megan's face.

"No. Really," he insisted. "I had a home. Several, in fact. Nice ones. Well, most of them. We had places we used just to party. But now..."

"Now this guy Jude is after you." Skepticism and confusion replaced disbelief.

"Right," he sighed.

"And they want Vivian because she belongs to Jude?"

"No more than you belong to me," Lukas said. He blushed at his slip up, but Megan didn't blink. If she noticed, she didn't draw attention to it.

"Why is she so important to him?"

They reached a bubbling fountain and took a seat on the brick edge. Lukas sighed and shrugged.

"Trophy? Control? All I know now is that she 'belongs' to the leader of the most dangerous group you can imagine, and she's on the road with Michael. And some of them think I know where they are."

"Do you?"

"I used to. Doubt they're there now. It doesn't matter; Jude knows where she is."

Megan sat in silence and pondered. Lukas crossed one tree-trunk-sized leg over the other and refused to think. He was tired of thinking.

"When will we have an idea of what's going on?"

A wave of depression washed over him. He didn't have any answers, and he was tired of saying, "I don't know" over and over again. He wished Michael was there. Michael always knew what to do. He heaved in a deep breath, and before he let it out and proclaimed his ignorance again, he heard a familiar noise.

He held up one large hand while searching for the source of the sound with the other. He found it and removed it from his pocket.

His cell phone was ringing.

"Lukas?" Michael yelled. His hand was over his right ear, and he was yelling into the phone on his left. Blu refused to turn the stereo down below the decibel level of a fighting match. As Michael heard his son's voice, he laughed with relief and joy.

"Yeah, yeah, we're fine for now. We're heading to South Bend, and from there to Savannah.... No, we got a flight.... Don't ask... Are you OK? ...You did? ... Oh.... No, they won't be after you, I don't think—not for a little while, anyway."

He paused, then laughed as Lukas shared the stories of his adventures with Gina and Megan and the cloud of vampires that flew off in their quest to find Michael and Vivian. It was several minutes before Michael broke into the conversation again.

"Look, Son, we need your help. No, I'm not worried about them tracking the phone. You saw—? Well, fuck. Blu, can you *please* turn this shit down? I can't think!"

Blu dismissed him with a limp-wristed wave. Michael did an exaggerated pantomime and put his hand back over his ear.

"I'm glad to hear your voice, too. Keep this phone charged. Find

Josh—you have his number, right? Yeah, find him and meet us at the airport. I'll be in touch."

Another pause. He chuckled.

"Yeah, me too. Hey Lukas? I love you. Bye."

ↂ ↄ

Lukas hung up the phone and stared at it momentarily as if it had flown in from outer space and landed in his hand. He'd forgotten he had put it in his pocket before he and Gina had left the Waters Avenue apartment. In case of emergency. It was almost funny. Here he'd been in the middle of the worst crisis in his life, and he hadn't thought to use the phone. He hadn't turned it on when he left to conserve the battery. He must have bumped the power button in the flurry of the last day's activities.

"Who was that?" Megan asked.

"My Dad. Michael."

"You're kidding! What are the odds of that?" Her amazed look, coupled with a smile, struck his heart like a defibrillator.

"About a million to one, I'd wager," he said. He hoped that sounded right. All at once, his language skills seemed to be on vacation. Man, she was gorgeous.

"Is he OK?"

Chill, Lukas. Breathe. Keep it cool.

"Yeah, he's fine. He told me to look for Josh."

His nervousness, which had begun to dissipate, returned full force. How had he managed to be so calm next to her for the last few hours? She was so beautiful!

Say something, shithead.

"I—I gotta make a call."

"Oh, okay."

He pressed a few buttons on his phone and put it to his ear. Josh answered. After taking a full five minutes calming him down and assuring him that he, his father, and Vivian were alright, he asked him where he was.

"I need you to come and get me," he said. He saw Megan sitting on the edge of the fountain and corrected himself. "And a friend."

There was no mistaking the look of resentment that time. *What'd I do wrong?* He lost track of what Josh was saying.

"What did you say? I'm sorry, I lost you somewhere."

He listened for a moment.

"No, I don't think they need the rental. They might, though. Don't return it, just in case."

Josh told him he had missed Michael and Vivian at the airport, and he informed Josh of what he'd heard. They spoke the broken language of vampires, telling just enough to explain but not enough that anyone eavesdropping would understand. They arranged for Josh to pick them up, and he ended the call.

Placing the phone in his pocket, he stood. "Time to go."

CZ   80

Jude reclined lazily in the Cleopatra chaise and let the images wash over him like a tropical breeze. He experienced the destruction of a house in Germany, and he enjoyed the thrill of a dozen vampires as they tore apart the former home of the woman vampire with the blood of gold. They'd hunted her like dogs, tracked her from her hunting grounds, then descended on the house, but she was gone.

They were furious at the missed chance to steal her power and her delectable blood. Their nearness to the smell of her drove them wild. More vampires tapped into the feral mindset and the link with Jerusha, which attracted them. Soon the neighborhood was teeming with vampires mourning the loss of the one with the blood they craved.

They were saddened and angry, but most of all, they were hungry. They crept into nearby homes as silent as specters and drained the occupants as they slept. It wasn't enough. The craving for the blood of Jerusha left them unsatisfied. They turned their anger on her home.

Jude felt them tear it apart like dry sticks. Their anger drove them to feats of incredible strength. He smiled at their rage, reveled in their fury. He felt the concrete break in his hands, and the tiles crush under his feet. He saw through their eyes as they shattered glass and ground it underfoot until it was fine powder mixed with their blood.

At the same time, he felt those nearest her closing in. With the snow on the roads, she'd never reach the airplane in time. And what if she did? Savannah International was surrounded by vampires waiting for them.

He sighed like a contented infant and settled deeper into the chaise. They would not make it through the night.

Chapter 46

Blu's radials were only two months old, and his car was a heavy eight-cylinder, but even so, the snow inhibited progress. He kept the speedometer near forty miles an hour, but he worried they were going too fast. Vivian would not allow him to slow down.

"Why don't you stop anybody who's chasing us?" he demanded after straightening the car out of a risky fishtail. "Why can't you deprogram them? Aren't you strong enough?"

"It's unlikely I can touch anyone who uses Jude's power—the Maleficence. And if they're weak enough that I could, Jude would go right behind me and reinstill it. Eventually, it would escalate to a mental battle to control them that'd drive them crazy. The best I can do is to defend us once they get here."

"How long until we reach the airport?" Michael wondered aloud.

Vivian focused, her eyes becoming vacant and frighteningly dead as her mind sent feelers out. The vacancy in her eyes vanished, and the woman who looked him in the eyes was more than in control. She was prepared to fight.

"At this pace, about ten minutes."

Michael was proud of her. He remembered the meek, terrified woman she had been. She'd completely changed, her attitude, her strength, her carriage. She had faced her past, and had allowed those memories to return because she was equipped to handle them. She chose to stand up to Jude—to the thing she knew as Joseph Cartaphilus—and she wanted to find a way to conquer him. Looking at the determined set of her chin, he knew that she would rid the world of Cartaphilus, even if it meant her life.

He hoped it never came to that.

℃ ℂ

Lukas and Megan sat near the river, which looked like flowing black ink. Megan took a sip of her beer and cringed.

"Yuk. I never was a beer drinker, but man. Double yuk."

Lukas agreed.

"Tell me about your family," Megan said.

So, he told her about his family and friends in Savannah, both vampire and human. The time passed quickly, and as Josh pulled up in his Tiburon, Megan saw that she had finished the tasteless beer.

"I didn't know I was drinking it," she laughed.

Lukas and Megan settled into the sports car, and Josh sped off. "What in the hell's going on?" he asked bluntly. Lukas froze, took a breath, and began the tale.

He shared his and Megan's conversion to vampirism, and Gina's decision to confront Jude, about Gina's struggle to control her body, her bravery, and how she died.

Josh listened without interruption. Megan admired his restraint.

"She and I were close," Josh explained to Megan once Lukas finished. "She came into the family two years almost to the day after I did. Michael found her in Forsyth Park, drained of blood. Whoever had struck had given her just enough blood to let her live 'til dawn. Sloppy bastard. Michael brought her home, and he and Lukas helped her survive. She was so sweet."

Megan thought he was going to break down. He paused once, and took a deep breath.

"I didn't think this would happen for a long time," he murmured bitterly. "She would've lived longer if she'd remained human."

"She'd have died in the park if it hadn't been for Michael," Lukas reminded him.

Josh nodded appreciatively. "You're right. I just can't believe she's gone."

He took a left on DeRenne and hit the accelerator, weaving through traffic like a mouse through a familiar maze, dodging early morning traffic with experienced ease. He plowed through traffic lights heedless of the color.

"What's the rush?" Megan asked from behind gritted teeth.

"Who's rushing? This is how he drives in general," Lukas said.

Megan clenched the seat and wondered how crumpled the car would become after the crash. Could vampires die in car crashes? If so, the backseat didn't strike her as the safest place to be.

Then again, no place seemed like a safe place.

ᘓ   ᙏ

Maysun's telepathic connections now floated in synchronicity, a symphony of communication. Finally, she had things, people, vampires, all where they needed to be or headed where her plan dictated them to be.

As usual, events began pulling together just as she had thought they were beyond repair. Just a few more minutes, a few more things to tie up. Her stomach churned as she thought of how the following discussion might go.

She reached out to Charles Dunning.

ᘓ   ᙏ

Charles.
Charles stared at the phone. He had pushed the end button, hadn't he?
Charles, get moving.
It was Maysun, speaking to him telepathically. But why?
A bombardment of images played in his mind, like a movie reel on fast-forward. Vivian meeting Rose Black. Her awareness of Jerusha, of Joseph. Cartaphilus' message to the dark undead.
Oh, hell. All this time I've been here when—Maysun, why?
He dropped the phone and leaped into the air, buoyant as a helium balloon. Doyle watched as Charles ascended, a mixture of confusion and relief passing over him.
"Man, I hate when he does that," he said. Doyle couldn't fly. Even the most basic shapeshifting was a few years beyond his ability. "Not even an explanation. How fucking rude."

ᘓ   ᙏ

They were only five miles from the airport. Michael wondered whether they'd know if they were speeding into a trap.
"Blu, hurry," Vivian coaxed. "I don't feel safe without people around."
"Woman, are you crazy?" he asked. "If I put this thing in the ditch, we'll be *walking* to the airport, unless you feel like tucking each of us

under an arm while you fly like one of those giant transporter vamps."

He was interrupted by a loud *thump* as a heavy object landed on the roof. It sounded like a body. Michael half expected it to slide off—the roof must have been covered in ice—but whatever it was stuck. Talons scraped the metal roof.

"Oh, hell," Vivian said. She didn't sound frightened. From the lack of concern in her voice, she might have burned dinner instead of hearing the approach of someone intent on killing her. She shucked her jacket, rolled down the window, and easily dodged the arm reaching in after her. She slugged it once when it got in her way, and it withdrew in obvious pain.

When the window was down all the way, Michael assumed she would perch herself on the sill and fight the thing from there. Instead, Vivian waggled fingers at them and floated out the window as though levitated by a magician.

"Look, Mom, no wings!" Blu wisecracked. When Michael shot him a curious look, Blu added, "Don't ask, I don't know, either." Michael closed his gaping mouth.

"Do we pull over and wait for her?" Michael asked.

"Hell, no. She can keep up."

The sounds of a scuffle ensued above. Michael had to conclude that Vivian did her damnedest to keep the battle directly above the car, for although he tried like hell to get a view of the fight from a window, he couldn't see a thing. It drove him crazy.

One of them landed on the roof with a loud *whump,* followed by a metallic scrape. Michael's feelings changed from curiosity to panic.

"I'm sure she's fine," Blu said. Michael wanted to know how in the hell Blu was so sure when his instincts were clouded with concern.

Vivian landed on the roof after the longest five minutes in Michael's memory. She leaned over the side, winded and bloodied, and poked her head into the window.

"Mind pulling over?" she asked. She was smiling. She was bloody, gouged, and disheveled, but she was smiling.

"Not at all," Blu said. He slowly steered into the drift on the side of the road. Vivian used the door to get in. Her shirt was in shreds, and the back was almost gone.

Blu guided the Ford back onto the road and resumed a cautious speed.

"So, is that it?" Michael asked. "We're sitting here, worried to death about getting attacked, and you float out the window and kill them? Is that what we were so scared of?"

Vivian shook her head and put her jacket back on. "There were only two of them, easy enough for me to take. Probably scouts. You probably could have killed them too, if you could fly."

Michael tried not to feel put off by how casually she stated his lack of experience.

"Speaking of flying," Blu interjected, "Mind explaining how you did that little number out the window? How'd you fly without wings?"

Vivian laughed and sighed at the same time. "It's the easiest and hardest thing in the world to explain," she said.

"Try me," Blu said.

Vivian contemplated it for a moment.

"It all breaks down to energy," she began. "It's kind of like thermo-dynamics, but on a spiritual level."

"Thermodynamics? Are you fuckin' serious?" Blu exclaimed.

"Think about it," Vivian continued, "Every time someone prays for world peace, every time someone performs a courageous act of love, every time someone ponders the wonders and the beauty of the universe, it focuses spiritual energy. Those are just a few extreme examples, but you get the idea."

"Focuses?"

"Like heat energy, spiritual energy is neither created nor destroyed. It just *is*. Why do you think prayer works? How do you think witches use spells effectively? Meditation? Law of Attraction? Do you think that all that spiritual energy is wasted? Some people know how to free it, but more importantly, how to harness it. It's like an unlit candle, waiting for spiritual heat to light it. Some people know how to make these things work for them."

"So, you rode spiritual energy out of here."

"In a manner of speaking, yes."

"How?" Michael asked

"I tapped into it in a way that most people can't."

"That's the first thing you've said since you got back into this car that makes any sense," Blu quipped. Vivian chuckled.

"I want more details," Michael said.

"Ok, think of it like this. People perform acts that concentrate posi-tive energy. It's like starting a fire. The energy has always had potential in the form of logs and matches, but it had never been released. Unfor-tunately for them, some folks release the energy, but it isn't doing any work for them. They release random positive energy with no direction. I tap into that unfocused energy and put it to work for me."

"Like putting a spit over the fire," Michael observed.

"Exactly."

"That makes sense, but I still don't know how you defied physics," Blu said.

Vivian smiled. "Neither do I," she admitted.

␣ ␣

In seconds, Charles reached the icy elevation of the clouds, but he didn't stop. Things had been going on for days without his knowledge, ever since the meeting in the cave. He didn't regret calling the *Shévet ha Dam* into play, but he wished he'd had an idea where it had gone from there.

Damn. I thought I had stayed in touch. How long have I been oblivious?

Too long. Of that, he had no doubt. He had been waiting for Jude to resurface to arrange a confrontation, but it seemed that Maysun had done all the arranging. But why?

He longed to reach Jerusha, to explain his plan to her. Even if he could have contacted her telepathically, what reason would she have to trust him? To her, he was *Shévet ha Dam*, a being who'd done nothing to save her for centuries. He was a criminal. Jude's executioner.

Now it was he who needed saving—along with the rest of the earth.

␣ ␣

Two more were dead. Not Renfields this time, but earnest bloodsuckers over five hundred years old. She had plucked them out of the sky like a Patriot missile. The others had sensed the ease with which she killed their scouts, and were backing off, their fervor subsiding in fear for their lives.

No! No. She's the one! Kill her! Forget about the fucking war! She's right there!

It was no use. At least fifty attackers turned south, headed to Savannah and the forces they knew were gathering. Jude sat up, incensed.

Damn. Damn. Damn it all to fucking hell!

Only a handful of diehards remained in pursuit. It looked like the battle would happen after all. Good versus evil.

Joseph against Jerusha.

Jude scoffed. It would be no competition. The concept of the good vampire was not a grass-roots movement. It was a ridiculous notion set into play by a handful of extremists. Vampirism had always been, and would always be, ruled by the dark and deadly. After all, they were his children. They had his blood.

I think I need to have a little fun before this "fight."

He wondered where Gina was.

Chapter 47

"I've been thinking," Vivian said as they pulled into South Bend Regional Airport.

"What's that?" Michael asked. He didn't like the look on her face.

"Why don't I head to Savannah without you?"

"Come again?" Blu said.

"If they knew I wasn't with you, you'd be safer. They aren't after you. They're after me, and they'll kill you if you're with me. They can't sense you. You're in the Source, so you're safe."

"Won't they be after us anyway," Michael asked, "for harboring you?"

Vivian shook her head. "I'm the one they want, not you."

"No way," Blu said. "I didn't kill all those vampires in New Jersey only to have you die on me now."

"Besides, we haven't developed a plan of attack," Michael added. "You have no idea what you're going to do once confronted with Cartaphilus. You need time to plan."

They pulled into a parking spot, and Blu stopped the car. The eerie silence that followed reminded Michael of a haunted house.

Vivian popped out like a jack-in-the-box. "I'm not worried," she said. "I haven't stayed alive this long only to fail now. I'll stay on the move until you get to Savannah, and we'll plan together once you're safe there. Meanwhile, if they want to kill me, they'll have to catch me," she laughed. She was in the air before they could move, and out of sight before they uttered the first doubt. She didn't even take her purse.

Michael and Blu exchanged bewildered glances.

"She's *your* girl," Blu said.

Blu and Michael leaned against the car for about five minutes, bracing for a strike. They remained tense, poised for action, ready to defend themselves from descending minions of the *Shévet ha Dam*. When none showed, they entered the airport feeling surprisingly let down.

They made it to their gate and waited tensely in the terminal for the flight, which was to leave in half an hour. Michael tried to call Lukas, but his phone would not work inside the airport. He gave a resigned sigh of frustration. At least there were no vampires to give them any trouble here. *No, they're all after Vivian.*

"Weird, huh?" Blu asked, breaking the silence.

"What's that?" Michael said.

"Where did she pick up all that knowledge? It's like she's another person now. Even the way she talks is different." His hands turned up. "How'd she do it?"

"How the hell am I supposed to know?" Michael laughed. The act felt good, if a little stressed. He hadn't laughed in too long.

"Well, you're the philosophy major," Blu retorted. Michael conceded.

"'Beware when the great God lets loose a thinker on this planet,'" he said. "Ralph Waldo Emerson. In all seriousness, I do have two theories."

"I figured you would," Blu teased.

"One: If she has access to energy the way she does, it's likely that she also has access to a collective unconscious."

"The Jungian thing you told me about?"

Michael nodded.

"It would explain how she knows things without knowing how. She taps into it whenever she wants to learn."

"And theory number two?"

"She can tap into people's minds. People, vampires."

"So do I," Blu said. "So do you, sometimes."

"She might be able to do it in a way that you and I can't," Michael continued. "You can pick up a conversation going on in someone's head. We can both understand intentions when we don't understand the language. Vivian may be different. I suspect she learns by telepathy. Kind of mental osmosis. She might be able to see inside someone's mind like it's a filing cabinet with folders of facts that she can sift through when she needs it."

"Creepy," Blu said.

"Not really," Michael said. "Not when you consider who she is. She'd never look anywhere that wasn't necessary."

"Which do you think it is?" Blu asked. Michael shrugged.

"I honestly think it's a little of both," he admitted. "When she first came out of it, right before we left for Germany, she asked me which side of the country we'd be entering with a lot of concern. It puzzled me for a minute since she'd been asleep for around fifty years, but I decided not to dwell on it at the time. I figured it would all come out, and it has."

"What's so weird about that?" Blu asked.

"Germany wasn't divided into two states until 1949, *after* World War II. She'd been 'under' since 1943. So, how'd she know that?" His pride in her was audible. "It was strange that she picked *that* up, and not that it was reunited, but maybe she hadn't read that far into whatever source she got her information from."

Blu peered at Michael with amusement.

"You care for her, huh?" he asked.

Michael chuckled and shifted his feet. He dropped his gaze, and if he could have, he'd have blushed. "Is it that obvious?"

Blu nodded. His grin showed his white, straight teeth. "I didn't get to be over five centuries old by not being able to read people," he said. "How long has she known?"

"Just a few days," Michael admitted.

This time Blu laughed in earnest. He gave Michael two solid and friendly pats on the back. Michael grinned as he remembered how Vivian rediscovered her shapeshifting ability.

"How long until we see her again?" he asked. Michael consulted the tickets in his hand as if he hadn't read them a thousand and one times.

"A little over four hours, including the layover," he said.

Blu heaved a frustrated sigh.

"Damn, that's a long time," he said. Michael only nodded.

ക്ക   ഇ

They came.

From the rafters and rooftops of Savannah, they took flight. Wings of leather or undead skin stretched and flapped. Elders tapped into spiritual sources and levitated against all laws of physics. Faces curled into inhuman snarls, and on each mind was a curious wonder of how much blood would be consumed tonight. From over two hundred miles around, they descended, in unison, on the airport. This would be the final battleground.

They came swiftly.

ക്ക   ഇ

Hurry, Charles. Hurry.

He wasn't sure if it was Maysun this time or his own mind urging him on. He was so cold that even his undead flesh felt it. He had to descend or risk turning into a chunk of ice.

He lowered his altitude slightly, but not his speed. He was nearly across the Atlantic now. Savannah was only a few hundred miles away.

He had the feeling his presence was needed. Vivian would be there. *I must try and speak with her. I'll plead if I have to.*

α β

Josh, Megan, and Lukas took what felt like their fiftieth sweep of the airport. A fog had crept in as they circled, and Josh squinted against the headlight glare.

"I'm tired of this," he said. "Let's park. I don't think whatever we're going to face can be any worse than another lap around this airport."

"It might not be as bad as we think," Lukas said. "We've been going slow enough. I imagine they'd've attacked if they were going to."

Josh took a ticket from the short-term parking machine and maneuvered the sports car into the closest well-lit parking spot. The fog turned the light from the streetlights into amber clouds. Few people flew out of Savannah International in the early morning hours, and the lot appeared deserted.

The three friends paused as the engine died, listened for the sound of leathery wings, footsteps, inhuman voices.

None came. The only arrival was the patter of misty raindrops.

"This is weird," Josh said. "Don't you sense that they're coming? I feel a presence out there."

"Me too," the others echoed.

The three of them heard it at once: a rustling sound, combined with heavy footsteps. Several footsteps.

"Oh, shit," Megan said.

In the rearview mirror, Josh saw them approach. They didn't fly, as he had anticipated. They crept up slowly, in a semi-circle, and blocked the car into its parking spot.

Makes sense. I can only hit so many of them before my car gets stuck on a vampire speed bump.

They stopped.

The friends made no move to get out of the relative safety of the car.

They exchanged worried glances, unsure what to do. There were at least a hundred vampires in the parking lot behind them, and who knew how many were in the fog ahead. It would be a short struggle.

Strangely, though, the looming crowd didn't exhibit aggression. They stood, poised like statues prepared to jump to life.

"It's the Welcome Wagon from hell," Megan quipped, but there was no humor in her voice.

A stirring among the ranks revealed a petite, darkly beautiful female who cautiously drew near the car as if she were approaching a frightened deer. She walked directly to Lukas's window and stood without moving.

"What do I do?" Lukas asked with clenched teeth.

"Roll down the window. See what she wants," Josh said. Lukas looked to Megan, who nodded. He opened the window a crack. Then, deciding that was pointless and only reflected his fear, he rolled it down to the ledge.

The female smiled an exotic, wicked smile, the tired smile of a woman who has seen too much. "My name is Maysun," she said. "We are here to help you."

She did nothing to veil her thoughts from him. In fact, she wordlessly encouraged him to test her sincerity and the sincerity of those accompanying her. In each mind, he found a bitter resentment for Jude Shepherd, who was known to many of them under different names. After that, the thoughts were so vehement, so hateful, that the message became jumbled.

"What is it?" Lukas asked. "What's going on here?"

"For centuries, these vampires have repeatedly been condemning their souls to hell for murdering humans," Maysun said, her Middle Eastern accent thick and beautiful. "Cartaphilus told us it didn't matter, that it was the vampire way, and we'd live forever, so the condition of our souls wouldn't matter. Now we know that he put our eternities in danger. We know what we've been doing is shameful. We wish to change that."

"My God," whispered Josh. "We're at war."

Chapter 48

Blu and Michael impatiently waited in line to board the plane. A burly man who looked like he would be more at home on a Viking ship approached them as brusquely as a bouncer at a club. Heads swiveled in their direction, and no wonder.

"Let's go," the Viking barked. Michael looked up. His son was an abnormally tall man: this Viking could have given Lukas a run for his money. He was dressed like a die-hard Harley-Davidson biker: engineer boots, leather pants, and a leather vest. He carried no coat. Winter in Indiana must have agreed with him.

Blu was not impressed. "Who the hell are you?"

"Airport security," the giant replied with a smirk. "Grab your bags,"

"Fuck," Michael whispered. They'd been so close! Who knew when the next flight to Savannah would be?

"Let me see some ID," Blu barked. The Viking growled like an angry tiger, revealing his pointed eyeteeth so only they could see.

Holy Fuck. I hadn't pinned him as a vampire! Michael thought. *How'd he do that?*

The giant tried to grab Blu by the collar to encourage him into cooperation. Blu flailed his arms wildly to brush him off.

"Hands off, Conan," he snapped. He and Michael picked up their bags and followed the burly bouncer. *Shévet ha Dam* or not, they knew it was best not to cause a scene in public.

Michael struggled to read the man's thoughts. It was like running into a concrete wall: painful, and it got him nowhere. He shot a look at Blu, who shook his head. Evidently, Blu, too, was stumped. This vamp was Tribe.

They left the terminal and retraced their steps out of the airport. Once outside, the man stopped them.

"My name is Krieg," he said. Michael released an exhale he hadn't known he was holding. Introductions were rarely made by people who intended to kill you. Maybe whatever had made him appear half-giant had stunted his ability to be read telepathically. "I am a transporter."

"Whoa. There real," Blu said. "I thought transporters were a myth."

Michael caught Blu's eye. *You think Vivian sent him?*

Gotta be, his friend replied.

"Drop your bags," Krieg ordered. Michael, who'd caught his drift, let go of his bag immediately. Blu followed suit with a wrinkled brow.

"Can I keep my backpack?" Michael asked. It contained the cell phone, his connection with his son, as well as Vivian's purse, which he had grabbed on impulse in case she needed it. Before tonight, she never went anywhere without it.

Krieg shrugged. "Can't weigh much," he conceded.

Krieg looked around for human life, but as he had evidently planned, he'd exited where there was none. With a slight groan, he extended enormous black bat-like wings from his back. Once freed, he smiled. It was a friendly smile, if a little crooked, and Michael found himself relaxing.

"There," Krieg said with noticeable relief, "That's better."

With arms the size and firmness of Michael's head, he scooped the two of them up as if they weighed no more than kittens. He required no running start, but jumped straight up and took flight. Despite his bat-like wings, the flight was smooth, easy, and as fast as an airplane.

"I've had fantasies like this," Blu hollered over the sound of the wind rushing past their ears, "But generally we're all naked."

Michael chuckled.

"Now, isn't this better than a layover in Detroit?" Krieg bellowed with a smile.

⚃ ⚂

Lukas, Megan, and Josh left the car as slowly as cornered criminals abandoning a stolen car. Maysun tried to placate them with a smile, but something about that smile disturbed them.

"You are her ally, Jerusha?" Maysun asked. They gave her a blank stare. "Forgive me... Vivian?" she corrected. This time Lukas and Josh nodded. Megan said nothing. Maysun nodded.

"She is our hope. I have known her for centuries—"

"Whoa, whoa, whoa," Lukas interrupted. He held up a palm in Maysun's direction. "Are we talking about the same person here?

Why'd you call her Jerusha a second ago? Do you know her? Who is she?"

"This woman, this vampire you know as Vivian, has lived many lives under many names," Maysun said. "Her first name was Jerusha. She is the blood daughter of Joseph Cartaphilus, whom you know as Jude."

"Cartaphilus," Josh said. He pondered the name for a moment. "Why does that sound familiar?"

"Pilate's gatekeeper. He struck Jesus as he carried his cross to Golgatha," Maysun clarified. She recounted the story of the curse. Megan became puzzled.

"He took her because he hated her, and then he kept her because..."

"It made him feel powerful to have control over a vampire who was his spiritual opposite," Maysun said.

"But he *is* powerful," Megan said.

Maysun smiled. It looked forced.

"He hasn't always been *so* powerful. Cartaphilus was once a man with a mortal, sinful soul. He viewed his curse as a blessing: he wouldn't have to face judgment for his evil life until much later. He might manage to live forever... or long enough to figure out a way out of an eternity in hell. Meanwhile, he corrupted or killed many, many humans. And, as you know, he fathered a race of vampires and instilled in them not only a thirst for blood but also a hunger for the Death Rush. In time, he came to think of himself as a god."

There was silence as they digested what Maysun had told them. It seemed incredible that their story spanned two millennia. This was an ancient war.

"When does this thing turn critical?" Megan asked.

"Any moment," Maysun replied. She turned her back to them and launched herself into the air. As a body, the army that had followed her took flight. They soared northwest, eager for blood and death. Those too young to fly marched like stone-faced soldiers headed to the battlefield. The friends watched them set off.

"That wasn't the answer I was hoping for," Megan said.

"You don't have to go," Lukas said. "I'd feel better if neither of you went."

Megan gave him a scornful glare.

"If you're goin', I'm goin', Mr. We're Descended from the Most Powerful Being on Earth."

He couldn't argue. He wanted to go, he wanted to be there, and he *knew* that Vivian and his father would be there. But one look on

Megan's face, and he couldn't argue. He would not risk her life, too. Not again.

"Fine," he snapped. "We'll hide inside with the humans." He turned on his heel and stormed to the airport entrance. The other two exchanged an unsure glance and followed him.

She was getting nearer. She was getting nearer, and she *knew*. Trying to read her was like deliberately placing his hand in a fire, but he sensed the rest. Although her thoughts were veiled, hiding how quickly she was approaching was tough. She had to be flying. If she was flying, she undoubtedly remembered.

Damn. This complicates things.

Cartaphilus had hoped for a long, drawn-out battle with plenty of pain, death, and suffering. But she had remembered, and now she was coming to confront him. Why? If she lost the battle, she would be his slave for another millennia or two as he abused her at his leisure. If she won—provided that Yeshua was right, and he had been so far—the world would face Armageddon, and billions of people would die. It didn't strike him as logical.

Wasn't she aware he had the advantage? He had Gina subjugated, Lukas was only a domino fall away, and with Lukas he surely had Michael. He was only perhaps an hour away from controlling everyone she had come to love. She gained no advantage by attacking, and still, she proceeded.

She was a fool.

Where had she found the strength for such an indomitable spirit after two thousand years of slavery?

You know that, Joseph. She's always had it. It's the reason you kept her so subjugated. You knew if she ever came to know who she was and who you were, it would mean combat. You've been lucky for two millennia. Your time ran out.

He kicked the side of the mattress. Gina had been slumbering heavily, sedate and aching after two hours of rutting. She lifted her head, barely raising it from the pillow. Dark circles colored the skin under her eyes.

"Get the hell up," he barked. "It's time to go."

☙ ❧

It was such a thrill to fly! Vivian soared over the earth and felt the wintry air, actually *felt* it, as it rushed past her body. She saw the shadows of the clouds across the landscape and the patchwork lines of the trees below. She dove into the treetops of a forest and dodged branches. She steered herself up again and back to a safe elevation and south. She knew she had a mission to carry out and was aware of the urgency, but she could not help playing around a bit. It was too luxurious an experience not to revel in it for just a moment.

South and east she flew, over unseen state and county borders. Dawn was three hours away, and she needed to make the most of her time.

The wind whipped her clothes more frantically as she increased speed. She had to be careful. If she flew too high or too fast, her body might develop problems from the cold, which would take precious time to recuperate. Time was one commodity she didn't have.

She closed her eyes and tapped into the Source. That was how she had come to recognize the font of knowledge and energy that she drew on whenever she needed guidance or wisdom. She intuited directions to Savannah, and a mental compass aimed her a little farther to her right. Savannah was now less than an hour away.

Where do I want to go once I arrive? She asked the Source. She sensed the airport or a location close to it. She received a mental picture of a field of blood, of flesh and gasoline-stoked flames so vivid she choked on smoke and gagged on a stench that didn't exist. She opened her eyes and saw no more than the earth passing beneath her.

Whatever that was, it wasn't good, she thought. She sensed the answer lay inside the Source, easily grasped if she tried. She didn't want to know. Not yet.

Vivian.

She was so shocked she dropped nearly two stories before recovering, righting herself, and regaining altitude. She spoke aloud as if he was next to her instead of in her mind.

"Charles?"

Vivian, we should talk. Things are happening much too rapidly.

She remembered him. Oisian Drummann. In her life as Vivian, she had once thought of him as the other Tyrone Power. She wondered how long ago it must feel to him. The memory was so fresh in her mind. She wondered how a member of the *Shévet ha Dam* had broken through her concentration when she was immersed in the Source. She wouldn't have guessed it possible for a man so devoted to Jude. To Cartaphilus.

"What do you want?"

I need to speak to you. I need to let you know about Jude.

"I know about Jude. Joseph Cartaphilus. I remember everything." Surely, he noticed that from her thoughts, and by the fact she was flying.

But do you know how to defeat him?

"It will come to me," she replied.

Are you certain? He dominated you for hundreds of years. What makes you so optimistic?

"I know, Charles."

Are you aware of the consequences if he dies?

Vivian inhaled sharply. It was true. Her confrontation with Jude might reach the ugly climax she dreaded. She held humanity in her hands. The cold air rushing by couldn't compete with the ice now in her veins. It was a weighty responsibility she did not enjoy.

Vivian?

"Yes. I know."

I do wish you would let me share with you what I know.

"Don't worry, Charles. Your mind has already shared everything. I can quite literally read you like a book," she said.

I don't doubt that. I always said you were amazing, he reminded her.

She broke contact.

Chapter 49

"Lukas?"

He looked at the top of Megan's head as they sat next to one another on the bench near the clock.

"Yes?"

"I watched a vampire movie once, and it said that if the head vampire dies, then all half-vampires go back to being human or something. And that you don't become a—pardon the expression—full-blooded vampire until you make your first kill."

"And?"

"And isn't Jude like the head vampire? He's the one who started this whole thing, according to Maysun."

Lukas hadn't considered the consequences of Jude's downfall. That is, provided it didn't bring about the end of the world. "I guess you're right," he admitted.

"Well, we haven't killed anybody. Does that mean we're going to turn back to normal?" She tried to keep the hope from her voice, but failed. Lukas gave her an encouraging smile and put his arm around her shoulders. He didn't care to remind her that, technically, he'd killed her.

"I don't know, Megan. I wish I could say."

She sighed. "No offense, but I hope so," she said.

He thought of his father and all the other vampires he knew who'd never killed. It humbled him, especially since he had survived such a short time before taking Megan's life, and he adored her. A pang of guilt sharper than blood, more painful than the transformation from human to vampire coursed through him. He pulled her closer. At least he'd done what he had to to keep her alive.

◕ ◙

Maysun's troop of *Shévet ha Dam* rebels flew to the field like athletes rushing a playing field. In the air, hunched in trees, buried in the earth, hiding in the long grass, they lurked. Their opposition—every dark soul that could attend—waited for them there.

It wasn't a shot but a shriek that announced the battle had begun. An unholy shriek coming from all corners of the earth, splitting the mind of everyone present into what felt like a thousand blood-soaked pieces. It was the battle cry of the father of vampires.

Joseph Cartaphilus had arrived.

At once, the sky was a furious flock of wings converging with no order, no discernible line of scrimmage. There were no colors to determine who fought whom—only the aura surrounding them determined which side of the line one resided. The mental ramparts fell as vampires from all ranks of the *Shévet ha Dam* revealed themselves as for or against their leader. There was no room for indecisiveness. Guttural cries and severed limbs filled the air as vampires clawed the air searching for opponents. Those who lost wings in the battle fought on the ground, bleeding until adversaries drained them.

Errando Medina doused the ground with an enormous can of gas and lit it swiftly before heading once more to the skies. Earthbound vampires on both sides of the skirmish ignited, crying in pain and despair as they filled the air with the stench of burning, undead flesh.

Jude floated through the madness like a man easing down a lazy river. Soul after undead soul ended under his powerful jaws. He drank until he was filled, then he let the crimson fluid drip from his bloody lips onto the ground. That holy fluid, that life-giving fluid was his to waste, his to spill, and he prized it.

If only *she* were here.

Battles between the undead have the potential to last centuries. This one died within the hour, the sides equally depleted in number, limping and flying to the shadows to recover from their injuries before regrouping. But still, she had not revealed herself.

Where in the hell are you, Jerusha?

☥　☦

A hundred feet below her and gleaming like a jewel lay the airport. Vivian looped around like a circling plane. The copious amount of vampire energy she picked up was astounding. She kept on her course and hoped to avoid detection.

Flying. Morphing into another physical body. She was amazed at the knowledge that was hers for the taking now that she knew how to tap into it. She felt brazen, uplifted, and *powerful.* Even now, with her memory restored, she could not recall a time when she felt so strong, so ready.

Ready for what?

She didn't know what it was she faced. She knew whom; oh, yes. She knew all about Jude, Joseph, the demon of a thousand names, but she didn't know what to anticipate. She remembered how he had subjugated her before, but this time was different. This time he wasn't coming at her from behind while she was unaware. This time, she was Jerusha, well-fed and gifted with all her facilities. And not just hers—she had access to all the Source had to offer.

She was terrified to face him alone. She may have the Source, but Jude had the Maleficence. The source of evil that had turned him into the father of the undead.

She felt the *Shévet ha Dam* tracing her flight like ants on a pheromone trail. Luckily, or unluckily, she could also tell that Cartaphilus was below.

A battle had ended nearby, and recently. She wanted no part of the violence. She flew away from the stench of burning dead and landed in a clearing about a mile away. Her first impulse had been to land, announce her presence to her recruits, and engage her forces to assist her. The Source was steering her clear of this idea.

But why not?

It certainly felt like the idea which made the most sense, but she felt the Source guide her until she grasped the full impact of why. What did Jude feed on? Blood, death, and pain. If she brought all of those vampires into a battle, she would be handing him the psychic energy he needed to feed on to overpower her. All the hate required to kill, all the agony of those who died within reach would be nothing more than an appetizer for him. He'd already glutted himself in battle and would be operating at his maximum potential. No, to defeat him, she would have to go alone.

She tried to tune in to his location.

"I'm already here, Jerusha," said a voice behind her, thick with contempt.

Chapter 50

There was no point veiling her thoughts. With Gina's wrists clenched tight in his hand, he stepped through the tenebrous fog. Vivian emptied her mind of distractions and filled it with the Source.

"That won't work," Cartaphilus taunted. "How are you going to fight with your mind cluttered with all that foolishness?"

Vivian smirked and clung to the Source, feeling its white-hot light flow through her like an ocean of love and knowledge. And she knew. She knew how it would end.

"Why should I fight you, Joseph?" she asked. "This is your battle. Not mine."

His brow wrinkled in confusion.

"Don't you understand?" she asked. She made the statement sound more like a plea than a question. "I'm not here to fight you, Joseph."

The fury he had bottled for months exploded. His expression darkened into a sneer of contempt, and he leaned forward like a mountain lion about to pounce. Vivian's heart leaped to her throat, and she became fearful for her life. Jude's expression was frightening, and she heard his thoughts with ease: *What does she mean she's not here to fight? If she isn't going to fight, why has she sought me out?*

He extended a hand, his face painted black with malice and hate. Vivian's mouth opened as his intention became clear. A ball of lightning flew from his palm as quickly as a bullet from a pistol.

This was more than vampiric talent. This was a gift from the power which bound him.

Vivian avoided it with an adroitness that came from her own Source of power. On her best day, she'd never maneuvered so quickly.

The blast struck two felled trees lying directly behind where Vivian had been.

Without a word, he pointed. Gina attacked.

❦

Krieg flew as rapidly as Michael had hoped he would. Doyle had told him about transporters, but this was better than he had expected. Krieg's wings were as strong as they looked and flew with incredible momentum.

They closed in on Savannah only moments after Vivian confronted Cartaphilus. He watched her swiftly duck a deadly lightning bolt with his heart in his mouth. He saw the trees catch fire and collapse. And to his shock, he saw Gina pounce catlike in Vivian's direction.

Oh my God! Gina!

"Krieg, thanks for the lift, man, but we gotta go," he said. His body wriggled worm-like in his haste to be at Vivian's side. He turned to deliver a gratified grin, but it froze when he saw the stern expression on Krieg's face.

Krieg shook his head with deliberate mischievousness. It was the face of a juvenile delinquent out on probation with a pocket full of firecrackers and a can of spray paint.

"Sorry. The trip does end here, but not until she dies," he said with a smirk.

"You can't be serious!" Blu exclaimed. Michael was too shaken to comment. *Until she dies.* It echoed ominously inside his mind.

"Nope," said Krieg. "Who do you think asked me to bring you? It wasn't Vivian." He was so smug, so sure of himself, that Michael would have gladly punched his face in. That was exactly what he did.

Krieg gave Michael another smirk and flew higher. Michael guessed he did so to discourage them from trying to escape. It might have worked. The injuries he'd suffer from the fall would slow him down from helping Vivian. He was willing to risk it for himself, but he didn't want to chance any damage to his friend. He gave Blu an inquiring look from where his head was latched firmly under Krieg's armpit. Blu nodded.

Together they wriggled like cats in a blanket and struck Krieg wherever their fists happened to land, barely taking care not to strike each other in the process. They kicked and fought and struggled with all their might. After about thirty long seconds, when Krieg showed no sign of an Achilles' heel, Michael bordered on giving up. That was when Blu managed a firm blow to Krieg's groin.

Perhaps it was because his testicles were proportionate to the rest of him, and the pain generated from hitting such a vital organ was that much greater. Maybe Blu hit it just right—or wrong. Whatever the reason, Michael and Blu were hastily released as the Viking of a vampire instinctively sought a protective grip on what were probably potato-sized family jewels.

Now airborne, Michael second-guessed his decision. They'd been at least three hundred feet above the skirmish when Krieg lost his grip, and the ground was coming up with frightening speed.

He heard a sickening tearing sound to his right. Blu shuddered violently as enormous blue wings tore and stretched through his shredded shirt.

"Fuck!" Blu cried. He extended his new appendages, grabbed Michael almost as an afterthought as he became airborne, and they drifted slowly toward the ground as if he had done it thousands of times before.

He has feathers, Michael noted with wonder. *The motherfucker has blue, feathered wings!*

"It's about Goddamn time," he teased. Blu smiled broadly.

"You're telling me," he agreed. "And you didn't lose the book bag."

Michael hadn't noticed. He held it up and inspected it as if it had magically appeared in his hand.

"Must be a sign," he said dazedly.

"Must be," Blu said.

ᘓ ᘔ

It happened so quickly. Her first impulse was for self-preservation, and her instincts shot along her nerves telling told her to raise her arms and fight, grab her neck and tear out her throat. She grasped a keen sense of anatomy and martial arts that floated in the knowledge available in the Source, but with it—

Can I do that?

—was another way for her to escape unharmed and without injuring Gina. She discovered another instinct—the instinct to protect those she loved, no matter what.

Trusting the Source to protect her, she inhaled deeply. Her body distorted, her bones wilted, muscles and skin morphed into a bloody jelly, and then her body was gone.

She remembered her dream about eavesdropping on the Table. At the time, she hadn't remembered making the change. This time, she was conscious of it. She was as amorphous as a sanguine cloud.

Gina nearly fell as she tried to grasp a body that was no longer there. Cartaphilus roared, and the ground shook.

Fifty feet away from the near-collision, Michael and Blu touched down. Cartaphilus smiled and beckoned to Gina.

He whispered into Gina's ear. She smiled a nasty smile and nodded.

ଔ   ଷ

"Where'd she go?" Michael asked in a panic. He'd watched her dissolve in disbelief and had expected her to materialize soon, but she hadn't.

"I don't know," Blu muttered. The two friends anxiously watched as Jude summoned Gina to his side. Michael could have cried at the sight of his friend beside Cartaphilus.

"God, tell me this isn't happening," he whispered. "What is he doing?"

"I don't know," Blu repeated. "But whatever it is, I sure as hell don't like the way he's looking at us."

ଔ   ଷ

Lukas felt a prick in the back of his head. At first, he assumed Megan was playing with him, and he reached around to grab her hand and steal a kiss, but when his hand found the back of his head, there was nothing there.

Who's Megan? A jealous voice inside his mind asked. Lukas hardly believed what he heard.

Gina?

That's right.

Can't be. You're... you died! Jude killed you!

Her voice rang through his head, the voice of a friend who'd been dead less than two days. The voice of a friend who had somehow lived, whom he could have helped if he hadn't been such a coward.

Lukas, I'm outside. I got away from Jude, but now I'm in a shitload of trouble. There's a lot of vampires out here who want to kill me, and I need your help! Please come!

Lukas saw with heartbreaking clarity the way his friend had been taken before his eyes, and he felt horribly at fault now, knowing she'd survived. Who knew what she'd gone through once he had turned tail and run?

My God, she's alive.

He would not let her die again.

He didn't say anything. He would not risk Megan's life. He excused himself and headed out the door at a sprint.

Ψ Ω

As much as she hated leaving Michael and Blu ignorant of her whereabouts, her cloudy form provided her with security. Cartaphilus could not kill what he couldn't strike, and although he may know *where* she was, he was powerless to do anything until she materialized again.

Blu and Michael were holding a frantic meeting in the shadows, consulting one another on a plan. Gina and Cartaphilus stood fifty feet away and did nothing.

What on earth is going on? What kind of battle is this?

Vivian heard a rustle to her left when Cartaphilus mimicked her disappearance.

Not good. Not good, she thought, but wasn't sure why. Her link to the Source peaked and dipped. *Is it that I am not using a physical form? No, that can't be right. The Source is everywhere. So why—*

Then she noticed Lukas emerging through the fog.

Ψ Ω

He sleepwalked down the steps, following Gina's voice through the mist. He was overjoyed she was alive, so overjoyed he didn't notice how remote her location was.

Michael cried out in alarm, and as Lukas turned to face his father, Cartaphilus took shape and grabbed him roughly. He didn't strike. He shot a glare in Vivian's direction and handed him carelessly over to Gina, who accepted him gratefully, caressing Lukas' neck with bladed fingernails.

Lukas's felt like a frightened cat. He knew now the depth of trouble he'd placed himself in. He wished he knew where Vivian was.

Wait... Vivian?

Suddenly it all came together. He felt a charge, almost electrical, sweep through him. His mind was shocked as if suddenly submerged in cold water. Knowledge he had never possessed charged through his mind crazily, and he wanted to laugh. He felt empowered, and his ears rang with the clarion sound of bells. He also heard a laugh, a delighted tinkle, sweet and fairylike.

Welcome to the Source, Lukas. Now let's see if I can keep you alive long enough for you to use it.

Chapter 51

A claw darted out of the fog and tore both the backpack and Vivian's purse open in a swipe. Michael's eyes grew twice their size as a single talon swooped and picked up a black velvet bag. "What the—?"

The bag soared across the field on unseen wings. It landed in Lukas's palm, and he heard these words in an unfamiliar voice: "This one will help you end it if you decide to finish the fight. Unless you want it all to be over, don't untie it."

He opened it without hesitation.

"Welcome to the Source, Gina," Lukas said as a glow, bright as lightning, escaped from the bag. Rays like sunshine through the clouds flew forth and touched everything in its path. As it reached Gina, she screamed and collapsed.

ʘ ʘ

The rays grew until the field was brighter than daylight, and everyone present was blinded. As it cooled, it assumed a physical presence, an antediluvian embrace of knowledge and love, of strength and mercy. Michael understood now how Vivian flew; he was so full of love and of the power of the Source he could have climbed to heaven on invisible steps. He breathed it in, felt it seeping into his pores, felt it charging his nerves like an electric current.

The Source. Now he understood.

Vivian sank into it like the embrace of an old friend. Her arms outstretched, eyes closed, as her soul quickened with the force that flowed through her flesh and blood. She knew Cartaphilus would not strike her now. Not when she was immersed in this power.

Maybe never.

She opened her eyes and looked at him. He stood apprehensively across the field from her. He didn't move. His expression of hatred and cruelty washed away in the flood of the Source, but now he looked unsure what to do.

She knew. What mattered now was her feelings toward Cartaphilus, Jude, Prince Rashad, Lucius, and the dozens of other names he had gone by over the centuries.

Why her feelings were the most important, she didn't know, but the Source said her answer rested there, and she submitted to its wisdom.

She looked at him now, a tragic being whose only joy came from death and pain. She saw now what she had never seen before; a frightened, frail creature who was terrified of dying and who hadn't wanted to die alone. Despite his apotheosis, he didn't honestly believe himself to be a god. He was a tool of the Maleficence—of evil and destruction— just as she was the tool of the Source. If it had not been so, Yeshua would never have issued the curse. It wasn't the man who had been evil; it was the force that drove the man, and now the creature that stood before her.

The Maleficence hadn't always owned him. It had used him. She remembered the man he had been, the beautiful creature whose nature had been overshadowed by the evil influence within him. She remembered his handsome face, his dark wavy hair and black eyes, his devilish smile. He had been charming, and graceful. And caring.

And she'd loved him. God, how she'd loved him.

She knew that he had a struggle within, a battle she intended to finish. The fight for balance had stretched over two millennia, and the time had come to end it and exorcise the demon.

jj

Jude watched her carefully, waiting for the attack. None came. Maybe she was serious. Maybe she had no intention of fighting.

Don't be ridiculous, a voice said. *No one flies a thousand miles to stare across a field.*

But that was just what she was doing. Jerusha calmly stood her ground across the barren field, her pale body glowed, and her dark hair shimmered behind her like lightning in a rainstorm.

She looks like an angel.

He berated himself for the mental slip and tried to step forward. His feet were cemented to the ground by an unseen force.

Damn her. Damn her!

He wanted to leap forward, to tear her head from her neck and drink blood from her skull. He hated her. A trickle of power grew inside him and threatened to swell. One of his feet detached itself from the ground and the effect surprised him so much he wavered, arms pinwheeling, before he set it down.

That's it! Just focus on your hate. Hate will give you what you need to move, to kill her.

He looked up, resolute, and made the serious mistake of looking into her eyes.

Within a split second, he was swimming in her psyche, trapped in her emotions, her mind, the Source. His body cried out and tripped over heavily, but he heard and felt nothing. All he knew was Jerusha, Vivian, Bettina, Katerina. All he felt was her love.

She loved him. She had always loved him, despite the heinous deeds he forced her to perform, despite how brutally he had treated her. She loved him with the love of the Creator, and had loved him for two thousand years. She knew the difference between Joseph and the Maleficence, had sensed what was him, and had loved that human portion.

The most shocking revelation was that he hadn't held her captive. The Source was hers to use, and always had been. He hadn't kept her chained by his side for all of those years... *she had chosen to stay!* She had stayed because the Source, the Creator, had loved him, and knew the only way he would come to see it was through her. The evil that had controlled him from the moment of his birth hadn't given him a chance to choose what path to take. Now, immersed through her in the Source, he had that choice. It was a relief and a horror, but he had that choice.

God, how he loved her.

He chose apostasy.

Jerusha!

♋ ♌

The false daylight died instantly, retreated to shadows unknown, and left even the oldest vampires temporarily blinded. Blu felt a faint tickle as the Source stopped singing along his limbs and slowly crept away, leaving only a hole he hadn't known was there. Before Blu's eyes recovered, he heard a horrible shriek.

"Joseph!"

He couldn't believe his ears. It was Vivian.

At first, he suspected the battle wasn't over, that Jude had duped Vivian somehow in this war of the mind—for that was what it had to be, no one was moving—into becoming Jude's slave once more. As his eyes recovered, he saw his mistake.

Vivian lay hunched over the charred remains of Cartaphilus' body. Her tears flowed in rivers down her cheeks and hissed as they landed on the cadaver. She stretched a hand over the blackened body as if she wished to embrace it but thought better of it.

She's mourning the bastard! He thought in disbelief.

Michael, Blu, and Lukas timidly joined her.

"Is he gone?" Lukas whispered. Vivian nodded with a sniff. Michael produced a handkerchief from his pocket and handed it to her with a nudge. She accepted it absently and promptly forgot to use it.

"Why are we still here?" Lukas asked. "I was told if he died, it caused the end of the world."

Vivian shook her head.

"He rejected the evil inside him that bound him to the curse. It was the Maleficence that Yeshua cursed. Not the man. When he rejected the evil, he rejected the vampire's curse and became a man. An ancient man whose time had come to die," she explained.

"He did?" Blu said. She nodded.

"He did it by admitting he loved me," she sobbed.

"Oh."

"The word *apocalypse* in Greek means 'lifting of the veil,'" Michael said. "Jude did that. He lifted the veil between himself and the Maleficence that bound him, and he cast the Maleficence out."

No one spoke after that. Michael offered her a hand up, which she accepted clumsily. The fight had left her exhausted. She wasn't sure how she would walk away from the burned corpse.

ଓ ଈ

"I see everything here is fine," a voice from behind them said. "We are all still alive, that is."

The friends turned around. Vivian indicated agreement, her head waggling so loosely it seemed ready to fall off.

"Yes, he found the way home," she replied.

Maysun nodded. "I suspected he would."

Maysun opened her arms, and Vivian found the strength to stumble the distance to her embrace.

"Shh... shh," Maysun cooed, stroking Vivian's hair fondly. "It will be alright now."

"Who are you?" Blu demanded. His new wings were spread wide, prepared to fly them all to safety if need be. Maysun beamed at his protectiveness.

"I think it is a good time to answer that," she said. She slowly released Vivian from her arms and backed away.

She trembled violently, and within seconds she transformed into Beth, the graceful witch. Another violent shaking spasm, and she was Rose Black. A third, and she was an Israeli woman, a stranger to everyone but Vivian, who had last seen her two thousand years ago.

"Meheitav'el?" Vivian asked. Maysun shook her head sadly.

"No, dear. Allow me to explain. I am the body of the Balance. I ensure the continuation of the Balance, and with it, the Source, and the Maleficence."

"But I don't understand. You were my best friend, and Rose Black, and Beth..."

"I was also a member of the Table and Sabine, one of Jude's lovers," she replied calmly, "As well as hundreds of other people throughout his life and yours, and in other lives, in other battles."

"But why?"

Her eyes reflected pools of knowledge that aged her centuries.

"Without Balance, there is no good or evil. Without Balance, there's chaos, or worse, entropy. Balance ensures the continuation of life and the quality of it."

Vivian was stunned.

"Thank you," she said.

"Don't thank me yet, Jerusha," Maysun observed. "The real war is just starting. There are vampires still loyal to Jude and the *Shévet ha Dam.*"

"What do we do to stop the Balance from shifting?" Vivian asked.

"Keep fighting," Maysun said. "Keep them from upsetting the Balance."

Chapter 52

Vivian insisted on burying Jude's remains, so everyone worked to dig a shallow grave.

"What about her?" Blu asked, motioning to Gina, who hadn't moved from where she had fallen.

"She's gone," Vivian said sadly. "She was too immersed in the Maleficence and can't be saved. She'll turn to ash come morning."

Lukas uttered a choked sob. Megan patted his shoulder, unsure what else to do.

"Where's Maysun?" Blu asked. They turned in all directions, scanning the field for her, but she had disappeared.

"I'm wondering," Lukas said, "I mean, I can tell the whole half-vampire going back to normal thing isn't happening. But I guess what I'm trying to say is, why are there vampires like us? If there's a Balance, that is. Aren't vampires all supposed to be evil? Hell, *she* was a vampire sometimes."

"I guess we have our place in the universe, just like everything else," Michael observed.

And somehow, it sounded balanced.

Epilogue

He was too late.

Below, the smoldering remains of hundreds of friends and former friends, of young vampires he had yet to meet, lay in stinking ruin. Body parts that would ash with the dawning sun were drained and lay in the bloodstained ground as if waiting to be reanimated.

Charles alighted with a flinch in the ash, mud, and blood. He cringed at the muck sticking to his Prada shoes.

He had failed to see the outcome of the battle, but in his heart, he knew that Jude had lost. Which was good, he supposed. Charles now had no career, no acquaintances he trusted, and no family, but it was good. The *Shévet ha Dam* was free from Jude, and the apocalypse had been averted.

A lonely, unmarked grave marked the resting place of one of the deceased. In a sea of nameless, faceless corpses, someone had seen to it that one carcass was properly buried. He knew beyond a doubt the undertaker was Jerusha, the body Joseph's.

Charles approached the freshly turned dirt with a grimace. He folded his arms across his chest and felt his body buckle in half. His guts were wrenched in pain, and a sob escaped his lips. The King of the Undead was dead, a testament that he cannot escape his fate no matter how hard one tries.

Everyone dies. Eventually.

He kicked a small clump of grass with a pointed toe and patted it into place. Jude had been his father, his mentor, and his friend. Despite his fear of the man, he had respected him, admired him, and he supposed maybe even cared for him a little.

Don't be a fool, Charles. You never cared for him. He scared the hell out of you—nothing more, nothing less. Don't develop feelings for him that were never there now that he's gone. If anything, you hated the bastard. You did what he told you, and only because you knew if you didn't, it'd be you under this dirt and not him. No more.

He stared at the pile of brown-red Georgia dirt, half expecting a bloodstained arm to reach through the earth and seize his ankle. But the dirt was as unmoving as the severed limbs all around him. He was glad. Jude was gone, and once he disposed of Maysun, he would be free to do whatever desired, free to manage the *Shévet ha Dam* as he saw fit, free to...

What was that?

A cold finger of dread tickled his spine, and he looked behind him. No one was there. His heart had leaped to his throat, and he shivered despite the unseasonably warm morning. The sunlight rose from its hiding place behind the trees, and bits and pieces of dismembered limbs hissed and smoked behind him as they ignited and turned to ash. Soon, the battleground would be a field again.

Relax, Charles. Jude can't hurt you now.

He forced himself to calm down, straightened his face, and stood facing Jude's unmarked grave once more, but now he could not concentrate. He'd been *certain* that someone—or something—had been behind him. He strained his ears for the faintest sound, but not even a breeze stirred. The only sound was the bodies burning behind him.

Damn you, Jude. Even in death, you scare the shit out of me.

As his thoughts swam, he felt a bottomless hatred swell in him. Hatred at Jude for turning him into a creature forced to consume blood. Hatred for this seemingly eternal life of darkness with no end in sight. Hatred at himself for his inability to choose a battle he was capable of winning.

The freshly-turned dirt at his feet attested to the futility of his life. When he had tried to help those resisting the allegedly irresistible force of Jude, they had won without his help.

His life was futile. All those centuries he'd devoted to the most powerful organization in the world, and now it was nothing more than a sandcastle in the path of an incoming tide. He was fooling himself. Killing Maysun would accomplish nothing. The *Shévet ha Dam* would crumble without Joseph's guidance, and where would that leave him? Nowhere. He had not a soul in the world he could count on, and centuries to dwell on his solitude.

Why didn't I die as a human? This isn't life at all, only existence. Century after century of trying to scrabble my way to the top, when the top was never mine to be had. And now what? The Shévet ha Dam will dissolve, and all my work will be for nothing.

God, he hated life. He hated Jude's life and was thrilled it was finally over. He hated the lives of all those he had worked alongside in the *Shé-vet ha Dam,* all those bloodthirsty demons with no more motivation than the next meal, the next stepping-stone to success, the next lie. And he had been one of them.

He wasn't sure he wasn't still.

Suddenly, his body was gripped by an enormous, invisible fist. His arms were pinned to his side, his lungs felt as if they were caving in, and he was grateful that he had no need for breath. His eyes brimmed with bloody tears, and he gritted his teeth to keep from crying out. His feet were lifted from the ground and dangled like marionette's. He struggled to escape, but it was futile. Whatever had a hold of him was more powerful than even Cartaphilus.

His thoughts swam with terror. Could Jude have found a way to live without his body after so many centuries of power? Was this his newest incarnation, his newest way to deal death?

Close, Charles, but not quite.

It wasn't the voice that startled him. He had almost expected to hear his attacker's voice, some revelation of who was about to slay him.

Just not from inside his mind.

His psyche felt like it was becoming an assemblage of hatred, rage, and the urge to kill. When it occurred to him what was happening to his body, he felt only a tweak of panic before it was quelled by a reassuring image of command and eternal life at the head of the *Shévet ha Dam.*

The *Shévet ha Dam* would not be without a leader. He had been Jude's right hand; he was the only logical choice for successor, and he would kill anyone who stood in his way without hesitation. He felt indestructible, and he did not care where his additional power was coming from. It was his to wield now.

He recalled with fury how Jerusha had shunned his offer of assistance, and he wondered how her blood would taste.

And now for an introduction into the next book in the Blood Tribe Trilogy: *Blood Trials*.

Through a fog of blood lust and ecstasy, Sana Huett heard two voices on the floor above engaged in an angry debate. It distracted her from the handsome young man between her thighs on the bed. Her lover's pale, cool body sent pleasure from her core to her slim fingertips as she writhed over him, but Sana was too unfocused to fully enjoy the experience.

She shook her head and tried to clear her mind, but her thoughts moved like water striders on the surface of a still pond. One minute, she was intent on her lover, awash in desire, enjoying his strength and boundless vigor; the next moment, the conversation above interrupted her thoughts with annoying, insistent words.

It wasn't until her lover placed his hands on either side of her rib cage that Sana noticed she was struggling to keep her balance. His hands on her sides held her steady as her shoulders and head swayed. She felt pleasantly drunk but had a hard time concerning herself about it.

I didn't have any alcohol, did I? Her mind reeled with the unsteady, disjointed pace of the inebriated. She struggled to remember, but her thoughts bobbed and tumbled in a sea of confusion. She couldn't recall her lover's name. Or where she'd met him. Or how they'd wound up naked in the finished basement room of... *It is my house, isn't it?* She giggled.

Her head lolled, and the young man sat up and caught it tenderly in his hand. Sana grinned, and he returned it with interest. His elongated eyeteeth sent excited chills from her neck to her toes, and the sight of his tongue against them only heightened the thrill.

Vampire! But god, he's so beautiful. So, so beautiful. Hair as dark as raven's wings, eyes like bright turquoise, his light skin contrasted against her toffee-color. *But what is his damn name? Why can't I...? This has to be a dream. Vampires aren't real. And I'd never sleep with someone I don't know.*

The sharp-toothed man below her drove his pelvis into her with earnest, sending waves of delight from her core through her body and making it impossible not to cry out. He gave her a smile that managed to be both shy and self-satisfied at her reaction.

The voice from the floor above spoke, interrupting her enjoyment.

Though the accent was English, the tone casual, it set Sana's heart racing, this time in fear.

That voice. I know that voice!

Sana jerked upright, but her lover grasped her with gentle hands and brought her focus back to him. He met her eyes in his wide blue ones, and she lost the impression that she'd been on the verge of an important realization. She couldn't resist her lover's pull.

And why would I want to? It's a dream. I might as well enjoy it. She relaxed, her body a puddle of bliss and desire as she stretched into a reclining pose. The man below her enfolded her in his muscular arms and entered her again.

Cedar-paneled walls surrounded her in the windowless room. Colors appeared ostentatious in the amber light of the bedside lamp: the off-ivory vase of the nightstand, the hazel swirls in the painting to her left, the yellow of the lamp, all of it blinding and frustratingly distracting.

The brilliance was fleeting. Soon, the colors dimmed, along with the throbbing of blood pumping in her veins, the smell of pine cleaner and laundry soap, and the musky, heady odor of sex. She blinked until the colors became less murky and wished her thoughts would do the same.

A voice growled, clearly frustrated. She'd know Thom's irritated tone anywhere.

Damn that conversation. I wish they'd stop talking.

The voices drew her with a slow but powerful force like a tide to the moon. The deepest voice unsettled her, making her heart flutter in a way that was both familiar and terrifying.

That voice. It sounds like the one that's always running inside my head, but it's talking to Thomas!

Thomas. Her husband. *My husband? Then why am I—?* Her breath caught in her throat, and her stomach clenched in guilt as her eyes dropped to the breathtaking young man she lay with. How had she forgotten she was married?

A sharp scratch on her breast set off another overwhelming wave of euphoria, but she fought the emotion. She tried to picture Thom, but all that came to mind was a muscular arm in a button-down shirt encircling her waist, a condescending voice, and a space where she assumed love belonged. No details. No face. No smile.

A familiar metallic odor hit her nostrils and, with it, a rapture that stunned her. Her mouth opened, and she felt an odd pulling at the gums above her eyeteeth. *What is that smell?*

She willed herself to block out all the hectic stimuli and shake the confusion, but it was as if she was under the influence of a hypnotic drug. Her vision blurred, and her muscles froze as she struggled to regain her senses.

Shutting her mind to the overpowering lust and desire wasn't easy. It was simpler to lie still and enjoy the carnal waves running through her body with her lover's every touch. The clearer her mind grew, the more panicked she became. She needed answers, but with solutions came a life-altering truth. She sensed more than she saw it, like putting her hand on a scalding doorknob and knowing a house fire lay behind the door.

I have to see. I have to! This can't be right. Was I drugged? Is this even real, or is it a dream? I have to fight it! Wake up, dammit!

The flesh below her was too genuine not to be real. When her eyes met her lover's concerned ones, she realized he didn't like the level of clear-headedness he saw there.

He sat up, pulled back the collar of her button-down shirt, and sank his sharp eyeteeth into her neck. Sana cried out in a mix of suffering and enjoyment, and the grip she'd had on reality slipped away.

David Sheen stood in the Huett foyer with Sana's husband, Thom, tied to a heavy wooden kitchen chair two feet away. A third man, Angelo Vargas, lazed on the couch, picking at his nails and letting the picked cuticle bits flutter to the rug. The man tied to a chair in the next room was not worthy of his attention.

"Sorry about the restraints," David said, allowing himself to come frustratingly close to kicking distance so he could feel Thom's ill humor. "Couldn't be helped, you know."

"So you say."

Dark-haired and dark-eyed, the three could have been mistaken for brothers: angular faces, all on the taller side of average, muscular, straight teeth. Handsome, David supposed. Their hair was a little different. Angelo had shoulder-length straight hair lighter than the others and dark green eyes. Both Thom and David had shorter, wavy hair, but David's was a tad longer than Thom's professional style. It was the way they carried themselves that made each of them distinct. Angelo's attitude was one of indifference to the point of soullessness. David had a feral quality that straitlaced Thom could never pull off. David often wondered if it was their similarity in appearance which initially drew

Sana to Thom. He suspected the woman remembered more about her fugues than she let on.

"Well, I couldn't have you running about the house mucking things up," David continued.

"Mucking things up? My wife's downstairs fucking a kid—"

"He looks young, but he's not. Physically, he's kind of stuck, but he's not truly seventeen."

"Seventeen? Aw, jeez. Statutory rape. Great. Fucking great. He's a damned kid, and you miscreants—"

"Gentlemen."

"Bullshit. None of you are fucking gentlemen. Gentlemen don't let women fuck children in basements. You and your friend are up here having coffee—"

"Tea."

Thom scowled, tired of his captor's persistent correction of trivial details during Thomas' remonstration.

"Shut the hell up," he snapped.

"Listen, Thomas. You're not in a position to quarrel now, are you? Tied up and all? I understand that you're cross, but if you'd let me explain—"

"There's nothing you can say that would explain this. Nothing."

David dragged a second chair away from the dining room table and sat on it backward, his chest leaning against the backrest and his elbows draped over the top. He raised his brows cockily and heaved an exaggerated sigh. Thom's head sank to his chest, and his nostrils flared like an angry bull.

"I told you, Thomas, He's not underage. But you've been a right arse since we arrived, and you won't listen. Are you ready to hear about how your wife met us?" he asked, "Or are you still too cross to hear? You might find the tale interesting."

Thom turned his chin to the wall. Although he tried to appear disinterested, his eyes gave away his curiosity, incapable as they were of not flicking back and forth from the other man's face to the wall and back. David smiled. This was the point in the script he'd been waiting for.

"Well then, allow me to fill you in on a few details about your wife she's never told you. What she couldn't tell you, because when she's with you, she can't remember."

About the author: Over the years, Iris Kain has called Michigan, Arizona, South Carolina, Georgia, and Germany home. She loves gargoyles, spiders, and black cats, as well as anything that makes you laugh while checking your closet for critters with teeth. Iris is a fan of horror movies and hard rock, and enjoys playing the piano (albeit poorly). She currently resides in Alabama with her son, cats and two adorable Swedish Vallhund dogs.

Follow Iris Kain on:
Instagram / Facebook / Twitter / TikTok
@ authoririskain

Goodreads: @goodreads.com/author/show/20996798.Iris_Kain

Bookbub: @bookbub.com/authors/iris-kain

And check out all the latest on Iris at **https://iriskain.com**!

Support

Indie

Authors

BUY

READ

REVIEW

www.ingramcontent.com/pod-product-compliance
Lightning Source LLC
Chambersburg PA
CBHW030359200726
48286CB00015B/1710